SILENT VOICES

PATRICIA GIBNEY

SPHERE

SPHERE

First published in 2021 by Bookouture, an imprint of Storyfire Ltd.
This paperback edition published in 2023 by Sphere

1 3 5 7 9 10 8 6 4 2

A CIP catalogue record for this book
is available from the British Library.

ISBN 978-1-4087-2852-9

Printed and bound in Great Britain by
Clays Ltd, Elcograf S.p.A.

Papers used by Sphere are from well-managed forests
and other responsible sources.

Sphere
An imprint of
Little, Brown Book Group
Carmelite House
50 Victoria Embankment
London EC4Y 0DZ

An Hachette UK Company

www.hachette.co.uk
www.littlebrown.co.uk

Patricia is the million-copy bestselling author of the DI Lottie Parker series. She always yearned to be a writer but between her full-time work and raising a family she could never find the time or commitment to fulfil that ambition. However, tragedy was to intervene which caused a r. jor shift in her life.

In 2009, after her husband died following a short illness, Patricia had to retire from her job and found that writing helped her cope thro gh her grief. She then started to write seriously. Fascinated by peoj e and their quirky characteristics, she always carries a notebook to s ibble down observations and ideas. Patricia lives in the Irish mid nds with her children.

www.patriciagibney.com

ALSO BY PATRICIA GIBNEY

The Missing Ones
The Stolen Girls
The Lost Child
No Safe Place
Tell Nobody
Final Betrayal
Broken Souls
Buried Angels
Little Bones
The Guilty Girl

For Ger Nichol
Agent and friend

Nine years earlier

The boy tried not to cry. He'd thought he knew the way home, but now he wasn't so sure. It was dark in the fields, far away from the lights of the house he'd just left. He'd been told to go home. They didn't want him there. Had even laughed at him. Big boys were not supposed to cry, but he was crying now. He hoped his mum and dad would be at home, like he'd just been told, even though they were supposed to be away for the night.

He walked across the field, up the lane, and gingerly stepped over the stile. He let his feet sink in the sandy ground. The dew was heavy underfoot and the distance ahead of him appeared shortened by the stubborn fog lying far too low. The trail should be familiar, bred deep in his mind from his treks with his daddy to check on the work at the quarry. Some days he never saw his dad. Long days and never-ending nights, the air punctured by the thud of drills and the hum of machinery. He loved that noise. His daddy had told him it was only a small operation but that one day the boy might make it great. He didn't like the way the green of the hedges had become grey with dust and stone after the summer and the nests had begun to empty. But his family didn't seem to worry about nature.

The silence wrapped itself around his shoulders and the fog dampened his hair as he trudged on. He wished he'd worn his wellington boots, because his runners were wet and sluiced up and down as he walked. Maybe he could have a look at the quarry before he crested the hill. There'd be no one there at this time of night, but he knew a way in. Anyway, that was the shortest way home. He eased through the gap in the wire fence and kept going.

1

He only realised he was close to the lip of the quarry when he heard the stones he'd kicked up as he walked hitting the water. The cavernous space opened up as all around him the fog rose mystically into the sky and the stone and grass split the earth before him. The boy felt he was alone with nature. Just then, he thought he heard a noise behind him. No, only silly people would come up here in the dark. Did that make him silly? There it was again. A rustle. Leaves shifting on the branches. The wind? No, the night was still with the fog hovering around him. Why did it have to be so dark? As he went to move away from the edge, the rustling came closer and stones crunched underfoot. He made to turn around, and felt a hand pressing between his shoulder blades.

'No!'

He thought he'd said the word out loud, but maybe he hadn't. Instead the air was filled with a hysterical laugh. Not his laugh. Then a choked scream left his body as the hand on his back pushed, and he was flying through the air.

The water was thick and viscous. It rushed into his screaming mouth and travelled into his lungs as quickly as his head dipped below the water.

He was strangely calm.

PROLOGUE

Saturday 25 November

It might only have been built in the last ten years but the little chapel house looked like it dated back to the time when the monks set up the first Christian churches in Ireland. At a push it held a hundred people, but today it was laid out for less than thirty.

Sprays of baby's breath interspersed with fragrant freesias were tied in little bunches with white satin ribbons on the backs of the chairs that lined the short aisle. When the first guests began to arrive and the door was opened, a miasma of scent wafted towards them in a wave of freshness. Light filtered through the small arched windows, casting rainbows on the stone walls and bathing the interior in a mystical aura.

A coolness permeated the inside of the chapel, even though outdoors the midday air was warm. Three pillar candles stood on the flower-draped altar, one each for the bride and groom, while the third candle had the names of dead family members inscribed in gold filigree.

Chatter preceded the guests as they took their seats. Family in the first two rows with friends behind them, followed by colleagues. The friends' section was mainly colleagues, but that didn't matter.

In the bedroom of the stone cottage adjacent to the chapel, Lottie stared at herself in the long mirror. She had to admit she didn't recognise the reflected image. Below a tight satin bodice, the chiffon cream dress floated out from her waist, and with the light streaming in through the window, she thought it looked magical. She hardly ever – never – wore dresses, and she would have got married in her jeans and T-shirt if she'd thought she could get away with it. But her daughters had been adamant, so she'd given in. A small victory for the girls, but she was surprisingly happy with her reflection. Her hair had been coloured a little lighter than normal – a box job last night; Chloe had insisted – though she wasn't sure if it was strawberry blonde or out-and-out blonde. She never fussed about such things. A few stray flowers placed strategically around her head hid the clips that held her hair in place. Katie had worked her magic with make-up and eyeshadow and a whole load of other shite Lottie had never used before, but she was pleased with the effect. At least it hid the bruises.

'It's smashing,' she said, hugging her elder daughter.

'You look ten years younger,' Katie said, a wide smile lighting up her eyes.

'Go away! I'm only forty-five,' Lottie said playfully. She'd turned forty-six in June. 'Is Louis ready?' Louis was Katie's two-year-old son, Lottie's grandson.

'He's ready, but I can't guarantee he'll do what he's supposed to do.'

'It doesn't matter. As long as Boyd is there, along with you, Chloe and Sean and little Louis, I'll be happy.'

'I know you haven't met Chloe's boyfriend yet, Mam, but he's not what you'd expect—'

'Not today, Katie.'

'Just giving you a little warning.'

'Thanks,' Lottie said. 'And I love your dress.' Katie was dressed in a fuchsia-pink floaty number from Macy's, while Chloe was wearing a similar style in blue (end-of-line sale). Lottie's own dress was from a charity shop, but they all looked quite expensive. No point in wasting money I don't have, she thought. 'Is Sean ready?'

'Sean is never ready,' Katie groaned. 'I'll go check on him.'

'Thanks. And Katie?'

'Yes?'

'Please don't let Granny Rose near me before the ceremony. She'll say something to upset me, and I can't be dealing with that today of all days.'

'Sure thing.'

Alone, Lottie felt her heart balloon with happiness. It was a feeling she'd thought she'd never again experience after her husband, Adam, had died five years ago. A period of hell had enveloped her then, and she'd floundered in the depths of addiction and sorrow, but eventually, with the help of her colleague, friend and soon-to-be husband Mark Boyd, she had arrived at this day, after a week of storms and torrential rain, with the sun shining brighter than she ever remembered at the end of November.

Sitting at the small dressing table, she stared at the gift her mother had given her. A gold locket. 'It was my mother's,' Rose had told her. 'It's an irreplaceable heirloom. Don't lose it. I put a photo in it, just for you.' There had been no expression of love or good wishes. Just that statement. *Don't lose it.* Lottie wanted to say, why give it as a gift if you're attaching orders? But she'd only murmured a thank you and let Rose off.

Opening the locket now, she stared at the small, crudely cut-out photograph of Adam's face. Her heart lurched in her chest before dipping dramatically somewhere into her belly, and her breath caught in the back of her throat. Tears threatened to override her sense of happiness. Was Rose just being her usual tactless self, or did she really think she was doing the right thing? Lottie snapped the locket shut and dropped it into Katie's make-up bag. Out of sight and all that. Not that she had forgotten Adam. She missed him and loved him still. But she loved Boyd in a different way. A new way. He was part of her present, not her past. He was here for her. She trusted him. Believed in him. Loved him. Didn't she? When she wasn't taking unnecessary risks and almost getting him killed!

Wiping away her tears before they ruined her make-up, she opened the lid of the blue velvet box that Boyd had given her. A thin silver chain with two interlinked hearts. Hand-crafted. Simple. Profound. Thoughtful. It was truly beautiful. Clipping it around her neck, she admired it in the mirror. A smile reached her green eyes which glinted like emeralds in sunshine. Enough! she admonished herself.

She slipped her feet into the cream silk shoes that Chloe had insisted she buy. Despite the price for something she'd never wear again, she'd given in and purchased them. Anything to keep her girls happy. Ready at last, she opened the door and stepped into the small living room, where her family awaited her.

'Oh my God! You look amazing,' Chloe enthused, grabbing Lottie's hands and twirling her round the room. A mesh of cream and blue chiffon swished in the air and Louis squealed with delight.

'What do you think, Sean?' Lottie said, regaining her balance as Chloe let her go.

Her son gripped his bottom lip with his teeth and his eyes glimmered with tears. His fair hair was cut tightly around his head, but his fringe still hung low towards his blue eyes. Adam's eyes. She felt her hand fly to her chest and gulped.

'You look stunning, Mam,' he said eventually. 'Beautiful.'

'Am I not always beautiful?' she joked, trying to release some of the tension which was in danger of simmering out of control.

Sean hugged her tightly, then stepped back. 'Are we Parkers ready to get this show on the road?'

An expectant silence descended on them, and Lottie inhaled the floral scent of her daughters' perfume.

'Who's got my bouquet?'

Katie took the bunch of wild flowers from the kitchenette sink and wiped the stems with a tea towel before handing them to her.

'I'm ready if you are,' Lottie said, and for the first time in five years, she felt truly happy. 'Let's get the next phase of our lives started.'

The nervy butterflies swarmed in the pit of her stomach as she stepped outside the door, walking behind her daughters and grandson. Sean grasped her elbow a little too tightly, then eased his fingers and let them rest softly on her arm.

'You okay, Mam?'

'I'm a little nervous. What if Boyd doesn't turn up?'

'Of course he'll turn up.'

As they walked across the cobbled stones of the courtyard, she glanced to the cottage where she hoped Boyd had arrived this morning to change into his new suit. It looked deserted.

'Stop fretting,' Sean said.

They rounded the corner and approached the chapel, and she felt the first wave of anxiety. Why was there a huddle of people outside? They should be inside. Chloe and Boyd had planned this down to the last detail, the last second. Boyd was like that. OCD. He'd drummed the schedule into her brain. 'Twelve noon. Not a second later.' How many times had he said it? Too many to count. She started to smile, but stopped as her mother approached with Grace, Boyd's sister.

'What's wrong?' Lottie said. 'The celebrant not shown up?'

'No, *she's* here,' Rose said, disdain greasing her words. She was old-fashioned and wasn't about to change.

Lottie caught Grace's arm. 'Where are you going, Grace? Boyd … Mark will be annoyed if we're a second late.'

'He's the one who's late,' Grace said.

Turning, Lottie saw Kirby exiting the cottage Boyd had been allocated. 'What's up?'

'We might need to hold off on the ceremony for a while,' Kirby said, lighting up a cigar. He looked unusually neat and tidy, though the buttons on his white shirt strained across his belly, and he'd put gel or something in his hair to calm down his unruly curls.

Her chest split in a schism of panic. 'Where's Boyd?'

'I don't know.'

'Weren't you with him this morning? To help him pin on his flower or something?'

'You know Boyd better than anyone, and you know that only he can do it right.' Kirby took a long drag on his cigar, topped it and palmed it. 'We agreed to meet at the chapel door at ten to twelve. It's now midday, and I just went to see why he was late and—'

'Oh for God's sake, Kirby, stop rambling.' Lottie shoved her bouquet into his hand and headed for the cottage. It was a studio-type design, neat and tidy. Typical Boyd.

His wedding suit hung on the back of a door, still in its plastic wrapping. Twirling around, she looked for a sign, for anything at all to tell her what was going on. She found it on the small kitchen table.

A note. Folded in two. Cream vellum paper. The name *Mark Boyd* on the outside of the fold.

She opened it up, and as she read, she could feel her blood turning to ice and her knees to jelly. Shivers ran up and down her spine.

The words blurred as she reread it. No signature. Hand-written in small, neat letters.

Before you make the biggest mistake of your life, meet me. If you don't, her blood will be on your hands. She is with me. You know where to find us.

Lottie sank to the floor in a whoosh of chiffon.

CHAPTER ONE

Sunday 19 November

The night was silent, birdsong no longer audible in the air. The birds had flown to warmer places, Ellen thought, as her feet squelched through the soggy dead leaves. Rain hung in the air.

Taking the damp washing in from the clothes line was a nightly chore. She wasn't sure why she continued to hang clothes out each morning and bring them in again at night. She supposed it gave the outward appearance that someone lived in the house. That her life was normal.

A soft sheen of mist settled on her hands as she threw the last peg into the plastic basket hanging on the line. She looked up at the dark sky, devoid of stars, the moon hidden by black clouds. The night her life had changed forever had been quite similar. Silent, damp and dark. The memory had haunted her every day since.

Shivering from the thoughts splicing through her mind, she turned towards the warm light breathing out through the back door, casting eerie shadows along the paving stones that cut the lawn in two. She kicked the leaves from the path onto the grass as she walked, telling herself that she would give it one last run-around with the mower tomorrow, if the promised rain decided not to fall.

She thought she heard a sound. Holding her breath, she listened. Crackling. The leaves were too moist to make such a noise. She couldn't see anyone about, so she shrugged and walked into the house.

She didn't realise how cold it was outside until she had shut the back door and felt the heat wrapping itself around her like a shawl. Still she shivered. Placing the clothes on the table, she flattened them out before draping them on the rack beside the stove. Maybe she wouldn't bother hanging them on the line in the morning.

Talking to herself as she worked, she wondered if she was going mad in the swamp of loneliness in which she found herself. At thirty years of age, she knew she should be happy with her life and out enjoying it, but things were never that simple.

She turned on the television for company and noticed the two mugs on the table, there since her visitor had left earlier. She had too much going on in her head, with the past tormenting her more and more with each visit. The mugs should have been rinsed and stacked in the dishwasher. As she lifted them, she glanced into the one she had used. A finger of whiskey slid around the bottom, so she drained it, even though she'd have preferred vodka, and brought the mugs to the draining board.

On the television, the familiar soap was almost over and she tried to remember what came on afterwards. She threw another stick in the stove and sat down with the remote control. It felt fuzzy in her hands.

Another sound. A door slamming. Upstairs? Ellen stilled, before dropping the remote, her hands shaking and her stomach suddenly gurgling. She jumped out of the chair. Her jeans caught on the nail she'd been meaning to hammer back in, and she heard the material rip. Her stomach was gripped with a merciless cramp. The pain burned up to her throat and she thought she was going to either puke or defecate or both. Another sound.

'Damn it to hell.' She muttered her late father's favourite curse as she tried to keep her insides together. Another cramp accompanied by an intense pain caused a shriek to escape from between gritted teeth. She had to get to the bathroom.

In the hall, the yellow shimmer from the outside light flickered in through the small pane of glass at the top of the door. Automatically she felt for the switch on the wall, but another sound caused her to pause. Was it from upstairs?

She could ring her friend to come over. To check it out for her. But she didn't want to be a burden. She wasn't easily frightened, but something warned her to be careful.

'I'm always careful,' she muttered, having learned the hard way. She climbed the stairs in the darkness.

Tomorrow she'd laugh about this, but tonight she didn't feel like laughing. She felt sick to her stomach, and the unknown noises weren't helping.

On the landing, she waited and listened. Not even a breath of air as she held her hand to her chest, gulping silently.

'Don't be silly,' she said out loud when at last she allowed herself to breathe normally. 'It's only birds on the roof.'

But there were very few birds around, she reminded herself. A bat in the attic? Yuck. Instinctively her hand flew to her hair. The idea of bats caught in the silky strands was almost more repulsive than a stranger hiding upstairs.

Her guts rumbled and another pain pierced her abdomen, shooting right up to her throat. She stood in the deathly silence, listening to her own laboured breathing. In. Out. In. Out. Imagining things.

'Maybe I am going mad.'

Doubling over, she screamed as the agony ripped her insides like a sharpened knife. She crawled into the bathroom, dragged down her jeans and hauled herself up onto the toilet. Her cries clogged her throat as the torturous throbbing clenched her lungs, squeezing them like plastic balls until she couldn't breathe at all.

She tried to pull up her jeans, but she had no energy. She kicked them down over her ankles and crawled out onto the landing. The

12

fetidness was tinged with something she could not have eaten. The taste was in her mouth. What was it? She struggled to put a name to the taste and smell. Her stomach was skewered once again. What was she to do? Phone. She must phone for help. Her mobile phone was on the kitchen table. The landline was at the foot of the stairs. Damn.

She dragged herself up along the wall and edged towards the stairs.

That was when she heard a whoosh. The flutter of material. Right before she felt the push between her shoulder blades. Then the thump-thump of her body as it tumbled, first against the wall and then against the steps, the hall floor coming towards her too quickly. Her hands flailed in front of her, trying to soften her landing on the hard tiles.

The crunch of bone on ceramic.

The crash of her head against the wall.

Two vertebrae in her spine snapping like chicken wings. From the torrid pain, she knew that she'd shattered her coccyx. Everything had happened so quickly.

She grabbed for the hall table and brought it down on top of her. The phone fell just out of her reach. Not that she could make a call. Her cranium smashed against the floor as she came to rest, one leg still on the stairs, the other twisted beneath her body, her nose broken. Blood poured out beneath her head for a time as her heart struggled to come to terms with the bodily assault. She couldn't breathe. Her airways constricted.

Air, she needed air. She tore at her throat, trying to bore a hole in it with her fingernails. But it was impossible. The pain was excruciating, but the feeling of suffocation made her hysterical.

It took some hours but eventually her heart gave up its struggle to pump blood through her damaged veins and arteries, and her soul exited her body in defeat.

CHAPTER TWO

Monday 20 November

Twenty-five-year-old Rachel Mullen's pet hate was tardiness, and here she was, half an hour late, walking into a group of people, most of whom she did not know. That should make it easier, but for Rachel, first impressions were key.

She rushed inside to a cacophony of voices, laughter and chat. Throwing her bags on the floor, she wriggled out of her damp coat. There was nowhere to hang it in the small vestibule, so she slung it over her arm. Her hair was falling out of the hastily tied bun on the top of her head, so she pulled off the bobbin and fluffed out the frizzy tendrils with her fingers. Picking up her laptop bag, she slung the strap over her shoulder, and draped her handbag over the other arm. She should have left them in the car or brought them home after her late-afternoon meeting. She felt a blush rise up her cheeks. Why had she had that drink with him? Feck it, she thought, it was worth it because things were progressing and soon her hard work would pay off. Yeah!

Plastering her best smile on her tired face, she pushed open the inner door and entered the buzzing room.

'There you are, Rachel.' The young woman approaching her was sporting an insincere smile. 'Glad you made it. Food is about to be served. Here, have a drink while you wait. I know you love Prosecco. Or maybe you'd prefer vodka?'

'Prosecco is fine.' Rachel wasn't fussed at the moment, though a shot would have been better. But not vodka. That resurrected too many bad memories.

'I know it was some time ago but I'm sorry about your mum.' The woman handed over a drink and disappeared into the gathered mass of people.

'I'm sure you are,' Rachel mumbled. She stared at the slim flute of sparkling liquid with its sad-looking strawberry swimming in it, then downed it in one go, strawberry too, and picked up another glass from a tray before making her way into the midst of the milling people. She felt out of place, and wrongly dressed. Though it couldn't be much later than 7.30, most people were dressed in party attire while she was still in her business suit.

She couldn't see anyone she knew, so she drifted back to the outer edges, parked herself against a wall and watched people interacting with each other. They're all fake, she thought. Very fake. But then if they were fake, what did that make her? She knew her life was built on one big lie and had spent the last nine years trying to absolve herself. But her mother's death two years ago had made her think about things differently. Could she right the wrongs of her youth? She could only try.

A tug on her sleeve caused her to swirl around.

'Hi there. You look as happy to be here as I do. Do you come here often?'

'Did you just make that up?' She forced a smile, looking him up and down. She noticed him swaying as he tried to stand still. She decided he was quite drunk.

'Ha, ha,' he said mockingly. 'You're very funny when you want to be.'

'You don't even know me.' She was bored already and tried to move away. He held on to her sleeve.

'Aren't you one of the Mullen sisters? I work for Hazel Clancy. You used to be friends with her, didn't you? She sent me here to represent her tonight.'

Rachel felt her throat go dry as the name conjured up an old memory. Why had Hazel been invited?

'Like a million years ago.' The words stumbled from her mouth.

'Come on, let's get out of here. We could catch a few at Danny's Bar. Doesn't that sound like a better night out than being stuck here with these bores?'

Swatting his hand away, accidentally spilling some of her drink on his shirt, she stepped backwards against the wall. The room was suddenly too warm, and she felt laden down with her bags and coat. 'Look, I don't mean to be rude, but I need to talk with these people. I have to make contacts for my new business. That's why I'm here. If you don't mind, I'd like to mingle on my own.'

'You're quite the tease, aren't you?' He smiled.

She relented a little. Anything for a quiet life. 'I'm Rachel.'

'Andy,' he said.

Ah, now she knew exactly who he was. The clown who invariably ruined everyone's night out by drinking too much. Nothing had changed, then, over the years. 'Could you get me a drink, Andy? A *proper* drink. Gin and tonic.'

'If you give me your phone number.'

'Deal.' She went to open her handbag.

'It's a free bar. Annie Fleming is being generous tonight. I suppose it's not every week Ragmullin has a new restaurant opening.'

'Here,' she said quickly, handing him a card. 'My number's on it.'

'Thanks.' He pocketed it. 'I'll be back in a tick.'

As he squeezed through the bodies, she breathed a sigh of relief. Immediately, though, a young girl approached her carrying a tray of canapés.

'Please take some,' she said, her eyes flitting about nervously.

'I've no free hands,' Rachel said, but she pushed her handbag further up her arm and politely picked up a canapé, wondering how she could balance it with everything she was already holding. Best to send it down the hatch. The girl offered the tray again; Rachel took another one. 'That's enough or I'll look like a whale.'

'You look just fine to me,' the girl said.

'I'm here to make an impression, but I'm afraid I'm the worse for wear. Think I've already had two Proseccos.'

'Oh, don't worry, everyone here is in the same boat.' The girl winked, her dark eyes muted, and headed off to find someone else to help lighten her tray. Rachel noticed a certain sense of isolation and loneliness in the way she carried herself. She herself had been there not that long ago, but now she was full of ideas and enthusiasm for her new venture after escaping from years working in a bank. She had to make this work.

'Here you are,' Andy said, a glass full of ice and a shot of gin in one hand, and a bottle of tonic in the other.

'Let me finish this first,' she said, indicating the cracker piled with pâté and a slice of cucumber on top.

'That looks gross,' he said.

'Chicken liver.'

He made a puking motion. 'Double gross.'

She smiled and swallowed before taking the gin and pouring the tonic to the brim of the glass. Andy was helping her to relax after the stress of her earlier meeting. She didn't really know him, hardly remembered him, so could he be confusing her with her sister? In that instant, she wished she had taken up Beth's offer to spend the night in Dublin, despite the fact she'd have had to endure a rock concert. For twins, she and Beth had quite different tastes, she conceded.

'Did you not get one for yourself?' she asked.

'I've a pint of Guinness resting. Be back in a minute,' he said, returning to the bar.

Sipping her drink, Rachel saw the evening's hostess, Annie Fleming, eyeing her through a bank of shoulders and hair. Tipping her glass in acknowledgement, Rachel turned away quickly, desperate to find someone to talk with. She didn't want to get into a conversation with Annie. That would be awkward, and she wasn't sure she'd be able to hide her guilty conscience. But she wanted to avoid Andy, who saw himself as her new best friend.

As she looked around, she discovered she knew very few of the people at the party. Much as it had seemed like a good idea in a business sense, she did not want to be here.

Her hand began to jitter and her drink splashed onto her red blouse and her leather handbag. She took a gulp to empty the glass a little. Ugh. It felt hot and tasted awful. Maybe the tonic was out of date? Her throat burned but she couldn't stop herself giggling like a teenager, without finding anything remotely funny.

Her bones creaked with exhaustion and she felt herself sway. Had the Andy fellow spiked her drink? Wouldn't surprise her, seeing as he knew Hazel. She could have done without that blast from her past.

Bending over in a fit of coughing, she tried to sip her drink. It was disgusting, but she swallowed deeply to stop the cough.

People. All around. Straightening up, she approached one group and began telling them about her business and how it was going to work. At least she imagined that was what she was talking about, but as she turned away to latch onto another small group, she had no idea what she had actually said.

She had to leave. It had been a mistake to come. She could have been at the 3Arena in Dublin with Beth, shaking her hair out to The Killers.

She placed the glass on the floor, feeling dizzy and sick and tired. Fumbling through her bag, she was unable to find her phone to call a taxi. She'd look for it when she was outside. She made her way quickly through the crowd and out the door. Pausing in the vestibule, she saw her reflection in the mirror there. A face she didn't recognise stared back at her. Her hair was wild, her skin streaked with mascara, her pupils dilated. Who was this person? She fled outside.

Sitting on the kerb in the spills of rain, Rachel found her phone buried in the bottom of her bag. Once she'd called, she prayed the taxi would arrive soon. She didn't know how long she could hold onto her belongings and her consciousness before exhaustion overtook her. She was doing her best to make it in the business world after all she'd been through. But now, sitting sopping wet on the pavement, she felt bereft, because all she could think of was her mother's last hours.

CHAPTER THREE

Tuesday 21 November

Boyd knew he should have kept on cycling. Don't stop. None of his business. Words of warning going around in his head, making him dizzier than he'd been for a while. His leisurely early-morning cycle before work making his days of pounding the roads prior to his illness a memory. But he was on the road to recovery from cancer, and a trip on the cycle lane on the outskirts of Ragmullin, along the old railway track by the canal, was a tonic. The Greenway, the council called it, though today there was little greenery on the bare branches and the November sky was a pasty muse of grey. Slime rested on the canal water. So why did he stop? Curiosity? Or pity?

Leaning his bike against the trunk of a dying tree, he wandered back to where the girl sat on the tarmac path, her oily fingers attempting to thread the chain back onto the High Nelly bike.

'Can I help you?' he said, crouching, his knees creaking. It was going to take some time to return to any kind of fitness. His course of chemotherapy had been harder to bear than the cancer.

She looked up, before returning her attention to the chain. He was stunned; not by her beauty, though he had to admit she was very pretty, but by the look that seemed to hollow out the depth from her eyes. Sad? Lost? Maybe. Definitely hostile.

'Are you okay?' he offered.

'Fuck off.'

What age was she? Maybe fourteen, fifteen? It was hard to tell nowadays. Her hair was jet black, like the blackbird that hugged the branch high above their heads. Her skin pale with the hint of a few freckles on her nose. He couldn't tell her true eye colour, but if pushed, he'd have said they were the darkest brown he'd ever seen. Shadows circled like bruises beneath her long lashes, and even though instinct told him to get back on his bike and cycle on, he remained where he was.

'Is this your bike?' Now why had he said that? Her shoulders hunched together so quickly he thought he heard the blades strike each other.

'What do you care? I can fix it myself.'

'It looks big for you.' He was thinking it was old-fashioned but didn't want to insult her. He had that urge again to leave. But he stayed, hunched down, unmoving, captivated by the darkness of her eyes.

'It was my granny's bike. Not that it's any of your business.'

'Don't suppose it is. But I think you're threading that the wrong way. I know a little about bikes. Let me help. Please.'

He was surprised by her sudden movement as she stood and thrust the bike towards him. The force of it propelling him backwards. She was a lot stronger than her razor-thin appearance led him to believe.

She wiped her hands on her faded jeans with the torn knees. By design or wear-and-tear? Probably the latter, he thought, as he assessed her red T-shirt at least two sizes too big and her Converse with no laces.

'What's your name?' He knelt to fix the chain.

'You talk a lot. My mammy always said I shouldn't talk to strangers.' She said this with a hint of sarcasm. Goading him.

'I'm Mark. My friends call me Boyd. You can call me Boyd.'

'I'm not your friend. I don't want to call you anything.'

'Fair enough. What can I call you?'

She toed the ground with the stained white sole of her shoe and bit her lip. Deciding. He continued working as if he didn't care. But for some reason he did. He cared.

'I'm Madeleine. My friends call me Maddy. You can call me what you like.'

'Well, Maddy, this chain is fixed for now. You need to oil it. Not too much, though. And don't leave the bike outside in the rain.'

'Where else can I leave it?'

'A shed or garage?'

She laughed then. The sound wasn't childlike. It was as if she'd once heard someone laugh like that and consigned it to memory until she found a time to use it.

'What's funny?'

'You.' She clutched the handlebars. 'Thinking I live in a house with a shed. We just about have a garden.'

He stood. 'Where *do* you live?'

'You ask a lot of questions.'

'You don't answer too many.'

'It's dangerous to talk to strangers.'

'I'm not a stranger now that you know my name.'

'You could be a murderer or a drug dealer for all I know.'

'I'm not.' He searched in the pocket of the pouch strapped around his waist. 'This is my card. I'm one of the good guys.'

He was surprised that she actually took the card but not surprised when a sneer spread across her face. 'You're a pig. Just my luck.'

He expected her to throw his card into the canal, but she didn't. She shoved it into her jeans pocket.

'What age are you?' he asked.

'Why do you want to know that?'

'You're out here alone at this hour of the morning. I know it's supposed to be safe, but still …'

'Would you ever piss off. I'm well able to look after myself.' She turned the bike around and threw her leg over the saddle. She looked awkward, as if she hadn't been cycling long. With one foot still on the ground, she pushed off, wobbled, then settled on the saddle and rode away from him.

Boyd watched as her hair floated behind her like the silky black mane of a thoroughbred horse and wondered where Maddy had been headed for when the chain fell off her granny's bicycle. He fetched his own from the side of the tree, but the need to cycle ten miles on the Greenway had deserted him. He got on the bike and rode in the girl's wake, heading back towards town.

He had a day's work ahead of him.

CHAPTER FOUR

After hanging her bag on the banister, Beth Mullen turned and banged the front door shut. In the kitchen, she found her flat sandals and slipped off her shoes. She filled the kettle with water and switched it on. The house was freezing. She looked at the heating control pad, knowing she really should be conserving the oil until one or other of them started making some money. She turned it on anyway.

'Lazybones, are you still in bed? I've the kettle on.' She spooned coffee from a jar into two mugs. Taking a milk carton from the refrigerator, she sniffed it, deciding it would have to do. 'We need to get some groceries.'

As the sound of the kettle rose to an ear-splitting roar, she thought they might also need to invest in a new kettle.

She was standing at the patio door, coffee in hand, looking out at their disgruntled garden, when she realised she was still alone in the silence of the morning.

'Rachel!' she yelled. 'I thought you had an early meeting with the bank. It's nearly nine, for God's sake.'

Swirling around, she frowned and placed her mug on the small table, then headed out to the hall and looked up the stairs, listening. Deathly silence.

Had her sister stayed out all night? Drunk, in some lad's bed? No! Though she suspected Rachel might have a mystery man. Maybe she had left for her meeting already.

She calmed her breathing and looked around the small hall, noticing what hadn't registered initially. The blue coat in a ball on the floor, and underneath it a handbag and laptop bag. Shit! Rage burned through her chest. This meeting had been their great chance at getting some more cash. And now everything was fecked.

Taking two steps at a time, her dress swishing around her legs, she climbed the stairs, her anger building with each step. By the time she reached the bedroom door, she was ready to explode.

'This is bloody ridiculous.' She pushed open the door. 'I can't believe you slept …'

Her voice trailed off as she looked at her sister lying on the bed. Body arched. Eyes rolled back in her head. Mouth open in a silent death scream.

She hesitated for a moment, then rushed to the side of the bed. Falling to her knees, she tried to take the hand in her own, but it was rigid and clutched to her sister's throat.

'Oh my God, Rachel! No!' Beth screamed the scream that her sister could no longer utter and realised in that instant that her life would never be the same again.

Rachel Mullen was dead.

CHAPTER FIVE

Boyd bumped the car up on the footpath between two parked vehicles, down the road from 36 Greenfield Drive, and switched off the engine.

'Before you say anything, I can't park any closer.'

'I'm not blind.' Lottie stared out through the rain-spattered windscreen. An ambulance and two squad cars were parked up in front. A long white station wagon with the technical bureau logo on the side caught her eye.

'Who called SOCOs?' she said. She opened the door and stepped straight into a puddle. 'Feck's sake.'

'Wasn't me,' Boyd said.

She smiled. It was good to have Boyd back by her side. And finally he was getting his wish. They were due to be married on Saturday. Four days away! He and Chloe had taken to the organisation of the wedding with gusto. She knew well enough to leave them at it. Despite being on the outside looking in, she still felt a flutter of excitement.

When the call had come to the station earlier, Boyd had just had a shower after his usual early-morning cycle and offered to drive her out to the scene, promising not to get too involved. Yeah, right! I'm a sucker for Boyd, she thought.

She took in her surroundings. The estate was made up of fifty or so two-storey houses, with well-kept gardens. As she hurried towards the house, Boyd followed. A uniformed officer stood by the gate with a clipboard in her hand and rain dripping from her heavy jacket.

'Good morning, Inspector Parker,' she said, grim-faced, but then a smile lit up her face as she saw who was standing behind Lottie. 'Morning, Sergeant Boyd.'

Lottie signed the page, headed for the door.

Boyd said, 'Not a great day for standing outside, Martina.'

'Hurry up, Boyd,' Lottie said. 'Time is evidence.'

'Where did you hear that?'

Ignoring his question, which was probably rhetorical, she took a forensic suit, gloves and booties from a SOCO. Standing under a small awning with rainwater pouring out over the blocked gutters, she began pulling on the over-clothes. She cursed herself for not having brought something to tie up her hair. It was longer now than it ever had been. Chloe's idea. For the wedding. She felt a pang of nerves settle in the pit of her stomach. Everyone seemed excited about it, but though she was looking forward to the day, she felt a sense of unease. Was she doing the right thing?

Shrugging off the moment of doubt, she zipped the suit up to her chin and pulled the hood over her unruly hair and a mask over her mouth and nose. Once she had on overshoes and gloves, she stepped into the narrow hallway.

There was a blue coat in a bundle on the floor and a couple of bags underneath it. There was plenty of space on the hooks on the wall, so why had the coat been left there?

'Someone was in a hurry,' she said over her shoulder. Boyd was still kitting himself out in the forensic overalls.

At the end of the hall was the kitchen, with white cupboards and a central island with steel-legged stools around it. A patio door had a white voile curtain dotted with stars. The wall held a massive abstract painting dazzling with all the colours of the rainbow, and in the corner stood an easel with a smaller canvas – a similar painting, unfinished.

Lottie nodded to a uniformed officer sitting in the living room with her arm around a distraught young woman who had her head buried in her hands. The sister who'd found the body. She should really be moved to the station, but for now she was out of their way, so Lottie decided to leave that conversation for later and headed back to the hall, where Boyd was standing at the bottom of the stairs.

'Body's up there,' he said.

'I gathered that.' She inched under his arm and made her way up, following the sound of voices to a bedroom. She spoke to one of the SOCOs. 'Is McGlynn here yet?'

'He's on his way,' the SOCO replied.

'Gerry, is it?' she asked the young man with a camera in his hand.

'Yes.'

As she couldn't think of anything else to say to delay the inevitable, she stepped into the room.

'Holy God, what happened to her?'

No one answered.

She moved closer, holding her breath. The young woman was on her back, her body arched unnaturally in full rigor mortis, heels dug into the mattress, head buried back into the pillow and her mouth open in a silent scream. It was hard to see, but Lottie could swear her bottom did not even touch the bed. She stared at the face and found it difficult to decipher the age, but the report indicated she was twenty-five. The brown hair was shoulder-length and frizzy. She was clothed in a short-sleeved red blouse, the buttons done up except for the top three, which appeared to have been torn open. Threads hung from the buttonholes and there was a definite rip in the material. Her navy trousers were unzipped, showing a distended belly and the top of white cotton knickers. Her feet were bare, the soles an unusual pigmented colour.

Exhaling her held breath, Lottie walked around the bed as SOCOs moved out of her way. She felt her head contract and a fuzzy feeling prickled behind her eyes. The atmosphere was brimming with a malignant presence. If she believed in the devil, she was sure he had visited this young woman.

'Don't you think we should wait for McGlynn?' Boyd said, remaining by the door.

'No,' Lottie replied. 'I don't see any evidence of a struggle having occurred with someone else.'

At the foot of the double bed, a pair of red shoes lay on their sides, and a navy jacket with silver buttons had been dropped on the floor. Lottie couldn't stop her eyes returning to the pillow. The young woman's eyes were rolled back in her head, leaving only the whites staring at her. She studied her mouth, which was twisted like the gnarled bark of an old oak tree. Froth and vomit were smudged on and around her lips, chin and neck, as if a fungus had taken root. There were marks like bruises around her nose and mouth. Had her nose been broken? There was no blood.

'Jesus,' Boyd whispered, breaking the deathly silence. 'What the hell happened to her?'

Before Lottie could reply, a voice bellowed behind them. 'What are you two doing in the middle of my crime scene?'

It shook her out of whatever trance had taken hold of her, and she glanced over Boyd's shoulder to see Jim McGlynn's green eyes glaring above his mask.

'For what it's worth, we didn't touch a thing,' she said.

'You're here, aren't you? Slap bang in the middle of everything. How am I supposed to do my job, eh?'

'Jim, tell me what it looks like to you.' Lottie ignored his ranting; she knew him well enough by now and they tolerated each other. But

29

she was aware that she needed McGlynn more than he needed her. He was the most professional forensic expert she had met in her career.

'How do I know? I can't see anything. You're standing right in front of me. The pair of you are like fecking giraffes that have escaped from the zoo, so you are.'

Stepping to the side, Lottie let McGlynn move forward. He took one pace and stopped. Assessing. Formulating. Visualising. He moved his head around, looking from the ceiling to the floor, at the curtained windows, across to the small cabinet with a blinking radio clock and a half-empty glass of a clear liquid. Eventually his eyes landed on the bed.

'Drugs, do you think?' Lottie ventured.

'Poison,' McGlynn said, confirming what she'd suspected. 'Most likely strychnine. That's rat poison for the likes of you, but we'll need a post-mortem to confirm it. Call the state pathologist.'

'I'll do it.' Boyd sounded relieved to leave the room.

'Self-inflicted?' Lottie asked.

McGlynn rounded on her. 'I told you before and I'll tell you again, Detective Inspector Parker, I am not God.'

She smiled behind her mask. McGlynn's mantra was old. And he always called her by her title when he was vexed, which was most of the time.

'But in your expert opinion, what do you think?' she said.

He blew air loudly out from his nose, his mask expanding and contracting like a balloon. 'In my expert opinion, you need to get out of my crime scene.'

'It's definitely a crime, then?'

'Of course it's a bloody crime. From the arching of the body and the rigor mortis, my best guess is strychnine poisoning within the last twenty-four hours. And because the substance is painful to ingest, it's not the usual choice for suicide.' He bent down and sniffed the glass

– 'Seems to be only water, but it'll be analysed' – then leaned over the body. 'There's evidence of bruising around her mouth, jaw and throat.'

Lottie took a step forward. 'Someone forced her to drink the poison?'

'Or someone speeded up the process by trying to smother her.' McGlynn called to his photographer. There had to be a record of the way the scene presented. 'Gerry, you know what you have to do; be quick about it.'

As McGlynn retreated to allow Gerry access to the bed, Lottie glanced at the woman's hands. One was like concrete, the fingers gripped around the bunched-up sheet. The other had clawed at her neck. She stared again at the bruises and the clearly visible scratches. The nails were painted a deathly black, as were those on her toes. As the camera flashed, she saw something that added to the confusion of the scene.

'Jim, is there something in her mouth?'

McGlynn pushed the photographer to one side and peered into the woman's mouth without touching it. 'I think you're right, but I'll have to wait for the pathologist.' He sniffed loudly and looked up at Lottie, but she was lost for words.

'One thing is certain,' she said eventually, 'this young woman died an awful, painful death.'

'And so will you if you keep standing there and don't let me get on with my job.'

'Thanks, Jim.' It was nice to be polite, she thought, even if the other person was rude.

Before she left the room, she gave a final glance back at the victim, her mind racing. *Why did someone kill you, Rachel Mullen?*

CHAPTER SIX

Maddy flung the bike behind the front wall and trekked into the house. Her jeans were streaked with oil and her hands and nails stained black. She walked into the kitchen, turned on the tap and held her hands under the dribble of water.

'Why is the water cold?' she yelled. Receiving no reply, she turned off the tap, went to the hot press and switched on the immersion.

'Don't turn on the immersion, missy.' Her sister's croaky voice came from the living room.

'I'm covered in oil, Stella. I need to wash my hands. The water's freezing.'

'You know we don't have enough money to cover the electric bill. It's due at the end of the month. Don't want the feckers turning off the power, so use the cold. Did you get my money from last night?'

Maddy dried her oily hands on the grimy tea towel and sauntered through the gap where once a door had hung. It was long since broken and flung into the back garden, where it hid the swampy patch in the grass. She lounged against the jamb.

'I got cash. Need me to buy anything with it?'

'Give it here.'

She placed the rolled-up notes on the arm of the couch. 'What are you doing there, Stella?'

'What does it look like? It's like getting blood from a stone, trying to squeeze milk from these useless tits of mine for this hungry little shit.' Stella's dark hair was matted to her scalp, her face flushed bright pink from the exertion. Her body seemed to flop as she moved slightly to find a better position for her baby daughter.

'Why do you bother?' Maddy watched her sister trying to feed her month-old daughter. Stella was only four years older than her, but already she had two kids. No way was Maddy having even one kid before she was nineteen. She glanced at the framed photograph on the mantelpiece and shivered, quickly returning her attention to her sister.

'It's cheaper than formula,' Stella said, her hooped earrings jabbing into her shoulders. 'I'm so tired of the little shits.'

Turning away, Maddy headed up the bare stairs. One of Stella's ex-boyfriends had ripped up the carpet and sold it. The wallpaper, which the council had pasted up before they'd been allocated the house, was in ribbons. In the bedroom, Maddy tore off her clothes and pulled on a pair of fluffy socks to protect her feet from the gnarled floor. She found a half-clean pair of jeans – or rather, as she realised when she had them on, half-dirty – and a T-shirt she'd only worn twice. She sniffed under the arms and decided she'd get another turn out of it. She searched for deodorant but couldn't find any. She looked in her sister's room which Stella shared with her two-year-old son.

When she was dressed, she shouted down the stairs. 'Stella, where's Trey?'

'Outside somewhere. And stop shouting, for fuck's sake. Ariana's just fallen asleep with my tit in her mouth. Peace for a few minutes before the little bitch starts bawling.'

Maddy grimaced each time her sister called the kids names. It wasn't right. They were breathing, living little people that Stella had brought into the world, and the least she could do was be nice to them and care for them. Her heart stuck in her throat at a memory … but she quickly blinked it away. Neither Stella nor she herself had been properly cared for growing up. They had different fathers and God himself only knew how many other siblings they had out in the world.

Sitting on her narrow bed, she stared out the window and wondered how her life had got to this state. Her mother had left them years earlier; it was rumoured by the neighbours that she lived somewhere in the countryside outside Ragmullin. Maddy didn't really know where and cared less. Her mother had been as heartless as Stella sometimes appeared to be. But Stella had good reason to be narky.

Their house backed onto another terrace, and beyond that were two more terraces. Further on was the field located behind the disused army barracks. Sometimes Maddy took Trey there and let him run around in freedom. It might not even be safe. She'd once met a local historian wandering around the perimeter searching for unexploded grenades. Still, there weren't many places she could bring a two-year-old without getting funny stares and snide remarks.

She heard the front door open and shut, and the plop of feet across the hall floor. Trey? She jumped off the bed and raced down the stairs.

But it wasn't Trey who was standing in the kitchen. She came to a halt, realising it was Stella's creepy boyfriend Simon. His hand reached for her arm and he ran a solitary finger up and down her bare flesh. She felt goose bumps of revulsion rise on her skin like pops of corn.

'How's my favourite sister-in-law?' His lips curled in a sneer.

'I'm not your fucking sister-in-law, Simon, and if you know what's good for you, you'll get out of my way.'

Before he could react, she dipped under his arm and flew out the door, leaving him standing there with his mouth open wide.

*

In the downstairs hall of the Mullen house, Lottie checked who the coat and bags belonged to, with a yell to the officer in the kitchen. When she was told they were Rachel's, she asked a SOCO to take care of them.

'Has all this been photographed?'

'Yes, it has.'

Under the coat was a black leather handbag and a laptop bag. She unzipped the handbag. Phone. Wallet. Tampax. Small linen purse with a lipstick and mascara inside, brands she didn't recognise. No perfume. In the wallet, she confirmed the victim's name from her credit card. She shook her head at how neat and tidy it all was. No car keys. No receipts. No bills in envelopes. No notes scribbled on bits of tissue or pages torn from notebooks. Very unlike the mess you'd find in her own well-worn handbag. She tapped the phone screen. It flashed brightly, showing 30% battery life. There were no missed calls or texts displayed on the lock screen, only a command to enter a PIN password. Damn.

The laptop case held no paperwork, just a MacBook Air. She asked the SOCOs to make sure they dusted everything for fingerprints before bringing the laptop to the station as a matter of urgency. She slipped the phone into a small plastic evidence bag and headed to the living room.

Boyd had replaced the uniformed officer beside the young woman on the couch. His arm rested loosely around her shoulders and Lottie felt an unnatural sense of jealousy. Not the time or place, she thought as she approached them.

The young woman looked up, her face tear-stained, and Lottie gasped involuntarily. If she hadn't just come down from viewing the body upstairs, she'd have said Rachel Mullen was alive and seated beside Boyd.

Regaining her composure, she brought over a chair, sat and introduced herself.

'I'm Beth,' the young woman replied, 'Rachel's twin sister. I can see your shock. We're almost identical.'

In looks maybe, but Beth was dressed totally differently from her sister. Her entire body seemed to be enveloped in the balloon of a black linen dress, and her feet were shod in brown leather Jesus sandals. Her hair appeared wilder and a little longer than Rachel's.

'I'm sorry about your sister,' Lottie said.

'I can't get my head around it.'

'Can I call someone for you?'

'Mam is dead, and Dad is a waster. Don't bother calling him.'

Lottie thought this statement was odd, but Beth was in shock, so she was liable to say anything.

'We will have to notify him,' Boyd said. 'You can give me the details later.'

'I know you've already talked to members of my team,' Lottie said, 'but can you go through it again for me?'

'I don't know what to say,' Beth said, her eyes brimming with tears. 'What happened to Rachel? Why does she look like that?'

'I'm not sure. But I need you to talk to me so that I can understand.' Lottie stared at the tear-filled hazel eyes and willed the girl to speak.

Eventually Beth said, 'I should have been here, but I wasn't.'

'What do you mean?'

'Last night. If I had been here, maybe she'd be alive.'

Lottie wondered if Beth thought her sister had killed herself. 'Where were you?'

'I was in Dublin. Travelled up on the lunchtime train yesterday. I was at The Killers concert in the 3Arena. Friends had got the tickets ages ago. I stayed over. I was singing and dancing while Rachel was … Oh God. What happened to her?'

36

'That's what I intend to find out.' Lottie fought an urge to cradle the young woman in her arms. Boyd had the comforter role for now and she was the inquisitor. 'What time did you arrive home?'

Beth wiped her nose. 'I'm not sure. I got a lift from the city with one of the guys who was heading home to Ballymahon. He dropped me off at the head of the road. It might have been eight thirty or so.' She shrugged her shoulders slowly. 'It wasn't long before I made the call, maybe fifteen minutes. You can check that, can't you? The emergency call.'

'We can. You were expecting Rachel to be here, then?'

'She had an early meeting scheduled with the bank, so when she didn't answer me, I thought she'd already left. Then I saw her coat and bag in the hall. She works from home. We converted the box room into an office space. She worked out of there and I painted in the kitchen.' Lottie remembered the canvases. 'I like to think I'm an artist. Rachel believes I can make it big, but I'm not so sure. The competition is …' As if realising she was rambling, Beth stopped and dropped her head. 'All this means nothing without Rachel. We might have been sisters, but we were also friends. Sisters argue and fall out, but we never did. We saw life differently to other people. We focused on positive things. Oh God, what will I do without her?'

'You last saw her at lunchtime yesterday?' Lottie said.

'She drove me to the station. She has a car, I don't. I got the one o'clock train.'

'What type of car did Rachel drive?'

'A red Toyota Yaris. Quite old.'

'The registration?'

Beth looked confused. 'I can find it for you before you go.'

'That's fine, thanks,' Lottie said, but then something struck her. There'd been a single Yale key on the hall stand, but no sign of car keys either there or in the dead woman's handbag. 'Do you know where she kept her keys?'

'Usually in her bag. Or on the table in the hall.'

She filed it away for later. 'Why didn't Rachel go to the concert with you?'

'Are you joking me? She hates rock music … hated it, I mean.'

'Did she have a boyfriend? Someone she was close to?'

'No. No one in the last two years. She was consumed with her work.'

'What did she do?'

'She set up her own cosmetics company. She's trying to finance it. All above my head, as I haven't a way with figures like Rachel has … had.'

'Okay. I'll need a list of her friends.'

'Sure.'

Lottie was wondering why someone would want to poison a young businesswoman, and immediately her mind filled with the horrific vision of Rachel's body. 'Beth, do you keep any sort of vermin poison in the house?'

'What? Rats and mice? Oh God, no. We have no problems like that at all. Why?'

'I'm just covering bases.' She made a note to check what her officers found in the cupboards and shed. 'Do you know anything about your sister's movements after she dropped you at the station?'

'I didn't phone or text her, if that's what you mean. I posted photos on Snapchat and Instagram but she never liked any of them. I knew she was busy, though.'

'Doing what?'

'She had a meeting in the afternoon, but I have no idea who with. And she was to go to a party later – around six or seven. It'll be in her diary. On her phone or laptop.'

Lottie wondered about this. 'That seems early for a party.'

'It was an official opening type of thing. A new restaurant. You know, the one beside the Credit Union? Used to be a mall at one stage, I think.'

She had probably walked past it a thousand times with her head buried in wedding preparations or work or her kids. 'What's it called?'

Beth shrugged and sniffed. 'Annie's Restaurant. We used to go to school with Jessica, who manages it. She's the owner's daughter. Annie Fleming.'

Lottie let the information sink in for a moment before asking, 'Do you know if Rachel attended the party?'

'I presume she went there straight after her business meeting. Upstairs … well, she's still wearing her suit …' The tears fell fast, like a river breaking its dam.

Lottie waited until Beth had composed herself before continuing. 'The business meeting. Have you any idea who it might have been with?'

Another shoulder shrug, the voluminous dress expanding and contracting with the movement. 'I honestly can't remember. Maybe she told me, but I was all abuzz for Dublin so I may have tuned her out. All I know is that she had the meeting at five yesterday and the bank meeting this morning, with the party in between. She was so anxious to finance her venture.'

'Tell me how she came to set up her cosmetic business.'

Beth let out a long, strangled sigh and Lottie thought she might fold into her dress in a stream of tears once again, but the young woman straightened up before leaning into the couch, causing her head to rest on Boyd's arm.

'Rachel used to be employed in a bank branch in Roscommon. She started work there after she did a college business studies diploma. But then our mother got breast cancer, and that changed everything. I was the one at home looking after her. Rachel felt guilty, so she gave up her job and came home to help.' Beth paused. 'It was my fault, because

I was always giving out and complaining about all I had to do, and that I wasn't a nurse and I had no time to paint. Selfish shit, I was. If I was a better person, maybe Rachel would still be alive and working in her boring bank job.'

'You both did what you thought best at the time,' Lottie said, memories of her late husband Adam's illness resurfacing like a rocket to explode in her chest. She shivered and caught Boyd staring at her. With a slight shake of her head to tell him she was fine, she continued. 'How long was your mother ill?'

'By the time it was diagnosed, it was already in her brain. Stage four. She died within five months.'

'Can I ask where your dad was during all this?'

'Dad was useless. Scared shitless when Mum lost control of her body. He packed up and left. Escaped back to his own mother in Dublin. He came to Mum's funeral, but Rachel had a go at him, shouted and roared that he was a traitor, and that's the last we saw of him. He was never around anyhow, so he wasn't much loss.'

This sounded particularly harsh, but Lottie didn't want to press Beth as it more than likely had nothing to do with her sister's death. She filed it away in case she needed to tackle it at a later date.

'Rachel changed after Mum died. Said life was too short to live with regret, and if she didn't follow her dream, she might never do it. No one knows what's around the corner, that was her favourite mantra …' Beth sobbed into a paper tissue, blew her nose.

'So, her dream was to set up her own company?'

'Yeah. She was developing an organic cosmetic range. I did the branding, logo and graphics for her, set up her social media accounts, all that kind of stuff. But Rachel had the business brain.'

'Is it up and running yet?'

Beth shook her head. 'She needed a financial backer. Dad stopped paying the mortgage, so it fell to us to find the money to keep the house. My paintings don't fetch what they used to, and Rachel was eating into her savings. She had the groundwork completed, but to rent a small factory unit and all that, she was still lacking a substantial cash injection.'

'And you think this was to be ironed out at the meeting yesterday?'

'Yeah. She was a bit secretive about it, but at the same time she was excited. Now … none of it matters.'

Showing Beth the phone encased in the plastic evidence bag, Lottie said, 'Do you know Rachel's PIN number?'

'It's 2810.'

'Has that some significance for her?'

'It's our birthday.' Beth drew in an unsteady breath. 'To activate her laptop, just put SmoothPebble in front of the numbers.'

'SmoothPebble?'

'Her cosmetic's brand name.' She looked up from beneath her long lashes and blinked away the tears caught on the fine hairs. 'It's all dead; her dream is dead, and Rachel is too.'

CHAPTER SEVEN

Maddy was glad to escape the house. Simon gave her the willies. He looked at her like he wanted to lick her face and stick his tongue down her throat. Yuck. She wasn't hanging around for him to pinch her bum when Stella wasn't looking.

Wandering around the town, she glanced through shop windows without seeing the displays. People were dipping in and out of shops, but she was oblivious to them all. She scratched at her arms, trying to erase the touch of Simon's fingers. She had no idea what Stella saw in him. He was big and ugly and uncouth. She liked that word because it described him perfectly.

'Uncouth bastard,' she murmured, shivering violently. She'd come out without her coat. But she'd suffer that so she didn't have to listen to Simon's slurping kisses all over her sister's mouth.

Standing outside Boyne's shop, she realised how far she'd walked in the cold and drizzle. It was all glitter and glitz, decorated for Christmas since before Halloween. A family-owned business that had started out as a tiny store selling debs' dresses, it had developed over the years into a fully fledged department store. Now it sold everything from shoes and jewellery to books and mirrors.

As the door slid open automatically, she stepped inside knowing she could lose herself here for an hour. A fantasy hour imagining herself dressed in red lace with bling necklaces, and stilettos designed by men who didn't know the pain that went into wearing them. Not that Maddy had ever worn them, but she'd heard her so-called friends talk about them. Maddy wasn't a party girl.

She let her fingers run over the soft material swinging from a rack and picked out a green number. Satin bodice with a lace skirt. It was beautiful. Pressing her nose against the material, smelling the newness, she mourned the fact that she never got new clothes unless she struck lucky in a charity shop. She glanced around, waiting for someone to tell her to put the dress back. But no one ever noticed her. I might as well be invisible, she thought.

*

As she became engrossed in the world of fine fashion, Maddy was unaware that she was being watched with interest. The watcher knew all about Maddy Daly and her past. Things she'd said and things she'd been told. Was Maddy dangerous? Time would tell.

CHAPTER EIGHT

Once Beth Mullen had volunteered to give a DNA sample, Boyd went to fetch a garda to escort her to a neighbour's house. She'd be brought to the station later for a formal interview.

Lottie went out to the hall to find Jane Dore climbing the stairs.

'What have you got for me this time, Inspector?' The state pathologist had protective booties on over her heels, which she wore to raise her diminutive height. She pulled the strings of her face mask around her ears and tugged the hood down over her hair. Lottie always found it uncomfortable conversing with only eyes for expression, but she was used to it.

'Looks like poisoning,' she said, 'and there's evidence of force. They'll need further examination, but I believe the marks around her nose and jaw were caused by gloved fingers and the victim wasn't wearing gloves.'

'I'll examine them, and I'll try to speed up the toxicology analysis. Anything else to point to it being suspicious?'

'Jim and I think it might be strychnine, but there's no bottle or packet in the room that would have contained it. That's suspicious in itself.'

'I'll head up. I'll let you know when I'm ready to conduct the post-mortem.'

'I appreciate that.'

Once Jane was gone, Lottie lingered in the hall. She glanced at Rachel's laptop case and handbag and called over a SOCO. 'Why are these still here?'

'We had to dust for fingerprints and swab for traces of DNA before we could move them.'

'I know all that. But can it be hurried up?' Seeing his eyes crease in a scowl, she added grudgingly, 'Please.'

'Sure thing.'

'And when you've completed the forensic work on the laptop, I want it bagged and logged and sent post-haste to my tech team, marked for Gary's attention. He's the best.'

She searched in the pockets of Rachel's coat. No car key there either.

After taking off her forensic suit, she waited at the gate while Boyd dumped his into a brown paper evidence bag. She made a phone call to the station and organised a team to commence door-to-door interviews and to determine if anyone had CCTV on their houses. When she had finished, she looked up and down the road. 'Where's her car?'

'What?' Boyd said.

'Beth told us Rachel's car was a red Toyota Yaris, but I couldn't find her keys in the house.' She glanced at the registration number she'd keyed into her phone. Beth had found it on a motor tax renewal form. She scanned the parked cars. There was no sign of Rachel's.

'Maybe she left it at the party and took a taxi home,' Boyd offered.

'Check it and find out who was at that party.' They got into the car and Lottie snapped on her seat belt. 'Let's go to the restaurant and talk to Annie Fleming, the owner.'

Boyd did a U-turn on the narrow road. 'I doubt it's open yet.'

'I want to have a look at it anyway.' She could feel Boyd glancing at her as he drove. 'What's on your mind?' she asked.

'I'm confused by the whole scene. What do you think happened to Rachel?'

'Some bastard poisoned her, that's what happened. Hopefully SOCOs can find us evidence, and if the gods are kind, one of the neighbours heard or saw something and will have good-quality security footage.'

'You might as well dream here as in bed,' Boyd said.

The town was quiet for a Tuesday, and he got a parking space right outside Annie's Restaurant. 'It's closed,' he said.

'So it is, Einstein.'

'You're very prickly today.'

'I've just seen the poisoned body of a twenty-five-year-old woman, so yeah, I'm prickly.'

'It's not that. What's bothering you?'

'In case you've forgotten, we're getting married on Saturday, and the last thing I need right now is a murder investigation landing in my lap.'

'I told you, you have nothing to do. Chloe and I have it all in hand.'

'I suppose if it all goes belly-up you can't blame me then.'

'Nothing will go wrong. My organisational skills are meticulous,' he laughed.

'I'll hold you to that.'

'You can hold me any time.'

She got out of the car and tried to peer through the restaurant's window. 'It's tinted. I can't see anything.' She had a good look up and down the street. Rachel's car wasn't parked up anywhere. 'Drive around to the back,' she said.

At the rear of the restaurant they found the gate locked with a two-inch-thick chain and padlock.

'Back to the station?' Boyd said.

'Hold on.' She rang Kirby and got a home address for Annie Fleming, then told him to go to Greenfield Drive and bring Beth in for interview and to get McKeown to check all the streets and car parks for Rachel's car.

'We're going to the lake,' she told Boyd.

'Bit chilly for a dip,' he said.

'Just drive the car, Boyd. Annie Fleming lives out there.'

CHAPTER NINE

As far as the eye could see, fields stretched into the distance, where the grass appeared greener.

'That's the golf course,' Boyd said as he took a sharp right.

'I know that, smart-arse.' Lottie gritted her teeth. 'Molesworth House should be up here somewhere.'

'Still think we're wasting our time. Rachel died in her own house.' Boyd eased his foot off the accelerator and allowed the car to glide around a corner.

'We have to account for her last hours,' Lottie said as she caught her first glimpse of Annie Fleming's home. 'And as the restaurant is closed at the moment, we need to speak with the owner. *Voilà!*'

Molesworth House looked majestic with the grey clouds clearing, bringing the rain off with them, and a mist was shifting up from the lake. 'It's been here since the seventeen hundreds, and was basically a ruin before being rebuilt and renovated,' Lottie said.

'And the golf club was established over a hundred and twenty years ago,' Boyd said.

'How do you know that?'

'I know my way around Google too, you know.' He laughed heartily, glancing at the phone in her hand.

The road narrowed as he took another right and parked. The area in front of the house had three cars parked in a triangle. Lottie checked to make sure none of them belonged to Rachel Mullen. None did.

Stepping out of the car, she looked up the concrete entrance steps at the massive black door with a brass knob and knocker. A silver bell hung to the right. It reminded her of her own family ancestral home, Farranstown House. Another thorn in her side.

'You don't think they knocked down the old house completely and rebuilt this on the site, do you?' she said.

Boyd scratched his head. 'I'd say it's a protected building.'

Glancing to her left, in the distance Lottie saw the sheen of lake water glinting as if fireflies were dancing on top as the sun broke through the mist.

She pulled on the bell and the door opened almost immediately. The woman appeared to be on her way out, cream woollen coat over one arm, keys in hand and an expensive-looking handbag swinging from the other.

Lottie showed her ID and introduced herself and Boyd.

'Annie Fleming,' the woman said. 'Call me Annie, everyone does.' A wide smile before a frown. 'What is this about?'

'Can we come in for a few minutes?' Lottie said, appraising the woman in front of her. Annie looked to be in her fifties. She wore a sleek black skirt to the knee with a matching blazer, a low-cut white silk blouse doing little to brighten the outfit. Her legs were expertly tanned, and her shoes were glossy black high heels that made her the same height as Lottie.

'I've to get into town. I need to work on tonight's menu. Time is money in my business.'

'Won't keep you too long, then,' Boyd said, flashing a disarming smile.

'I suppose I can give you five minutes. I'd really like to know what it's about, though.' She opened the door wider and allowed them to walk in, closing it behind them.

Standing on the black-and-white diamond-shaped tiles, Lottie took in the magnificence of the hallway. 'Wow!'

A stone staircase wound its way up towards an oval stained-glass window set into the wall at the turn of the stairs. The kaleidoscope of colours glinted off the white walls, casting rainbows about her head.

'That's the original staircase, and we restored the flooring,' Annie said, and pointed to a room to her right.

Lottie entered.

A young woman rose gracefully from behind a desk like a swan raising its head out of the water, eyes wary, no smile. Mid twenties, also dressed in a black skirt suit. Her hair folded around her neck as she turned towards Lottie. Silken black hair kept away from a smooth forehead with a pearl-studded hairband. Chloe had taken to wearing one recently so Lottie concluded they must be back in fashion.

'My daughter, Jessica,' Annie said, 'manager of Annie's Restaurant.'

'Pleased to meet you,' Boyd said, holding out his hand.

'That's what we want to talk to you about,' Lottie said quickly.

'I hope there's nothing wrong. Please sit.' Annie frowned and indicated a row of chairs by the wall, above which hung monster-sized portraits of people Lottie thought must be the woman's ancestors. As Annie pulled over an office chair to sit in front of them, Lottie felt like she was the one being interviewed.

'This is a fantastic room,' Boyd gushed.

'Thank you. I have to admit, it has the X factor. The wallpaper is hand-blocked. Created and shipped in from the UK. The chandeliers are French. See that painting over the mantelpiece?'

'It transports you back in time,' Boyd said.

'You're a man after my own heart,' Annie said, sweeping her hand around. Clear polished nails, manicured and pristine, Lottie noted, and a large diamond glinted on her ring finger.

Behind Annie, Jessica rolled her eyes, and Lottie couldn't help smiling. Her own daughters used to do the same when they were children. Even though they were no longer children, she supposed they still rolled their eyes behind her back. Her eldest, Katie, was currently in New York with her two-year-old son, Louis; they'd be home on Friday for the wedding the following day. They were having a ball, if the FaceTime calls were anything to go by. She supposed Louis's grandad, Tom Rickard, was spoiling the little boy. Katie was independent. Knew her own mind. When she wanted something, she went for it. Chloe wasn't much different. She worked in Fallon's pub in Ragmullin. It had recently changed ownership and Lottie had to admit it was decidedly more upmarket now, which eased her worries about Chloe working in the pub trade. She wondered what Adam would say if he was still alive. Then there was sixteen-year-old Sean. Still at home. Still grumbling. Still swinging through phases of being upbeat and downbeat. She was learning to recognise the moods and how to react. Or not to react at all, which was most of the time.

Feeling Boyd nudge her, she realised she'd been in a trance thinking of her family. She shook herself physically.

'Annie, we need you to tell us everything you can about the party held at your restaurant last night. We need a list of everyone who attended as guests, and your staff.'

'Whatever for?'

'We're investigating the suspicious death of a young woman whom we believe attended your party.'

'Oh my God. That's awful. Who was it? How did she die?'

'At the moment I just need you to tell me all you can remember about the evening.'

Annie squared her shoulders, and Lottie figured the woman was not used to being spoken to in such an authoritative manner. She cast a glance at Jessica, who had now seated herself back behind her desk. 'Were you in attendance too, Jessica?'

'I was.' It was the first time she'd spoken since they'd entered the room.

'In that case, join us over here. I need all the information I can get.'

Jessica's eyes darted towards the back of her mother's head, as if she was waiting for approval.

'For God's sake, Jessica, move,' Annie growled, 'and bring the lists the inspector asked for.'

If Lottie had spoken to her own girls that way, there would be hell to pay. But Jessica grabbed two sheets of paper from the desk and wheeled her chair across, sitting dutifully beside her mother. Annie took the pages and handed them over.

'I'm anxious to get to the restaurant, so what do you want to know?' Annie knotted her hands into each other on her lap, like a nun.

With the battle lines drawn, Lottie glanced over the guest list and noted Rachel Mullen's name. 'Did everyone who was invited attend?'

'Not exactly.'

'What do you mean?'

Annie sighed heavily. 'Some people sent colleagues or friends if they themselves couldn't be there. We had intimated on the invite that this was optional. I wanted to make a positive impression on the business community.'

'There were people there who aren't on the list? Was anyone taking names at the door?'

'No, but I'm sure we can add names to the list and email it on to you.'

'There are about forty names here. How many people attended altogether?'

Jessica glanced sideways at her mother as Annie shook her head. 'Maybe thirty or so. Jessica spent this morning taking bookings as a result of positive feedback. Plenty of photos on Instagram. A success is what I'd say.'

'Did all the guests arrive and leave at the same time?'

'Are you joking? Champagne and a free bar? It must have been eleven o'clock by the time I got to lock the door.'

'You locked up the premises yourself?'

'Yes. I only had staff hired in until nine thirty, so I let them go on time. Now I must hurry and let the cleaners in and prepare dinner menus for tonight. I'm not starting lunches until next week.'

'There's only one staff member on this list,' Lottie said. 'A chef, David Crawley. Did you have waiting staff?'

'Are they not on there? Jessica will email the full list to you. We hired in casual staff just for the party, including Darren, who usually works in Cafferty's. David Crawley is our full-time chef.'

'Haven't you got full-time waiting staff?'

'Not yet. I needed to see how our bookings took off.'

Jessica smirked and Lottie read between the lines. Annie was paying cash under the counter. But that didn't concern her now. She had a murder to solve.

She handed the guest list to Boyd and looked at Annie. 'Do you know Rachel Mullen?'

'Why do you want to know about her?' Annie said.

'Rachel's in the process of setting up her business, but most of the people listed are established businesspeople or local councillors. Seems odd to me that she was invited.'

'We knew her years ago. She went to school with Jessica. Recently she contacted me to see if I would help fund her new business.'

'And did you?'

'Good God, no. I'm struggling with finance after all the work I've had done to Molesworth. I told her over the phone about the party.

Said it would be a good opportunity to network. I never thought she'd turn up. I'm not sure she's even on the list. Jessica compiled it.'

'But you didn't offer to assist—'

'Inspector,' Annie cut in. 'I really need to get going.' She stood.

'Sit down, please,' Boyd said sternly.

Annie glared, but sat.

Boyd continued. 'Rachel Mullen was found dead in her home this morning. We are trying to trace her last known movements. For that, we need your help.'

Lottie's gaze moved between the two women. Jessica's hand flew to her mouth while Annie's jaw dropped.

'Oh my God! That's just awful. Why didn't you tell us it was Rachel at the start? I'll help you in any way I can.'

'I feel sick,' Jessica said. 'Can I be excused?'

'Wait,' Lottie said, thinking it was an odd way for a twenty-something-year-old woman to speak. It was like she was still in school. 'Did either of you see Rachel arrive?'

Jessica said, 'I … I did. She arrived just before we started serving the canapés.'

'Did you speak with her?'

'Not really. Maybe a few words.'

'What did you talk about?' Lottie said.

Jessica shrugged a shoulder. 'I just welcomed her and gave her a glass of Prosecco. I was busy and hadn't time to stop and chat, to be honest.'

'Any idea why she was late?'

'No. She wasn't that late anyway. It was around seven, I'd say.'

'Was she alone?'

'Yes.'

'Did you see her over the course of the evening?'

'I was mingling with the guests. Networking. I didn't notice who she was talking to or that.'

'And you, Annie? Did you see her or speak with her?'

'I was busy all evening. I may have seen her, but I can't honestly say I spoke with her.'

Lottie figured this meant that Annie had spent her time with people she assumed to be more important than Rachel. 'What time did she leave?'

'I have no idea,' Jessica said.

'I don't think she was with the stragglers I had to hunt out at eleven o'clock,' Annie added, her voice now devoid of its confrontational tone.

'Did you find a set of car keys when you were locking up?'

'No, but the place is a mess. I really have to let the cleaners and my chef in.'

'We'll need you to let us in first.' Lottie was thinking Annie would have no need for a chef today.

'Whatever for?'

'Because your restaurant is the last place we know our victim was seen.'

'Was Rachel murdered?' Jessica asked.

'For the moment we are treating it as a suspicious death,' Boyd replied.

'Oh that poor girl,' Annie said.

'Poor Beth.' Jessica hung her head. Trying to hide her tears, Lottie thought.

'Were you close to the Mullens?' She directed her question to Jessica.

'No. It's just that I never knew anyone who was murdered before. It's so sad.'

'It is that,' Annie said, and put a hand on Jessica's. It was the first affectionate gesture Lottie had seen between the two women since she entered the house.

'Can I have the restaurant keys?' she said. 'I need to have a look around, and we may need to let our forensic team in.'

'Surely you don't think anything happened to her on my premises?' Annie asked.

'We need to check everything.'

'I'll go with you then. There are security codes I need to enter.'

As she stood, Lottie gave one last look at the portraits hanging on the wall and wondered how Jessica could work under such watchful eyes.

CHAPTER TEN

While Jessica stayed behind to email the guest and staff lists to the station, Boyd followed Annie's Mercedes and Lottie rang Kirby. He confirmed that Beth had made her formal statement and was back at the neighbour's house. She told him to get a team together to follow up with those named on the Fleming lists and to get Lynch to check Instagram for the party photos. They needed to know if there was a suspect among them or if they had witnessed anything unusual about or around Rachel last night.

At the rear of the restaurant, they followed Annie to the back door. After dealing with a series of boxes requiring entry codes and the swipe of a card, she stepped inside and switched off the alarm.

'Hold on a minute,' Lottie said. 'I want you to stay out here.'

'I have things to do. David and the cleaners are due any minute.'

'Just wait here until we've had a look around, okay?'

Annie nodded and returned to her car.

Lottie and Boyd pulled on overshoes and gloves and walked along a narrow corridor that led to a kitchen kitted out with stainless-steel equipment. Everything appeared to have been cleaned. No utensils, plates or trays visible, and no left-over food anywhere. Further on, they entered the restaurant through an arch.

'It's bigger than I thought,' Lottie said.

'Really?' Boyd said.

Lottie glanced at him. 'Is there an innuendo in there somewhere?'

'You have a warped mind, Lottie Parker.' He walked ahead of her. She grinned and followed.

'It's quite tidy for the aftermath of a party,' she said. 'Annie did say it hadn't been cleaned, didn't she?'

'She certainly made enough fuss about letting the cleaners in this morning.'

Two rows of square tables and cloth-backed chairs lined the walls. The centre aisle was long and narrow. A few helium balloons had escaped their moorings and clung to the ceiling. Ribbons and streamers covered some of the tables, and glasses were lined up on the counter of a small bar halfway down the room to the right.

'It's dark, isn't it?' Lottie looked around for a light switch but couldn't see any. She took another step and felt her paper-thin overshoe sticking to the floor. Maybe the cleaners would have a job after all.

Boyd was scanning the glasses on the bar counter as she made her way towards the front door. She glanced out the window at the street beyond and noticed everyday life cruising past.

'Will we get SOCOs in here?' Boyd said.

'Could do, though I think Rachel was murdered in her own home.'

'She might have got a spiked drink here.'

'True. A sweep of the area wouldn't do any harm. Are you okay?'

'I'm fine.'

'I need to organise an incident team. You can go back to the office and start on it if you want. You look a bit tired.'

'I said I'm fine, Lottie.'

'Okay, if you say so.'

She retraced her footsteps, careful not to leave anything for McGlynn to lose his hair over later on if this place did indeed offer them some evidence of wrongdoing.

At the rear door, she saw Annie talking earnestly with a small man dressed in check trousers and a white tunic. He turned and held out his hand. Lottie pulled off her gloves and let him shake her hand. His grip was firm and dry.

'David Crawley. Head chef. The only chef at the moment,' he chuckled. 'Can I help you?'

She forced a smile at the squat man with his shaved head and puffy face. A tattoo trailed around his neck. What was it with men and their tattoos? As he released her hand, she noticed his fingers were chubby and a series of cuts traversed the backs of his hands. Was he even a good chef? She was sure that Annie would only want the best.

'Mr Crawley, we'd like a word. Can you come to the station with us? Won't take long.'

'If you think it's necessary, and you can call me David.'

Lottie sent him in Boyd's direction and called for a squad car to come with uniforms to cordon off the restaurant. After a short conversation with Annie, the woman handed over the codes and keys and headed off huffily in her Merc without a wave.

At the station, they brought David Crawley into an interview room. Boyd sat beside Lottie with Crawley facing them.

'Am I under arrest or something?'

'Not at all. We're just getting a feel for last night's event.'

'Annie told me what happened to that poor girl. Tragic.'

'Where do you live, Mr Crawley?'

'David will do. I live in Ragmullin with my wife and daughter.'

'I'll need the address.'

'Number 29 Campfield Drive. We have a nice house there. Terrific neighbours. We're good people.'

'I'm sure you are.' Why did he feel the need to say that? Lottie wondered. 'What time did you arrive at the restaurant yesterday?'

'Four on the dot. I had to prepare finger food.'

'Could anyone have interfered with the food?'

'No way on earth. I oversaw the pass. Food placed on trays, sent out and served.'

'What time did you leave the restaurant?'

'Must have been nine thirty by the time I was happy with the kitchen. I left straight away.'

'Did you have any interactions with the guests?'

'None at all. Annie was very excited. Big night for her.'

'You didn't notice anything out of the ordinary?'

'I'm not sure I follow you.' He leaned over, his head like a turnip between his hunched shoulders. 'I was in the kitchen. I prepared the food. That's all. What happened to that poor woman?'

'I'm asking the questions, Mr Crawley.'

'Sure thing. Sorry. I saw some people arrive and Miss Fleming was all biz. She doesn't let me call her by her first name like her mother does. She told me she would give me the nod when to bring out the food, so I was standing at the arch. I thought all the guests were there, but then I saw a woman arriving late. All flustered she was. That's when Miss Fleming told me it was time to serve the food.'

'What time was this?'

'Around seven, I think.'

'Did you notice anything in particular about this guest?'

He pushed his bottom lip over his top, thinking before he answered. 'Not really. Tall and pretty. Can I say that? Her hair was damp like she'd been caught in the rain.'

'What did you do then?'

'I called the waiting staff to begin serving the food and handed out the trays. There wasn't a whole lot. I think there was to be about forty guests.' As he talked, his flesh rippled and his tattoo seemed to crawl around his neck as if it was alive.

'It was just canapés, then?' Lottie said, and he nodded. 'Can you be more specific?' She was almost certain Rachel hadn't been poisoned by the food. More people would be sick or dead if that was the case.

David sighed and closed his eyes as he recited. 'Puff pastry, which I made myself, topped with smoked salmon, chicken liver pâté, Parma ham, prawns, tomatoes, goat's cheese and halloumi. Sour cream and salsa dips freshly made. Oh, and guacamole cones.' He opened his eyes.

'I want you to write out a list of all the ingredients you used. Where it was sourced from and anyone who might have had access to it.'

'I can do that.'

'Who else helped prepare the food with you?'

'I didn't need help. I'm an expert chef.'

'I don't doubt that, but I need to know who else had access to the food you prepared?'

'The waiting staff after I put the food on trays.'

'And the drinks? Who served those?'

A shrug. 'I don't know about that. The bar was open. Servers went round with trays of glasses. You can get a staff list from Miss Fleming. I think she used local people.'

'Okay. If you think of anything else, anything unusual about last night, please let me know.'

'I can go now?'

'You can.'

He stood, bowed as if she was royalty and rushed out of the interview room.

CHAPTER ELEVEN

Lottie got ready to set up an incident team. They had so little information. Why had Rachel been murdered? She hoped Jane commenced the post-mortem today. She needed answers. Nothing presented as logical. But then murder rarely was.

She stuck a photo of Rachel, one they'd pulled from one of her social media accounts, onto the whiteboard. Her blue eyes sparkled, and her hair hung loose about her shoulders in a style that looked carefree, though knowing her own daughters, Lottie guessed it was the work of straighteners. In reality, Rachel's hair was more frizzy than straight. Her nose was speckled with freckles and her mouth had perfect butterfly lips. It was a better image to have on display than that of the death mask.

Detective Lynch had been tasked with trawling Rachel's social media accounts. There was only business stuff to relate so far.

'Most of those who were at the party probably have private accounts,' Lynch said.

'Try a hashtag search. Use your head.' Lottie had no time for pandering to anyone today, plus she felt her skin come out in hives whenever Maria Lynch was close. Following her last case, someone had reported her for, among other things, taking shortcuts to reach closure of the investigation. Though she had no proof, she was certain it had been Lynch.

On the board Garda Brennan had attached the lists of the staff and guests that Jessica Fleming had sent over. One guest name stuck out, but Lottie parked that conversation for the moment and went in search of Gary, her technical guru.

He was already working on Rachel's laptop. He raised his glasses and acknowledged Lottie beneath the steel-framed rims before replacing them on his nose. He was young and enthusiastic, but craved recognition.

'You're doing a great job here, Gary. Helped solve more cases than I've had breakfasts.'

He laughed. 'I don't think you have a reputation for eating breakfast, Inspector. Now if you'd said more cases than you've had McDonald's coffees, then I'd be rightly chuffed.'

'Whatever you say, but I do appreciate your work.'

His cheeks seemed to glow with pride, and he stuttered and stammered. She couldn't make out a word he was saying.

'In plain English,' she urged.

'Yeah. Right. Sorry. Definitely onto something.'

'Really?' Lottie pulled over a chair in the cupboard-like office that Gary inhabited along with a collection of half-empty paper cups and Diet Coke cans. Could Rachel have been killed because of some major discovery she'd made in the course of her business?

'She'd developed brilliant business plans and strategies,' Gary began. 'Top of the game, if you ask me. Very organised, and to the point. This lady knew the beauty world.'

'Explain?'

'Her business is called SmoothPebble. Organic beauty products. I know it's been done before, but her plans make it look like she had her head screwed on.'

'Beth, her sister, told me that Rachel was developing a cosmetic line, but that concept has been on the go since Adam and Eve.'

'I know, but she was espousing the use of natural products mined from the earth. Ground stone and gravel to make body scrubs. Plants and leaves for face masks. That kind of thing. Might not be new, but the way they're manufactured is innovative. Very technical. Not sure you'd understand it, so I can dumb it down for you. That's if you need it?'

'Not now. Write up a note on it.'

'Before I start work on the phone, there's one other thing. Rachel was planning to get funding to develop some kind of facial recognition app to determine which product would be most suitable for your skin type.'

Lottie hardly had time each morning to wash her face and slap on moisturiser, let alone stare into her phone until it told her the correct product to use.

'New and innovative enough to be killed for?' When she saw confusion flit across his face she added, 'It's okay, that was a rhetorical question. What do you know about strychnine?'

'Haven't seen it mentioned in her plans, but I know it's used to kill rodents.'

'Where's the best place to buy it?'

Gary leaned over the laptop and pulled one of his many keyboards towards him. 'Mmm,' he said.

'Mmm what?'

'You wouldn't find it on the shelf in Boots, but you'd probably be able to get it in any hardware store.'

She knew that, so why had she asked such a stupid question? 'I've barely had time to look at her phone. Her sister said she had a meeting yesterday. Can you find out anything further?'

'Hold on a minute.' He tapped Rachel's laptop and brought up her calendar. 'Here we are.'

Peering over his shoulder, Lottie read, *Finance meeting with Matthew Fleming*. Interesting. He was Annie Fleming's husband. Time: 5 p.m.

Leaving Gary to his work, she returned to the incident room, but before she could properly think over Rachel's meeting with Matthew Fleming, she was accosted by Superintendent Deborah Farrell.

'Tell me what's going on.' Farrell pointed a chubby finger towards the board, where Garda Brennan had added photos of Rachel's bedroom.

'Can we talk in your office?' Lottie said.

'What's all this got to do with Annie Fleming? I was at her restaurant yesterday evening.'

'That's why we need to speak in your office.'

Farrell stood transfixed in front of Rachel Mullen's photograph. 'I remember her. Saw her there.' She turned on her heel. 'Follow me.'

Lottie tracked her superintendent's footsteps down the corridor. Once they were both seated, Farrell folded her arms.

'I should have been informed without having to find out like this. I'm waiting for an explanation.'

Deciding to skip an insincere apology, Lottie cut to the kernel of the morning's events. 'At around nine o'clock this morning, the body of a young businesswoman was found by her sister at her home. The dead woman has been named as Rachel Mullen. It appears she was poisoned. The post-mortem should verify it fairly quickly. We also know she attended the party in Annie's Restaurant.'

'Okay. Go on.'

'Can you remember anything about her?'

'I spoke with her briefly,' Farrell said, unfolding her arms and leaning them on the table. 'I remember she was very animated describing some technical aspect of her business. When she mentioned cosmetics, I switched off and she drifted away to speak with someone else.' She looked at Lottie earnestly. 'You think one of the other guests poisoned her?'

'No evidence to suggest anything yet, but we'll be interviewing everyone who was on the premises last night and checking their social media posts. We might discover something interesting from their photos or videos, plus we have some CCTV footage to peruse. We don't know what time Rachel left the party or if she went anywhere else after Annie's before heading home. But it was a Monday night, so it's unlikely. We haven't located her car, or her keys. We're checking taxis.' Lottie crossed her fingers, praying that the little they had might throw up a lead. 'Her laptop and phone are with the tech guys. SOCOs are still working at her house, where the body was found. Hopefully they'll discover DNA or fingerprints that don't belong to Rachel or her sister. We need something to point us in a direction to follow.'

'What about the sister?'

'We're verifying that she was in Dublin where she said she was. Initial perusal of her Snapchat and Instagram tell us she was at a concert in the 3Arena, but in order to tick all the boxes, we need to check what time she returned to Ragmullin.'

'Right, so. Go ahead.'

Lottie made to rise from the chair, but sat back down again. 'Superintendent, can you tell me anything else about last night?'

'What do you want to know?'

Easing a breath out through her lips, she made herself comfortable. 'What was the nature of the event?'

'Annie Fleming sees herself as an up-and-coming entrepreneur. She's in her fifties, so I find what she's doing admirable. I'm all for women making a success in business, but …'

'But what?'

'I believe she just wants to rub it in her soon-to-be-ex-husband's face. The grapevine says he pushed her for a divorce, but she wouldn't agree. Proceedings are held up in the High Court, as far as I know.'

Lottie wanted to ask how Farrell knew all this, but she let her superintendent continue.

'In case you're wondering, I knew the family years ago. Matthew lives just outside Ragmullin, but he ran a quarry near Athlone, among others he had scattered around the country. I had a run in with him a couple of times when I was based there.'

'Rachel Mullen had a meeting with Matthew Fleming before she attended the party. Does that strike you as odd?'

Farrell scrunched up an eye, thinking. 'One of Matthew's daughters works on environmental issues for him. She'd be about Rachel Mullen's age. Maybe she arranged the meeting?'

'Maybe,' Lottie said, thinking this was the first she'd heard of another Fleming daughter. Making a note to investigate them further if anything significant pointed towards the family, she parked the idea for now and said, 'I'm troubled by the use of poison, and there's some evidence Rachel might have been smothered. That sounds personal to me.'

'Did she have boyfriend troubles?'

She remembered asking Beth for a list of Rachel's friends. 'I have to follow that up.' She paused to think for a moment. 'Once the pathologist can give me time of death, and maybe an indication to the time of ingestion of the poison, I'll know whether we need to concentrate on the venue. But it's going to be difficult, as the guest list is incomplete.'

'Have everyone checked out and have a look at the CCTV. Interview the staff who were on the premises too.'

Lottie wanted to say she knew how to do her job but bit her tongue. Farrell continued, 'And take a long, hard look at Matthew Fleming.'

'But he wasn't even at the party.' He might not have been on the guest list, but had he turned up?

'I can see your brain clicking away. For your information, as I was leaving around nine thirty last night, a silver BMW almost ran me down in the car park. I was so annoyed, I memorised the registration number and ran it through the system this morning.'

'Matthew Fleming?'

'Yes. Now why would he turn up at Annie's party? I presume he wasn't invited. I warn you, he's a slippery customer. I should know; like I said, I had a run-in with him before over his quarry business.'

'Okay,' Lottie said. 'Can you tell me if you noticed anything else out of the ordinary last night?'

'It was a very stilted affair. Awkward. Who holds a party with a free bar on a Monday night?'

'Not well thought out,' Lottie ventured.

'Annie Fleming wouldn't spend Christmas if she thought she wasn't going to benefit. She just wanted to show off.'

'But wasn't it only a small affair?'

'Nothing is for nothing where she's concerned. Watch your step on this one, Inspector Parker. Particularly with Matthew and Annie Fleming. There's an odd dynamic between them.'

'Thanks for the advice.' Lottie stood.

'And Parker?'

'Yes?'

'After your last case, you may have slithered out from under your suspension without a blemish on your record, with the chief superintendent banging drums in high places, making sweet music for you and your reputation, but let me tell you, I'm not a fan of music. Dismissed.'

CHAPTER TWELVE

Lottie called Boyd, McKeown and Kirby together to the incident room. She left Lynch to finish trawling through social media, following which she was to collate the information coming in from door-to-door enquiries.

'We could do with a bigger team,' Kirby said, and Lottie knew he meant she should include Lynch.

'Why don't you see if you can round up some of the footballers from Ragmullin Shamrocks then?' McKeown said with a smirk.

'Shut up,' Kirby growled.

'I'll be quick,' Lottie said. 'I want your feelings on this before we get down to specifics.'

'What's the motive?' McKeown asked. 'That's what I can't get my head around.'

'Yeah.' Boyd nodded. 'What made her a target?'

'And,' Lottie added, 'if her car isn't on the street or in the car park, where is it? Did the killer take it? Any luck with the taxi she called?'

'Working on it,' Kirby said.

'Get all the CCTV you can,' Lottie told them. 'I want to know everything there is to know about Rachel Mullen's last movements. At the moment, all we have to work on is the party, so find out who knew she was attending it.' She marked off her questions on her fingers. 'Did she get a bit tipsy at the free bar, cause a scene that we've yet to hear about? Did someone follow her home? Talk to her sister again. Find out who Rachel was friendly with.'

Boyd said, 'We need to find out if she had a boyfriend.'

70

'We already asked her sister, but follow it up. And find her father. Let me know of any developments on that score.'

'We need to interview the other guests face to face, not just over the phone,' Kirby said.

'That's going to take time,' McKeown pointed out.

Kirby shook his head. 'It's not like there's an army to interview.'

'Yeah, but we only have the invite list. We don't have the names of those they brought along with them.' McKeown glared at him and Lottie groaned inwardly.

Animosity was growing between these two detectives and she felt powerless to defuse it. McKeown had been drafted in when Lynch was away on maternity leave and he had been retained when Boyd got leukaemia. She was glad to have him on her team. The tall, shaven-headed detective was smart and intuitive, but also adept at riling Kirby, who had his own struggles. Losing his partner during a case, losing his home due to gambling, and now trying hard to get things right. She had to admit she had a very squishy spot for him.

She turned to him now. 'Have you contacted those we know about to make sure no one else is ill?'

'Most of them have been contacted by phone.' Kirby shifted his weight on the chair, causing it to squeak. 'Some sent replacements and others have volunteered the names of those they brought along. More follow-ups required. Can't I bring Lynch in on—'

Lottie cut across him. 'I've already spoken with the chef; what's the story on the staff hired in for the event.'

'I think there's only two or three,' McKeown said.

'Think? You should know!' Lottie paced a small circle.

'I had a word with Darren the barman,' Kirby said. 'He is a sound bloke. I know him from Cafferty's. Says he didn't notice anything unusual.'

'Any security footage in yet?'

McKeown again. 'We have the CCTV footage from the street outside the restaurant. But inside, the only camera is in the bar area, trained on the till. I have the disc to check, but I need to follow up on the rear car park CCTV.'

'Maybe we'll strike lucky.'

'Boss,' Kirby said, 'about Lynch …'

'Not now.' She didn't want to talk about Lynch, to whom she had allocated the drudge work. It would keep the meddling busybody stuck to her desk during the investigation.

Once they all knew what they had to do, she went back to her office. Lynch curled her lip but remained silent. Good.

As the day wore on, Lottie became more frustrated with their lack of progress. The CCTV threw up nothing new. When they eventually received the footage from the restaurant car park, she could see Super-intendent Farrell leaving and then a car speeding in before stopping at the rear wall. There was no image of whoever alighted from the vehicle, as it was parked in a dark corner. They couldn't make out the registration number, but she was happy with the super's evidence. After getting a list from Beth of Rachel's friends, she handed it to McKeown to follow up. Beth reiterated that Rachel had had no current boyfriend.

Lottie phoned upstairs to Gary to see if he'd found anything further on the laptop or phone. No joy there. McKeown reported that so far no one had any reason to murder the young woman. Everyone spoke admiringly of her drive and enterprise and all were shocked by her death.

She located the Mullen girls' father in Dublin and received confir-mation from his employer, Aldi, that he'd worked the night shift in their Sandyford warehouse and clocked out at 8 a.m. She was surprised when Bill Mullen remained stoical at the news of Rachel's death; he didn't offer to come to Ragmullin to comfort Beth, but said he might attend the funeral if she wanted him there.

Lottie was growing weary with hard-hearted and self-centred people.

'Kirby, any information forthcoming from the guests?'

'Still making calls, boss.'

'Well hurry up.'

Glancing around, she spotted Boyd. 'Time to talk to Matthew Fleming.' She had found lots of information about Fleming online, not all of it complimentary.

'Why?'

'He had a meeting with Rachel at five o'clock yesterday. And then he turned up at Annie's party at nine thirty. We need to rule him in or out of the investigation.'

'Okay. Isn't he better known as Bones Fleming?' Boyd said.

'Why would he be called that?'

'Wait till you see him.'

'Okay,' she said.

'Fleming is a big fish. Hands in a lot of pots, so I've heard,' Boyd said. 'Had his eye on becoming a politician at one time.'

'A dangerous fish, so. What if he tried to sabotage Annie's success by bringing this to her doorstep?'

'I heard he comes across as a hard businessman, but murder?' Boyd shook his head. 'I doubt even he would take it that far. Too risky for his own interests.'

'Let's see what he has to say for himself.'

Matthew Fleming's office was all glass and steel, situated in a new business park housing mainly garage showrooms. Three floors, including an atrium filled with plastic plants. A totally different image from the dust, gravel and heavy trucks Lottie associated with quarries. She assumed Fleming's thinking was that by locating here, he could alter that mindset. Somehow, she felt that mattered to the quarry man.

When he stood to welcome them, Lottie stopped for a beat. He was over six feet tall and knitting-needle thin, a sharp grey suit hanging on a skeleton. A shock of white hair stood out on his head as if he'd been hit by a bolt of electricity, and his face … She did a double-take. It was pale, almost transparent, but his eyes were the colour of slate. Despite her initial shock, she had to admit he carried a certain charm, even if his nickname, Bones, was apt.

'Lovely to meet you both,' he said, indicating the chairs. Red velvet. Fancy.

Before they sat, Lottie glanced out through the large window to her right and noticed how quickly the day had darkened. Returning her gaze to Fleming, she watched as he folded his tall frame into the large ergonomic chair behind an enormous desk.

'I know what you're thinking, but I'm not dying,' he said. 'Want to get that out of the way. People assume I've some terminal illness because of my physique. I blame it on my wife. She bleeds me dry! But that's another story.'

He glanced at his laptop screen, presumably reading their names, which his secretary had emailed him. Concentrating his attention on Boyd, he said, 'Detective Inspector Parker, how can I help you?'

Lottie bit her tongue.

Boyd said, 'Sorry, sir, I'm Detective Sergeant Boyd.'

Instead of looking uncomfortable, Fleming inclined his head towards Lottie. 'Only joking, Inspector Parker. You can call me Matt.'

Shrugging off the insult, she said, 'Can you confirm that you were at your ex-wife's restaurant last night?'

'Stupid woman.' He snorted and hastily wiped a hand under his nose. 'Have you seen what she's done to her old family home out by the lake? Been in her father's family for generations. It had gone to rack and ruin, but Annie being Annie decided it was up to her to bring it back to life. There were many objections to that venture, mine being the loudest and most vociferous. Not that the council listened; they were only interested in the right of way through the estate being maintained because it allows the public access to the golf club and the lake. Sorry for the rant. I tend to blow fire when her name is mentioned.'

'I need to know why you were at—'

'I wasn't. I have nothing to do with whatever that woman does. She was a pain in the arse from the day I married her, and she still is. The only good thing to come out of our marriage was my daughters.'

'We met Jessica; who is your other daughter?' Lottie asked.

He was gazing at the ceiling as if he hadn't heard her question. 'I love Jessica, but I think when she looks into a mirror, her mother stares back at her. That's hard to swallow.'

Lottie thought back to her interaction with Annie and Jessica. She could not recall any similarities between the two women. 'Tell me about your other daughter?'

He refocused his attention.

'Tara.' The name seemed to soften the sharpness of his eyes. A father filled with pride, Lottie thought, and immediately felt sorry for Beth Mullen, whose father showed little interest in travelling down from Dublin to comfort her. 'There's only eleven months between the girls. Irish twins, as people like to say. Jessica is the elder, but it's Tara who likes to accentuate their differences. Always dying her hair blonde and—'

'Where is Tara?' Lottie said.

'She was home at the weekend. Was due to fly back to London on Monday night for an early-morning meeting on Tuesday, but I believe she took ill at the airport and returned to her mother's house. No matter what I can offer, I suppose she still yearns for a mother's love, though I'm not so sure she'll get much of that from Annie.'

'And what exactly is Tara's job?'

'I have many business interests. Concrete, quarries, developments. Tara did environmental studies in college and I've employed her as my environmental officer. She's developing my Chiswick office. She is a true asset to my company.' A flash of admiration shot across Fleming's eyes, a look that was totally absent when he mentioned Annie or Jessica.

'Do you know Rachel Mullen?' Lottie kept her gaze glued to Fleming to note a reaction. And she got it. It was the first time his colour heightened since they'd entered his office. Dots of red on his transparent cheeks.

'What about her?'

'I'm asking the questions here, Mr Fleming.'

'So you are.'

'And I expect an answer.'

'What has Rachel got to do with you?'

'You know her, so?'

'I had a meeting with her yesterday.'

'Tell me about it.'

'She emailed me some time ago. An approach about a business proposition. We arranged a meeting. So yes, she was here in this office yesterday afternoon.'

'What did you discuss?'

'We discussed her business. She presented me with a strategy. I told her to email it on. I wanted Tara to look over it. Rachel's proposing mining for the base material to manufacture cosmetic products. It has great growth potential for my company. She's on to something there.'

'Mmm, you're thinking of branching into the beauty business, then?' Boyd said. 'Huge disparity between quarry blasting and developing cosmetics.'

'Rachel's plans are private, and I can't say much more about them because I actually think she is very inventive and forward-thinking. There was something in her proposal that clicked with me.'

'When did you last speak with her?'

'She was on time for her five o'clock appointment.' He scrunched up his eyes. 'I suppose she left here around six thirty. She had another appointment in town.'

'At Annie's?'

'She didn't say where. Why all these questions about Rachel?'

'Did she arrive here by car?'

'She did.'

'And did she leave by car?'

Fleming smiled, upturned pink lips almost feminine against his pale skin. 'No. We had a couple of drinks here. Business and pleasure. I booked her a taxi. She was to pick up her car this morning.' He glanced towards the floor-to-ceiling window. 'No sign of her yet. Her car is still in the car park out the back.'

Lottie tried to hide her surprise. 'Do you have the keys?'

'Why would you think I have her keys?'

Now was the time, Lottie thought, to wipe the pink-lipped smile off his face.

'Because Rachel's car keys were not amongst her possessions when we found her body.'

If it was possible, she would have said his face paled considerably. 'Body? What do you mean?'

'Rachel Mullen was found dead this morning.'

'What?' He ran a hand through his hair, causing it to spring even more upright. 'Oh my God. That's just terrible. What happened?'

Lottie kept her mouth shut, waiting to see what conclusion he would jump to.

Fleming straightened his back and tapped the desk with a thin, impatient finger. 'Because there are two detectives in my office, I assume her death was suspicious.'

'You assume correctly Mr Fleming. Can you account for your movements after Ms Mullen left your office?'

'This is such a shock. I need a drink.' He stood and opened a steel cabinet behind his desk. 'Would either of you care for a stiff one?'

'We're on duty,' Boyd said.

As Fleming filled a tumbler with brandy, Lottie skimmed her eyes around the office. She knew Rachel had not been killed here. She'd been at the party afterwards. But had there been something in the drink he'd given her? Had she returned to this office after the party?

'Was six thirty yesterday evening the last time you saw Ms Mullen?'

'Yes, or thereabouts.' He swallowed a good slurp of the amber liquid. 'Surely you don't think I did anything to her? We were on the brink of a business deal, financially profitable for both of us. I had no reason to harm her.'

'Had you met her before yesterday?'

'What's that got to do with anything?'

Maybe everything, Lottie thought. 'Why were you at the restaurant at nine thirty last night?'

Fleming refilled the glass and sat back down. 'Do I need a solicitor?'

Shit, not that old chestnut. 'Do you?'

'Don't take me for a stupid man. I lived with Annie for over twenty years and I know the way she can spin things. I gather you've spoken with her, so you know what I mean. I assume she brought my name up. And I can bet she told you I was out to sabotage her new business.'

Lottie kept her expression stony. 'I can't divulge the content of conversations I may have had with anyone in connection with our investigation.'

'You don't need to. Annie is a vindictive, bitter bitch.'

'Then why were you at her restaurant last night? A witness saw you arrive around nine thirty. What were you doing there?'

'That is none of your business.'

'I'm afraid everything is my business until I find who killed Rachel Mullen. Who did you speak with when you arrived, and what time did you leave?'

'It had nothing to do with Rachel.'

'Mr Fleming, I need full disclosure of your movements and a synopsis of your discussion with Rachel Mullen.'

'My solicitor will be in contact with you.'

Lottie rose. 'Thank you for your time.'

At the door, she waited for Boyd, who had remained seated. In the soothing voice he used from time to time, he said, 'Mr Fleming, we need the keys to Rachel Mullen's car.'

To Lottie's surprise, Fleming opened a drawer and slid a key ring with three keys attached across the desk. 'It's in the car park. The red Toyota Yaris. My secretary will show you the way.'

CHAPTER THIRTEEN

Tara Fleming lay on the bed, ignoring her mother who'd entered the room, and stared at the ceiling. She thought about the web of lies in which she'd become embroiled and how there was no one she could discuss it with. At twenty-five, she still found it difficult to speak civilly to her mother. The reason being she suspected Annie could see through the pretence.

Her mother crossed the room and placed a tumbler of water, along with two paracetamol, on the bedside cabinet. Tara grimaced. Annie was able to play the motherly role when she wanted to.

'You don't need the pills,' Annie said icily, 'but they may help you maintain the *illusion* of illness.'

'You are too kind,' Tara said, unable to restrain the irony in her voice.

'That's priceless coming from you.' Annie stood at the window and faced the rain-swept lake. 'Where were you last night?'

'Told you. I had a flight to London booked and was at the airport.'

'Sure you were.' Annie half turned and raised a quizzical eyebrow. 'Does your sister know you're home?'

'Haven't seen her yet.' And I don't want to, Tara thought, turning on her side, ignoring the pills and her mother.

'Jessica is upset with all this business about Rachel Mullen. You remember Rachel, don't you?'

Tara wanted to drag the quilt up over her head, but instead she remained still.

'I'm talking to you,' Annie repeated.

'Yeah, I remember her. Like I remember all the lies and secrets I've been forced into since I was a little girl.' Her words sounded as if another voice had uttered them. A voice dredged from a childhood nemesis. 'Why would you even invite her to the party?'

'Jessica put her on the list. Plus a few others of whom I didn't approve.'

'You should have taken a more hands-on approach then, shouldn't you, Mum?' Tara said, feeling the sneer that curled her lips seeping into her words.

'Those Mullen girls never did do much with themselves, did they?' Annie drew back the curtains and secured them with the tiebacks. 'What is it with your generation? Starting one thing and never finishing it.'

'It was Dad who wanted Jessica and me to study chemistry, even though I never had an aptitude for it,' Tara said. 'I'm glad now that I stood up to him and did environmental studies.'

'A waste of money, guzzled up by the Trinity coffers.' Annie sat on the windowsill and shook her head. 'At least Jessica tried out chemistry before switching to business studies. Isn't that what Rachel studied?'

'How would I know? I haven't seen her for years. You and Dad put a stop to that friendship. And the others too.' Tara sat and swung her legs over the edge of the bed, her feet swallowed up by the thick carpet. 'You think we're still children that you can mould to your will.' She held her mother's gaze. Annie's eyes darkened into a squint.

'Nothing stopped you licking up to your father, though. I could never understand why you favour that man over me.'

'You'll have to accept that there are some things over which you have no control.' Tara pulled on a sweatshirt and stood. 'Now leave me alone and continue your mission of trying to shape Jessica into your image. Though I have a strong suspicion you won't fare much better with her than you did with me.'

'I wish you hadn't dyed your hair that awful blonde. Cheapens you, you know. Makes your face thinner than your father's and that's some feat.' Annie sniffed loudly. At the door, she turned. 'Tara, can I ask you one question?'

'Can't stop you, can I?'

'Why did you come here last night instead of going to your father's?'

Tara toyed with a lie but decided on the truth, knowing it would hurt the most. 'Dad has a new woman in his life.' Catching sight of the shock on Annie's face, she laughed. 'Oh, you didn't know, did you? That's just hilarious.'

She laughed to the sound of the door slamming.

CHAPTER FOURTEEN

They left Matthew Fleming's office and walked to the car park. The afternoon sky was beginning to darken and sensor lights flashed on when they crossed the yard. Lottie noticed Fleming's silver BMW parked in an extra-wide space where *Company Director* was inscribed on a blue plate nailed to the wall. Beside it was a black Range Rover; two cars further down she spied the red Yaris with an oval pebble hanging from the rear-view mirror.

Walking around the car, pulling on gloves, she said, 'Superintendent Farrell was right.'

'About what?' Boyd said, taking out his phone to take a photo of the car.

'Fleming is a slippery customer.'

'He's a little obnoxious, to be honest.'

'A little? If I was Rachel Mullen, I'd be taking my business plans to someone else.'

'She can't do that now,' Boyd said, 'and Fleming has all her plans. Nothing stopping him handing them over to his daughter Tara to set her up as the glossy side of his company. It grated on my skin the way he talked.'

'I know what you mean. Remind me to contact Tara Fleming,' Lottie said. She stuck the key in the driver's door lock. 'And Boyd ...'

'What?'

'We need to find out what time Rachel left that party. I think it's possible that Matt Fleming was looking for her.'

'Her phone says she rang the taxi at eight thirty-six p.m.'

'But until we get confirmation from the taxi company, we don't know if she actually left at that time.'

She leaned into the Yaris. It was pristine. No food wrappers or containers. No rubbish like she herself had scattered in the footwell of her Hyundai. The interior smelled of lavender and she saw an air freshener clipped to the air vent. She opened the rear door. Spotless. She went to the boot and unlocked it. Inside lay a cabin-sized suitcase.

'That's an overnight bag,' Boyd said.

'Clever clogs,' Lottie said. 'We can take it with us, as we know this is not a crime scene. I'm sure Rachel was murdered in her own bed at her own house.'

'What if she came back here after she left the party but before she went home?'

'We know Matt Fleming arrived at Annie's around nine thirty. I'll tell McKeown to continue searching the CCTV to see what time he left. We also need to find out who Fleming spoke to when he was there.'

'Okay.' Boyd lifted the case out.

'I'm thinking it might not have been the first time Rachel met Fleming.'

'What makes you think that? A hunch? Gut?'

'Bit of both. If she was here with her dream business plan to secure investment or funding, why would she risk ruining her chance by drinking with him?'

'Maybe he was persuasive? Maybe she felt she had no option but to join in?'

'No, that's not it. I'm sure she knew him before that meeting. She'd been at school with his daughters, and the image Beth painted of her doesn't gel with her taking a risk like that. According to Beth's interview, Rachel was dedicated to getting her business up and running. She wanted to make her dream a reality.'

'You might have a point,' Boyd conceded.

Lottie closed the boot. 'Arrange for the car to be impounded. We need it out of here before anyone tampers with it.'

She looked up at the modern building. At one of the windows, she saw Fleming staring down into the car park. He smiled and waved at her. A shiver ran all the way down her spine.

*

Matthew Fleming turned away from the window, the smile slipping down his face. All around him the glass walls mocked him, his skeleton shimmying this way and that. His world was contained in this one room. His life. He shuddered. What if it all came crashing down around him? Everything he'd worked so hard to create would be shattered in an instant. The illusion would disappear. His vision blurred, the glass turning opaque as he imagined what could go wrong. He had to do something, and quickly.

From his breast pocket he pulled out his second phone, an old Nokia, and clicked on one of only three numbers he'd saved.

It was answered on the first ring.

For a moment, he listened to the breath coming down the line. Then he spoke, his voice harsh and sharp. 'I've just had two detectives in my office.'

The breathing appeared to stall.

Fleming hissed, 'What the fuck have you done now?'

*

Back at the station, Lottie told McKeown to check what time Matthew Fleming's car left the restaurant car park and to determine if he'd been alone or not.

Kirby held up a hand. 'I traced the taxi driver who brought Rachel home. He picked her up outside the restaurant at eight forty p.m. and

85

brought her to her own front door. She was alone. The driver says she wasn't talkative, and he thought she looked a bit disorientated. He concluded she'd had too much to drink.'

'Dead end there,' Boyd said.

'Where and when was she poisoned?' Lottie said. 'Did someone follow her? Did she let that person into her house? Did she know them? The fact is, if someone got into her house, we need SOCOs to find that evidence.'

'We haven't yet found any neighbours with CCTV, and no one reports hearing screams or calls for help,' McKeown said, returning to the office. 'But I found Matthew Fleming's car leaving the restaurant at nine forty p.m., though there's no way of knowing if he was the person behind the wheel.'

'See if the footage can be enhanced. If we take it that Fleming was driving, it means he was inside the restaurant for less than ten minutes,' Lottie said, leaning against the wall. 'I want to know what went on in those ten minutes. He refused to enlighten us, so will you speak to Jessica? I'll have a word with Annie.'

'Will do,' McKeown said.

'But Rachel had already left by then,' Boyd said.

'Yes,' Lottie said, 'but Matthew Fleming had her car keys in his office. Why did she leave them with him? Even if she left her car there, she should have brought her keys.'

'Maybe she wanted him to drop the car to her house or something.'

'Get someone to check the other keys on the ring. One might be a spare key to her house. If it is, Fleming had it.'

'How did she get into her home?'

'There was a key on the hall stand; Beth confirmed that Rachel always kept it in her handbag for emergencies.'

'Right,' Boyd said. 'What about the overnight case from the boot of her car?'

'I had a look and it contained just a silky nightdress and a change of clothes along with some make-up. For a night away with someone? Contact Beth and confirm that Rachel already knew Matthew Fleming.'

'What will I do?' Kirby said.

'How are you getting on with checking the guests and staff?'

'Most of the guests are accounted for, except a couple I've yet to call. No illness among any of them, and those I've spoken to can account for their movements from the time they left the party. I asked about Rachel and most had little recollection of her, though one person thought she looked unwell and another remembered her arriving late and talking to a young man for a while.'

'Find out who that was. What about the staff?'

'Next on my list.' Kirby moved over beside Lottie at the wall outside her office door and dropped his voice to a whisper. 'Boss, can I let Lynch do it?'

'No, you cannot.' She shoved away from the wall with a push of her foot and threw a glance at Lynch's bowed head in the far corner. The woman could burn in hell for all she cared. She went into her office and shut the door. Then Jane Dore rang.

CHAPTER FIFTEEN

Hazel Clancy was being watched from behind a rack of clothes on the opposite side of the shop.

The voyeur was confident that no one had any idea who they really were. Especially not Hazel, with her immaculate golden hair held up in a carefree ponytail. It probably took twenty minutes with a half-tin of hairspray to make it look that way. Not to mention the tan. The latest experiment from a bottle. Long-lasting, smear-free, non-stick, just like a fucking frying pan. Jesus! But the tan, fake or not, accentuated her pale blue eyes.

And the clothes. Hazel would call them smart casual. That was what the designers labelled them too. A black leather biker jacket with sparkling zips and a red floral dress to her ankles with glossy black slingbacks, heels an inch thick and two inches high. Hazel didn't need the extra two inches. She was already five foot ten. Imposing and well structured. Carefully constructed. It took time, and a lot of effort, to look as effortless as Hazel did. Every fucking day. Well, Ms Hazel Clancy, I know something you don't, the voyeur thought. This might just be your *last* fucking day. If that's the case, maybe you should be doing a job that's a little more exciting than bossing your staff around in a poxy flea-ridden department store.

*

Hazel loved her job. She knew some people thought working in a department store was boring, but she relished the power of being manager, and being surrounded by clothes all day long. Not that she had time to try them on, but she loved the smell of them, the look of them, the feel of the material between her fingers. She had landed the job by skipping two rungs on the career ladder. She smiled when she thought of how she'd achieved that at twenty-five years of age. She knew it rankled with some of the older members of Boyne's staff. Sod them. She was better than the lot of them squashed in the canteen together.

Behind the glass panel, she sat at her desk with an eye on the shop floor and tapped the screen to bring up her online diary. She had a meeting with one of her staff in a few minutes. A reprimand for Andy Ashe. Some of the staff called him AA behind his back. His own fault. Andy never hid the fact that he was a recovering alcoholic. Too young, at thirty, Hazel thought, to be wasting his life. And it was a waste. Not that she could talk, but that was her business.

He'd helped her out last night by attending that champagne party for her. Not that she'd wanted to accept the invite, but being secretary of the Chamber of Commerce, she was forced to at least send someone in her place.

When she'd asked him, Andy had jumped at the chance. Maybe it wasn't such a good idea to send a reformed alcoholic to a free drinks party. But it was done now, she thought, cringing.

He knocked on her glass door. Hazel liked to be able to see out to the shop floor, to keep an eye on the staff and the stock and, of course, the customers. You'd be surprised at how many people shoved dresses into their shopping bags without paying. Her ex-boyfriend had thought there were many better things worth robbing than clothes. She'd nearly dumped him that night. But the sex was good, and it kept her body trim, so she put up with his ignorance.

Andy sat without being instructed to do so. He was unshaven, and his fair hair, normally cut short at the back and sides, now hung in a greasy mop over his forehead. He wore his trademark sunglasses, even indoors. He looked like one of the creeps you'd see in a 1930s gangster movie. He was single and boring. She wondered why he didn't just resign. She had no time for wasters.

'I've received a complaint,' she began in her most authoritative voice, and then realised it was actually her normal tone. She had decided not to ask him about the party. As he pushed his sunglasses up onto his head, his bleary eyes told her enough. He'd slipped into his old habits. He was off the wagon more than he was on it. Hopefully he hadn't made a show of himself; it would reflect badly on her. Not that she really gave a hoot what the Flemings thought of her any more.

'She was an ignorant old cow,' he muttered, dribble sticking to his stubble.

'Who?'

'Mrs Conway. Ninety-nine if she's a day. Don't know how she can even see with those glasses. They're like the bottom of milk bottles.'

Hazel had no idea what the bottom of a milk bottle was like. She got her milk in a carton like everyone else. 'I am not at liberty to say who made the complaint, but—'

'I know it was her. The old bitchity witch.'

'I beg your pardon?'

He fiddled with his sunglasses and dragged them further back on his head, bringing his hair with them. 'What did she say about me?'

'I'm not at—'

'Liberty, yeah, yeah. Spare me the HR speak, Mizz Clancy.'

Hazel bristled. Andy insisted on calling her 'Mizz' knowing it irritated her because she had yet to snare someone to put a ring on her finger. She felt her cheeks redden, and a burst of anger lit a fire in her belly, quicker than a spark igniting butane gas.

She stood, took off her leather jacket and hung it on the back of her chair. The swish of her expensive dress made her feel powerful.

'This complaint states that you were rude to a customer. You accused them of removing a dress from a rack and leaving without paying. At the time, you had no proof. You hadn't even verified it on our CCTV. You used vulgar language and made the customer cry. What do you have to say in your defence?'

He leaned across the desk, his breath a stinking mixture of alcohol and cigarettes, causing her to recoil a few inches. Definitely a mistake to send him last night.

'I don't need a defence,' he said, 'because she stole the fucking dress.'

Hazel remembered that she was in charge and resumed her position of authority. Squaring her shoulders, she sat and tapped her screen. 'It says here that you called her, and I quote, "a dried-up vagina".'

Andy laughed so vigorously his sunglasses hit the floor. 'I never said that, but I wish I had.' His laugh dissolved into a rattle of hiccups as he bent to pick the glasses up.

Now that she thought about it, he probably wouldn't have been able to come up with anything so offensive without having sat at a bar for an hour with a few pints beforehand.

'Would you care to enlighten me as to what you actually did say?' Hazel was getting bored of this conversation. She just wanted to issue a warning and tell him to get the hell out of her office, taking his stink with him.

He sniffed and swallowed. 'I told the thieving cow I'd check the CCTV and then call the guards if she didn't take the dress out of her wheelie bag and place it on the counter. That's all I said. Then she burst into a flood of false tears and everyone within earshot rushed around her. All she wanted was an audience. I'm a worse fool to have given her one.'

'Do you have any witnesses to the incident?'

'I'm sure you have plenty of names on her complaint form to back her up. The only colleague who could help me is Lucy, who at that time was watching the fitting rooms. God, I could tell you a thing or—'

'Andy! I can see what goes on in my shop.'

'Can you, though? You didn't see that old witch playing to the grandstand, did you?'

'It was my day off.' Hazel fiddled with her dress buttons, annoyed to feel it tight across her bust. 'I've watched the security footage, but there's no sound, which might be helpful for your defence. Maybe you were acting in good faith, but you can't go around accusing people, so I'm issuing you with a warning. Your second one in six weeks. Andy, you have to improve your manners with the public, because if anything like this happens again, I will refer the matter to Human Resources.' She hoped he didn't know that HR consisted of one person rather than a team.

'I'm not afraid of the hairy runts.' He stood, shoved the chair noisily against the desk and headed for the door. 'And that old prune is a liar.'

'Andy?'

'What?'

'A little deodorant under the arms and a mint in your mouth would go a long way to improving your image.'

'We can't all look in the same mirror you do, Hazel.'

He slammed the door so hard she was afraid the glass had cracked. Sitting back in her chair, she noticed he had sucked the tension out with his exit. Was he wearing the same shirt and chinos as yesterday? Probably wore them last night too. Dear God! She held her head in her hands and laughed. She'd have loved to be a fly on Annie Fleming's restaurant wall last night.

Her phone rang before she could fully relax.

CHAPTER SIXTEEN

The drive to Tullamore through torrential rain failed to dampen Lottie's mood. She called Annie Fleming from the hands-free in the car. Annie said she could tell her plenty about Matthew, and after checking the time, Lottie agreed to meet her in the morning.

She raced across the hospital car park with her jacket over her head. The Dead House was icy cold and the white wall tiles seemed to shimmer with the souls of the deceased. Shivering, she pulled on protective clothing and entered the cutting room.

'You might need vapour rub under your nose for this one,' Jane said.

'The body's not decomposed, so it shouldn't be too bad.'

'Trust me. The poison turned the stomach to mush and the gases are toxic.'

'Maybe I should leave you to it,' Lottie offered, but really there was no way she was leaving without an armful of answers.

'You're here now. Stay.'

'Thanks for getting to Rachel so quickly. I really appreciate it.' She liked to personalise the victims. It reminded her she was dealing with real people.

'I had no one else waiting to be cut open.' Jane fixed her visor and picked up a scalpel. After recording her preliminary introductions, she paused. 'Where is Boyd?'

'He's had enough of hospitals to last him a lifetime, and a mortuary's not the best place for him.'

'You're right there. I'm ready to begin.' Jane had lowered the table to suit her height. She walked around and shone the light down on Rachel Mullen's face, speaking quickly into the microphone as she leaned over the dead woman.

'What is it?' Lottie said, craning her neck to see but staying by the wall, close enough to hear but far enough not to get in Jane's way.

'I'll explain it simply. I can see, under the microscope, indentations around her lips and chin. Suggests to me she was held quite tightly. It's possible she was suffocated by the hold.'

'McGlynn did mention bruising. Does it mean that someone held her face and poured a drink down her throat?'

'Let's not jump to conclusions. I don't offer opinions, only facts. Fact – she did not poison herself.'

Lottie felt a rush of excitement.

'Initial findings,' Jane continued, 'determined that the glass on the bedside cabinet contained only water. If she had administered the poison to herself, we would have found a vessel with traces of it. Jim fast-tracked the fingerprints on the glass. Only Rachel's. The fact is, it has no trace of poison, but it's been sent for further analysis.'

'When do you think you'll have toxicology reports back?'

Jane turned and stared over her mask. 'I've hardly begun. I'd appreciate it if you let me get on with the job.'

'Sure. Sorry.' Lottie folded her arms and waited while Jane continued her methodical examination. She glanced from time to time at the large digital clock on the wall. Inactivity drove her berserk. Fidgeting from foot to foot, she sensed her frustration seeping into the room.

Standing on the opposite side of the body, Jane stopped her work and stared over at her.

'There are no visible wounds on the body other than the markings around her mouth, nose and throat. The scratches definitely match her own hands, and I've taken samples from underneath her fingernails. Without toxicology, I can't positively say, but the physical state of the deceased – arched body and rigor – prompts me to concur with your initial observations. This young lady was poisoned. I will analyse her stomach contents, but she died within four hours of consumption of a strong dose, and suffered a particularly painful death.'

'Okay, right. Why didn't she call for help? Could alcohol have inhibited her?'

'You mentioned in your report that a witness said she appeared intoxicated, so that might have affected her. Again, I'll need toxicology to determine the blood alcohol level.'

'Was she sexually assaulted?'

'No outward physical evidence, but I'll take swabs.'

'Right.' Lottie stared at Rachel Mullen's face, twisted in a last deathly scream. Her hair, damp and flat, was spread out on the cold stainless steel on which she lay naked. She was no more than bones and skin. Lottie's heart broke to see her in this state, and she did not want to watch the scalpel cut into the dead flesh.

'Are you staying or leaving?' Jane said.

'I think I'll leave you to it.'

'That's grand. Can I continue?'

'Yeah.'

Lottie walked to the door as Jane switched the recording device back on, and was already at the receptacle for disposing of forensic suits when she heard Jane call her.

'What have you found?' she said as she rushed back.

Jane stood behind Rachel Mullen's head, holding something with a pair of tweezers. 'A shard of glass.'

'I'd totally forgotten that I'd noticed something in her mouth,' Lottie said.

'A message of some sort, do you think?'

'I don't know what to think.' Studying the piece of glass, Lottie noted that the edges were crooked, it was about two centimetres in diameter and it reflected the light like a mirror. In fact, she thought once the bodily fluids were cleaned from it, it might even be a piece of mirror. 'Was Rachel alive when it was … you know …'

'She was dead at the time.'

Lottie knew what that meant. 'Someone watched this young woman die an excruciatingly painful death, then stuffed a piece of glass down her throat.'

'Exactly.'

'Oh God, Jane. Fecking hell. Did the killer leave any evidence when it was pushed inside?'

'I will examine everything thoroughly, but I suspect gloves were worn.'

'Thanks, Jane. Let me know what you find.' Lottie left the pathologist to her task.

CHAPTER SEVENTEEN

Cafferty's bar was Andy Ashe's regular haunt.

'Pint of Guinness and a half-one,' he said, hauling himself onto a stool beside a man called Mick who was filling out betting slips with the *Daily Mirror* open on the racing page.

'Bad day, Andy lad?' Mick said. He said that to everyone, so Andy ignored him. 'There's a horse called Frilly Dress in the six forty-five at Waterford. Fancy a flutter?'

'Shut up, Mick.' Andy downed the whiskey in one gulp and sat with the glass mid-air as he felt the liquid warm up his belly. He pointed the glass at Caroline behind the bar. 'Another one, when you're ready.'

'Slow down a bit,' she said. 'Darren's off, and I don't want to have to get the trolley to carry you out the door.'

Mick laughed into his pint. Andy felt his blood boil, and not from the whiskey. This was all Hazel Clancy's fault. Humiliating him. He couldn't remember what he'd said to that old lady the day she'd stolen the dress. It probably wasn't what Hazel had written down on the complaint form, but he was certain it was something in that vein. They were all out to get him.

The pint arrived, its creamy head still settling as the bubbles floated through the dark liquid. He leaned on his elbows and watched it, inhaling the alcohol fumes.

He put a fifty-euro note on the counter and Caroline placed the second whiskey beside his hand.

'You know Hazel Clancy, don't you, Car?' he said.

'I do. We used to go to the same gym. Not that I go now.' She patted her obviously pregnant tummy.

'What's she like when she hasn't got a poker up her arse?'

Caroline laughed. 'That poker keeps Hazel ramrod straight. It's always there.'

'Thought so.'

'She giving you a hard time?'

'You could say that.'

'Turn on the telly, love,' Mick said. 'The racing's on.'

'Why don't you go next door and place your bets?' Andy said.

Caroline glared at him. They both knew Mick hadn't placed a bet in six months. He was a reformed gambler, just like Andy was a reformed alcoholic. Andy tittered to himself.

'Feck you, anyway.' Mick drained his pint, folded his newspaper, thrust the betting slips into his pocket and stomped out of the pub.

'You didn't have to say that,' Caroline said. 'He's gone straight to the bookies to do just what you said.'

'As if I give a damn.'

'What's up with you?'

'Nothing.'

'I guess it's to do with Hazel. She's a bitch, so quit moping over her.'

'I'm not moping, I'm planning an extremely painful death for her.' He pulled the sunglasses from the top of his head, down over his eyes. The grease from his hair smeared the lenses, but he wasn't about to clean them in front of Caroline.

'You're hilarious, Andy Ashe.' She laughed and went to the till.

'I'm serious.'

He looked at the pint. Lifted it and eyed it again, before slowly raising it to his lips and swallowing it in three gulps. Delicious. Just like Hazel Clancy would be if she was lying dead beneath his body.

CHAPTER EIGHTEEN

Hazel swapped her slingbacks for her polished Doc Martens. Once she had them perfectly laced, she zipped up her leather jacket. Pulling on a black knitted hat with a large fluffy bobble, she let her hair hang loose beneath it, sweeping out over her shoulders. She knew she looked good and this feeling made her stand taller as she locked the shutters.

It was a ten-minute walk home, and with the rain pouring down, she wished she had a car. By the time she reached home, her dress was sopping, sticking to her legs. Home was a luxury apartment block situated on the old Dublin Road. A large red-brick affair, comprising twenty exclusive residences. She lived in a ground-floor apartment with her own front door and a set of double doors off the kitchen leading out to a small patio area, overlooked by trees lining the main road. She'd recently noticed a *For Sale* sign outside one dwelling and had checked it on the estate agent's website. Almost a million euros! She was glad she'd bought hers when she did, with an affordable mortgage and a nice inheritance after her parents died.

Unlocking the door, she stepped into the narrow hall that led to the living area.

'Hello! I'm home. Is dinner ready?'

She hung up her jacket and brought her hat to the sink, where she wrung it out before placing it on the radiator to dry. 'I hadn't a great day today. I had to give Andy an official warning. He's his own worst enemy.'

Listening intently, ear cocked, she heard only silence in the apartment. She knew she was being silly, but she talked out loud to keep herself company.

'I'm sorry now that I didn't go to that party last night. I got a phone call from a detective looking for information. It seems one of the guests died. Imagine, the guards rang me to see if I saw anything or if I was feeling unwell. And I wasn't even there.'

She opened the patio door and let her cat in. He was shivering, his fur saturated. She fetched a towel and rubbed the wet animal.

'It was exciting to get the call from the gardaí, but then I realised it was Andy who'd shared in the actual excitement. Just like me to miss all the fun, isn't that right?'

Releasing the cat, she filled his bowl with dry food and topped up his water. Her stomach growled so loudly the cat looked up. She opened the refrigerator and peered in. It was almost empty. She was hungry and she wasn't hungry, both at the same time. She closed the door and took the Chinese takeaway menu from under a fridge magnet.

'Think it will be chow mein tonight,' she told the cat, as she phoned in the order.

Feeling the wet of her dress seeping into her skin, she made her way to the bedroom. Peeling off the dress and her underwear, she grabbed the towel from the radiator under the window. The blinds were up and she realised she was naked. She smiled to herself and raised her arms in a series of stretches before pulling down the blind. As she did so, she thought she saw a shadow move around one of the trees through the spills of rain. Whoever it was, she'd given them a full-frontal view.

'Hope you liked it.' The blind flipped down on the windowsill and she drew the curtain over.

In the shower, she sang out of tune as she lathered her hair for two minutes. She left the conditioner in for another three to ensure a perfect shine, then shaved her legs. She was making good money, but why waste it in a salon when a razor cost only a couple of euros? Her father had once said that if you looked after the pennies, the pounds would look after themselves. A saying from before they had euros and cents. She didn't miss her dad, but she missed his handouts.

Ablutions completed, she stepped out of the shower and dried herself. Her stomach growled again as the doorbell chimed. She pulled on a pair of navy joggers and a white hoodie and accepted the order at the door.

The smell wafted around the kitchen as she opened up the cartons. A wave of nausea swamped her. She needed to eat, but she needed something else too. Something to take the edge off.

'This is all your fault,' she cried in her empty bedroom. 'If you hadn't left me, I wouldn't be in this state.'

She'd put the little packet under a basket in the top drawer of the dresser. She shoved her underwear out of the way and searched. Surely this was where she'd left it. She rummaged through the second and third drawers. Her stash was gone. Had she actually used it all? She tried to recall if she'd had any left when she'd used it last night. She never let it run out. So where had she put it?

After going through every drawer and pocket in the bedroom, she repeated the exercise in the living room and kitchen. Nothing. The food was now cold, but she took a fork and started to stuff it in her mouth anyway. Maybe it would help her remember.

As she ate, the cat suddenly arched his back, his ears pricked; even his fluff stood upright.

'What's up, Cat?' She'd never got around to giving him a name.

Putting down the fork, she walked to the patio door. With the light on inside, she could only see her own reflection. Switching it off, she put her nose to the pane and peered out. A shadow suddenly appeared, causing her to jump backwards with a scream, step on the cat's tail and almost fall.

'Stupid fucking cat!'

She shooed him out of the way and slowly approached the patio door, checking to see if it was locked. It wasn't. Had she left it open? Surely she hadn't been that irresponsible. She was paranoid about security. Especially now she was on her own.

She opened the door fully and stepped outside as a gust of wind whirled around the apartment wall. No one there. At least, she couldn't see anyone. As she went to return inside, the patio door slammed shut. Now she was outside, half dressed, getting soaked. It had slammed so hard the door was jammed. She tugged and pulled, but no joy. She'd have to either find the complex manager or delve into the flowerpot two apartments down for the spare key she'd hidden. Fuck. Fuck. Fuck.

Climbing over the low perimeter wall, she stepped onto the sodden grass in her bare feet. As she turned the corner, a shadow appeared in front of her.

'What the hell?' Hazel said, mustering bravado from a place usually reserved for her cocaine-induced bravery.

'Shh ... it's me.'

CHAPTER NINETEEN

Back in the office, Lottie was still thinking of the shard of glass the pathologist had held in the tweezers. She hoped something would show up in the analysis. Making a note on the incident board, she found that very little else had been added in her absence.

Kirby stuck his head round the door. 'I was talking to Hazel Clancy earlier. She's one of the guests on the party list. She couldn't go last night and—'

'Cross her off, then,' Lottie said sharply, her irritation growing with the lack of progress.

'She sent one of her staff instead, and I know him. He used to drink regularly in Cafferty's.'

'Why are you telling me all this?'

'She said he's clocked off for the day and is probably in the pub. I thought I'd go have a word with him. I need to leave shortly anyhow. I'm expecting a furniture delivery.'

'What did you buy?'

'A bed.'

'What were you sleeping on for the last few months?'

'The floor.'

Kirby shuffled off. Boyd was talking animatedly on the phone and McKeown was eyeing Garda Martina Brennan, who'd dropped a report on his desk. Lottie heard the rain beating against the window and figured there wasn't much else she could do this evening.

'I'm going home to cook my son his dinner. All okay here?' When no one answered, she grabbed her bag and left. Maybe she could go through Chloe's wedding plan and familiarise herself with all she had to do before Saturday. A tiny tingle of excitement took root as she headed out of the office.

*

Kirby had spent almost six months squatting on Boyd's couch, followed by months moving from cheap hotels to B&Bs until he'd eventually saved enough for a deposit on a rental. No way he could get a mortgage. He'd developed a gambling habit after the death of his girlfriend, and the bank had repossessed his house. The furniture delivery was due that evening, but after the phone conversation with Hazel Clancy, he took a detour via Cafferty's.

He took in his surroundings while his eyes became accustomed to the dark interior. His vision settled and he lunged for the counter and pulled out a stool.

'Pint of Guinness, Caroline.' Kirby turned to the man beside him. 'Andy! Just the man. Back on the sauce, I see.'

'You're not blind yet, anyway.'

'What's biting you?' Kirby slapped him on the shoulder. Andy turned away. 'Seriously, though, I thought you quit a few months ago.' He settled his bulk on the narrow stool.

'I un-quit. Happy?'

'None of my business,' Kirby said, taking the pint from Caroline. He left it on the counter to settle for a few more moments.

Andy folded his arms. 'Why are you making a song-and-dance about it if it's none of your business?'

'Will you lighten up, Andy? It's like an undertaker's wake since you came in,' Caroline said, slamming Kirby's change on the counter.

'See, you've upset my only friend in the world,' Kirby said, and slurped his pint.

'At least you've got a friend,' Andy said. 'I've only got enemies.'

'The job?' Kirby enquired.

'Nail on head.'

'Think yourself lucky that the only dead bodies you see are the ants in the fitting rooms. I'm surprised I can stomach a pint after what I witnessed today.'

'Another murder in Ragmullin?' Andy said.

'Yes.'

'It must be six months since we had a murder here. I was afraid we'd lose our title of Killing Town of Ireland.' Andy's voice was mocking but more alert now.

'This is a bad one.' Kirby felt his chest swell with importance. The news seemed not to have reached the local grapevine. 'Say nothing to anyone. We only found the body this morning.'

'I heard there was a lot of activity up on Greenfield Drive,' Caroline said, folding her arms on the counter once she'd twisted her hair behind her ears. Her eyes were wide in anticipation of a good gossip story that she could spread.

'I can't say any more.' He concentrated on his pint and took another gulp. He should have kept his mouth shut.

'You can't start something and not finish it.' Caroline leaned in closer to him.

'Course I can. Though I'm definitely finishing this pint. Put another one on, please, and then I have to be off.' He checked the time to be sure he could fit in a chat with Andy before his furniture delivery.

'Who was murdered?' Andy said quietly when Caroline had moved away to the taps.

'That's what I want to talk to you about.'

'Me?' He pushed his sunglasses up on his head. 'Why?'

Kirby glanced at the other man's watery eyes. 'We're talking to everyone who was at Annie's Restaurant last night, to see if they …' He stalled. The pub was not the place to conduct an interview; that kind of thing, off-the-books stuff, had got his boss into trouble before.

'If they what?' Andy pressed. He had abandoned his drink and twisted round on the stool to look at Kirby.

'If the guests noticed anything unusual in relation to the victim.'

'Who was murdered?' Caroline said as she returned with his pint.

Kirby made up his mind and turned to Andy. 'Can I get you one?'

'If you're buying, I'll have a Jameson.'

Picking up his pint, Kirby stood. 'We'll be over in the snug.'

When they were both seated, he said, 'Tell me about last night.'

Sunglasses down over his eyes once again, Andy said, 'Just to set the record straight, I did nothing.'

'Will you lighten up? I only want to know what kind of gig it was. Who was there? What went on? That kind of thing.'

'Might cost you more than one whiskey.'

'Feck off. You probably earn more than me, and I've rent to be paying now.'

'You and me both.' Andy wet his lips with the drink and put the glass down. 'It was a fancy enough sort of affair, even if it was an after-work do.'

'Who was there? What was the chat?'

'Corporate shites. The cream of Ragmullin in their own minds. Spreadsheet this, graphs that. Shares and money. I earwigged until I got bored. Anyhow, champagne doesn't agree with my gut, especially since I've been off the drink for a few months. But who would be able to resist when it's free?'

'I wouldn't,' Kirby agreed. 'Anyone you know there?'

'Not a one. My manager was invited, not me, but she's a cute hoor. Probably knew it would bore the arse off of her, so she sent me instead. Then she had the cheek to give me a bollocking today over an unfounded complaint.'

'No love lost there, I take it?'

'You're right. Pity she didn't go last night; maybe she'd be the one with a knife in her throat.'

Kirby tried not to appear shocked by Andy's words. 'No one ended up with a knife in their throat.'

'Oh? Who died, and how?'

Andy was clever, and no pushover, Kirby thought, as his eye caught the time on the bar clock.

'I've to head off soon.' He put the glass to his mouth and swallowed the pint.

'At least I got myself a date out of last night,' Andy said.

'That right? Who?'

'To be truthful, it's not a verified date, but she gave me her number.' He struggled to get a business card out of his back pocket.

Kirby noticed the stains on the other man's beige chinos. His own trousers were not much better. He'd have to go to the dry cleaner's soon. Not a good idea to put his second-best suit in the washing machine. If he had a washing machine, that was. He was thinking of the cost of setting up his new home in an unfurnished rental when Andy handed him the card.

'Holy Mother of God!' Kirby said. 'You have to talk to me, and fast.'

'What?' Andy said.

'I need you to come to the station to give a statement.'

'No way. I'm half cut.' Then his face blanched as realisation dawned. 'Is she dead? Is that what has you looking like a balloon about to pop? Come on, I never touched her.'

107

'Maybe not, but it appears that you're one of a few who actually had a conversation with our victim.' Kirby turned the card over. Rachel Mullen smiled at him from the top right-hand corner. He concentrated on Andy staring into the dregs of his whiskey.

'I can't believe I was just talking to her last night and now she's dead. That's awful. And you think someone killed her?'

'We don't know yet.' He wanted to keep things vague for now. 'All I can say is that I need you to come to the station and make a statement.'

'Look, I've had … what … three half-ones and a couple of pints. There's no way I can give a statement now. I'm liable to say something to incriminate myself, and I swear on a stack of Jerusalem Bibles, I never even shook hands with her.'

Kirby sighed. Andy was correct about making a statement under the influence of alcohol, but still, he had spoken to the victim, and for all they knew, he was one of the last people to see her alive. He had to get some information out of him.

'You're going to have to make yourself available for an interview in the morning, Andy. But I really need you to tell me everything you remember about last night.'

He noticed the shake in Andy's hand as he lifted the tumbler to his lips. He sipped and placed it gingerly on the edge of the low table.

'There isn't much to tell. I had a couple of freebies in my belly when she walked in. Tall, elegant, hair to her shoulders. But I think it was the red shoes that did me in. A *Wizard of Oz* moment.'

'A what?'

'The movie. The one where Dorothy takes the shoes from the dead witch and clicks her heels to get home.'

'I'll take your word for it. So Rachel's red shoes turned your head, did they?'

'I waited until she was alone, and with champers for courage I went over to chat.'

'What time was that?'

'I've no idea. The free drink was my undoing. But she was striking. Asked me to get her a real drink.'

'Real drink?'

'Gin and tonic.'

'Where did you get it?'

'From the bar. When I came back, she was eating a cracker with what looked like shite spread on it. Chicken liver, she said. Gross, I said. And it was.'

'Who served her the food?'

Andy shrugged and gulped down a mouthful of alcohol. 'One of the waiting staff. She was young. Not my type.' He winked, and Kirby felt his stomach flip.

'What did you and Rachel talk about?' He sipped his pint, feeling a little uneasy. This was a conversation to be held under caution, at the station. But he needed the information.

'Didn't really talk about much. I gave her the drink and headed back to get my Guinness, and when I looked for her again, I couldn't find her.'

'Did she talk about her business?'

'I told you, we didn't really talk. Anyhow, it'd probably be double Dutch to me. I looked at her business card. Something about using stones to make skincare products.'

Kirby found his notebook in his pocket and jotted down what Andy had said. There was no knowing what the man might remember tomorrow.

'Were you in her company for long?'

'Time means nothing when I've a good few on me. You know how it is.'

Kirby knew all too well. 'Did you leave the party with her?'

'It wasn't like a real party. Just a bunch of suits milling about sculling free booze.'

'Just like you?'

'Just like me.' Andy swallowed the remainder of his drink and indicated to Caroline for another. 'To answer your question, I didn't leave with her. I drank as much as I could and at some stage I headed for home. I swear I never saw her after I gave her the gin and tonic.' He took the drink from Caroline.

Kirby noticed that Andy hadn't offered to buy him a drink. He checked the time again. He really had to leave. He hoped Andy had no involvement in Rachel's death. If he'd been as drunk last night as he was now, there was no way he could have carried out the murder.

He stood. 'Nine o'clock tomorrow morning.'

'I start work at ten.'

'No excuses. I want you in the station at nine.' He headed for the door.

'Bright-eyed and bushy-tailed,' Andy said, and his glasses fell off his head.

Caroline sighed. 'I'll see that he goes home after that one.'

'Rather you than me,' Kirby said.

CHAPTER TWENTY

Detective Sam McKeown left a message for Jessica Fleming to contact him for a further interview, then sought out Garda Martina Brennan before she clocked off. She was in the locker room, hauling off her vest and heavy equipment.

'It's such a relief to get rid of this stuff,' she said.

'I know a way to relieve the tension from your delicious shoulders.' He stood behind her and feathered her neck with a line of kisses.

'Stop! Jesus, Sam, not here.'

He pulled away. 'You don't like it down here in the dungeon? There's no one here, only ghosts.'

'The walls in this place have hyper-alert ears.' She shoved her work-issue stuff into the locker and put on a red fleece jacket.

'That brings out the colour in your eyes,' he said.

She laughed. 'My eyes are not red.'

'They're full of passion.' He dragged her into his arms. Her head only came to his shoulder, and she squirmed.

'I'll see you later if you like, Sam. I can cook something. You like my Madras chicken breasts.'

'I love your—'

She stopped him with a finger on his lips as if he were a child. 'Shh. See you at eight?'

'Eight it is.'

He watched her tight bum shimmy out of the room and noted how the light dulled once she had left. His phone vibrated in his pocket.

'Hi, love. Yeah, I meant to ring you earlier. We've a new case, looks like murder. I'll be stuck in Ragmullin for a few nights.' He listened for a few moments then said, 'Love you too. See you at the weekend all being well here.'

He hung up, then ran a finger over Martina's name on her locker and blew it a kiss. He whistled as he climbed the steps back to the office. His phone rang again with a number he did not recognise.

'Hello,' he said.

'Detective McKeown, this is Jessica Fleming. You wanted to speak to me. I can see you now; that's if you have nothing else on?'

He heard a laugh and possibly a touch of innuendo. 'Can you come into the station now?' he asked.

'I'm having dinner in about half an hour, so it would be better if you called out to me.' Her tone was officious, but then it lightened with a short laugh. 'Are you hungry?'

'I'll be there in ten minutes.'

Garda Martina Brennan would have to wait until another night.

CHAPTER TWENTY-ONE

Maddy fidgeted, biting the hard skin around her thumb. Bumping into the lanky detective that morning was playing on her mind, and she still had to bring the bike back.

She made her escape as Simon waltzed from the kitchen to the sitting room holding a plate stacked with what looked like ten slices of buttered toast. He placed it on the arm of the chair and kissed Stella, the baby crushed between them. Trey came in from wherever he'd been playing, stole a slice of toast, jumped up on an armchair with muck on his shoes and began fiddling with the television remote control. All three of them, plus the baby, were oblivious to her existence. She felt a bit peeved; after all, she was doing the jobs Stella couldn't do since she'd had the baby. But now that she'd handed over the money from last night, she was invisible.

Outside, she picked up the bike from the bald wet lawn where she'd thrown it. Ellen wouldn't be so nice as to lend it to her again if she let anything happen to it. She wouldn't be too pleased either to hear that Maddy had said the bike belonged to her granny. Maddy wondered what age Ellen was. Thirty, maybe, she concluded as she sat up on the saddle and headed off.

Pedalling down the street, across the canal and under the railway bridge, she thought of the man who'd helped her with the bike chain that morning. She'd have to remember to tell Ellen to oil it properly in future.

Her hair blew out behind her and the rain fell hard and sharp, and she cursed not having put on a hat, or a jacket with a hood. The wind was rising, and leaves and paper bags smacked her in the face. Then she remembered that she'd have to walk home in this deluge. Two fecking miles. It was all Stella's fault. Maddy would have taken the bike back last night, but Stella had asked her to do the job for her. She could piss off the next time she asked.

She rode through the industrial estate, which was being transformed into a retail district. She rode past the electrical shop with its newest tech gadgets, and past the twenty-four-hour garage with the smell of coffee tickling her wet nose.

After dipping under another railway bridge, she was almost in the countryside, though it was still part of the town. She passed the fields to her left with a new housing estate sprouting up beyond the grass swirling in the wind. To her right she whizzed by the line of old bungalows with their cute gardens and stone walls. She slowed down as she reached Ellen's house, one of only three two-storey houses on the road, and skidded into the yard.

The sky was black, storm clouds crashing into each other. She leaned the bike against the pebble-dashed wall and ran to the back door. Knocking, she turned to look at Ellen's garden. It was neat, with no broken bits of furniture like her own house had, and the clothes line fed between two bare apple trees. Ellen's car was parked out front, so she must be home; she'd hardly gone for a walk in this weather.

She knocked again, then depressed the handle easily and pushed the door inwards. She stuck her head inside.

'Ellen? I've returned your bike. Thanks.' No reply. Maybe she was in bed.

Turning to leave, Maddy felt the rain trickle down the inside of her T-shirt. She shivered. The only sound inside the house came from the television in the kitchen. Ellen wouldn't go out for a walk and leave it on. She wouldn't forget to lock the door either. Where was she?

It was no business of hers, Maddy thought, but at the same time, Ellen had been good to her. Offered her the bike and gave her apples and stuff. And listened to her. Ellen was one of the nicest people Maddy had ever met, probably *the* nicest, because in Maddy's world, most people looked down on her and laughed at her or turned their noses up in disgust. None of that was Maddy's fault, Ellen had told her. She had to remember she had no control over how other people acted; she only had control over how she reacted. Good advice, Maddy thought, but it was hard to put into practice when everyone was either a bitch or a bastard.

Ellen was good for her. Talked with her, not at her. Listened to her when she felt she had spent her life talking to a brick wall. Maddy wondered if she saw her as the mother she'd never really had. Though she was at least fifteen years older than her, Ellen had never talked down at her or reprimanded her.

She'd only hurt Maddy once in the three years she'd known her. Not physically, but by her words. That day during the summer when Maddy had offered to cut the lawn. She wouldn't have offered but she was stuck for money and knew Ellen would throw her a few euros. Before she'd even plugged in the small electric mower, Ellen had said she should take a shower. It wasn't Maddy's fault she hadn't taken a shower before she left home. It was Simon's. He'd been stone drunk the night before and had fallen asleep on the bathroom floor. Shrugging off that image, she replaced it with a picture of Ellen. Tall and beautiful, with her hair always shining, the ginger streaks sparkling in the sunshine. But there was no sunshine now. Only the dark and a damn storm.

Maybe she should just leave.

'Ellen, are you upstairs?'

No reply.

'I dropped your bike back. It's at the side of the house. I don't have the key to the shed. You better put it in before the weather gets any worse.'

Even as she said this, Maddy knew the bike was liable to be a rust ball by morning. Not her problem if Ellen didn't trust her with the key to the bloody shed.

Stepping outside, she shut the back door, hunched her shoulders and prepared to run the whole way back home. At the front of the house, she paused, thinking there was no way Ellen had gone out walking without locking up her house, and especially not in the rain. She was fastidious about the weather. She'd have known rain and wind were in the air. Just then, a streak of lightning lit up the evening sky.

Maddy lifted the letter box on the front door for one last yell. First, though, she hunkered down and glanced through the small brass rectangle,

'Ellen? Shit! Ellen!' She screamed and dropped the brass flap. 'Oh my God!'

Racing around the side of the house once again, she skidded on the shingle and fell to her knees. She stumbled, righted herself, opened the back door and lunged through the kitchen into the hall.

Kneeling beside the half-dressed, twisted form of her friend, she said, 'Did you fall down the stairs, Ellen?'

She put out her hand to rouse the woman, but stopped as she noticed the chalkiness of her face. Ellen's mouth was open in a frozen scream, and though she had never in her life seen a dead body, Maddy knew Ellen was dead. A pool of blood on the floor had dried to a circle around her head. And the smell! The air was clogged by a repressive odour, like rotting vegetables in a bin under the sink. It couldn't be coming from Ellen's body, could it? Recoiling, Maddy pressed her hand to her nose and mouth.

'What do I do?' she cried. 'Why did you have to die on me?' Anger replaced her sympathy. 'Fuck you. Everyone leaves me. Every fucking person in my life is a leaver.' Her voice echoed like a chant screeching back at her.

Shivering from the fright, and the wetness rapidly soaking into her bones, she sat back on her bottom and wondered what she should do. Call the emergency services? Then, an awful thought entered her head. If she called them, the guards would think she'd done something to Ellen. They'd take one look at her and think she'd tried to rob her and maybe pushed her down the stairs or something. That was exactly what they'd think. People in authority looked down their noses at the likes of Maddy Daly.

But she couldn't just leave Ellen here, dead, like this. Maybe she could phone the detective, the one she'd met that morning? He'd seemed okay. He'd fixed the chain on the bike, hadn't he? She felt about in her jeans pocket for his card, but of course she didn't have it. She'd changed her clothes.

Tears spilled down her cheeks and she cursed the world into which she had been born. Through her tears, she saw the telephone on the floor. Couldn't she make an anonymous call to the emergency services and then get the hell out of there? No way was she using her own mobile, because that could be traced. Buoyed with a sense of purpose, she lifted the receiver and punched in 999.

Forcing calm into her voice, she recited Ellen's name and address before telling the voice on the end of the line that she thought Ellen was dead. Then she hung up.

'You're the same as everyone else,' she said to the twisted body. 'Everyone leaves me in the end.'

Then, without a backward glance, she walked slowly along the hall to the kitchen. Only when she'd pulled the back door shut and was out in the pouring rain did she break into a run.

CHAPTER TWENTY-TWO

The house was quiet when Lottie got home. Sean was in the sitting room watching a quiz show, his most recent addiction. She was certain this was preferable to hours in front of his PlayStation. Her sixteen-year-old son was as tall now as his dad had been, and he'd inherited Adam's eyes and hair too.

He looked up from under his fringe, eyes wide in greeting. 'Hi, Mam. What's for dinner?'

'I'll check with the chef,' she said, and eased the door closed behind her.

In the kitchen, she began washing the lunchtime dishes, racking her brain to see what she could concoct from the scant foodstuff in the refrigerator and cupboards.

She had half hoped her mother might have dropped off something she'd made earlier, but no such luck. It had been a curse of a day and she craved a glass of wine, a cushion under her feet and her head on Boyd's shoulder. She shuddered out of her musings and opened the fridge door. With only four sleeps (in Chloe speak) to her big day, she felt a muted excitement but was simultaneously terrified. Excited to be able to acknowledge her love for Boyd at last and terrified of what the future would hold for them. They still had to sort out living arrangements. Katie and Louis were due home on Friday and then the chaos would truly erupt. But that made her happy. She missed her daughter and little grandson terribly.

She found a lonely-looking pork chop under a bag of wilted spinach. The chop would have to do Sean. She'd have a sandwich. If she had any bread left in the house. Switching on the hob, she poured oil to heat in a pan, turned on the oven and crossed her fingers that there was a bag of chips in the freezer.

After sweeping the floor, she just had the chips in the oven when her phone rang. Superintendent Farrell. Now what?

'You better get your coat on again,' Farrell said.

'I'm cooking Sean's dinner.'

'Isn't he big enough to cook his own?'

It was bad enough getting lectures from her mother; now her boss was at it. 'What's up?'

'Suspicious death. SOCOs are there already.' Farrell recited the address.

Lottie hung up and wondered what had happened. Her mother lived out that way. Should she call her? No.

She stared at the cooker. Switch it off and order a takeaway for Sean? No way. She went to the hall, and shouted while pulling her jacket off the banister, 'Sean, turn off that television. I have one minute to tell you how to cook your dinner.'

'It's like a mud bath out here,' Lottie said as she tugged booties over her sopping wet shoes. She dragged the zip of her forensic suit to her chin and waited until Boyd was similarly attired before fastening her face mask and pulling the hood over her drenched hair. They stepped into the kitchen. SOCOs had placed small steel pallets on the ground. Lottie could see why. Footprints along the floor. Gerry was busy with his camera, snapping evidence at the scene.

'It's late,' Boyd said.

'So it is.'

'Why are we even here? I heard the woman fell down the stairs. Stone-cold dead.'

'If that's the case, how did she make the emergency call?' Lottie stepped into the narrow hall. The caller must have made the footprints. 'There's the phone, and the body is there. According to the paramedics who arrived with the ambulance, this lady has been dead for some hours, if not days.'

'What time was the call received?' Boyd said.

'Seven twenty-three this evening.'

She waited, Boyd close behind her, as Jim McGlynn assessed the body. The paramedics had left the scene once the gardaí arrived, followed quickly by a fire engine.

'Why were all the emergency services here?' Boyd said.

'The caller didn't provide any information other than the name and address of the victim and the fact that they thought she was dead. Then they hung up. So the agent sent out everyone bar the army.'

'Any idea who the caller might have been?' Boyd asked.

'The report says nothing other than it sounded like a young distressed female.'

'It might have been a robbery.'

'The place doesn't look ransacked,' Lottie said.

'Maybe Ms Gormley disturbed the burglar, or he disturbed her, and she fell down the stairs,' Boyd said, with a yawn.

McGlynn raised his head, green eyes flashing angrily. 'Maybe she fell or maybe she was pushed, but take a look at the area around her mouth.'

The stale air in the narrow space shifted as McGlynn drew back, allowing them to have a better look. Lottie stared at the partially dressed woman with her mouth open in her final anguished death throes, a dried substance stuck to her lips and chin. And a considerable amount of bruising. She could feel Boyd's breath through the thin fabric covering her neck.

'Oh my God,' she said.

'Poisoned?' Boyd said.

'It can't be a second one.' She hunkered down beside McGlynn, who blew out heavily, his mask expanding with his breath.

'We'll need a post-mortem to determine that and to tell us if this death is connected to the woman discovered this morning. My guess is poison, and if it is, I'm inclined to believe the two deaths are connected. But cause of death is the pathologist's remit, not mine.'

'Shit,' Boyd said.

'How long has she been dead?' Lottie said.

McGlynn shook his head. 'Don't know, but I'd estimate longer than twenty-four hours.'

'Can you see into her mouth from there?' She explained about the piece of glass the pathologist had found in Rachel Mullen's throat.

'Ah, I did think there was something lodged there but like I told you then, it's a job for the state pathologist.'

'Okay.'

The space was too small for all of them, so Lottie hunted Boyd back into the kitchen and followed him. She looked around.

'No sign of a struggle in here,' she said and touched a blouse hanging on the clothes rack. 'These clothes are dry. The neighbours might know when they last saw her out and about. Her mobile phone is on the table.' She touched the home key with her gloved finger. 'Needs a PIN. Put it in an evidence bag. Gary can have a look at it.'

She resumed her scan of the kitchen. 'The television is on. There are two mugs there by the sink. She might have had a visitor.'

'Or maybe she just didn't wash the first mug and took out another. Who knows?'

'Or the person who made the call was here all along. Or maybe they left then returned. Oh, I don't know. It makes no sense if she's been dead for a day or more.'

She picked up one of the mugs and held it to her nose. 'Whiskey, I'd say.' She sniffed the second one. 'Same.'

'The poison may have been in it. But wouldn't you still smell it?' Boyd said.

Lottie shrugged. 'Once the mugs are analysed, we'll know.'

'So she had a drink with someone. Then what?'

'If it was poison, she might have felt ill. After the visitor left, she went upstairs to the bathroom. There's no toilet down here.'

'Or she was getting ready for bed. Lottie, we have no idea how long she's been dead.'

'We'll just have to wait for the post-mortem. I want to look upstairs.'

'It'll be morning before McGlynn lets us step over the body.'

'So be it.'

'Do you know the victim?' Boyd asked.

'No. Why? Should I?'

'Your mother lives on this road.'

'Doesn't mean I have to know her neighbours.'

'She might be able to fill you in.'

'*We* will do the work, not my mother.'

'Just thought it could be a short cut. Rose knows everything and everyone.'

'Right.' Lottie found the kitchen too small to have a row with Boyd. 'Ellen is in a state of undress. Just wearing her knickers and a blouse. Maybe something disturbed her while she was upstairs getting ready for bed?'

Two more SOCOs entered the kitchen. Even though they knew their job, Lottie said, 'Bag those mugs and dust everywhere and everything for fingerprints. There must have been someone else with her at some stage.'

'First responders say the back door was unlocked,' Boyd said. 'Maybe the person who was drinking with her left but came back tonight, and that's who made the phone call.'

'If Jim is right, she's been dead longer than twenty-four hours. Is it possible whoever poisoned her hung around that long looking at a corpse? I don't know, but I have a gut feeling the person who made the call is not the individual who drank out of that mug.'

'Stranger things—'

'Her car is locked, but there's a bicycle outside in the rain.' One of the SOCOs came in from outside. 'At the side of the house.'

'You know about bikes, Boyd.' Lottie went to the back door, eyeing the torrential downpour, and braced herself for a soaking. The exterior wall light blazed brightly, highlighting the raindrops like diamonds. She hadn't noticed the bicycle on the way in; she'd been trying to avoid getting drenched.

'Wait a minute,' Boyd said. 'I saw that bike recently, or one very similar to it.'

'Really?' Lottie turned to look at him. 'When?'

'This morning. When I went on my bike ride before work.' He walked closer to inspect it, hovering a gloved finger over the wet handlebars and down to the chain. 'Yes. It's the same one. A young girl was stopped by the canal. The chain had come undone.'

'And you helped her?'

'I did.'

'Did you find out who she was?'

'I'll have to think what name she told me. Don't think she mentioned a surname. Aged about fourteen or fifteen. Maybe older. She said the bicycle belonged to her grandmother, which was probably a lie. Come to think of it, we don't even know if this bike *is* Ellen Gormley's. It might just happen to be leaning against the side of her house.'

'Neighbours or family will know.' Lottie wiped rainwater from her eyes. 'The dead woman looks early thirties, so she's hardly old enough to be your girl's grandmother.'

'You're right. And we need to find Ellen Gormley's family and inform them of her death.'

'We'll do that back at the station,' Lottie said. 'It's awful to think of that poor woman lying dead in there for a day or two and no one missing her.'

'Shocking.'

'We need to locate that young girl, Boyd. If this bicycle does indeed belong to Ellen Gormley, we have to find out when the girl was here.'

'You think she could be the last person to see Ellen alive?'

'It's possible, or …'

'I don't like where you're going with this, Lottie.'

'I never said the words.'

'But you're thinking it.'

'I suppose I am. Whoever she is, that girl might be crucial to discovering what happened to Ellen Gormley.'

CHAPTER TWENTY-THREE

It seemed that Simon had gone. The bathroom was free. Stripping off her clothes, Maddy stood into the shower. As usual the water was little more than an icy trickle, but she didn't care. She needed to free her skin of the smell from Ellen's house. It clung to every pore. She scrubbed with her nails, raising red welts and scratches, but she couldn't get rid of it.

Switching off the useless shower, she wrapped a threadbare towel around her body and lay down on her narrow bed. She hadn't the energy to draw the covers up over her and shivered violently as the rain drummed a noisy beat against the window. She hadn't turned on the light and she could see the black sky outside with the rain falling in sheets.

Her heart spasmed with palpitations as anxiety took root. Could she be traced by her voice on the 999 call? She didn't think that was possible. But if a neighbour had seen her, the guards might be able to find her. Shit. Would they think she'd pushed Ellen down the stairs?

She jumped up, grabbed her oily jeans from the floor and found the detective's card. She'd have to ring him and tell him before things got out of hand. He might understand. He might even believe her. But he'd seen her with the bike, he'd remember that, and she'd lied. Said it belonged to her grandmother, the first thing that'd come into her head. Why hadn't she told him the truth? Because Maddy knew that the truth mostly got her in trouble and fabricating things into fiction usually worked better.

She searched the floor for her phone, then glanced at his card and tapped in the number. She paused. What was she going to say? *Hey, Mr Mark, remember me? We met on the canal line this morning. I had this High Nelly bike and I know you thought I stole it, but I didn't, and the thing is, the woman who owns it is dead.* She felt a tear search for escape at the corner of her eye. Yeah, right. Like she could tell him that. Still her finger hovered over the call icon.

Don't be a fool. She shoved the phone under her pillow. If they eventually connected her to the bike, she would tell the truth. Or not. Whatever.

The rain continued to beat violently against the window, the baby howled in the room next door, and two-year-old Trey groaned, cried out and was silent once again. Eventually Maddy drifted off to sleep.

CHAPTER TWENTY-FOUR

The state pathologist phoned to say she wouldn't get to Ragmullin until first thing the next morning, so once McGlynn's team had carried out a preliminary sweep of the area, Lottie and Boyd made their way up the narrow stairs. Lottie emphasised that it was imperative to get a handle on things despite McGlynn insisting there was nothing upstairs to indicate suspicious activity.

Once she'd looked into the three bedrooms and the bathroom, she had to agree with the SOCO leader. A handbag by the bed offered up bank cards in the wallet confirming what the caller had told the emergency operator. The dead woman was Ellen Gormley.

'Since I heard the name, I've been thinking it's familiar. Why is that?' Lottie said as she looked through the bedside cabinet.

'Your mother will know,' Boyd said.

'Feck off, smart-arse. That bookcase is stocked to the gills.'

Boyd walked along the shelving that lined the length of the wall at the foot of the bed. 'There's quite a few medical books. Maybe she's a nurse or a doctor.'

Lottie went back to the handbag and opened an interior zip.

'Dr Ellen Gormley.' She held up a lanyard with an ID badge swinging on the end of it. 'That's why I know the name.' She read the back of the badge. 'She has a practice in Ragmullin, specialising in psychology. A starting point.'

'If it turns out she was poisoned, what's her link to Rachel Mullen?'

'First of all, we can't make any assumptions until the post-mortem is carried out. Ellen might have just fallen down the stairs and ruptured a lung, which caused the foaming at her mouth. Secondly, we need to trace her next of kin and inform them. Thirdly, we need to find out who made the call. And fourthly, we need to find the girl you saw with the bike. She told you a fib. Ellen Gormley's date of birth on this badge means she is thirty years old, and even though I'm terrible at maths, I don't think she could have been the grandmother of a teenager.'

'As always, you're absolutely right, Lottie Parker.'

Boyd humphed down the stairs and Lottie tried to figure out if he was being sarcastic or not. There was still a lot she had to figure out about Mark Boyd.

It was getting on for midnight by the time they got back to the station. The office was as quiet as a morgue. Lottie was about to call it a night, but she felt an urge to trace Ellen Gormley's relatives and inform them of her death before the Ragmullin grapevine sprung into life.

Ellen's phone and laptop had been dropped off to the station. The phone had been on the kitchen table and her laptop zipped into a briefcase in the living room, where there were two high-backed black leather chairs, a small coffee table with a box of tissues, and a desk with a stack of books ready to topple over.

'I'm trying this phone before I send it to the technical team,' Lottie said.

'Thought it needed a PIN?' Boyd said.

'True.' Lottie tried the first four digits of Ellen's date of birth, which she'd found on the reverse side of her ID tag. When that didn't work, she worked from the end and tried the last four.

'Bingo. I'm in.'

'Oh, I'm surprised,' Boyd said.

'Why?'

'You can't even remember your own password.'

'Duh.' Despite the late hour, she felt a surge of adrenaline as she stared at the phone screen. 'No social media apps. It's possible she had no online profile. A load of phone calls and a few texts. Numbers appear random. Could be patients. Her contact list is sparse too.'

'I googled her name. She kept a low profile. No golf photos, or speeches. The kind of thing I'd associate with a doctor.'

'You're pigeonholing her. If I call out the first names of the females on her contact list, will you see if you recognise the name that girl gave you?'

'I think it was something like Paddy, or … wait a minute … Maddy. Yeah. Maddy. That's it.'

Lottie scrolled though the contacts. 'Neither name appears here.'

'It's possible she stole the bike and then had a fit of conscience and returned it.' Boyd yawned loudly.

'After meeting you, you mean?'

'I did tell her I was a detective and I gave her my card.'

'Gallant as ever.'

'What do you mean by that?'

'Nothing.' Who was the girl and what was her relationship to Ellen? 'SOCOs will take fingerprints from the bike. They might throw up a name.'

'Jesus, she's only a kid. I hardly think she poisoned that woman and flung her down the stairs.'

'You're in a ratty humour.' She glanced at the time. 'Thought you were a morning person, Boyd.'

'I am, but I don't count ten minutes past midnight as morning. We haven't found any obvious family members and it doesn't look like she was married or had kids, so why don't we leave it until the *real* morning?'

'You're right. It's been a long day and I'll only make mistakes at this hour.'

'Come here and give me a kiss,' Boyd said, reaching for her hand as she stood.

'I think you need to go home, and I need my beauty sleep.' She grinned. Kissed him on the cheek.

'You're grand the way you are. You know, we're like an old married couple and we're not even married,' he grumbled.

'Not long now.'

'I can't wait.' He pulled on his wet coat.

'How is the wedding prep going? You haven't killed Chloe yet anyhow.'

'All you need to do is turn up.' Boyd winked at her.

'Don't forget to get Grace to Ragmullin on time.'

'Ah, Grace. That's a whole other ball game.'

'How's she doing?'

'Brilliantly, to be honest. She loves being on her own. Connemara is in her bones. I asked a few people I know to keep an eye on her. Did I tell you she got a job?'

'No, you didn't,' Lottie said.

'She's only just started. She's working in a pub.'

'Your sister, Grace, in a pub? That can't be right.'

'It's quiet in the west this time of year. She's just doing a few evenings a week. Switching on the glass washer and then stacking glasses back on the shelf.'

'She picks up dirty glasses? I thought Grace abhorred anything dirty.'

'As far as I know, the bar staff have to pick them up and put them in the washer because Grace refused. So you're right there. She only handles the clean glasses.'

'Gosh, she won't last long in that job, but I hope it works out for her.'

'Me too.'

The hazel flecks in his eyes sparkled under the lights and Lottie leaned up and kissed him gently. Then she took his hand, switched out the lights and left the world of murder on her desk for the night.

CHAPTER TWENTY-FIVE

Tuesday nights in Fallon's pub were as quiet as Mondays and Wednesdays. The busy period ran from Thursday to Sunday. Chloe Parker preferred to be busy. Tonight, time was dragging. She had polished the same glass for the second time before she noticed what she was doing. The door opened and closed, and he walked in. A physical lift occurred in her body from her toes to her mouth, which curved in a smile.

'Hi there,' she said as he sat on the stool at the counter.

'Quiet night, I see,' he said.

'It sure is. Pint of Heineken?'

'I think I'll have a vodka and Red Bull. No ice.'

'That kind of day then?' She turned to the optics and poured the spirit. Taking a can of Red Bull from the shelf, she put the drinks in front of him and leaned her chin on her hand. 'You look tired.'

'Bad day at the office.'

'You don't have an office,' she laughed.

'Smile more often. It brings out the blue in your eyes.' He leaned over and kissed her lips.

'You've made my night,' she said. 'Hey, I've been meaning to ask you, and there's no obligation or anything ...' Letting her voice trail off, Chloe wondered if she was doing the right thing. She'd only been seeing him a few weeks, and he was older than her. A lot older. Her mother would have a fit. She'd kept him secret, which was easy in her house with Lottie out all day at work and then spending her time with Boyd.

She heard the click of fingers in front of her eyes. 'Oh, sorry, I was miles away.'

'What were you about to ask me?'

'Would you like to come to a wedding on Saturday?'

'Who's getting married?'

'My mother.'

'That's some way to introduce me to your family.'

'Will you come?'

'Let me sleep on it, okay?'

Biting the edge of her thumb, she felt an itch of irritation just beneath the skin. Sometimes he talked like an old man. But she'd had her fill of spontaneous youths who'd bored the life out of her. The fact that someone older had taken an interest in her at all infused her with excitement.

'Alone?' she said.

He winked, held her arm, drew her gently towards him. 'You can join me if you like.'

She wished the counter wasn't between them.

*

Standing in the unlit room, staring out the window of what her mother called the penthouse suite on the top floor of the house, Jessica Fleming listened to the rain pound the lake. She sipped a Pinot Grigio. The night was as dark as coal, but the lights from the golf clubhouse cast eerie shadows through the sheets of rain.

She smiled to herself thinking back on the day's events, and in particular how her attention had been held by Sam McKeown, the tall, bald, good-looking detective. He'd taken his time interviewing her. He was cute in a rugged sort of way. Jessica was no fool, especially where men were concerned. He was either married or divorced but she felt he was still married and on the prowl, hence the absent wedding ring. He had the look of a hunter, wily and alert. And he'd got more information out of her than he needed in order to investigate Rachel's death.

Seeing Rachel arrive at the restaurant party had sent a shiver down her spine, though she had to admit, her own part in the invite list had been genius. The look on her mother's face! Priceless. Sometimes it paid to be bold. And then this morning, just hours later, Rachel was found dead. Pity.

Sipping more wine, Jessica walked around the room, feathering the designer quilt with her cold fingers. She shivered. So much waste. Her mother was a fool. Pouring money into the renovation of this old shell of a house and then opening up the restaurant in town, all just to spite Daddy. Did she not realise that he didn't care what she did? She was shoving them all into the quicksand of bankruptcy just to get one over on him. I wish you luck, Mother, Jessica thought.

She glanced at the time. It was late, but she was wound up.

Turning towards the door too quickly, she felt a sharp pain tug at her scalp. She took off her tight hairband and shook out her long straight hair. Standing in front of the floor-length mirror, she wondered why she had dressed up for the interview with Detective McKeown. Maybe she should have curled her hair and worn her black chiffon dress, the one she'd bought in Brown Thomas. Next time, she thought. Maybe she could get him to invite her out. Her dating history was a little too sparse. Men never lived up to her expectations. Was that her father's fault also? She turned away from the mirror, afraid of her own reflection.

With one more glance at the rain on the lake, she was about to leave the room when she heard a car pull up outside. She pressed her nose to the window pane and curved her hand over her brow to see better. Who was calling so late?

Damn, she thought. It was Tara. What was she doing home? Wasn't she supposed to be in London, or was that just another one of her lies? Jessica dug her nails into her palms. Tara always got what she wanted. Ever since they'd been children. Was she now back to take away the little ground that Jessica had gained? Was she about to drive a wedge into her relationship with their mother? She sighed loudly. With Tara, she knew she had to expect the unexpected.

Drawing away from the window, she drained her drink, placed the glass on the ledge and left the suite to get ready for bed. Tomorrow is another day, she said to herself, and laughed thinking of the line from *Gone with the Wind*. Well, she was no Scarlett O'Hara, but was Tara strong enough to destroy her future?

Damn Tara.

The first time the little girl saw her father having sex, she was nine years old. The woman was not her mother. The little girl had no idea what it was that she was watching until many months later, by which time she had become adept at spying on her father. But this first time, she hadn't meant to spy. She had been about to knock on the door, but it was slightly ajar, the sound of laughter coming from inside. She rarely heard her father laugh, and that was what made her stop and watch. Maybe she should have walked away. But she was rooted where she stood, as if someone had glued her feet to the floor. Her eyes growing wider as she watched.

The woman was more like a girl. She seemed to be a lot younger than her mother. A teenager then? She certainly laughed like a teenager. Like the teenager who babysat for them on the rare occasions her parents ventured out for a meal or a party.

The little girl watched with childish fascination as her father kissed the teenager roughly, and he must have pulled her hair because there was a screech, but it was quickly followed by a high-pitched giggle.

The little girl knew she should turn away, but it was as if some unnatural force had stuck her nose to the crack in the door to her father's study. She was not allowed to go in. No one was allowed into his 'manly domain', as he called it.

When the pair moved behind the desk, she saw that the teenager wore a short white denim skirt and a red flowery blouse tied in a knot exposing her stomach. Her father was unusually dressed in that his shirt was open and the belt of his trousers hung open too. Maybe she should back away now. But a small flutter in her belly held her in place. She knew she was about to witness something forbidden.

Once they were positioned behind the desk, he pulled down his trousers and the woman pulled up her skirt and shimmied out of her knickers, flinging them over her shoulder. The little girl wondered what was going on. She stood there unable to move, unable to look away. A statue, staring in shock and horror.

The grunting and grinding came next, her father's head buried in the long loose hair of the teenager as they moved in rhythm to some beat only audible in their own ears. After a few moments, her father let out a loud moan and the teenager gasped, then giggled again. At that moment, the little girl locked eyes with her father. His lips parted in a sly smile and his eyes were bulbous in some kind of weird ecstasy.

He'd seen her, and as he thrust his body into the teenager one last time, he smiled again at his daughter. It was an unusual smile. The little girl had never seen such an expression on her father's face before and she was sure she never wanted to see it again, but of course she did. Many times after that first instance.

She raced down the stairs. In the hall, she noticed the teenager's striped and fringed cloth bag on the coat stand. Filled with feelings she didn't know how to put her finger on, she began to rummage through the bag – wallet, receipts, a hair tie – until she put her hand on a bottle. A heavy black perfume bottle.

Her father only purchased the most expensive gifts for the women in his life, which until now the little girl had thought meant her mother. The name on the black bottle intrigued her. She had seen it written on a dark brown bottle in the shed, though painted on that one was a skull and crossbones.

CHAPTER TWENTY-SIX

Wednesday 22 November

Andy Ashe woke up with the mother and father of a hangover.

He couldn't figure out where he was. Groaning, he sat up. In his own bed. Alone. Fully dressed. He wasn't sure if that was good or bad.

Shit. He dragged off his clothes and showered for ten minutes. By the time he was dried and dressed, he felt worse. And he still had to face into work.

He flicked through the news app on his phone and immediately saw Rachel Mullen's bright face smiling out at him. Double shit.

And then he remembered Detective Larry Kirby. Treble shit.

Hazily he recalled he was to be in the station at nine. It was now nine thirty. Any minute he expected the riot squad, or whatever they were called, to break down his door and barge in, snap handcuffs on his wrists and haul him off in a van with bars on the windows in front of all his neighbours. Give them something definitive to talk about at least.

He was late for the interview, but not late for work. He'd give Hazel the news that he needed an hour off and then he'd traipse up to the garda station and get it over with. He could do with the hair of the dog. He opened all his cupboards but couldn't find anything containing alcohol except for white wine vinegar, and that was definitely a no-no.

Why wasn't his life simple?

With his jacket on, he dipped his finger in the empty holy water font, a habit he couldn't shake off from childhood, and went out to face whatever the day was about to throw back in his face.

*

Hazel had fallen into bed having taken two codeine for a headache and the nausea that raged through her stomach, and half a bottle of cough mixture for the rasping in her throat. After her visitor had left, she'd felt truly awful. Too many memories; too much wine.

Standing before the mirror, she felt dizzy and knew she couldn't go to work today. Black circles rimmed her eyes and there were scratches on her cheeks. She recalled falling into a bush with the fright she'd got.

The coffee wasn't doing her much good. Her head was fuzzy as hell. She needed a shot of something stronger. She searched the drawers again but still couldn't find her stash. She needed a hit, and quickly. She pulled her phone towards her and tapped the number saved under 'Mum'.

'Answer, please,' she willed the inanimate object in her hand. But it went to a message, which was more usual than not.

When it beeped, she said, 'It's Hazel. Can you come around? You know what I need. Bring it now. I'll pay double the usual.' She ended the call, then held her head in her hands and wondered how she was ever going to escape the hell she had created for herself.

Her ex-lover had seemed like her saviour, but when he'd dumped her, her life had spiralled like she was falling down a deep dark well. And whenever she tried to climb back out, she slipped further into the abyss.

She was drowning in her own misery.

CHAPTER TWENTY-SEVEN

Jessica Fleming hated the kitchen her mother had created in the basement of Molesworth House. It felt as though it had been plucked out of a *Downton Abbey* set. Massive white ceramic stove, copper pots hanging overhead waiting to be used, a twelve-foot oak table in the centre surrounded by hard wooden chairs. Two walls of cupboards jutted out over a black granite counter. The window was narrow and long, with small stained-glass panes, taking up half of one wall.

Seated at the table, her mother held a cafetière in her hand as she poured freshly brewed coffee into a mug. Some luxuries did not lend themselves to the old-world atmosphere, and a hi-tech coffee machine was one of them. As Jessica took the mug offered and leaned against the sink, she heard footsteps on the winding stairs.

Annie studied the steam from her coffee, her own mug gripped between both hands. 'I don't want any more rows, Jessica.'

If your blood could freeze in your veins, Jessica was sure hers had suddenly turned to ice as her sister stepped off the bottom stair and breezed into the kitchen. She'd been right last night. Tara was home.

'Good morning,' Tara said, zipping up a black satin Michael Kors jacket over a white shirt and black jeans.

'I thought you were supposed to be in London.' The vision of her sister sweeping her recently streaked blonde hair back from her face into a ponytail caused Jessica's words to die in her throat. Without any make-up, the scar running from Tara's left lower eyelid to her chin flared bright red.

'I wasn't feeling well,' Tara said. 'There was no way I was going to be stuck on a plane vomiting into a sick bag.' She raised an eyebrow. 'I'm wondering if perhaps I caught whatever Rachel Mullen had.'

'Rachel did not catch anything,' Annie said. 'She was murdered.'

'*You're* not dead though.' Jessica couldn't keep the venom from slipping out with her words.

'Ha! Are you sorry?'

'Shut up.' Turning away, Jessica tipped her coffee into the deep Belfast sink and made to leave the room.

'Sit down,' Annie said, her voice low and forceful. 'We need to talk.'

'I have absolutely nothing to say to her.' Jessica folded her arms.

'Sit down!' The window panes rattled with the timbre of Annie's voice and the rainbow from the stained glass shimmered out over the room.

Tara complied. Jessica reluctantly and noisily dragged out a chair, fixed her spectacles tight to her nose and sat opposite her sister.

Annie remained seated at the head of the table and poured fresh coffee. Waiting in a silence broken only by the tick of the large clock hanging on the wall at the turn of the stairs, Jessica wished she was anywhere but here.

'Tara,' Annie said, 'you know about Rachel's death. You know what that means.'

'Enlighten me.'

'She'd been at my launch party. At the restaurant. The gardaí will be suspicious of everyone who was there. I've spoken to the detectives and been as helpful as I can. A detective even called here yesterday evening to grill Jessica.'

Tara opened her mouth and laughed loudly, her scar creasing and stretching with the movement of her lips. Jessica felt her stomach turn.

'Oh Jessica,' Tara said, 'have you been a bold girl?'

'Shut up.'

'Girls.' Annie's voice was calm now. 'Stop acting like five-year-olds. We need to be unified. I don't know who killed her or why, but I can do without the guards crawling all over our affairs.'

'Affairs? That's a good one,' Tara said. 'Does Daddy know?'

'Tara!' Annie's voice was rising again, and Jessica wondered where this was leading. Why the hell was her sister even here?

Annie said, 'You will find this difficult to contemplate, Tara, but I think your father might've had something to do with that girl's death. I have no proof, but he arrived at the party in a right tizzy on Monday night, and we all know he is rarely rattled.'

'I saw him for a brief moment,' Jessica put in, 'but I was engaged in conversation, and when I looked for him, he'd left.'

'He didn't stay long,' Annie said. 'But the thing is, he was looking for Rachel Mullen.'

'What would he have wanted with her?' Tara asked, and Jessica noticed that her eyes had narrowed, cat-like, ready to pounce.

'Only your father can answer that,' Annie replied.

Tara's eyes narrowed further. 'She used to be our friend when we were teenagers, that's all. I can't understand why Daddy would have been looking for her.'

'Maybe she owed him money,' Jessica suggested.

'She contacted me seeking funding for some project she's involved in. It's possible she also contacted your father though I'm confident he wouldn't lend anyone a cent.'

'Interesting,' Tara said. 'Daddy never mentioned that to me.'

'What will the guards have to say about it all?' Jessica said.

'I don't know.' Annie shook her head. 'I presume they've spoken with him. But my concern is how this will affect my business.'

'Typical,' Tara said. 'Money always comes first with you. What about Rachel? What about her family? Oh God, poor Beth.'

'You didn't think much of them when you were fifteen; why on earth would you worry about them now?' Annie said.

Tara folded her arms and remained silent.

'Look, girls, I have enough to worry about with my own family. I'm just asking you to be alert. Like I said, I fear your father could be involved in this in some way. I can't have him ruining everything for me now that I'm on the brink of success at last.'

'Sounds to me like Daddy had a bit on the side,' Tara said, her mouth curved in a malicious smile, causing her scar to crease once again. Jessica turned away and concentrated on her mother.

'Enough!' Annie snapped. 'I want you both to act like proper sisters. Don't give the gardaí anything that will draw attention towards us. I need my restaurant to flourish or I'll end up defaulting on my business loans.'

Jessica kept her mouth shut, not because she was afraid of inflaming her mother's anger but because she really had nothing to say.

Tara's squeaky voice filled the silence. 'What do you want us to tell them? You're always putting words in our mouths, so off you go.'

The slap caught Tara unawares, but the noise of it reverberated in the old kitchen, causing Jessica's spectacles to slip down her nose. She hesitated to raise her hand to fix them as she watched the pulse spreading across her sister's face, inflaming her scar.

'Bitch!' Tara screamed, shoving back her chair. She was on the bottom step of the stairs before she turned. 'You will be so fucking sorry you did that.'

And then she was gone.

As Annie fell back into her chair, Jessica stood frozen. Afraid to move. Afraid to say anything. Because she knew that in circumstances like these, no matter what she said or did, it would be wrong.

CHAPTER TWENTY-EIGHT

Once the forensic team had completed their work, Beth Mullen received a phone call to inform her she was allowed back into her home. She thanked her neighbour for her kindness and hurried down the road to the empty house.

Inside she saw evidence of the work that had been carried out over the last twenty-four hours, but she was surprised at how neat it had been left. The only absence she felt profoundly was the spirit of her sister. Between the walls, the place was a shell. Lifeless. Soulless. Rachel was dead. Things they'd shared for twenty-five years were now a memory, never to be shared again.

She tried to shake off Rachel's ghost. She had to shower and change. Then there were things to do. Affairs to be put in order. Her father to contact, even though Detective Boyd had informed her that he wasn't in any hurry to travel to comfort her.

She also wanted to visit her mother's grave, because by a cruel twist of fate, today was the second anniversary of her death. Rachel would have wanted her to buy flowers. Surely the florist would have something fresh and appropriate, even though it was November. Then she realised she'd have to organise her sister's funeral.

Slumping onto the armchair, she felt as if a void had opened up in her chest. Something that her twin sister had filled since the day she'd been born. She wasn't thinking straight.

Expecting to cry and scream, she was surprised that her eyes remained dry. So far, she had shed her tears at the correct time and in front of the right people. She had kept the facade intact. She had played the shocked, grieving sister to perfection, of that she was sure. But now she was alone, in the house that was totally hers because Rachel had organised through the bank for the mortgage protection to transfer to her following their mother's death. Rachel had sorted out all that kind of thing. She was good at administrative work, whereas Beth was the creative soul of the family, the silent partner behind her sister's drive and enthusiasm. Now, though, it was Beth's chance to shine. In the perfect cliché, she could emerge from the shadow of the perfect twin.

Was Rachel's death the beginning of this metamorphosis? She wondered about the one thing Rachel had forbidden her to talk about. The secret that had brought a darkness to her eyes from time to time. Therapy worked for a while, and at first it had returned light and joy to Rachel, a sparkle so bright that Beth had been blinded by it. Then, in an instant, one winter's day, the light was extinguished. It was only with the prospect of her new business that the true Rachel began to emerge once again. Maybe if Beth could delve into that secret, she might get somewhere close to discovering why her sister was dead. Should she have explained all this to the detectives? No, because she couldn't even explain it to herself. Rachel had been so hard to understand, and more so after their mother's death, when she'd abandoned her old friends.

The doorbell rang and Beth jumped out of the chair, knocking her knee against the coffee table. She stood still. Was it the detectives again? Hadn't she told them enough? She'd told them all she thought they needed to know. She'd been truthful. Except for one lie.

Glancing in the hall mirror, she tried to flatten some of the frizz from her hair, then gave up and opened the door.

The man in front of her jutted out his clean-shaven chin, skin as smooth as slate and his eyes two pools of darkness, hair swept to the back of his neck in a short ponytail. His black parka jacket made him appear weighty, but Beth knew he was slim and toned. Confusion swept through her like a blizzard, and eventually she got the words out.

'Brendan, what are you doing here?'

She glanced past him, up and down the road. Seeing a garda car parked a little further down, she beckoned him inside. No one had mentioned they'd be watching the house. She'd refused the help of a family liaison officer, but did they think she might be in danger from whoever had killed her sister? Did they think the killer might return? If so, why hadn't they warned her?

Her mind racing with questions, she followed Brendan into the living room. How to act? Normal? Huh, she thought. Nothing was normal any more.

'Coffee?' she said, to give herself time to think.

'No thanks.' His voice sounded older somehow. 'I just want to talk to you.'

'Why are you here?'

'Jesus, Beth, why do you think?' He pulled off his jacket and dropped it on a chair. 'Last night I heard Rachel was dead, and you ask me why I'm here?' He sank onto the couch, his hair flipping over his high forehead. He left it there, hiding his eyes, which appeared darker and more menacing than she'd thought a pair of eyes could be.

'I think I'm entitled to ask what's brought you here. You terrorised her when she was alive, so I don't understand why you've turned up on our doorstep now.'

'You always were the more abrasive of the two of you. It took me a while to work out the differences in personality, but I got there. The hard way. You made my life shit. You and Rachel.'

'What are you talking about?'

'You know right well, and now that she's dead, I think you owe me an explanation for what you did.'

'Brendan, I have no idea what you're referring to.'

'Make the coffee and I'll refresh your memory.'

Busying herself with mugs and spoons and watching the kettle boil, Beth wondered if Brendan had had anything to do with her twin sister's death.

CHAPTER TWENTY-NINE

When they got out of the car at Cusack Heights, Boyd looked around to see who was watching them. Lottie shook her head.

'What?' he said, buttoning his coat.

'No one is going to steal your car.'

'I'm not stupid. I'm just surprised Maddy Daly lives here. She was cycling along the canal when I met her, and it was only seven o'clock in the morning.'

'And what exactly has that to do with anything?'

'I'm wondering why.'

'Perhaps she needed to escape the doom and gloom of living in a high-density, overcrowded, littered housing estate.' Lottie fanned her hand around, justifying her words.

'Yeah, but—'

'Come on and we'll ask her.'

They had found out from a neighbour of Ellen's that she'd been seen recently in the company of a teenager from the Cusack Heights estate. Another neighbour informed them that she'd often seen Maddy Daly riding Ellen's bike. Initially worried that the girl had stolen it, the neighbour had spoken to Ellen, who'd told them to mind their own business.

Lottie felt admiration for Ellen Gormley as she walked up the cracked pavement to the open front door. It was cold and damp out and she wondered why the door wasn't closed to keep the heat in.

'Hello? Anyone home?' She rapped her knuckles on the jamb.

A baby's cry emanated from upstairs, but no one came down to welcome them. Lottie stepped into the concrete-floored hall, remnants of linoleum adhering to the skirting board.

'Hello,' Boyd said, louder.

'Do you have to yell?' Lottie shrugged him away from her shoulder. She was on edge, not having slept well. Chloe hadn't arrived home from work until after 2 a.m. Work? Yeah, pull the other one. Lottie had had to force herself to stay in her bed, her anger denying her sleep until it was almost time to get up.

Before she could take another step, a dishevelled, barefoot young woman clothed only in a bra and tracksuit bottoms walked down the stairs carrying a baby in her arms. A little boy peered through the bars of the landing banister.

'Hey! What's the racket?' the woman said. 'You've woken the baby.'

Lottie could dispute this as untrue. She'd heard the baby cry before she'd entered the property.

'Are you Maddy Daly?'

'Who wants to know?'

'She's not Maddy,' Boyd said, and the girl turned up her nose at him.

'I'm Detective Inspector Parker. My colleague is Detective Sergeant Boyd. And you are …?'

'Stella. What's Maddy done?'

'Nothing as far as we know. We'd like a quick word.'

As if she was used to two gardaí strolling into the house, Stella stomped up the stairs, yelling, 'Maddy, there's two guards downstairs and they want to talk to you. I warned you to stay out of trouble.'

The little boy gave a weak wave and disappeared.

'Let's wait in the kitchen,' Boyd said.

In the small room with no door, Lottie looked around.

'It's surprisingly clean,' she said under her breath.

'We are a civilised family!'

Swinging around, she saw a teenager standing in the doorway, arms by her sides, hands clenched in fists. She was wearing a long blue T-shirt to her knees, her legs bare. Her hair looked like she'd slept on it while it was still wet. It stood up and out all over her head, the darkest shade of black Lottie had ever seen. Her face was pale, almost white, but there were dark rings under her eyes.

'Sorry for barging in, but we did knock,' Boyd said holding up his hands as if warding off an onslaught.

The girl stomped barefoot across the compact kitchen and filled a glass with water. She gulped it down before saying, 'You've made Stella mad. What do you want?'

'Can we sit? We just want to ask you a few questions.' Boyd pulled out a chair. Maddy walked over to him and Lottie thought she was going to push the chair back in, but she just stood staring at him.

'I know you. Yesterday morning. You fixed the chain on my bike.'

'Your bike?' Lottie said quickly.

'What's it to you?' The dark hair swung wildly as the girl twisted her head away from Boyd. She skewered Lottie with a pair of threatening eyes.

'Maddy—' Lottie began.

'How do you know my name?' The girl stepped closer.

'We can do this here or at the station. Up to you,' Lottie said, gritting her teeth.

'You sound like one of those cops on the telly.' A sly grin spread across the girl's face, but she slid onto the chair. 'Sit down if that's what you want.'

Boyd sat. Lottie remained standing, wondering what dynamic was at play.

'Do you need an adult present?' Boyd said softly. 'Your mother, or that older girl we met at the door?'

'My sister? Are you joking me? I'm fine on my own.'

'Okay then. Tell me, how do you know Ellen Gormley?'

Maddy chewed her lip. 'Don't know her.'

'You were riding her bike when I last saw you.'

'Told you, my granny left it to me.'

Without admitting that she knew this was a lie, Lottie said, 'What's your granny's name?'

Maddy bowed her head. 'She's dead.'

'Really?' Boyd said. 'The thing is, Maddy, we know the bike belonged to Ellen Gormley. Did she lend it to you?'

Maddy instantly dropped the hard act and, looking like the child she was, said, 'So what if she did? I left it back. I always leave it back.'

'Did you leave it back last night?'

A shrug of the shoulders. 'Don't know.'

'Listen to me,' he said. 'Ellen is dead.'

'What?' Maddy's hand thumped the table. 'You're telling me lies.'

'I'm afraid it's true. But you knew that already, didn't you?'

'How would I know?' She bared her teeth. 'You're only after telling me.'

Lottie was tired of the charade. She moved to sit opposite the angry girl. 'What time were you at Ellen Gormley's house last night?'

'Are you deaf as well as stupid? I wasn't there.'

Boyd cut in with his irritatingly soft voice. 'I saw you early yesterday morning with Ellen's bicycle out on the Greenway. And last night that same bike was parked against the side wall of her home. Explain that.'

'Maybe someone stole it from me. You see where I live. Nothing is safe here.'

'We have the voice recording of the emergency call made from Ellen's house phone at seven twenty-three last night,' Lottie said evenly.

152

'I think it was you who phoned but I don't believe you had anything to do with Ellen's death.' She had no proof one way or the other, but logic told her that if Maddy had returned the bicycle last night, she'd found the body and made the call. 'Tell me about Ellen.'

The act instantaneously disappeared. Maddy slumped, and her hair brushed the table as her head fell forward. 'Ellen was my friend. I'd never hurt her.'

Lottie nodded for Boyd to resume his questions.

'How did you two become friends?' he asked.

'I met her when I was going through a tough time.'

'When was that?'

'I suppose it was a few years ago. I know it was sometime after my thirteenth birthday.'

'Why is that so significant?'

'Don't want to talk about it. Nothing to do with Ellen being dead.'

'We don't know that,' Lottie said, wondering what had sent this young girl to seek a psychologist when she was just thirteen. It brought to mind the years of therapy her son had undergone since his dad had died.

'Fuck you,' Maddy said. 'I never touched her. She was the only person I ever met who was good to me.'

'What age are you now, Maddy?' Lottie said, quietly.

'Sixteen.' The dark eyes stared at Lottie as if challenging her.

'You look younger.' She knew Maddy was fifteen. They'd checked.

'Whatever! You can think what you like.'

'Did Ellen take you under her wing?'

'Her what?'

'Did she look out for you?'

'Suppose so.' A shrug of the shoulders. 'She was nice.'

'She lent you her bike?'

'Yeah.'

'Why did you need it? You live in town.'

Maddy clenched her hands together, interlocking her fingers until the skin turned white. 'Ellen would give anyone anything they asked for and I never asked for nothing. She just lent me the bike now and again, so I could visit her. Saved me a two-mile walk out to her house. Not that I minded it. She was a good person.'

'What made you return the bicycle yesterday evening?'

'I'd had it since Saturday so I thought she might want it back.'

'Did you phone her or anything?'

'No.'

'Last night, when you returned Ellen's bike to her home, you found her … erm …' Lottie struggled for the right words to use. 'What way was she when you found her?'

'Dead.'

'Can you expand a little?'

'She was on the floor. At the bottom of the stairs. I didn't touch her because I knew she was dead. I put my ear near her mouth. I couldn't hear a breath.'

'Did you make the call?'

Maddy cried then, the tough-girl act melting as fast as the tears fell down her cheeks and onto the table. 'Yeah. I used her hall phone. It was on the floor. Didn't want my mobile number traced. But you found me anyway.'

'We did. Why didn't you stay with her until the emergency services arrived?'

'Because I knew you'd blame me, and I was right.' She ran the back of her hand under her nose and then swiped at her cheeks, trying to dry them. Her eyes flashed defiance.

'We're not blaming you, Maddy. We're trying to determine the timeline of events. How did you and Ellen become friends, if she was your therapist?'

'I packed in the therapy after a few months, but I think maybe she thought she was being a mother figure or something like that. She continued to make appointments for me. But those were just chats and coffee.'

'When did you last see her?' Lottie wondered about the ethics of this arrangement, but if Maddy wasn't under therapy rules, she supposed Ellen had been within her rights.

'Last night. She was dead, like I told you.'

'I mean before last night.'

Maddy lifted her head and closed her eyes as if she was thinking hard. 'Saturday. We had tea and scones in the Bank Café and then she drove me out to the lake to show me some old house that had been rebuilt or something.'

Lottie exchanged a glance with Boyd. 'Which lake?'

'Don't know.' Maddy thought for a moment. 'There's a golf course near it.'

'What was the reason Ellen wanted to show you this house?'

She bit her lip and shrugged. She looked about three years old. 'She never said.'

'You sure?'

'Yeah. I think she just wanted to see it because it was done up.'

'What did she talk about when you were out there?'

'Nothing much. We got out of the car and walked round the back of the house. Ellen was interested in seeing the stables. But they'd been turned into cottages. She seemed a bit shocked by that.'

'She knew something of the history and layout of the building?'

'Seemed that way.'

155

'Did she say how she knew about it?'

'No. She was a bit silent really. And that's not like Ellen. She normally talks non-stop. She's good fun for an old woman.'

Lottie cringed. Old at thirty? What must Maddy think of *her*, then, on the wrong side of forty?

Boyd leaned in closer to the girl. 'Maddy, this is very important. I want you to try recalling everything you can about that visit. Anything Ellen said. It might be very important in finding who killed her.'

'Someone killed her? I thought she'd fallen down the stairs.'

'We need the post-mortem to confirm it one way or the other, but I'll be honest with you because you've been honest with us, haven't you?'

Maddy nodded her head. Lottie wasn't buying this crap. She felt the girl was putting on a very good act, but she let Boyd continue.

'We suspect Ellen may have been poisoned.'

Lottie kicked him under the table and glared. They shouldn't give out this kind of information, especially to a minor, someone they suspected might have been involved in a suspicious death. But he'd it said now. Shit!

'Poisoned? That's so awful.' Maddy looked shaken. 'Why would someone do that to her?'

'That's what we're trying to find out,' Boyd said. 'Can you tell me anything else about last night?'

'When I saw her, I panicked, like. I thought she'd fallen down the stairs and that you'd think I pushed her. But poison? That's like something out of a novel.'

'You read a lot, do you?' Lottie couldn't help herself.

Maddy narrowed her eyes, pupils shrinking. 'You think I'm a dumb kid? I might not always go to school, but I read. I can't afford to buy books, so I get them from the library, where it's free to *borrow* them.'

Lottie knew the emphasis was for her benefit, informing her that Maddy wasn't a thief. Wow, this girl was carrying a serious plank on her shoulders.

'You will have to make a formal statement at the station,' she said.

'Why? I've told you all I know.'

'You might have been the last person to see Ellen alive, so that makes you a very important witness.' But Lottie knew they needed confirmation of time of death in order to trace Ellen's contacts.

'Shit,' Maddy said.

'And you'll need a responsible adult with you. Can we speak with your mother or father?'

'If you can find them, sure, talk to them.'

'Where are they?'

'How would I know? Never had a dad, and my ma might be in a pub somewhere.' Maddy sighed and twisted a lock of hair around her finger. 'Suppose I could ask Stella.'

'Your older sister?'

'Yeah,' Maddy sneered. 'The one with two kids and she's only nineteen. She's an adult, but I don't know about the responsible part.'

Boyd stood. 'We need to take the shoes you were wearing last night, plus you will have to have your fingerprints taken and a DNA swab.'

Maddy was about to protest, but then her shoulders slumped in acceptance. 'Hold on.'

When she returned, she handed him a pair of trainers. He placed them in an evidence bag. 'When do you think you can come in?'

'Whenever Simon turns up. He can mind the kids. As long as he doesn't sell them.'

'Who's Simon?' Lottie said, scrunching her eyebrows.

'Stella's boyfriend. Not sure if he is Ariana's daddy or not. He definitely isn't Trey's.'

'Trey?'

'Stella's son. He's two.'

'Okay, thanks, Maddy. You definitely have to come to the station to make that statement. Today.' Lottie zipped up her jacket and made to leave. Boyd walked on ahead of her. At the door she turned back to Maddy. 'What do you mean, sell the kids?'

CHAPTER THIRTY

The shower was still freezing cold and Maddy had no option but to shiver under the drip-drip of water. She stood for one minute before giving up. It was too damn cold.

She dried herself with the thin damp towel she'd used the night before and slipped on her jeans and a sweatshirt. Bundling up her dirty clothes, she brought them to the kitchen. After loading the machine, she couldn't find any washing powder, but she switched it on anyway.

She didn't hear him enter the house or walk up behind her. But she felt his breath on her neck, and when she turned, he was standing so close her breasts brushed his chest. Goose bumps pulsed on her skin and the hairs on her arms stood up like tiny black needles. She tried to dip under his arm. He caught her and twisted her flesh through the worn threads of her sweatshirt. He breathed out a vile mixture of nicotine and alcohol, and something else. Something earthy and stinking. Cannabis. How could Stella stand it?

'Let go of my arm, shithead.' She tried to twist away.

He shoved his face into hers. She gagged as he stuck his tongue straight into her mouth. Trying to fight him off, her hands thrashed uselessly against his. She was going to vomit right into his mouth if he didn't stop. He pulled away and pinned her to the vibrating washing machine.

'What have you done, you little shit?' he hissed.

Struggling for breath, she spat his saliva out of her mouth. 'Don't know what you're talking about.'

'Those were detectives I saw leaving. What did they want?'

'Nothing.'

'Don't be smart with me. I hate people who shit on me.'

She screeched as he twisted her arm and imprisoned her against the counter. Her skin burned and pain drove directly into the bone. Had he broken it? The intense throbbing told her something was definitely wrong. He lowered his head and bit her on the neck, then sucked hard on her flesh.

'Piss off, Simon! You're a nutjob.' She flailed wildly, trying to escape, the pain in her arm intensifying. Spasms flashed warning signs through her body. Willing the cry to die in her throat, she thought she was going to pass out when she heard footsteps on the floor, followed by a loud smash. With an animalistic screech, Simon pulled away, nursing the back of his head.

'What the fuck?' he roared.

Stella stood with the handle of a mug in her hand, the remains of the crockery scattered across the floor. 'What's going on?' she screamed.

'Stella, babe …' Simon drew his hand away from the back of his head, blood smearing his fingers. 'For your information, your bitch of a sister came on to me. She was up for it, begging me for a shag.'

'Like hell she was. She can't stand the sight of you. And come to think of it, I don't know what I see in you either, you stinking slop of piss. Get the fuck out of our house.'

A sneer creased his face in two. 'That's not what your mother said when I rode her a few nights ago.'

Stella picked up another mug and made to smash it into his face. He caught her arm and squeezed until she let the mug drop. Then he slapped her hard across the face. As she fell to the floor, his bulk seemed to expand and retract before he stepped over her and headed for the door.

'Pair of nutters. That's what you are. If the guards come near me or touch my stuff, I swear to God I'll kill the two of you.'

Maddy knew he would have banged the kitchen door if there had been a door in the frame. Instead, he made do with slamming the front door. He'd be back. Stella always took him back.

Upstairs, the baby screamed, and Trey ran into the kitchen crying.

Maddy wandered into the sitting room, clutching her arm. She stared at the photo on the mantelpiece and felt tears flow down her cheeks. She picked up the frame and kissed the photo before returning it to its dusty home.

She wondered how she could ever escape the chamber of doom in which she found herself, especially now that Ellen was dead.

CHAPTER THIRTY-ONE

On the way to the station from Maddy Daly's house, Lottie read a message on her phone.

'According to Kirby, there's still no word on the next of kin for Ellen Gormley, and Jane has scheduled the post-mortem for later this morning. No tox results back on Rachel yet.'

'The deaths have to be connected,' Boyd said.

'SOCOs found no evidence of poison at the restaurant or in Rachel's home. They're continuing to search the rear of the restaurant and another team are going through Ellen's home and garden. But I don't think they'll find anything there. This killer is meticulous. I can't get my head around the message they're sending us.'

'What message?'

'The shard of glass in Rachel's throat.'

Boyd remained silent. Lottie studied the worried line of his jaw. 'What's up?'

'That girl ...'

'Maddy Daly? Do you think she had anything to do with Ellen's death?

'No, but I'm getting an unnatural feeling to protect her.'

Lottie smothered a laugh. 'You're going soft in your old age.'

'I'm serious, Lottie. She reminds me of that girl we found dead a few years ago. In the water barrel. I don't want the same thing to happen to Maddy.'

'She was at a murder victim's house last night. She is involved either directly or by association. I'll get Kirby to run a search for her in the PULSE database.'

'Do what you have to do, but I'm going to check on her later.'

Back at the station, Lottie found Kirby waiting to interview Andy Ashe.

'He was supposed to be here at nine, but he's only after arriving. Said his boss didn't turn up for work at Boyne's department store and he had to open up.'

'Give me a minute and I'll sit in with you.' She threw her bag and jacket on her chair. In the general office, Lynch looked up at her from under her fringe, a scowl lining her forehead.

After glancing at the lists on Kirby's desk, Lottie picked one up.

'Andy Ashe is not on this.'

'His boss, Hazel Clancy, was invited but couldn't go, so she sent him.' Kirby chewed on the end of his biro. 'I spoke to her on the phone yesterday. Bit insensitive sending him in her place, if you ask me. Andy's an alcoholic.'

'And the casual staff who worked the night of Rachel's death, have they been contacted and interviewed?'

Kirby nodded. 'No one saw anything unusual and none of them are sick. It had to be a targeted attack on Rachel.'

'Of course it was. The piece of glass shoved in her throat confirms it. I wish I knew what it meant.' She was about to return the list to the mess on Kirby's desk when a name caught her eye. 'Stella Daly?'

'Yeah. I phoned her. The same answer as the others. Three wise monkeys.'

'But ... Boyd! Come here a minute. Look at this.'

Boyd ambled over and took the list. 'Why didn't you tell us, Kirby?'

163

'Tell you what? I'm lost.'

'The girl we just interviewed, Maddy Daly, found Ellen Gormley's body last night. She rang 999 and then fled. She has a sister called Stella. The same Stella who is listed here as having worked at Annie's on Monday night. The night Rachel Mullen was murdered. We are looking for connections. That is one, in black and white.' She jabbed her finger onto the page and threw it back on the desk.

'We need to go back and talk to Stella,' Boyd said.

'Give me fifteen minutes to interview this Andy Ashe, then we'll go. See what you can dig up on the Dalys in the meantime.'

Grabbing Kirby by the elbow, she steered him out the door and along the corridor. 'I'm sorry, Kirby. It's not your fault. I'm just not myself.'

'Wedding jitters?' he said.

'Don't even go there. Did you and Boyd have your final fitting for your suits yet?'

He blushed and his hair seemed to spring up in surprise. 'What final fitting? No one mentioned anything about a final fitting to me.'

Lottie looked around for Boyd and caught sight of him disappearing down the corridor. 'I'm going to kill him.'

The interview room stank to high heaven, the air suffused with stale alcohol fumes. Lottie would have opened a window if there had been a window to open.

Kirby started the recording device, reading out details, names and titles.

'Am I under arrest or something?' Ashe said, sunglasses perched on his head.

'You're just helping us with our enquiries,' Lottie said.

'I don't know anything about Rachel Mullen or how she died.'

'Unusual choice of words.'

'What do you mean?'

'Do you know how she died?'

'Not a clue. I only saw her at the stupid party for a few minutes.'

'Tell us about that evening.'

Lottie waited patiently. Ashe sighed, brushed his hair away from his eyes and rubbed them vigorously. She could see he was hung-over. Not the best recipe for a coherent interview, but he was all they had.

'There's not much to tell. I arrived there straight after work, around ten past six. Couldn't resist the free champers, even though I was off the drink. But temptation, you know …'

'Go on.'

'I saw her come in late. I'd sculled a good few drinks by that stage. She didn't seem to know me, and I wondered if I'd mixed her up with her sister, Beth. It wasn't until she gave me her card that I knew I was talking to the right twin. I hadn't seen them in ages. After their mother died, Rachel dumped all her old friends.'

'Were you one of those friends?'

He shrugged one shoulder. 'Not a friend as such. I knew Beth and I used to see her around with Rachel some weekends. The odd few that Rachel actually returned home. Don't know what she saw in Roscommon to keep her there, so yes, just the weekends she was home. Mainly from a distance. I had a drink problem, so I wasn't that welcome.'

'Who was in this circle of friends?'

'I'd have to have a think. It's been two or three years. Before her mother died. Not so much since. I thought Beth had turned her into a hermit. It felt a bit odd when I met Rachel Monday night. I don't think she actually remembered me.'

'You don't have much time for Beth?'

He blushed and fanned at his cheeks. 'Don't get me wrong, now. She's a nice girl but a bit up her own hole, if you get my meaning.'

'I don't, so explain.'

'Jesus, you're an old fish, aren't you?'

Kirby leaned across the table. 'Show some respect, Andy.'

'I'm sorry, Inspector.'

'You were telling us how you didn't like Beth.'

'I never said that. It's just … you know …'

'I don't know. I'm a bit of a dinosaur,' Lottie said, knowing exactly where he was going with this. She had two daughters and a sixteen-year-old son, so she was well aware of the dynamics of friendships. Not that she herself had a friend in the world other than Boyd. This suddenly made her feel lonely. She shook off the feeling and concentrated on Andy Ashe.

'Beth liked to lord it over all gatherings. Even in the pub. She dictated how much Rachel could drink. Bit of a control freak.'

'You're older than the twins. How did you become friends?'

He stared at the ceiling, then lowered his head with a squint in his eye. 'You know what, I can't actually remember. Must have been in a nightclub or something.'

'How long ago did this happen?'

'Must be five or six years.'

'Did you date either of them?'

'Good God, no.'

'Why not?'

'I'm not gay, if that's what you're thinking. We were just acquaintances. Bumped into them now and then when I was out. That's all. No big mystery.'

'Okay. On Monday night, so, you saw Rachel arrive late. What happened then?'

'Nothing. That's it.'

'You told Detective Kirby here that you spoke with her, fetched her a drink. That's not nothing.'

'She had a glass of champers in her hand, but she wanted something stronger. She asked me to get her a gin and tonic from the bar.'

'And did you?'

'Yeah, and a Guinness for myself. There's only so much watered-down sparkle I can swallow.' He waited, and when Lottie said nothing, he continued. 'I brought back her drink, and while she was eating, I went to fetch my Guinness, which was settling on the counter. When I returned to where I'd left her, she wasn't there. I spotted her a while later, talking to a group near the kitchen door.'

'Who was in this group?'

'No idea. Probably people more important than I was, anyhow.'

'Did you see her at all after that?'

'I was three sheets to the wind. Truthfully, I forgot about her. I hope I didn't make a show of myself.'

'Did you see her leave?'

'No.'

'Do you know Matthew Fleming?'

'Jessica's dad? Everyone knows Bones.'

'Did you see him that night?'

He scrunched up his face, thinking. 'He wasn't there early on, but I've no idea about later.'

'You didn't see him arrive around nine thirty and leave ten minutes after?'

He shook his head. 'I don't even remember leaving the place myself.'

Lottie glanced at the scant notes she'd scribbled. A whole lot of nothing. She looked at Kirby to see if he had anything to add. He shook his head. Scanning through her notes, she noticed a word she had circled.

'You mentioned that Rachel was eating when you brought her the gin and tonic. What was she eating?'

'Some ugly piece of shit. Chicken liver. Ugh.'

'Did you see who served her?'

'Staff were floating around all evening with trays of that shite. Couldn't say which of them served her.'

'Try to think. It's important. Were they male or female? Young or old?'

He took a deep breath and closed his eyes, and for a moment Lottie thought he'd fallen asleep. Then he said, 'A girl. I only saw her back as she moved away from Rachel, but I remember seeing her a few minutes later by the bar and thinking to myself that she looked too young to be working.'

'Too young? How young?'

'I'd say she wasn't more than fifteen or sixteen.'

'Her name?'

'No idea.'

'Hair colour?'

'Black. Yeah. Very black, tied up in a ponytail.'

'Eyes?'

'Haven't a clue.'

'If I get you a photo, do you think you could identify her?'

'Probably not.'

'Your boss …' she looked down at the file Kirby had open, 'Hazel Clancy. Why didn't she go to the event?'

'You better ask her. She hardly speaks to me, stuck up b——. Anyway, I really have to be getting to work.'

'Is there anything you want to add about Rachel that might help us find the person who killed her?' Lottie had a feeling Andy might have had something to do with Rachel's death, but if he couldn't remember going home, she'd have to dig around to trace his movements on Monday night.

He was half standing, his hand on the back of the chair, but he sat down again and clasped his hands on the table. He stared at Kirby, then at Lottie, then back to Kirby before his eyes rested on hers.

'I'm not one to rat out my friends. Or ex-friend, even if we hardly recognise each other …'

'But …'

'But if I was you, I'd have a long, hard look at Rachel's stalker ex-boyfriend.'

CHAPTER THIRTY-TWO

Lottie stormed into the office and came to a stop at Boyd's desk. 'Didn't you ask Beth yesterday if Rachel had a boyfriend?'

'I'll check my notes and—'

'I know you did, and she said there was no boyfriend. She failed to mention an ex who stalked Rachel for a year after they broke up.'

'Really? Who?' Boyd leaned into his chair and folded his arms.

'Some guy named Brendan Healy. Check him out. Find out where he is now and where he was on Monday night.'

'Will do.'

'And I found out something about your little friend.'

'Who?'

'Maddy Daly. We know Kirby spoke to her sister, Stella, yesterday because her name was on the list of casual waiting staff. But she failed to mention that it wasn't her who worked Monday night. It had to be Maddy.'

'How do you know that?'

'I don't know for sure, but the description Andy Ashe gave us matches Maddy, not Stella. Pair of liars.'

Boyd stood. 'Hold on a minute. Maddy didn't lie to us. We never asked her a single question about Rachel or Monday night's party.'

Lottie sniffed away his explanation. 'Get your coat on. First we'll talk to Beth about this Healy guy, and then we'll call to the Dalys'.'

In her office, she took a few deep breaths and pulled on her jacket. When she turned around, McKeown filled the doorway. 'What now?'

'I spoke to Jessica Fleming yesterday evening. She told me her father arrived at the party looking for her mother. He had a short conversation with Annie and then left.'

'Okay. What else?'

'Annie Fleming phoned earlier. She said you'd arranged to meet her this morning.'

Lottie had forgotten about it. 'I have so many irons in the fire, McKeown, I'm going to get burned.'

'I told her you were busy, but now she's downstairs waiting to talk to you.'

She paused, yet to get her second arm into the sleeve of her jacket. She pulled it on fully, zipped it with a snap and rushed past McKeown, muttering under her breath, 'Do I have to do everything myself?'

Annie Fleming was pacing around the small tiled reception area, her nose in the air, a black Crombie coat on her shoulders with a grey skirt suit underneath. She looked as if she'd just stepped out of a hair salon. Lottie caught a glimpse of her own face in the Perspex surrounding the front desk. She looked like someone who'd been pulled screaming from a clogged sewer. She ran a hand through her hair to spring some life into it, but quickly gave up.

'Mrs Fleming, I'm sorry. I was busy earlier.'

'Annie, please. Would you like to join me for a cappuccino? This place gives me the creeps.'

'Honestly, I'm extremely busy. I was actually on my way to interview someone.'

'Please. Indulge me. I might be able to help you progress your investigation.'

Did she just bat her eyelashes? Lottie thought she must be seeing things. 'I haven't my bag or wallet …' She floundered for an excuse.

Annie waved a leather clutch bag in the air. 'I have my cards.'

Sure you have. Lottie followed her out the door, letting it swing shut behind her as she tramped down the steps.

They settled on the Bean Café, a minute's walk. It was probably a step below what Annie was used to, but Lottie hadn't time to pander to anyone's whims. She had to talk to Maddy Daly again, and Beth Mullen. Both had lied, even if it was only by omission, and if there was one thing she hated, it was liars.

As they entered the tiny café, the smell of freshly ground coffee, with a hint of caramel and home-baked bread, suffused the air. Lottie realised she was starving.

'This is so quaint,' Annie said. 'I've never been here before.'

'It's handy, and the coffee is good,' Lottie said once she'd ordered two coffees, and a toasted croissant for herself because Annie was paying. 'It gets a steady trade from the station. Would you like something to eat?'

'I had a good breakfast this morning. The key to a healthy day.'

'I had a McDonald's muffin at seven,' Lottie said. They sat at a small table inside the window, which looked out on the narrow street. 'What did you wish to talk to me about?'

'I wanted to get an update on when I can reopen my restaurant. I have loans to pay and stock to use up, and suppliers ready to deliver more. I can't possibly leave the doors shut for a week.'

'It won't be anything like a week.'

'That's not what one of your detectives told me last night. The tall, good-looking guy who came out to have a word with Jessica. Nice young man. Bit of an eye on him, though.'

'Detective McKeown?'

'Jessica was very taken with him.'

'Really?' Lottie had pinned McKeown down as professional in his work life. 'I must apologise if he was in any way discourteous to you or your daughter.'

'Not at all. On the contrary, he was very gentlemanly. But I can't accept what he said. Please tell me I can return to my premises today. I want to open up tonight.'

'Unfortunately we have to wait until the scene-of-crime officers finish their work.'

'But the young woman didn't even die there. She died in her own home.'

'That may be so, but your restaurant is the last known place she visited before she returned home. We have to check it out in order to get a full picture of Rachel's movements on Monday night.'

'This whole thing is a disaster,' Annie said as the coffees were placed on the table. A plate with a delicious-looking croissant was slid in front of Lottie. When they were alone again, Annie added, 'Of course I'm sorry for that poor girl and her family but her death has nothing to do with me or mine.'

'I have to investigate every avenue available to us.' Lottie was dying to take a bite of her food but didn't want to be talking with her mouth full and crumbs sticking to her chin, so she pushed the plate to one side. She'd bring it with her when they left. She caught Annie staring at her ring, which, now that she looked at it, seemed like a third cousin twice removed of the gigantic diamond weighing heavily on the other woman's hand.

'Are you married?' Annie said.

'Widowed.' Lottie cringed saying the word, with all the grief it magnified. 'My husband died some years ago, but I'm engaged to be married again.' What made her give away that piece of personal information?

'I'm so sorry about the loss of your husband, but it's reassuring to hear you found a new love. Any date set?'

'It's supposed to be Saturday, but now, with this case, I'm not so—'

'Stop. We both have a motivation to get everything sorted quickly.' Annie sipped her coffee and gently wiped the froth from her top lip with a napkin. She seemed happy that it was cloth and not paper.

'Can I ask you a few questions?' Lottie said.

'You can ask me anything that might help get my business open again.'

'Now that you've had time to digest all that happened, do you remember anything else about Monday night?'

'Like what?'

'You tell me.' She wondered if Annie was being deliberately obtuse or genuinely slow on the uptake.

'I was busy all day getting ready for the party and busy that evening too. I talked to so many people, my head was buzzing. It's like a blur to me. It was a huge success, but now, with the murder and all … Bookings are good, but I'm not so sure of the longer-term consequences.'

Lottie bristled. Was Annie Fleming so caught up in her own world that she was insensitive to the fact that, besides the taxi driver, she and her guests might have been the last people to see Rachel Mullen alive? The young woman might even have been poisoned at the party. Or had someone been watching her there and then followed her home? With no forced entry, it had to be someone she knew. Or someone with a key to her house. The piece of glass found in Rachel's throat pointed to it being personal.

'Inspector? May I call you Lottie?'

Lottie shook herself out of her reverie. 'Sure. Please, Annie, think back to Monday night and tell me about your husband arriving. You weren't expecting him, I gather.'

She focused on Annie's face, which remained as still and rigid as the white ceramic plate on the table. Only her eyes betrayed a distinct distaste. They slanted downwards, narrowing into tiny slits.

'Matthew turned up unannounced. Of course he knew about the party, and he has a habit of trying to steal my limelight.'

'And was that what he did?'

'Thankfully, no. It must have been around half nine when he arrived, because I was in the kitchen and had just paid the casual staff. He barged in through the back door.'

'He has the door code then?'

'Unfortunately.' Annie sniffed loudly, as if the mention of her husband's name had discharged a rancid stench. 'I worked in that man's business for twenty years. I gave Matthew and his company my heart and soul, and now … I wouldn't give him the steam off my piss.' Her cheeks reddened. 'I apologise, there's no need for crudeness, but Matthew Fleming evokes such hatred in my heart that I can't control the words that are liable to burst out of my mouth. I'm sorry.'

'Why'd you give him the code if you didn't want him around?'

'Our daughter Tara gave it to him. She and her father are like this.' She crossed two fingers. 'Jessica saw through Matthew and his ways. She sticks by me. But Tara … she's a lost cause where I'm concerned. She works with him and stands up for him in every argument.'

'What reason did he have to be at the restaurant?'

'I've no idea. He charged in like a deranged bull, nearly knocking down one of the waitresses. I accosted him, shouted at him. But he shoved me out of the way and stormed into the restaurant. I'm sure he was up to no good. Wanted to disrupt my evening. At least the most important people had left by then. He must have realised this, because the next time I saw him, he was rushing out the door again.'

'And he said nothing to you?'

'Not really.'

That's not a direct answer, Lottie thought, her senses heightened. 'But he said something, didn't he?'

'Yes.' It was the first time Annie had appeared disconcerted. She twirled the diamond ring on her finger, but the stone was so large it wouldn't twist round fully.

'What was it about?'

She pursed her lips before speaking. 'He was looking for Rachel Mullen.'

'What?'

'I know. I'm sorry. I should have told you before now, but I thought if I mentioned it, he'd pull me down with him. Matthew is a bullish man and I know his main aim in life is to sabotage everything I try to achieve. Even our daughters. He gave Tara the well-paid job of environmental officer in his company, and she's now helping him expand his business interests in the UK. I'm doing my best to keep Jessica on my side.'

Lottie had had her fair share of confrontations with pig-headed men, so she got what Annie was saying. That didn't excuse withholding information, though.

'When he couldn't find Rachel, what did he do?'

A gold earring studded with a hanging pearl swept against Annie's shoulder as she shrugged. 'He left in a huff. That's all I know.'

'Were you aware that he'd had a meeting with Rachel earlier that afternoon?'

'What? No, I didn't know that. Whatever was it about?'

Lottie ignored the question. 'Do you have any idea why Matthew would be interested in financing Rachel's new business?'

This time Annie's chin visibly dropped. 'Are you telling me he was actually going to finance that young woman's enterprise? That's totally absurd! He wouldn't lend me a cent; why would he offer money to a nobody? The hypocrite.'

'Why do you refer to Rachel as a nobody?'

'I don't mean it in a derogatory manner.'

That's exactly what you mean, Lottie thought. 'What can you tell me about Rachel? And this time I'd appreciate honesty.'

Annie delayed answering by sipping her coffee, wiping her lips, leaving a stain of red lipstick on the linen, and taking a deep breath. 'Rachel and her sister, the artist one, were in school years ago with my girls. They never got along.'

'Do you mean the Mullen sisters didn't get on with each other or they didn't get along with your girls?'

'With my girls. There was a time when they used to be friends. Must be ten years ago, when they were teenagers. The Mullens would come to our house to do homework and have tea and then they'd stay half the night. This was when I was still with Matthew, long before I refurbished Molesworth House. We lived on the outskirts of town. I remember their mother would drive them out. But then, all of a sudden, they stopped coming over. Jessica told me they fell out over an essay or something.'

'What did Tara tell you?'

'Tara never spoke about it. But I imagine it was serious enough at the time. You know what teenagers are like. Best friends one minute and sworn enemies the next.'

'Were they enemies?'

'No, no. They just fell out of friendship. Kids move on.'

Digesting this information, Lottie tried to work out if Annie's revelation was important to the investigation. At this stage, she had to assume everything was relevant until it wasn't.

'Do you think Matthew might have been in talks with Rachel to somehow get back at you? Doesn't seem like good financial sense to me.' Lottie didn't know where she was going with this. Rachel was a minion in the business world compared to Annie.

'Nothing makes sense where Matthew and his prejudices are concerned. We're separated and the divorce is going to be messy. He's out to ruin me.'

'You think your ex-husband would murder someone solely to bring down your business?' Lottie couldn't see any logic in this statement but voiced it anyhow.

'I never said that.'

'You implied it.'

'Maybe I did.' Annie picked up her bag, ready to stand. 'It's up to you to see what dirt you can dig up on him. And I'll do my best to help you.'

'How?'

'I'll talk to my girls. See if they can tell me anything.'

'I would prefer to do the interviewing. I haven't met Tara yet.'

'Come out to Molesworth House for dinner tonight and we can all talk. Bring your partner, if you like.'

'That's not really how these things work. Could you and your daughters come to the station later today?'

'I really want you to see all of Molesworth. And Tara hasn't been well, so it's best she stays at home. Do say you'll come, and please try to have my restaurant returned to me as soon as possible.'

'I'm sure it will be released to you later today.'

'Brilliant. Dinner will be ready by seven.'

Lottie wasn't sure she had agreed to dinner, and she didn't like being manipulated, but she wanted to meet Tara Fleming. She'd ring her mother to see if she'd feed Sean. Chloe was able to look after herself, but Lottie couldn't trust her to cook for her brother.

'I better get back to the station.' She dragged her jacket off the back of the chair and made to stand. 'By the way, do you know Ellen Gormley?'

'Name doesn't strike a bell.'

'She was a doctor. A psychologist.'

'Was? Don't tell me she's dead too?'

'I'm afraid so.'

Annie's face seemed to turn grey. 'Oh God. Was she from Ragmullin?'

'Yes. Do you know her?'

She lowered her eyelids demurely. 'Can't say I do. I'm sorry.'

Lottie stood up. 'I'll be in touch.'

Annie grabbed her arm, pulling her close. 'Please listen to me. When you're dealing with Matthew, you have to be at your best. You have to be careful. He's lethal.'

CHAPTER THIRTY-THREE

Maddy knew she suffered from some form of repetitive cleaning syndrome. Ellen had told her the clinical name, but she could never remember it. She thought of it now as she stood under her third cold shower of the morning, gently washing the bite mark on her neck. God knows what disease Simon had implanted into her body. How had he ever wriggled his way into Stella's life? They were poor, not desperate, but he had brought them lower than earthworms. Stella had claimed to be in love. Not any more, I hope, Maddy thought.

She dragged her nails up and down her legs, across her stomach, trying to ignore the piercing pain in her arm. Tears flew down her cheeks. She thought her arm was broken. Her heart was broken too. She'd lost everything she'd ever cared for, and the one person who had recently brought light into her life was dead.

She stood for another three minutes under the dribble of cold water until she could no longer stand it. Stepping onto the bare bathroom floor, she attempted to dry herself with the wet threadbare towel. She dragged her clothes on over her damp body, everything sticking and snagging on her skin. Then she sank to the freezing-cold floor, leaning against the door with a boot hole smashed through it from years ago, and sobbed and sobbed.

As she sat there in the cold, screaming silently inside her head while her body shuddered in pain, she heard the patter of little feet on the floorboards outside.

'Mads? Play with me.'

She was unable to answer him. She couldn't form the words.

He knocked gently on the door. 'Sorry, Mads.'

The poor child. He thought it was all his fault. Like she'd thought everything was her fault when she was just thirteen. She felt his tiny fingers poke her through the hole in the door.

'Can we play now?' he whispered.

Her throat convulsed with hiccups, she dragged herself to her feet and opened the door. She tried to pick Trey up, but winced as pain surged up her arm, making it throb like she'd been stung. She'd have to go to a pharmacy for painkillers.

As she followed him down the stairs, listening to the sound of Stella crying in her room along with the baby's shrieks, Maddy suddenly thought of something. When Simon was mauling her, what had he meant when he said the guards better not touch his stuff? He only stayed over with Stella occasionally. So what stuff was he talking about?

CHAPTER THIRTY-FOUR

Beth Mullen's face was like a translucent map. Lined, tired and drawn. The black rings under her eyes accentuated the dark brown irises, which flashed in annoyance when she opened the door.

'This won't take long,' Lottie said, stepping into the hall. 'A couple of questions.'

'I told you everything yesterday.' Beth followed them to the living room.

Lottie stood in the inner doorway, feeling a knot of confusion. A young man was lounging on the couch as if he was relaxing in his own home, without standing to greet them.

Beth hurried over to him, eyes wide. In warning? Lottie wasn't sure.

'These are the detectives I told you about. They're investigating Rachel's death.'

Lottie held her hand out to the man, expecting him to stand and shake it. He didn't.

'What's your name, sir?'

His dark eyes, pinpricks in the muted light, stared back at her. Though she knew nothing about him, she immediately disliked him. Unprofessional of her, she knew, but it was a human reaction nonetheless. She waited him out.

'This is Brendan Healy.' Beth spoke up for him, twisting her hands together. 'He's a … a family friend.'

Lottie glanced at Boyd. He gave her a slight nod. They recognised the name. Sitting in front of them, like he hadn't a care in the world, was the man mentioned by Andy Ashe as Rachel Mullen's ex-boyfriend and alleged stalker. And what was Beth's role in his appearance at her home?

'What brings you to Ragmullin?' Lottie said, keeping her voice even.

'He heard about what happened to Rachel,' Beth said quickly, 'and called to see how I was coping.'

'Very considerate of you, Mr Healy. When did you last see Rachel?' Lottie cut to the chase. She was not giving this lug enough rope to shimmy down and escape.

When he spoke, Healy's voice was soft and sweet. Too bloody sweet.

'I heard the news. Very disturbing to think that a young woman could be murdered in her own bed, her own home. Nowhere is safe nowadays. Doesn't say much for the policing in this country, does it?'

'I asked you when you last saw Rachel.'

He turned his head slightly, glanced up at Beth as if to check whether she was about to contradict him. Was that a slight movement of her head? It was clear she was going to play along with whatever lies Healy was about to spin. But why?

He swept the black fringe away from his dark eyes and ran his tongue along his gums. 'My friendship with the Mullens goes back a long way. I used to live in Ragmullin. That was before I moved to the city. Dublin, in case you were wondering.' He smirked, his lips in a thin line displaying cynicism rather than mirth.

Lottie had an urge to get him alone in a dark alley and beat ten shades of shit out of him. Irrational thoughts about someone she'd only met sixty seconds ago, but that was the reaction he evoked.

'My parents still live in Ragmullin. I visit them now and again, to catch up on the local gossip.'

'You were friends with Rachel?'

'Some might say that.'

'Intimate friends?'

'I like to think so.' The smirk turned salacious. As if he had awakened a memory that excited him. It turned Lottie's stomach. Beth bowed her head; unable to see any reaction in her face, Lottie concentrated on Healy.

'Back to my original question. When did you last see Rachel?'

He glanced towards Beth again. 'When was it? I'm sure *you* remember.'

He was passing the lie onto the dead woman's grieving twin. Lottie couldn't get her head around Beth's duplicity.

Shrugging a shoulder half-heartedly, Beth said, 'It must be a good few years ago. Before Mum died, I'd say.'

'Nothing more recent?' Lottie pressed.

Healy said, 'I couldn't say for sure. When I come home, I often frequent the local pubs, so there's no way of knowing if Rachel was in the same hostelry as I on a particular Friday night.'

'I can be more specific in my wording then.' Lottie was now truly pissed off with his manner. 'When did you last speak with Rachel? As in actually opening your mouth and saying words to her, in person or on the phone.'

'Are you trying to trip me up?'

'If you're innocent of any crime, why would you think that?'

'It's always the way. The ex-boyfriend appears, and you stick the knife in.'

Taking a step closer, Lottie was surprised when Healy rose quickly from the couch to stand in front of her. He wasn't a tall man, about an inch below her five foot eight, and when he turned, she noted he had a short ponytail at the nape of his neck.

With his back to her, he stood facing one of Beth's paintings.

'The talent of these sisters always intrigued me. They never recognised it. Maybe you could help me in persuading Beth to exhibit in my gallery.'

'You own a gallery?' Boyd said derisively. Evidently Healy was having the same effect on both of them.

'I actually run one. In the Temple Bar area of the city.'

'That's Dublin, is it?' Lottie said sarcastically.

'Very funny.'

'Murder isn't funny.'

'I don't suppose it is. There's been a lot in this town recently. You really should do a better job.'

What the hell was he getting at? Confusion thwarted Lottie's mental capacity to ask another question. Boyd stepped up.

'Were you in Ragmullin on Monday?'

'How could I be? I was curating an exhibition in my gallery. Isn't that right, Beth?'

'Er, I suppose so.'

'You don't sound very confident,' Boyd said.

'Everything's a blur since I found Rachel's body.' Beth was standing with her arms wrapped around herself, as if she was shielding herself from some invisible force. From Healy? Or something else?

Lottie said, 'We're talking about the night before you found your sister dead upstairs.'

'Look, the thing is, Brendan invited me to view the latest work at his gallery. The invite came out of the blue, but I couldn't go. I had tickets for the concert in the 3Arena. It finished around ten thirty so I assumed the gallery would be closed by then and I didn't go over there. Are you satisfied?'

'Far from it.' She'd had enough of this fudging the truth. 'You both need to come to the station for formal interviews.' She moved closer to

185

Healy, who remained staring at the painting. 'Your name has already come up in our investigation, Mr Healy. I'd like you to accompany us now.'

He turned quickly. 'Am I under arrest?'

'No.' She wanted to add 'not yet' but held her words back.

'Then I don't see what you could possibly ask me there that you can't ask me here.'

'It's protocol.'

'Please,' Beth interrupted. 'I couldn't face going to the garda station again. Not today.'

'I need to use the bathroom first,' Healy said. 'And then I'll contact a solicitor before I go anywhere with you. I believe you are harassing me, Detective Inspector.'

He'd used her title in a tone that implied he viewed her like a Nazi war criminal. When he'd left the room and moved upstairs, she said, 'Beth, what is going on with him?'

'There's nothing going on, now or ever. He invited me to the gallery on Monday, but I didn't go. That's it.'

Letting that rest for now, Lottie changed tack. 'Did Rachel know Matthew Fleming?'

'The quarry owner?'

'Yes.'

'I … I don't think so.'

'Really? You went to school with his daughters. I'm sure over the course of the years you must have met their father.'

'It's possible we did, but why would Rachel *know* him?' She made air quotes around the word. Was she reading something more into Lottie's question?

'I'm not sure if you know it or not, but the meeting your sister had on Monday afternoon was with Matthew Fleming.'

Beth's face paled significantly, and Lottie could see thin blue veins beneath her skin.

'She never mentioned who she was meeting.'

'Why not?'

'I … I don't know.'

'Would there be a reason why Rachel didn't want you to know who she was sourcing funding from?'

'She kept her business affairs separate from mine.'

'But you're sisters. Twins. You lived together. And you told us you were involved with some of her work. Graphic design. Her social media accounts …'

'That's the creative element. I knew nothing of the business side. I've been busy with my art, building up a portfolio to exhibit. Rachel was always talking about tapping into the pockets of wealthy people, and everyone knows Mr Fleming is rich. She might have played on the fact that we knew his daughters when we were teenagers. I honestly don't know.'

Boyd moved out to the hall for a moment. When he came back, his eyebrows were knitted in a frown. 'Healy's a long time in the bathroom.'

Pushing past him, Lottie rushed into the hall and flew up the stairs. The bathroom was empty. She ran back down the stairs and dashed out into the road, looking frantically up and down. The area was quiet. No one around. She checked with the driver of the squad car and he hadn't noticed Healy leaving.

She came back inside and stared hard at Beth. 'He's gone. Now, Miss Mullen, you better tell us what is going on.'

CHAPTER THIRTY-FIVE

Maddy found an old scarf and tied it around her arm, hoping it might secure the damaged bone. It did nothing to ease the pain. She tucked Trey's small hand in her other one and they walked across the field that backed onto Cusack Heights.

'Forgot my ball,' Trey said.

'I can't play ball today,' she said. 'We'll go for a walk, then we can watch cartoons. Okay?'

'Okay.'

His little hand felt like the soft flesh of a baby. But it instilled not an ounce of longing in Maddy's heart. In fact, it repelled her a little. She could not understand Stella and her pregnancies. Did she not know how to use the pill?

'Hi, Maddy.'

She'd been so lost in angry thoughts that she hadn't seen him approach. David Crawley stood in front of her, two pit bull terriers straining from a chain-link leash. Trey's hand tightened in hers and she instinctively lifted him into her arms, wincing with the pain.

'Hi, David, not working today?' She didn't have much time for the chef, with his puffy face, bald head and neck flesh crawling with a horrible tattoo.

'Restaurant's closed up. Did you not hear about it?'

'Hear about what?' She moved away a little. She didn't like dogs and she definitely didn't like David Crawley. He never lost an opportunity to stop and talk. On Monday night he had been a little too familiar with her. Nothing sexual, but enough to give her cause for concern. Even though Maddy knew she was well able to look after herself, she tried not to put herself into situations that could spiral out of control.

'The murder,' he said.

'What murder?' Did he mean Ellen?

'One of the party guests was found murdered in her own bed. Can you believe it?'

'In her bed?'

'That's what the guards told me when they interviewed me.'

So it wasn't Ellen. She stiffened her grip on Trey. She'd worked in place of Stella, and David knew who she was. She'd have to be careful. 'Who was it?' she asked.

'Some young one you wouldn't know,' he said. 'The likes of her wouldn't mix in your sort of circle.'

'And what circle would that be?'

'Oh, something has got your knickers in a twist today, young Maddy. Is it boyfriend trouble?'

'I don't have a boyfriend,' she said.

'A gorgeous young one like yourself, surely you have hordes sniffing round you?'

'I'm not like your dogs.'

'Oh, definitely touchy. Maybe if you got a bit, you'd be nicer to people who are nice to you.'

His arms strained with the dogs pulling on the leash, and Trey nuzzled deeper into Maddy's collarbone, his little fingers picking at the Spider-Man plaster on her neck.

'Shut up, David.'

'Quid pro quo. That's Latin, I think. It means you scratch my back and I'll scratch yours.'

'I don't have time for riddles.' She went to move away, but he caught her arm. Her sore arm. She screamed.

'I barely touched you.'

'I fell. Hurt my arm.'

'If it's that bad, you should see a doctor.'

'I will,' she said.

'Mind yourself, so.' He reined in the dogs, wrapping the chain around his chubby fingers. 'Remember, your secret is safe with me.'

She stopped. Turned. Looked at him. 'What secret?'

'You're just a kid, Maddy. You worked Monday night instead of Stella. I said nothing to the guards when they interviewed me, and if you're nice to me, maybe I won't tell them when they come asking again. But if you're not, who knows what I might say.'

She wanted to walk off. To leave him standing there with his ugly dogs in the middle of the field. But she couldn't move. Instead, he turned away, laughing loudly, and disappeared down the rubbish-strewn alley between the two housing estates.

'Can we get my ball?' Trey said.

'Later.' She held the child closer, as if he could shield her from the evil she knew was surely coming her way. After a few moments, she turned for home, and followed David down the narrow alley.

*

'Brendan's an oddball,' Beth said.

'What do you mean by that?' Lottie crossed her legs and waited.

'He tries to fit in, but his personality, it's a bit skewed.' Beth gripped her mug of black coffee tightly. 'And that annoys people, so they make it even harder for him.'

'And that matters … why?'

190

'He tried too hard with Rachel. She was having none of it. They dated for a while, a month or so, but he couldn't accept it when she didn't want to be with him any longer. He pestered her. Followed her. Drove to Roscommon and waited outside the bank for her every evening. I think she even had to call the guards once. It might be on your records somewhere.'

'That's when she accused him of stalking her?'

'Yes.'

'But he gave up eventually?'

'I suppose so. He turned his attention to me.'

'And did he harass you too?'

'I could handle him. I knew how to make him believe he was winning when in fact I was totally in control.'

'Like turning down his invite to his exhibition?'

'Exactly.'

'And you don't have feelings for him?'

'I like him. As a friend.'

'Even after he stalked your sister?'

'He can't help himself. Brendan is his own worst enemy.'

'Why do you humour him?'

Beth swirled the coffee around in the mug and stared at it for a moment. Then she raised her head. 'It kept him away from Rachel.'

'Do you think he could have harmed Rachel?'

'You mean killed her? I doubt it.'

Boyd walked over and sat beside her. 'You told us you were in Dublin on Monday night. Are you sure you didn't go over to the gallery and see Brendan? He kind of implied you were his alibi.'

'I told you. The concert finished at ten thirty and I went for drinks with my friends. I'll give you their names to validate that. I hadn't seen Brendan in months before he turned up here this morning.'

'Thanks, Beth. You'll have to make a statement at the station.'

'Later. Please. I need to get my head around all this.'

'I'll send a car for you,' Boyd said. 'Is that okay?'

'If I have to, then—'

'You do,' Lottie said. She grabbed her coat and headed for the door. 'Boyd. Come on.'

'You have my number, Beth,' he said. 'Ring me if you think of anything else, or if Brendan comes back.'

Lottie said, 'If he comes back, don't let him in. Call us immediately.'

'Okay.'

'By the way, do you know why Rachel had an overnight bag in the boot of her car?'

Beth raised her eyebrows in surprise. 'Maybe she had planned to go somewhere else after the party. I honestly don't know.'

Lottie drew Rachel's keys out of her bag. There were three keys on the ring. One of them was for the Yaris. On the way out, she tried one of the others in the door. It worked.

She showed Beth the third key. 'What is this one for?'

Beth shrugged. 'I have no idea.'

*

Maddy dropped Trey back to Stella. She had to find a doctor, or at the very least a pharmacy. Feeling her heart breaking all over again at the thought of no longer having Ellen around, something shifted inside her brain. Had Ellen been murdered like the woman David had told her about? That scared her even more. She'd read loads of true-crime books about serial killers. Didn't it take three murders to class someone as a serial killer, or something like that? If so, did that mean someone else was a target? She shivered, skimmed five euros from Stella's purse and grabbed her jacket, though she knew it was useless against the rain that had started pouring down again.

She could walk around Boyne's store, caress the luxurious dress materials, something to make her feel good. Or she could go to the library and find a corner to lose herself in a book. But her arm screamed for attention.

If she went to the hospital emergency department, they might send her for an X-ray, and she had no money to speak of, no medical card because her mother was AWOL and Stella hadn't bothered with the paperwork. Shit. Her life was total shit.

The rain mingled with her tears as she found herself outside Annie's Restaurant. Crime-scene tape was secured across the front door. She'd worked there Monday night for fifty euros, which she'd handed over to Stella without a cent for herself. She thought about David again. What had he really meant when he'd said her secret was safe with him?

She drew away and walked slowly through the puddles, water seeping into her well-worn trainers. She crossed the road at the traffic lights. The library would be warm, and she would be dry.

Hurrying down Gaol Street, she noticed a man walking on the opposite footpath. He seemed vaguely familiar with his small stature and dark hair sleeked back in a ponytail, but she couldn't place him.

Before she could react, he had crossed the street and gripped her arm. Her good arm, luckily. Or unluckily, she thought later, because if it was her bad arm, she'd have screamed.

'What the hell are you playing at?' she said.

'You're Maddy Daly, aren't you?'

'So what?' It was the middle of the day, in the middle of the street, in the middle of town. She was safe, wasn't she?

'I need to have a chat with you,' he said.

'Who are you?'

'You can call me Brendan. Keep your mouth shut and come with me.'

'You can shag off if you think I'm going anywhere with you.' She struggled, but his grip was firm. People sidestepped them out onto the road, oblivious to her silent terror, minding their own business. She twisted her body, trying to escape his clutches, but it was useless. Through clenched teeth she said, 'I don't even know you!'

'You're going to know a lot about me soon. Just do as I say.'

'Piss off.'

'I know about Ellen.'

That made her stop struggling. 'What about Ellen?'

'I know things you need to hear. But I also need to know what she told you.'

'She told me nothing about anything, shithead.'

'What did you do to her?'

'She was my friend. I never did a thing to her.'

'That's funny.'

'Why?'

'Because that's not what she told me.'

'You're a liar.'

'I'm not lying about this. Now, I'm loosening my grip and if you want to know the truth about Ellen, you will follow me nice and quietly.'

Maddy stood on the pavement, confusion paralysing her. He walked on ahead, going back the way he had come. He seemed confident that she'd follow. What did this Brendan person know about Ellen?

Curiosity and fear collided in a whirlpool, rocking her empty stomach. Her head was dizzy. She needed to get her arm looked at. But he was disappearing down the street and she had to know what he was talking about, so she went after him.

CHAPTER THIRTY-SIX

Before they'd left the Mullen house, Boyd had put out an alert for Brendan Healy, but so far there was no sighting of him or the car that was registered to him. They'd sent a uniformed duo round to his parents' house, but he wasn't there, though his mother said he'd called into them that morning. After her earlier conversation with Annie Fleming, Lottie decided to have another chat with Matt Fleming about Rachel.

At the forecourt of the Fleming office building, she jumped out of the car, pulling up her hood.

'Matthew Fleming, the very man. I'm glad we caught you before you disappeared.'

Fleming jingled a large bunch of keys in his hand and pressed a fob. She glanced over at the Range Rover as the lights flashed and the doors automatically unlocked. Where was the BMW she'd seen him driving on the CCTV on Monday night?

'I'm in a hurry,' he said. 'Back-to-back meetings in Dublin. I should be on the road.'

'Won't take long. Can we go to your office? Or—'

'I'm in a hurry.'

'Or you could come to the station.'

'What is it you want?' He pulled up the hood of his black padded jacket as the rain began to pummel his white hair.

'After our previous conversation, you were supposed to supply me with your itinerary for Monday night. To date I've received nothing from you, and that pisses me off. I don't like being pissed off, Mr Fleming. Can you account for your whereabouts on Monday night or not?'

'What the hell are you talking about?'

'Don't play silly buggers. I know you were at Annie's Restaurant at nine thirty. I also know you left ten minutes later. Where did you go then?'

'Home.'

'Are you sure you didn't go to Rachel's house and let yourself in with this key?' She held up the key ring.

'You're delusional. Her keys were in the desk drawer in my office all night. I totally forgot I had them until you mentioned her car yesterday.'

'Selective amnesia is common among murder suspects,' she said. 'Do you know that?'

'I know this: you are barking up the proverbial wrong tree. If you'll excuse me, I have a meeting to get to.' He made to open the car door.

Lottie slammed her hand on the side window, causing him to flinch. She thought she heard his bones rattle. 'Why did you suddenly appear at the restaurant and leave ten minutes later?'

He sighed and ran a hand over his brow. Rain dripped down his nose. 'You're not going to leave it alone, are you?'

'I'm not.'

'It had nothing to do with Rachel.' He sighed and relented. 'I had business to discuss with Annie, but she was well oiled with Prosecco and I couldn't get a word in edgeways between her calling me a bastard and a bollox. So I left.'

'Annie said you were looking for Rachel.'

'She'd say anything to land me in the soup.'

Lottie let it go. 'Did you talk to anyone else?'

'No.'

'Not even your daughter?'

'As far as I knew, Tara was at the airport, and Jessica was busy.'

'Where did you go after that?'

He turned his head towards the inky clouds and allowed the rain to cool the ballooning red of his cheeks on his otherwise pale face. 'I went home.'

'Can anyone verify that?'

'What do you think?' He moved a step closer, black eyes skewering through her. 'I'm separated from my wife and she is hell-bent on splitting up my family. She's trying to turn my daughters away from me. I live alone, except when Tara decides to stay.'

'No girlfriend to add validity to your statement?'

'I told you, I was on my own. Don't you listen?'

'I listen for what is not being said, and you, Mr Fleming, are not telling me something.'

'I've told you the truth.'

'I will find that out. Just so you know, this key opens Rachel's front door.' She held it up. 'Someone got into her house without breaking in. That same person poured poison down her throat and stuffed ...' She caught herself. The information about the glass had been held back from the media and the public.

'Stuffed what?'

'Suffocated her.' She glanced at his hands to see if he had any scratch marks, but he was wearing black leather driving gloves. She tried to think if she had noticed any marks on his hands when she'd spoken to him yesterday. She didn't think so. She wanted to have him forensically examined, but from what she'd learned about Fleming, there was no way he would voluntarily consent to any request. She needed evidence before looking for a court order.

'Can I go now?' he said.

'Your daughters were in school with Rachel and her sister Beth. You must have met them during their teenage years. I believe they were all friends and visited your home.'

'You are relentless.' He sighed, the sound whipped away by the wind and rain. 'I worked in Athlone for many years. I was busy building up my business. I was away a lot, so I missed out on my daughters growing up. At weekends some of their friends stayed over, but with work calls and Annie constantly fighting with me, I never knew who was who. Therefore, to answer your question, I have no idea if I met the Mullens back then.'

'I find that hard to believe. I'm sure two pretty girls, similar in appearance, would have caught your wandering eye.'

The rain increased in strength, along with Fleming's anger. 'What are you implying, Inspector Parker?'

Lottie smiled. 'I'm not implying anything, but it seems to me you're reading something into my words, something I had not intended, and you know what? That makes me think you are definitely concealing information relevant to my investigation. But it doesn't matter, because I'll find out what it is.' She moved into his personal space as his hand squeezed the car door handle. 'You're lying to me, and I don't even need to be this close to you, because I can smell a liar a mile off.' She stepped away.

He grunted, opened the door and sat in. With the door still open, he started the car, the engine as silent as a kitten. A soft purr. Rich bastard.

'I'm sure Annie has painted me with the blackest paint she can find,' he said. 'That's why you're after me, Inspector Parker. But you're mistaken if you think I had anything to do with Rachel's death. Good day.'

Lottie spoke before he could close the door. 'What do you know about Dr Ellen Gormley?'

He was momentarily wrong-footed, his brow knitting into a white V. 'What about Ellen?'

'You know her?'

'Professionally.'

Lottie frowned. What business could he have had with her?

'Why do you want to know about her?'

'She's dead. Murdered. Can you tell me when you last saw her?'

'She was a psychologist, and therefore the reason I knew her is confidential. Now, I've had enough accusatory shit from you. If you require anything further from me, talk through my solicitor.'

As he drove off, Lottie felt more confused than ever. She moved back to her own battered car, where Boyd was leaning like a drowned rat beside the bonnet.

'What?' she said grumpily.

'I never opened my mouth,' Boyd said.

'But you're thinking I said something wrong there?'

'Nope, not a thing. You rattled his cage good and proper.'

'No, I did not. Matthew Fleming doesn't have a cage around him to rattle. He *is* a bloody cage. I just need to find what or who holds the key to it.'

'You have that mysterious key on Rachel's key ring. That might work.'

'Smart-arse. Let's go back to the station. I should be hearing from Jane soon. I need to attend Ellen's post-mortem.'

*

Maddy was still ten paces behind the Brendan man with the ponytail. Why was she following him, after all that had happened?

Her mind was filled with images, and emotions rocked her heart with palpitations. She'd found her good friend Ellen dead last night, and a woman had been murdered after attending a party where she had worked illegally on Monday night. Suddenly she recalled her musings about serial killers. Could she be a potential third victim? A series of tremors shook her body while nausea rose to her throat. With her arm clutched tight to her chest, she stalled.

He had turned the corner at the theatre, heading towards the public car park. Was he going to bundle her into a car and abduct her? Take her somewhere and flay her alive? But he'd said he knew something about Ellen. Taking a deep breath, Maddy put her head down and tracked his steps, even though he was now out of sight.

As she reached the corner, she collided with someone with such force that she fell back against a lamp post.

'Watch where you're … Oh, if it isn't little Miss Spitfire!'

'Simon!' His stocky figure loomed over her. Had he been following her? No, that wasn't possible. He had come around the corner in front of her. She tried to regain a little composure while her heart continued to beat too fast. She couldn't see Brendan, or whatever his name was, anywhere.

'What are you doing here?'

'Nosy Parker Daly,' Simon said. 'You'd make a good detective, you know.' He laughed and ran a hand over the back of his head, as if feeling the bump made earlier by the broken mug. 'If you want to know, I was over there at the social.' He pointed to a building. 'Where are you off to in such a hurry?'

Maddy hesitated. She knew she was acting irrationally. She wanted to follow Brendan, but it might be dangerous. Simon was dangerous too – her arm and neck bore witness to that – but now she considered asking him to walk with her until she found the other man. Which was the lesser evil?

'Simon, will you do me a favour?'

'You want me to go and fuck myself?'

'Can you walk me through the car park?'

He laughed, a loud and ugly sound. 'You want a quick shift between two cars?'

'Don't be so obnoxious.'

'Ha. That's a big word for a small girl.'

'Will you walk with me or not?' she said, straightening her back. She was not a *small* girl!

He leaned in closer, his breath acrid. 'What's up, hun? Do you want me to help you smash someone's head in? I don't see a mug in your hand, so what's the Daly weapon this time?'

'Oh piss off, Simon. You're such a pain in the hole.' She marched around him and turned the corner. But she was relieved when she sensed his presence beside her.

'What or who are we looking for?' He lit a roll-up, the weedy smell wending towards her.

'Just some guy with a ponytail.' She walked up and down the rows of cars like a traffic warden, peering in through windscreens. But there was no sign of Brendan. He had vanished.

'What will we do now?' Simon said, a vulgar sneer pasted on his face as he made a pumping gesture with his hand near his groin.

'You can piss off,' she said, feeling none of the bravado her voice conveyed. She dragged her hood up over her dripping wet hair. 'I have to find a pharmacy to get painkillers for my arm. The arm you broke.'

'Hey! Hold on a minute. I broke nothing—'

'If you ever touch me again, Simon, I'll report you to the guards for assault.' Her whole body trembled. Shock or fear? But she knew she had to stand up to this bully. Ellen would have told her to, if she was still alive.

'You can be funny when you want,' he said, taking a long drag from the damp, crumpled rollie.

'I'll tell them about your stuff.' His face physically drooped and his eyes took on an unnatural gleam. She supposed his *stuff* was his precious weed. 'And if you touch me now, I'm going to scream my head off.'

Looking around, she was glad to see a couple of men in sharp suits walking towards their cars. They'd probably come from the courthouse. Solicitors maybe. They might not help her if she screamed, but at least it would cause Simon to run off. Hopefully. What was she thinking when she'd asked him to walk with her? Silly girl.

He shook his head, water flying everywhere, and his voice dropped to a whisper as he gripped her good arm. 'What do you know about my stuff?'

'Nothing. Just taking the rise out of you.'

Stepping away, he held up his hands in surrender. 'Fuck you, Maddy Daly. You know what? I regret the day I ever got involved with you lot. Bad-news family. Should have known by the state of your alcoholic mother. Bet you don't know she's shacked up with a farmer out in Ballydoon.'

'Leave my mother out of this.'

'With pleasure.' He stomped off, wending his way unevenly through the parked cars.

She remained where she was until he was out of sight. Only then did she exhale a relieved breath, but she felt a cold sweat break out on her forehead. She didn't want to know anything about the woman who'd staggered away and abandoned her to Stella's care.

Making her way back through the car park, water flowing in rivulets around her feet towards blocked drains, she mounted the steps that led to Gallagher's Lane to bring her out on Main Street. Up ahead, leaning against the wall, she noticed someone hunched over, trying to protect the cigarette he was smoking.

She stopped with one foot in front of the other, off balance physically and mentally.

It was the ponytail man – Brendan.

As she felt her feet adhere to the wet ground, his lip curled menacingly. 'What took you so long? You have to come with me.'

A warning signal lit up her brain. She didn't want to go anywhere with this stranger.

She turned and ran.

CHAPTER THIRTY-SEVEN

The state pathologist had left a message for Lottie to say she was commencing Ellen Gormley's post-mortem. That had been an hour ago. Shit.

Leaving Boyd at the station to follow up with Maddy Daly about her interview, Lottie headed off for Tullamore. As she drove, she called back to base for updates. There was still no luck in tracing next of kin for Ellen. Her PA could give them no information either; they'd need a court order to release her patient records. Lottie knew that would take time and concrete evidence, and even then she would have to request particular files rather than asking for all of them.

She recalled that not one of Ellen's neighbours had registered seeing anything out of the ordinary in the days leading up to her death. No one had any recollection of a visitor Ellen might have entertained with whiskey in her kitchen while she folded her laundry. Had it been young Maddy Daly? One or two people recognised Maddy as being a friend of Ellen's and knew that Ellen often loaned Maddy her bicycle. Ellen was a kind soul. That was all anyone had to say. So why had she become a target for a murderer? And had Matthew Fleming anything to do with her death? So far, he was one of the common denominators between the Gormley and Mullen murders.

As she pulled into a parking space outside the Dead House, Chloe rang.

'Where are you?'

Lottie told her.

'Ah, Mam!'

'What? I'm working two murders. I'll be home when I can. Granny—'

'You forgot, didn't you?'

Shit, what had she forgotten now? She racked her brain, but Chloe cut through her ruminations.

'Your hair trial! You never turned up. I'm standing here like a spare prick and Ashley is moving on to her next client.'

Her hair? Oh God. For the wedding. Her own wedding. Chloe seemed more excited than she was. The daughter who'd almost scuppered her relationship with Boyd at one stage was now full of enthusiasm, plans and ideas. It was good to see a smile on her face these days.

'Chloe, I'm sorry. I've been so busy. It never entered my head. Can you rearrange it for Friday? These cases should be more advanced by then.' She crossed her fingers in hope.

'Mother! The wedding is Saturday! This week!' Chloe was verging on hysterical. Over a hairstyle?

Rubbing her hand across her forehead, trying to think how she could fit in another appointment, Lottie said, 'Calm down, love.'

'I'm organising this wedding for you single-handedly despite Boyd's fussiness, and you're refusing all input and—'

'Chloe, it's only for thirty people.'

'You know what, Mam? I don't care any more. You can turn up with your hair in a knitted hat for all I care. You're always the same. Thinking of no one but yourself.'

'That's unfair. I—' But she was talking to air. Her daughter had hung up. Damn.

Struggling out of the car, Lottie wondered how she could manage to fit in a trial for her poxy hair. Who cared? Boyd wouldn't notice.

But as she walked through the disinfectant-smelling tiled tunnel to the cutting room, she felt that maybe she should make an effort. Her once-in-a-lifetime event was on a second chance, and she couldn't afford to muck it up.

Sighing, she pushed through the double doors and suited up. As she tightened her face mask, she shed Chloe's criticism and donned her professional mode. Entering the cutting room, she found Jane working on Ellen's corpse.

'Anything interesting?'

'If you're asking whether I found something similar to the glass I took from Rachel Mullen's throat, the answer is yes.' Jane pointed to a sharp piece lying in a stainless-steel kidney bowl.

Lottie stared at it, noting that it was larger than the first shard. 'It reflects like a mirror.'

'You're right. It could be a sliver of mirror.'

'Was it placed in the throat after death?'

'Yes.'

'And does it match the shard from Rachel's throat?'

'It will be sent for analysis. Then we'll know.'

'Thanks. Found anything else?' Lottie was tuned into Jane's tone and way of relating information.

'Ellen Gormley was poisoned. If she hadn't fallen down the stairs, I reckon she would have been able to get help. She was dead at least thirty-six hours before her body was found.'

'Her mobile phone and house phone were both downstairs. Perhaps she was coming downstairs to make a phone call when she fell.'

'Fell? I'll get to that soon. However, as death wasn't instantaneous, this woman suffered. Two broken vertebrae and a smashed coccyx bone. She cracked her skull as she came down the stairs. But the worst thing is that the poison in her system would have smothered her lungs in fluid. Along with her painful injuries, she'd have struggled to breathe.'

'That's horrific.'

'That's not all.' Jane turned Ellen's naked body onto its side.

Walking around the table, keeping at a distance, Lottie saw what Jane was pointing at between the victim's shoulder blades. She leaned in closer. 'Is that a bruise?'

'Yes. It occurred a few hours before death and is not consistent with the bruises sustained in the tumble down the stairs. Did you find evidence that anyone else had been upstairs in her house?'

'No.' Lottie said the word confidently before immediately doubting herself. She'd have to check with SOCOs to hear if they'd discovered anything relevant.

'Go back to the scene, check it out. Someone else had to have been there.'

Not liking being told how to do her job, Lottie bristled. 'It could be an old bruise.'

Jane peered over her mask, her rimless spectacles covered by plastic goggles transforming her into an alien. It was her turn to bristle. 'The lividity and skin tone tell me it occurred shortly before the bones were broken in the fall.'

'Not an old bruise, then,' Lottie muttered in agreement. The pungent odour of death mingled with the silence of the room.

'I'm looking forward to Saturday,' Jane said, turning the body onto its back, breaking the tension.

'Going anywhere special?'

She laughed. 'I thought I had a wedding to attend, but maybe I'm wrong.'

'I've been so busy these last few days,' Lottie said, still smarting from Chloe's earlier words. 'I could have done with a simpler lead-in than all this. I haven't a clue what's left on the to-do list.'

'You better check it out then. I want somewhere to show off my new outfit.' Jane winked beneath the double layer of glass and plastic.

'I might postpone—'

'Don't you dare, Lottie Parker. Where else am I going to wear a custom-made fascinator complete with feathers and tulle?'

Lottie laughed, releasing some of the stress that was holding her together. She suddenly felt very tired. 'I can't imagine you dressed up like that.'

'The only reason I'm wearing it is because it adds six inches to my height. You and I know I need every inch I can get.' Another wink.

Lottie returned her gaze to Ellen Gormley's bruised and broken body lying on the cold slab of steel. Her heart contracted.

'She was a psychologist, Jane.'

'Okay.'

'Did you ever meet her? Know anything about her? We can't find any next of kin. Her PA knows nothing either.'

'I didn't know her, but I'm sure she was professional in her work and kept things private.'

Lottie thought for a moment. 'How would a woman who kept relationships on a strictly professional footing have befriended a fifteen-year-old girl?' She explained about Maddy Daly.

'Did you ask the girl?' Jane said.

'She mentioned that she'd been friends with Ellen since she'd been a patient, when she was aged thirteen.'

'Is that relationship relevant?'

'I don't know. Why?'

'Perhaps you should get a court order for Ellen's records. Specifically, the records pertaining to said teenager.'

'I doubt that can happen.'

'Get the girl's consent.'

'Easier said than done.'

'You love a challenge, Lottie Parker, don't you? If someone tells you something is impossible, what do you do?'

'Make it possible.'

'There you go. You know what you have to do.' Jane turned back to the corpse. 'Dr Ellen Gormley. Aged thirty. Death by asphyxia, caused by ingested rat poison.'

The mood in the office was grim when Lottie returned from Ellen's post-mortem. No progress on either of the murder investigations.

Sitting at her desk, she made notes of what she'd found out so far as she prepared for their evening team meeting. The piece of glass or mirror had her puzzled. What was the killer trying to say? She was disappointed there were still no sightings of Brendan Healy or his car. The officers in the traffic cars fitted with the ANPR system had reported back to base that it was possible Healy had changed his car's number plates.

She sent Kirby and McKeown back to Ellen's house to carry out another search, particularly upstairs. The only evidence that someone had been in the house around the time the victim had been poisoned was the extra mug smelling of whiskey, and now the bruise Jane had discovered on Ellen's back. She told them to also search the shed for evidence of any packets or bottles that could have contained poison, though she knew SOCOs had so far found nothing incriminating.

They'd matched the damp footprints to Maddy Daly's shoes, where she'd stopped beside the body and exited again. Maddy had not been upstairs. Unless she'd taken off her shoes, Lottie thought.

She filled Boyd in on the post-mortem details, and as Maddy hadn't turned up, he went to fetch her to bring her in for her formal interview. Hopefully the girl might now be more forthcoming on her relationship with Ellen.

As she made a list, Lottie sensed someone staring at her. She expected to see Superintendent Farrell armed for a confrontation. Instead, it was Maria Lynch.

'Detective Lynch, what can I do for you?'

'May I sit down?'

'Of course.'

Lynch sat, her face pinched, hair cut shorter than usual but still snagged back with a bobbin.

'I want to tell you something …' she began.

'I hope the children are okay?' Lottie didn't dare ask after Lynch's husband Ben. She wasn't about to get burned twice.

'Kids are grand. Baby is growing so quickly. All good.'

'What did you want to see me about?' Lottie's tone sharpened. She was sure it had been Lynch who'd run to Superintendent Farrell with tales of how Lottie had cut corners with her previous investigation in order to get quick results. The snitch had succeeded in getting her suspended during an investigation that found no wrongdoing. She could never forgive duplicitous behaviour. If Lynch had an issue, she should have spoken to her about it before bringing it upstairs.

'I want to set the record straight.'

'What record would that be?'

'I did not report you to Superintendent Farrell.'

'I believe you did.' Lottie could not disguise the contempt in her voice.

'Did she say so?'

'No. The superintendent knows better than to reveal her snitches … I mean sources.' God, but she needed to ease up.

Lynch looked up from beneath her fair lashes. 'You've been giving me the shit jobs since you returned, so I know you believe it was me. But I am telling you here and now: even though I may have thought of it – many times, in fact – I did not report you for mismanagement of cases or illegal conduct.'

'Mismanagement? Illegal conduct? Don't make me laugh. Anything I did, I did for the good of our cases, to catch calculating and dangerous criminals and murderers. I work hard to achieve positive results and keep the superintendent's spreadsheets balanced. Don't go all Mother Teresa on me. We've worked together a long time. You know how I operate. I know how you operate. We never saw eye to eye, but we got results. Results are what matter to those upstairs. So, what changed with you?'

'McKeown.'

'What about him?'

'It was Detective McKeown who reported your unorthodox work practices.'

'Look, Maria, blaming someone else is not going to elevate you in my eyes.'

'I'm telling you the truth. I want proper duties. We have two murders and you need me out on the ground and active on the team. I'm a good detective and you're wasting my skills having me stuck behind a desk staring at a monitor. This … being here … begging you … it goes against all I stand for. But that's it. I am begging you to please reinstate me on the team.'

If Lottie didn't know how much Lynch hated her, she would have sworn she saw remorse in the detective's eyes. Remorse for what, though, if she hadn't been the one to report her? Then it came to her. It was guilt.

'What did you do, Lynch?'

'I don't understand.'

'I think you do.'

'Honestly I don't, boss.'

'Don't "boss" me. You hate my guts. You were gunning for my job at one time, probably still are, so if you didn't report me to Farrell, did you put McKeown up to it?'

'I did not. It was him. I had nothing to do with it.'

'If you have nothing further to add, I advise you to think long and hard about your career in this station. And if you value it, you will come back with the truth.'

Lynch's eyes flared with something Lottie couldn't quite decipher. But she was sure it was more than anger.

She watched the detective stand, shove the chair under the desk and walk out with her head held high. She left the door wide open and marched back to her desk, the meek mouse act well and truly gone. But she had given Lottie someone else to worry about. Someone she'd mistakenly thought was on her side. Sam fecking McKeown.

CHAPTER THIRTY-EIGHT

The afternoon was turning into a dull, misty evening. Boyd parked outside Maddy Daly's house and sat with the engine idling. He looked up at the dirty windows and the front door with its peeling paint and wondered when he and Lottie would ever get the time to renovate Farranstown House to make it their home.

He was shaken out of his musings when Stella, Maddy's sister, came out the door, manhandling a buggy down the three steps. Exiting the car, he moved to help.

'Here, let me do that,' he said.

'Piss off,' Stella growled.

The baby was wrapped up well, at least. The misty rain spread over the see-through plastic covering keeping her dry.

'What's her name?' Boyd hoped he wasn't making a rookie mistake just because the baby was wearing a pink knitted hat.

'It's none of your business what she's called.'

With the buggy safely on the cracked wet concrete path, Boyd smiled.

'What's funny, cop face?'

'Nothing. I'm looking for Maddy. Is she inside?'

'She's not, and you've upset us enough already, so get the hell away from us.'

Stella tugged at the zip of her jacket, snagging it on the light cotton material, which was already becoming saturated. Boyd toyed with the

213

idea of grabbing a navy garda rain jacket from the boot for her, then discounted it as a bad idea. 'I need to speak to her. Where is she?'

'I don't know where she is. She was supposed to mind Trey while I brought Ariana for her injections.'

'Who's minding Trey then?' Boyd recalled seeing a small boy looking down the stairs that morning.

'He's with a neighbour, not that it's any of your business. Now let me pass. I'm bloody late already.'

Standing to one side, Boyd said, 'Will I shut the front door?'

She flushed, and he thought she was about to let fly with another stream of invective, but her face hardened, and she looked like someone thirty years older than her nineteen years.

'Do what you like. I'm late.'

He watched her negotiate the buggy out onto the footpath and hurry away. The open door was an invitation to have a look inside. He had no idea what he was looking for, but he wasn't about to pass up the chance to have a snoop.

Dampness and residual cigarette smoke greeted him as he stepped inside. He glanced into the living room, recoiling at the state of the couch, with its torn fabric and stuffing spilling out. The grate looked like a fire hadn't been lit in it in years. It was piled high with cigarette butts. The room was so bare it made him feel lonely for the girls and the children living here. He backed out to the hall and climbed the stairs.

Fully aware that he was invading their privacy for no good reason, he quickly looked into each room. The bathroom was surprisingly clean, though the shower curtain was ripped, and the taps were corroded. The next room must be Stella's, as it had a cot for the baby. The double bed was made up. The linen looked fresh. But Maddy's room was a mess, clothes strewn about and the bed unmade.

Lifting the pillow, he found the space beneath it empty. He ran his hands under the mattress. Nothing. Guilt swamped him as he searched the pockets of the jeans and cut-offs lying on the floor. Nothing.

He didn't know what he was looking for, and even if he found something relevant to Ellen's murder, wasn't this in fact an illegal search despite Stella leaving the door open?

There were a few books stacked on the floor at the foot of the bed. Some were psychology journals, obviously loaned to her by Ellen. Nothing fell from the pages as he flipped them upside down. Kneeling on the floor, he scanned the area beneath the bed.

'What the fuck are you doing?'

He turned swiftly, catching his forehead on the base of the bed. 'The door was open. Stella said—'

'I don't give a shit what she said; you're in my room.' Maddy shook her head wearily. He could see tears in her eyes and noticed the way she clutched one arm across her body while her hand held a pharmacy paper bag. The girl was distressed, and he sensed it wasn't entirely because of his intrusion.

'I can explain,' he said, standing, moving towards her.

Maddy flinched and stepped around him into the room. She threw the bag on the bed and sat, resting her head against the wall. 'Why are you here?'

'Like I said, Stella—'

'Forget Stella. What do you want with me?'

'Can I sit down?'

Motioning to a spot on the floor a few feet from her, Maddy acceded to his request. He sat awkwardly and nursed the bump swelling on his forehead.

'You told us this morning that Ellen was your friend. I'm trying to find out why someone would want to kill her.'

'By looking under my bed? Come on, I'm not a dope. You think I killed my only friend? Ellen and I … well, we had some sort of … I don't know what you'd call it.'

'A connection?'

'Yeah. Maybe she saw me as her child or something. I don't know. I would never have hurt her. Never. You have to believe me.' She swiped at dark strands of wet hair that hung over her eyes and scrunched them to the nape of her neck. Tears moistened her eyes again, eyes he'd first thought were hard as marbles. 'I miss her already.'

'Can you tell me how you first came in contact with Dr Gormley?'

'I … I had mental health issues. Around the time I turned thirteen. I was referred to Ellen and she worked with me until I was a little better. Then, when I quit the sessions, we became friends.'

'Are you okay now?'

'I'll never be okay. I have a lot of … problems.'

'Is that why Ellen befriended you?'

'Whatever. You can think what you like.'

'Did she talk to you much about her family and friends? We can't trace anyone belonging to her.'

Maddy bit her lower lip. 'Maybe they're all dead. I don't know.'

Boyd kneaded his fingers, thinking. He had to be careful. Now that she was opening up to him, he didn't want to say anything that might cause her to clamp her mouth shut. 'What did you talk about?'

'That's my business. And Ellen's. Though I suppose she doesn't give a shite now she's dead.'

'Did she ever mention anything about someone who might want to harm her?'

'No.'

'Ever mention the names of any of her other patients?'

'Are you for real? She was a professional. Sworn an oath … or something.' Maddy sighed loudly and winced when she rubbed her arm. 'We talked mainly about my shitty life. Happy now?'

Boyd decided he had trodden that thin line enough for now. 'We know you worked at Annie's on Monday night. Can you recall anything unusual happening?'

Her pale cheeks flushed bright red. 'How'd you find out about that? Bet it was big-mouth David.'

'David?'

'David Crawley. He's a chef. Lives on the estate round the back from here, the creep. He knew I was underage and that I was filling in for Stella, but he promised he'd say nothing. Should have known he couldn't keep his mouth shut.' She folded her arms and let out a cry.

'Are you hurt?'

She shook her head, biting her lip.

'You're in pain. What happened?'

'Nothing.'

He decided she'd tell him when she was ready, and made a mental note to have a word with David the chef. 'Did you know Rachel Mullen?'

'Read about her online.' She slid her phone out of her jeans pocket and showed him the cracked screen. 'And before you ask, yes, I remember seeing her at the party.'

'What can you tell me about that evening?'

'Not much. I was busy. The trays were heavy. I was doing my best not to let everything fall. Kept my head down and did my job. Got paid and left.'

'Tell me what you recall about Rachel.'

'She was very beautiful, her hair wild and frizzy. Wish I could get mine cut like that.' She ran her fingers up and down her dark mane.

'She had the most amazing red shoes. Took some canapés from my tray. She seemed hungry and maybe a bit drunk.'

'Who was she talking to?'

'Some drunk dude. Good-looking. Sunglasses on his head. Like hello, it's bloody winter and pissing rain outside and he's waltzing around with sunglasses on.' She smiled and it lit up her face like sunshine over a placid lake. Boyd wished she had reason to smile more often.

Fighting an urge to mother her and tell her everything was going to be okay, he said, 'I know about him. Andy Ashe.'

'Oh, he works in Boyne's department store. Thought I recognised him.'

'You shop in there?'

'I like to look.'

He noted the blush creeping up her pale skin, highlighting her few freckles. 'Did you see Rachel with anyone else?'

'She might have spoken with Jessica Fleming. Or maybe not. I was trying to offload the food from my tray.'

'Think, Maddy. Anything else?'

'She just seemed to be mingling. I didn't notice anything unusual. Just people talking too loud and drinking too much. I didn't see her leave.'

'Do you know the Flemings?'

'No. That was the first night I'd worked for Annie.'

'What about Matthew Fleming?'

'Who's he?'

'Doesn't matter. You told us this morning that Ellen drove out to the lake and Molesworth House on Saturday. That house belongs to Annie Fleming. Have you thought any more about that visit?'

'Are you for real? Of course I have. It's the last time I was with Ellen …' Maddy closed her eyes. 'The last time I saw her alive, and I can't believe I'll never see her again.' Her long wet hair stuck to her clothes and Boyd resisted getting up from the floor to place an arm around her heaving shoulder to comfort her.

'Can you remember anything she said? What she talked about? Something to give us a clue as to why she drove out there.'

'She seemed nostalgic. You don't have to look surprised. I know big words.'

'It's not that at all,' Boyd said, shamefaced.

'She was upset when she couldn't find the stables. That's all. She never spoke about whoever's living there now.'

Boyd gingerly got to his feet and leaned against the wall to iron out his creased back muscles. 'Do you know Brendan Healy?'

'Brendan?' Her body stiffened. 'No.'

'What's up?'

'Nothing. I don't know him.'

'I think you do.'

'Can you leave now, please?'

'Maddy, there have been two murders in the space of a few days, with no suspects. I believe you can help me.'

'I don't know anything else. I'd like you to leave.'

'Who hurt your arm?'

'Si …' She seemed to catch herself in time. 'No one. I fell off the bike the other day. My arm is only acting up today.'

'Si? Simon?'

'It's no one. Leave me alone.'

Boyd paced a little, then hunkered down so that his face was level with hers. 'Maddy, I can help you, but only if you tell me what's going on.'

'Just go,' she said.

He took a card from his wallet and left it on the bed beside her.

'You gave me one already.'

'I know. And I'd like you to use it if you want to talk or if you need me for anything. Don't be afraid. I want to help you,' he said, though he'd never felt so helpless.

He walked down the bare stairs and pulled the front door shut behind him. As he went down the cracked path, he was aware that something of Maddy's sadness had settled on his shoulders, and he didn't know how to shake it off.

At the car, he paused with the keys in his hand and looked up at the windows again. He couldn't help wondering what it was she wasn't telling him. The spaces between her words had been filled with an uneasy silence. And that bothered him.

*

Hazel Clancy sniffed more of the delicious white powder up her nose, allowing the sensation to flow directly into her brain. Wow! That was so good. She giggled and went into her bedroom, falling onto the bed. She had to get straight. She had to work tomorrow. She couldn't afford to miss any more days like this. She needed to keep up the impression.

She closed her eyes, letting herself float on the fumes of euphoria.

A noise.

Was that the apartment door opening? No one had a key. That's weird, she thought, unable to keep her eyes open.

Then ... footsteps creeping softly across the floor.

'Hello?' She tried to get up but was too high to move. Eyelids drooping once again. Was that a spider web falling across the bed? Forcing her eyes open, she tried to look around.

The doorway darkened. Something reflected in the mirror. A light? Or a shadow? It moved, didn't it? Was the shadow actually someone standing there?

'Wha ...? Who ...?' She couldn't form a sentence.

The shadow moved closer. One step at a time. And stopped at the edge of the bed.

With great effort, Hazel got an elbow under her body. Tried to sit up. To move. She wanted to be frightened but she couldn't muster that emotion. She felt herself smiling, though nothing was funny. No message would go to her brain to tell it to be fearful.

A bottle. Held to her lips.

A hand across her nose, forcing her head into the pillow.

The liquid trickled down her throat.

*

Kirby followed McKeown up Ellen Gormley's stairs.

'This is a waste of time,' McKeown grumbled. 'The boss and Boyd and SOCOs have been through this place.'

'When I'm asked to do something,' Kirby said, 'I do it. All part of the job.'

'Yeah, but does she even know what she's doing any more?'

'What do you mean?'

'She was suspended for inadequate work practices ...'

'Not proven, and she was reinstated.'

'... and she hasn't changed how she does the job,' McKeown said. 'I hate to say this, but I don't trust her ability.'

'You don't know her. You haven't worked with her for as long as I have, so shut your mouth.'

'Just a warning salvo.'

Kirby watched McKeown enter Ellen's bathroom, where he opened the medicine cabinet noisily. Once he had his breathing under control, Kirby marched into the bedroom. He blotted out McKeown's insubordinate words and concentrated on the search. In a way, he hoped he found nothing the boss had missed, but conversely, he wanted to discover something. It was frustrating having bodies with no clues as to the perpetrator.

After fifteen minutes, he'd drawn a blank. He'd opened each of the books on the bookcase and flipped through the pages until his wrist was sore. Nothing.

As he listened to the sound of McKeown mooching through cupboards, he ran his hand absent-mindedly along the top of the bookcase, which seemed to have been made from odd bits of timber. Then he noticed it wasn't flush to the wall. Maybe, just maybe, he thought. He grabbed the corners at one end and inched it out slightly. Was that something wedged between the wall and the timber? Maybe a book had fallen down.

It appeared to be loose pages. Tugging the bookcase out further, he reached in and extracted them. Then he stepped backwards and fanned them out. He should put them into an evidence sleeve and bring them to the station, but he wanted to see what they were about first.

Sitting on the side of the bed, he shouted, 'McKeown! I've found something!'

CHAPTER THIRTY-NINE

A long time ago, a mirror was Tara Fleming's best friend. Now it mocked her.

She finished applying her eyeliner, deciding she didn't need mascara on her false eyelashes. Interlaced among her own long lashes, the tiny fake hairs made her eyes appear bigger and wider than normal. But her foundation wasn't doing its trick today. Normally, the heavy-duty stage make-up that she had resorted to layering over the scar succeeded in making its garish impact minimal. It did not work when she was stressed. The deep red line refused to remain hidden. The scar seemed to sprout up of its own accord, with the make-up settling into the crevice, unable to dam the hideousness. Even her blonde highlights were in need of a touch-up.

'Not looking particularly beautiful this evening, are you?'

Tara swung round. Jessica stood there, flawless as usual. Her statement pearl hairband holding back her dark hair and circling her perfect face. Not perfect, no, but beside Tara's it was blemish-free. Jessica's eyes were sharp stones behind her spectacles.

'What are you doing in my room?' Tara snarled. 'Get out.'

'No need to be so tigerish. And why do you need a room here? You've got one at Daddy's house. And a new one in London, though as far as I can tell, you're never there. What do you do for him anyhow? Environmental officer could mean anything. Not like me. Business manager. Now that's a proper job.'

'Why are you always so bitchy, Jessica?'

'You may be younger, but I learned many things from you. Perhaps I should thank you.'

'You always were a pain in the arse. I think you're getting worse. You want to be careful, or whoever killed Rachel might come for you next.' Holding a hairbrush as if it were a gun, Tara pointed it towards her sister.

'I think your brain is mush again. Maybe you need to make an appointment with your shrink.'

'Get out.'

'I just wanted to let you know that Mother has invited detectives over to dinner this evening. You need to be on your best behaviour. That's if you can manage it.'

'God almighty, I'm not nine, Jess.'

'And don't abbreviate my name.'

'Whatever.' Tara turned back to the mirror. She sensed her sister moving further into the room. 'What do you really want?'

Jessica sat on the end of the bed and twirled the fringe of the throw around her fingers. 'What do you make of these murders?' Her voice was softer, almost cajoling.

Tara brushed her hair methodically, trying not to let Jessica see the tremble in her hand. 'I don't make anything of them because I'm not interested.'

'I heard Rachel had a meeting with Daddy on Monday afternoon shortly before she arrived at Mum's party.' Jessica's voice had taken on an icy tone.

'So what?'

'Did you know about it?'

'Why would I? I'm not his PA. But you and I know that he can't resist a pretty lady.'

'Lady? Ha. The thing is, that little meeting will project him onto the guards' radar.'

'Don't be ridiculous. If he didn't do anything, he has nothing to fear.'

'Tara, you shouldn't be so naive. We both know what happened in the past and how things deteriorated in our family. Who knows what he did to Rachel.'

Swinging around on the stool, Tara faced her sister. Even discounting her vivid scar, they were still unalike. 'What do you mean?'

'You should know. You've been little more than his secretary these past few years—'

'How dare you! Daddy gave me a highly paid job in his company, while you were lumbered with Mum and her ridiculous restaurant ideas.' Tara laughed, knowing it made her scar scream fierceness. Sometimes she welcomed that transformation. Like now. She saw how irritated Jessica had become. 'I get it. You're jealous of me.'

'In another life maybe.' Jessica unwound the blanket fringe from her finger, leaving behind a ridge of red marks. 'Since you were not on your way to London on Monday night like you led us to believe, where were you?'

'I felt ill at the airport and couldn't face the flight. I came home here to recover. Not that it's any of your business.' Tara wondered why she was even having this conversation.

Jessica's brows knitted into a frown, narrowing her eyes. 'If this murder brings down Mother's restaurant, then everything you do is my business.'

'You think *I* killed Rachel? Oh my God. You've really lost it this time.' Tara shook her head with a laugh. 'I had no problem with Rachel or anyone else Dad brought into his life.'

'That's beside the point,' Jessica said tetchily. 'I saw her at the party. She seemed to be either drunk or drugged to the eyeballs. And I know what you went through after … your accident. Prescription drugs. Painkillers. Valium. All that. I suspect the detectives will find out about that episode in your life and then they'll ask you the same question. Where were you Monday night?'

Tara's stomach churned and she clenched the muscles as she felt bile rise to her throat. How dare Jessica bring up that painful period of her life. A time when she'd lost so many memories. A time when she'd floated in and out of reality. Her 'disappeared' time, until her dad had rescued her and brought her back to life. How dare she! Digging her fingernails into the palms of her hands, she tried to quell her rising anger.

'I told you, I was here, and now I'd like you to leave. And don't expect me to be the perfect sibling at dinner. If the detectives want answers, I'll gladly talk to them. But I don't owe you an explanation for anything.' She narrowed her eyes into slits, the glue of her lashes sticking until she could hardly see her sister. 'Go on, get the fuck out of my room.'

Jessica balled up the throw, flung it to the floor and left, slamming the door. Tara thought this was a childish act of defiance. The mirror rattled in its frame as a clash of thunder echoed from outside.

At the window, she watched the storm gather over the lake. A flash of lightning streaked across the sky and lit up one of the cottages. A place of buried secrets. One of the places that bound the family in silence.

CHAPTER FORTY

Pacing around the incident board, Lottie felt totally alone. Lynch sat in a corner along with a few uniformed gardaí, but there was no sign of Boyd. She watched Garda Brennan pin up the details from Ellen Gormley's post-mortem. She tried to see the significance of the two pieces of glass that had been left in the victims' throats. It had to mean something, besides confirming both women had been killed by the same person.

Kirby burst in, waving two clear evidence bags. He bustled to the front of the room. McKeown followed him.

'What in the name of God is the rush for?' Lottie said as Kirby shoved the bags under her nose.

'I found them behind the bookcase,' he said triumphantly. 'In Ellen Gormley's bedroom. SOCOs missed them.'

'What are they?' She tried to read through the plastic.

'We couldn't decipher the words,' McKeown said, towering over Kirby, 'but it matches Ellen's illegible handwriting. We compared it to notebooks we found on her desk.'

'No signature, though,' Kirby said, regaining his limelight. He held up another page. 'And this is an outline map of a piece of land. No place names noted, but there are coordinates.'

'Try to find out where the land is. Have the pages been fingerprinted?'

'Not yet,' Kirby said.

Spreading the pages out on the table, Lottie was glad Kirby had put each page into an individual bag. 'The handwriting is impossible to read.'

She couldn't understand what she was looking at. Were the pages notes from a counselling consultation? She scanned her eyes over each one, but no name jumped out at her. She'd have to spend time trying to decipher them. 'Could there be pages missing?'

'We looked,' McKeown said. 'There was nothing else behind the bookcase.'

'We did a thorough search of the entire house, but found nothing else.' Kirby ran his hand through his hair, which refused to lie down.

'Has anyone had any luck tracing next of kin for Ellen?' Lottie asked.

Maria Lynch said, 'I found out that she had a brother, but he died years ago. Parents are dead also. No other relatives that I can find.'

'Thanks,' Lottie said grudgingly. 'I'll go through those papers later, Kirby, and well done. But let's not waste any more time.' She was thinking of giving the pages to Lynch to work on, but held off for now.

As the detectives took their seats, she said, 'Where's Boyd?'

Shoulders shrugged and heads shook. She tried phoning him. No answer. She left a message telling him the team meeting was about to begin. The day was getting away from her and she still had to go to Molesworth House for dinner with Annie Fleming.

'Anything of note from Ellen Gormley's post-mortem?' McKeown asked.

'She died from asphyxiation due to ingesting poison. Samples have been sent for analysis. A shard of glass, possibly a piece of mirror, was found in her throat, which confirms a link with Rachel Mullen's death. The pathologist found a bruise between her shoulder blades. She believes this occurred before Ellen tumbled down the stairs. Did someone push her? If so, there was someone else in the house the night she died.' Lottie read through the preliminary report Jane had emailed. 'Death occurred sometime between Sunday night and early Monday morning. Have we checked if any of the residents have security cameras in that area?'

McKeown said, 'Not that we found so far. Most of the neighbours have alarms on their houses, but Dr Gormley didn't.'

'Check over our traffic cam footage for, say, Saturday evening into Monday morning.'

'There's no cameras on that road.'

'Then try the main road leading to where Ellen lives. There's a camera located over the roundabout at the old tobacco factory.'

McKeown groaned. She didn't blame him. It meant hours in the cupboard-sized office going through hazy tapes. But it had to be done and someone had to do it. She could ask Lynch, but something was telling her there were only so many shitty jobs she could dump on her.

'Has Brendan Healy been located?' she said. More blank faces and head shakes. 'Remind me what his parents had to say?'

'They only see him now and again. They were at pains to tell me he's a thirty-year-old adult who lives in County Dublin and works in the city.' McKeown consulted his iPad. 'I've had our Rathfarnham colleagues check his apartment, but he's not there and his neighbours don't even know him. Life in the suburbs, huh?'

'It's important we find him, to either implicate him in or eliminate him from our investigation.' She heard movement at the door, and Superintendent Farrell walked in, leaned against the wall, folded her arms and scowled.

Shit, Lottie thought. Farrell remained tight-lipped, so she continued.

'Rachel Mullen's keys were in Matthew Fleming's possession because she'd had a few drinks at the meeting with him and left her car at his office. Can we up our game and try to prove where he went after he left Annie's at nine forty? He says he went home. Scour the traffic cams and see what they throw up. And another thing, it's possible Rachel already knew Matthew Fleming well. It's unlikely she went to a business meeting and had drinks with a man she'd never met before. She was friends with his daughters in school, but we need to tie her to him more recently. See what you can dig up. I'm meeting Annie later on, so I'll quiz her.'

McKeown piped up. 'Maybe it was normal practice for Rachel to have drinks with business contacts.'

Kirby said, 'Her plans for SmoothPebble cosmetics demonstrate that she was anxious to connect with him for raw materials as well as funding. Plus, Fleming is well established. Joining up with him would have given her business the recognition that otherwise might take years to build.'

'According to her sister,' Lottie said, trying to defuse the argument before it found legs, 'it would have been out of character for Rachel to drink at a meeting like this. And we know she previously had association with Fleming's daughters. So what happened at that meeting? Fleming has invoked the solicitor trick, so we need to dig up dirt to get him talking. Another thing: he told me he knew Dr Ellen Gormley in a professional capacity.'

'Matthew Fleming spilling his guts to a therapist?' Superintendent Farrell said, unfolding her arms. She marched to the head of the room to stand beside Lottie. 'That I cannot imagine.'

'He didn't elaborate on his connection to her, but he knew she was a therapist. We need to get consent to access her files. Otherwise we have to show evidence of criminal activity in order to seek a court order.'

'I wonder what Matthew Fleming could have to discuss in a therapy session,' McKeown said dubiously.

'Every which way I turn, his name crops up,' Lottie said. 'We need to monitor his movements. And backtrack over what he was doing, what he's involved in and who with.'

'Did the forensic team discover any DNA or fingerprints at either scene or in Rachel's car?' Farrell pressed.

'They found plenty of fingerprints, but nothing compares to anything on PULSE. Those they could identify belonged to the victims, and Maddy Daly and Beth Mullen. They lifted Maddy's from her shoes. The rest are unidentified.'

'Then you need to find a suspect for comparison purposes.' Farrell straightened her back and flipped her tie. 'You're working at a snail's pace. Everyone needs to smarten up and do some real police work.'

'We still don't know why Rachel had an overnight suitcase in her car,' Lottie said. 'Her sister couldn't offer any explanation.'

'Maybe she planned to travel to Dublin to meet up with Beth after the concert finished,' McKeown said.

'Not likely,' Lottie said. 'They would have discussed that. What else have you got?'

'Her laptop and iPad only contain business details. There are a lot of photos, which appear to be of paintings. Beth's work.' McKeown paused and tapped his own iPad. 'There's a report just in from SOCOs. Unidentified fingerprints lifted from Rachel Mullen's front door match ones found on her bedroom door and bedside cabinet. But here's the thing. They also match some found inside Ellen Gormley's house. Namely on one of the mugs that contained whiskey.'

'Good,' said Farrell. 'Something else to tie the two crimes together.'

'They might have had the same visitor who may not have been their killer,' Lottie said cautiously.

Farrell grunted and turned to look at the lists Lottie had made on the whiteboard. 'What's this about a third key?'

As Lottie explained about Rachel's key ring, a thought occurred to her. 'This is a long shot, but we should see if the unidentified key works on Ellen's door.'

'What's your logic?' Farrell said.

'Something else to link the victims, maybe,' Lottie said doubtfully.

'Keep me informed. I have a media briefing at nine in the morning. And if I hear a serial killer mentioned, I might turn into one. They're scrambling for headlines.'

Lottie knew they needed three deaths to formally classify them as serial killings. Didn't stop the media bandying the term about.

After Farrell had left, she picked up the pages Kirby had brought from Ellen's house just as her phone vibrated in her jeans pocket.

At last. Boyd.

CHAPTER FORTY-ONE

The psychedelic colours on the wall danced to their own tune. Pinks. Yellows. Purples. But wasn't her wall plain white?

Hazel tried to bring the room into focus, but her stomach lurched wildly, so she shut her eyes. She reached out to grab the glass she knew was beside her, and her hand flew through the air, connecting with space. Her throat burned, then tightened. She felt as if a cement block was pressing down on her lungs. She tried to cough. Her throat constricted. She needed to cough up whatever was clogging her airways, but she couldn't catch a breath. She tore at her neck, her fingers swiping wildly in the fetid atmosphere.

Hadn't someone been in the room? Forced something into her mouth? Were they still here? Watching her in her agony? Oh God, no. She thought she'd cried out, but the air was silent.

She was alone. All alone in the world. She wondered how she could wallow in self-pity when she might be dying.

A sound. Movement. Someone trying to be silent?

She heard it again. The soft flutter of material, like silk or satin. Was she in the shop, at work? Was she so high she was unaware of having worked through the day? God, Andy would have a smug mug on him now if he was close by, viewing her demise. At least she'd have succeeded in wiping away the sycophantic expression he normally wore. She felt her eyes bulge with tears. But she couldn't breathe, so how could she cry? She tried to call out, but her throat just gurgled and a soft foam filled her mouth.

She didn't know if she was lying down or sitting up. She definitely wasn't standing. A flutter like butterfly wings breezed over her face. Her eyes were open, she thought, but she couldn't see a thing. She sensed herself floating on a cloud before her stomach clenched in on itself.

She seemed to remember fingers prising her lips apart. She'd been powerless to refuse as the liquid was poured down her throat. Had that been a dream?

Her throat tightened again; her stomach rebelled. Pain cut like a scythe through every muscle and tendon in her body. She tore at her neck, attempting to knife the pain out of her throat with her fingernails. Her back arched and she screamed a silent scream as her body began to shut down.

*

Boyd's face was pale, and dark rings circled his eyes. They settled at a small table in the Bean Café. Lottie ordered a double espresso for both of them, plus two doughnuts.

'For energy,' she said, setting the plate down between them.

'What?'

'The doughnuts.'

'You won't fit into your wedding dress, Mrs Parker.'

'I'm going to wear an old suit.' She winked, but he remained stony-faced. 'What's the matter?'

'Maddy Daly. I know you're normally the one with the gut feelings, but I sense it in my bones that she's in danger.'

'What evidence do you have to support your theory?' Lottie gulped her coffee, willing life back into her body. The day had been so long.

'I have no evidence as such. But when I called to her house to collect her for her interview, she wasn't there. And when she did turn up, she was flustered and in pain.'

'In pain?'

'Clutching her arm, like this.' He demonstrated for her.

'Did she fall?'

'I don't know. She started to tell me, then clammed up. Mentioned the name Si.'

'Could be Simon Wallace, Stella's boyfriend. He doesn't live with them but does, if you catch my drift.'

Boyd said, 'Maybe he beat her up.'

'Why would he do that?'

He shrugged. 'When I told her that we knew she'd worked at the party, she immediately blamed David Crawley, the chef, for snitching.'

'But that's not what's bothering you.'

'I mentioned Brendan Healy, and she blanched, then denied knowing him.'

'Is that what's worrying you?'

'Yeah.'

Lottie paused, thinking. 'I still can't understand how Healy went to ground so quickly. He has to be somewhere. Drink your coffee. You need to be awake; you're coming to dinner with me at Annie Fleming's.'

'Really?'

'It's work, Boyd. We need to get as much information as possible.'

'I think we should organise someone to keep an eye on Maddy.'

'I doubt we can authorise it. She found the body, but we don't have any hard evidence to connect her to Ellen's death. Not yet, anyhow. Listen, I'll get Traffic to do a drive-by at her home every hour. That okay?'

'Okay.'

She watched him as he downed the strong coffee and felt in her heart that he wasn't okay at all. Maybe they should postpone the wedding. It wouldn't be easy, plus she really did want to marry him.

She'd watch him carefully over the next few hours and try to figure out what was going on.

When he put the cup down, she reached for his hand.

'We're going to be fine, Boyd.'

And she said a silent prayer that her words were true.

CHAPTER FORTY-TWO

'I don't know why we had to come out here for dinner,' Boyd grumbled. 'I hadn't even time for a proper shower. I swear to God my back is still wet and my shirt is stuck—'

'Will you stop complaining?' Lottie said. 'We might get lucky and discover information to help us progress our investigations.'

'You think?' Boyd sounded sceptical.

'I honestly don't know what to think. At least we'll get food. I meant to ask, did you reschedule your suit fitting?'

'Changing the subject doesn't work. Did you reschedule your hairstyling?'

Touché, she thought, and looked at him as he rang the bell on the impressive door of Molesworth House. 'Did you know you have a bump on your forehead?'

'Walked into a door.'

'Likely story.'

'It's true,' he said, rubbing a finger over the protrusion. 'Almost. Lottie, I'm wondering if we could have a word with the council. See if they can rehouse Maddy and her sister and the kids. Away from Simon.'

Lottie leaned over and pressed the bell again. 'You've a soft spot for that young one.'

'I just feel for her, living like that. She's a good kid.'

'You know nothing about her.'

The door opened before he could reply. A young woman Lottie hadn't met before stood in the bright light of the hallway.

'You must be the detectives,' she said.

'We've been called worse,' Boyd replied with a smile that transformed his face from the grouchy mask he'd sported seconds earlier. Lottie glared at him. How could he switch on such charm in an instant? After he'd introduced them both, they stepped into the hallway.

'I'm Tara, by the way. The forgotten child.'

'Really?' Boyd said, interest lighting up his eyes.

'Yeah.' She dropped her voice to a conspiratorial whisper. 'Mum and Jessica like to think I don't exist. You'll see for yourself over dinner. Come this way.'

Lottie was intrigued to know how Tara Fleming had received the wicked scar on her face. It would be impolite to enquire. Matthew had spoken glowingly of his daughter, so why did the young woman sound so disgruntled?

The dining room appeared to be catering for a party of twenty. Hopefully not, Lottie thought. The long mahogany table was dressed with fine bone china, silver and enough cutlery for fifteen courses, interspersed with large floral arrangements. The candelabra, each with ten candles burning brightly, could have come direct from Buckingham Palace.

Lottie whispered into Boyd's ear. 'Are they expecting the Queen?'

'Don't mind all this,' Tara said, waving her hand over the elaborate display. 'Mum likes to show off.'

A door opened at the opposite end of the palatial room and Annie Fleming floated towards them in a green sea of a dress. 'I'm so glad you came. Gives me a chance to show you all I've done with the house.'

'In case you hadn't noticed, Mum is proud of this monstrosity,' Tara said. She pulled out a velvet-backed chair and sat.

'That's not your seat,' Annie said. 'I've you placed further down.'

'I'm fine here. I'm bloody starving. Can we get this circus on the road?'

Annie flushed brightly. It was clear there was friction between mother and daughter. 'We have to wait for Jessica.'

Next to Annie, Lottie felt dowdy and frumpy in her black skinny jeans and white blouse. At least it was ironed, compliments of Rose. Maybe she should have robbed one of Chloe's party dresses. No, there was no point in turning up like mutton dressed as lamb. That was what Rose would say, thought Lottie, as she wondered about the dynamics at play in the Fleming household.

'Wine?' Annie asked, holding a crystal decanter.

'Not for me,' Boyd said. 'I'm driving.'

'I'd love a sparkling water,' Lottie said politely. She'd sworn off alcohol and preferred to avoid temptation.

'I'll have water too,' Boyd said.

'Tara, pet, would you fetch the water from the kitchen? And see what's keeping your sister.'

'Sure, if I have to.'

Lottie couldn't help but hear the falseness in both women's tones. When Tara had left, Annie poured herself a generous amount of red wine into a crystal goblet.

'Do you have staff in tonight?' Boyd said.

'Oh God, no. I can just about pay the casual staff at the restaurant. My girls will be doing the waiting tonight. I hope you like pheasant.'

Lottie glanced sideways at Boyd, who was nodding his head enthusiastically. 'I've never eaten it, but I love a challenge.'

'It's beautiful meat,' Annie said. 'Shot only yesterday. Shooting season is so short, which is a pity. But you're lucky it's on at the moment.'

Lottie wondered if she could ask for a cheese sandwich. She found Boyd eyeing her as if to say 'don't you dare'. Smiling, she turned to Annie. 'I'll try anything once.'

'Let's sit. The girls will be here in a minute. Have you made any progress on the murders?'

'We're working flat out,' Lottie said swiftly.

'That's good.' Annie sat at the head of the table, with Lottie and Boyd either side of her.

'You mentioned this morning, Annie, that you thought Matthew might have been involved in Rachel's death. Do you have any evidence to support that?'

'No. I was merely expressing a fear that my ex-husband might have been trying to jeopardise my shot at success. He's a vindictive bastard. Sorry if I spoke out of turn. I don't think even Matthew would go so far as to use murder to thwart my restaurant. Speaking of which, is there any word on when I can reopen? Did you find anything there to help your investigation?'

'I can't tell you anything about the case,' Lottie said, knowing that nothing had been found at the restaurant to prove Rachel had been poisoned there. 'But SOCOs have completed their work, and your property can be released back to you.'

'That's fantastic. I'll get Jessica to restart advertising, and she can call David to compile the menus.'

'How long have you known David Crawley?' Boyd asked.

'Forever.'

'Really?'

'No, that's a euphemism. David used to work in a hotel in town until recently. He left that job to join me. He's a good man.'

'Did he recommend the casual staff to you, or did you use an agency?' Lottie said, wondering how Maddy could have infiltrated herself in Stella's place.

Annie shrugged one shoulder. 'David knows everyone in the trade. He recommended the staff. We only needed a handful for the party.'

'Did he vet the staff or did you?'

'David and Jessica did. I have enough to be doing, as you can imagine.'

Lottie couldn't, but she said, 'I know Tara works for her dad, but does she help you out?'

For a moment Annie seemed at a loss as to how to respond, waving a hand in the air dismissively before saying, 'Tara works full-time with Matthew as his environmental officer. That's important in the quarry business nowadays. Her job takes her abroad a lot.'

Boyd said, 'Is that why she didn't turn up to support you on Monday night?'

'She was supposed to be on her way to London for a business meeting. Unfortunately she felt ill at the airport and returned home.'

'Home being here?' Boyd questioned.

'Tara has a room here and one in Matthew's house. She's finding it hard to settle at the moment.'

Lottie said, 'Why is that?'

'I prefer not to talk about it while Tara may be in earshot, but suffice to say she has suffered with her mental health over the years.'

Wanting to delve further but knowing the girl might walk in any moment, Lottie said, 'Annie, I asked you earlier today if you knew of Ellen Gormley. I've a feeling that you do know her.'

Annie sipped her wine slowly, then she put down the glass and looked squarely at Lottie, her tone even, her voice almost a whisper. 'I've heard of her, but I don't know her personally.'

'Could she have had some connection to your home here, to Molesworth House?'

'I have no idea, but I doubt it. She was just a therapist, wasn't she? Why do you ask?'

Lottie flattened her mouth as if what she was about to say was painful. She wanted to gauge Annie's reaction. 'Ellen Gormley drove out here on Saturday afternoon to have a look around. Apparently she was interested in the stables, and I've been told she seemed shocked that they'd been turned into cottages. Do you know anything about that?'

'Saturday? I'm sure I was in the restaurant all day, getting things ready for Monday night. You do know there's a public right of way across the land? Anyone can drive or walk around.'

Lottie tried to keep her tone even, though it was becoming increasingly difficult with Annie's haughtiness. 'But have you any idea why Ellen would want to see the stables? Was there anything special about them?'

'The stables were in as ruinous condition as the house was. I wanted to knock them to the ground, but as this is a listed building, the blasted council wouldn't allow it. So I turned them into self-catering cottages. I hope to be able to rent them out.'

'Ellen seemed to know something of the history and layout of the building.'

'Really?'

'That's what we've been led to believe. Has she a connection to your family apart from on a professional level?'

'What do you mean? I don't know her personally or professionally.'

Annie was so quick to pick up on things, Lottie knew she would be unable to trap her into disclosing information she preferred to keep locked away.

Deciding to be direct, she said, 'Ellen was last seen on Saturday, the day she drove around your property. I don't know if there is a relevant connection to your house or not, and I accept that coincidences happen, but I don't like them. They pose more questions than there are answers. I'd appreciate it if you could be totally honest with me at this stage.'

'I am being honest with you.' Another gulp of wine and the crystal glass was empty. Annie refilled it.

'Perhaps, but I think you're being economical with the truth,' Lottie persisted.

Annie lowered her head, her chin almost touching her chest, and chewed on her bottom lip. After a moment, she seemed to shake herself out of whatever fugue state she'd slipped into. She glanced over her shoulder at the door, then put a hand out and grabbed Lottie's fingers. 'Before my daughters arrive, I want to tell you something. It's strictly confidential. Can we agree on that?'

'It depends on what you tell me,' Lottie said, feeling her hand sweating under the other woman's chill fingers. She dared not look over at Boyd.

'I suppose I can't ask for much more.' Withdrawing her hand, Annie said, 'A number of years ago, Tara suffered a breakdown. She needed psychological care. Matthew heard about this psychologist, Ellen Gormley, and she treated Tara for twelve months or so.'

'Out here?'

'God, no. The house wasn't even finished then. But she sometimes brought Tara out here for a drive. For respite. To help her mind recover. Tara found the lake soothing. Perhaps Dr Gormley saw the work that was being carried out at the time, and maybe that's why she returned, as you said, looking for the stables.' Annie shrugged. 'I honestly don't know, and I shouldn't even be telling you. I'd appreciate it if you didn't mention it to Tara. She's still fragile.'

'Do you mind telling me what happened to leave her in such a state?'

Annie shook her head slowly. 'I'm not sure I …' She stopped as the door creaked open behind her, then plastered a smile on her face and stood to take the bottled water from Tara. Jessica followed her sister in, carrying a tray laden with what looked like roast chicken. Pheasant, Lottie reminded herself. Tara left the water, exited the room and returned with two dishes of veg and potatoes.

Annie dished up the food and they began to eat, cutlery clashing against white bone china. Lottie was no longer hungry. She noticed that Tara ate little, shoving her food around the plate like Sean did.

'Tara,' she said, 'I hear you weren't well Monday night and had to cancel your London trip.'

'That's right. A tummy bug.'

'Are you better now?'

'Almost.'

'And you came here from the airport that night?'

Tara nodded.

'What time was that?' Lottie pressed.

'Must have been around eleven.'

'I find it interesting that you came here rather than going to your father's house; I believe that's your primary residence.'

'You sound like a teacher I once had,' Tara said.

Jessica looked up from her plate. 'You skived off school half the time.'

'And whose fault was that?' Tara slammed her fork down.

'Oh, we are sensitive tonight,' Jessica sneered.

Tara touched her cheek and turned to Lottie. 'I had an accident when I was fifteen, and I missed a lot of school. That's what my sister is referring to.'

'Was it Jessica's fault?' Lottie chanced.

'How dare you?' Jessica said snappily.

'Girls, girls. Mind your manners in front of our guests. Apologise to the inspector.'

'Sorry,' Jessica said. Tara remained tight-lipped.

Lottie decided to continue now that Tara seemed rattled. 'You were a patient of Dr Gormley's. How long did your therapy last?'

'Really? You can sit there and ask me about a private health matter? I take offence at you even bringing up the subject.' Tara folded her arms across her chest, but Lottie caught Annie staring disapprovingly in her direction.

'The reason I'm asking is that Ellen was out here last Saturday. Looking for the stables.'

'The stables?' Tara's face paled and she shot an anxious look over at her sister.

'Do you know what significance, if any, they held for her?'

'How ... how would I know that? We had a strictly professional relationship.' Tara balled up her napkin, pushed back her chair and stood. 'I don't think I've fully shaken off the bug. Excuse me. I'm going to bed.'

As she made for the door, Annie said, 'Tara, bring your plate with you and then help clear the table. You and Jessica can stack the dishwasher. Lottie, let's take a walk outside before dessert.'

'Fresh air would be nice,' Lottie said, thinking an industrial fan couldn't shift the uneasy feeling that had settled in the room. She turned to Boyd. 'Are you coming?'

'I'll pass, if you don't mind.'

She did mind but threw him a weak smile as she thought of the conversation that had just transpired. Tara Fleming had catapulted herself onto Lottie's shortlist of suspects.

CHAPTER FORTY-THREE

'I'd like to see the cottages,' Lottie said as she stepped outside with Annie.

The sky was black, but the rain had eased, leaving a smell not unlike decomposition rising from the concrete footpaths. Overhead, a bird flapped its wings in alarm and flew off. The only other sound was the wind on the lake and the distant hum of traffic over on the main road.

'You've done a fantastic job on the house. It looks great,' she said as they moved away from it.

Annie lit a cigarette and walked along a cobbled pathway that skirted around the side of the house.

Lottie inhaled the cigarette smoke, taking a good hit, and dismissed the idea of asking for one. No point in resuming that habit again. She had to duck her head for a few moments beneath a canopy of bushes sheltering the path. Once they emerged on the other side, the grounds opened up in an expanse of lawn, wet from the day's rain and dotted with clumps of wild flowers. Lamps embedded in the path lit the way.

'Beautiful, isn't it?' Annie said. 'Natural flora and fauna. We reclaimed the land with the house. The cottages are this way.'

Lottie looked back at the house, lit up like a Christmas tree. She seemed to recall from her childhood, when she'd been brought out to the lake, a ruin with no roof and numerous chimney stacks jutting skywards.

They wound their way along the path.

'Did it cost much to refurbish the estate?' Might as well be bold, Lottie thought.

'A lot,' Annie said, surreptitiously, inhaling deeply on her cigarette. She blew out smoke and added, 'The council insisted on retaining the historic nature of the place. They dug out old paintings and a couple of faded black-and-white photos that demonstrated its past grandeur. I'm glad now, because it will work well for small civil ceremonies. I have great plans for Molesworth House as well as for my restaurant.'

They had reached an arc of stone cottages in a courtyard. Annie approached the nearest one and doused her cigarette in an ashtray situated at the door. She took a key card from her pocket and slid it into the lock. Pushing open the heavy wooden door, she waited for Lottie to step inside ahead of her.

'These were stables? You've done a massive job.'

'Molesworth was a stud farm in the thirties. My great-grandfather owned it, actually, but he went bankrupt. The estate was handed down through the generations until I inherited it.'

'You must be proud of your achievement.'

Annie leaned against the wall and folded her arms. 'I've been privileged in life, but my separation from Matthew broke me. However, between the house and the restaurant, good things were happening until the death of that girl.' She began walking around the rustic living room, trailing her hand along the stonework with pride.

Lottie digested her words. 'It must have cost you a fortune,' she said eventually.

'My family were once wealthy.' There was a shard of annoyance in Annie's tone.

'Not any more, then?'

'My grandfather was a gambler and lost his shirt, as the saying goes. But my father worked tirelessly to keep the estate in the family name. Then I married a wealthy but stupid man. Events occurred that forced me to separate from Matthew.' Her eyes twinkled dangerously. 'If we get divorced, I am due very little. I'm up to my ears in bank loans. I cut some corners, literally. The stone used in places where the old walls had crumbled came from one of Matthew's quarries. That makes me smile. The irony of it.'

'It's a great job,' Lottie said, thinking she was repeating herself a lot.

Annie opened the door, and a gust of wind entered, blasting wet leaves along the stone floor. Lottie shook her shoulders into professional mode, ready to ask what might have disturbed Ellen about the old stables, but before she could pose the question, the night air was pierced by a scream from the big house.

*

Feeling awkward in Jessica's presence, after Annie and Lottie left, Boyd sipped his water. He wished he had a bottle of Heineken in his hand. There was something unnerving about the beautiful young woman clearing the plates from the table.

'Are you looking forward to getting back to working in the restaurant?'

'I don't work in it, I manage it.' Jessica's voice was as sharp as the knife she brandished before clattering it on top of the pile of dishes.

'That's what I meant.' Boyd vowed not to be intimidated by a girl twenty years his junior. 'Can you sit for a moment? I'd like to chat.'

'I'm sure you get enough chat in your boring job.'

'My job is far from boring,' he said. 'I'm not long back from sick leave, if you want to know.'

She placed the dishes on a tray but didn't lift it. She sat and clasped her hands around a glass of wine. 'I hope you're okay now.'

'I'm getting there.'

'You work with Sam, don't you? I'd love to know more about him.'

'Sam?'

'Detective McKeown.'

Boyd squinted in puzzlement. 'Why are you asking about him?'

'He called out to interview me yesterday. I was half hoping he might have come back tonight for dinner with the inspector. We got on really well. He was so nice.'

Boyd thought of the back-biting that went on between McKeown and Kirby. Nice? Mmm. Interesting.

'Did he give you his number?'

'He did.'

'If I were you, I'd give him a call then.' He wasn't sure Lottie would agree with this, but it might be a way to extract information from Jessica.

'That could be construed as being a bit forward.' She lowered her eyelids.

Boyd smiled. 'Jessica, what are you really after?'

'Is he married?'

He wasn't sure how to answer. The truth was, he knew very little about McKeown. 'He hasn't been based in Ragmullin all that long.'

'And?'

'I don't know much about him.'

'Pity.' Jessica drained her glass and stood, taking up the tray of dirty dishes. 'Detective Boyd, what are *you* after?'

He smiled. She'd turned his own question on him. 'I was wondering if you can tell me anything about your father and Rachel?'

'I knew you stayed back for a reason.' Jessica returned his smile and he was unsure if it was sincere or not. 'I have nothing to tell, though Tara might know. I'll bring this lot to the kitchen and see if she's feeling any better. She might talk to you.'

'That's great. Thanks.'

'No problem.'

'By the way, do you know Maddy Daly?'

'Who is she?'

'She worked at the party on Monday night.'

Jessica squinted, thinking. 'I think there was a Stella Daly on the list. Don't remember a Maddy, though. Where is she from?'

'Ragmullin.'

'Sorry, don't recognise the name.'

'Grand, so.' Boyd patted his pocket for cigarettes he no longer smoked.

At the door, Jessica glanced over her shoulder at him before exiting the room.

After a few minutes sitting alone, he wondered if she had been checking to make sure he wasn't following her. He hoped Lottie wouldn't be long, because he was knackered.

That was when he heard the scream.

It was coming from downstairs. He flew down to the kitchen, where he found Tara sitting on the floor holding a hand aloft, blood dripping down her arm.

'She's insane,' Jessica yelled.

'What happened?' Boyd asked.

Jessica curled her lip. 'Bitch attacked me, and I fought back.'

He pulled a tea towel from a hook and knelt beside Tara. 'Keep it raised,' he told her. 'Jessica, do you have a first aid kit?'

'I'm not sure,' she said.

'Would you mind looking?'

He wound the tea towel around Tara's hand while her sister opened and shut cupboard doors.

'Are you okay?' he asked.

'Feel faint,' Tara said.

'Stay on the floor a little longer. I might be able to stem the bleeding, but I think you should go to the hospital.' Looking around for Jessica, he said, 'Any sign of that kit?'

She returned from the pantry with a red box. Boyd opened it and cleaned Tara's hand with an antiseptic wipe. 'It's deep. How did you do it?'

'We were loading the dishwasher,' Jessica said, staring hard into her sister's eyes. 'Somehow she cut herself with the carving knife.'

'I thought you said she attacked you?'

'I made a mistake.'

Boyd stared at Jessica for a moment before returning his attention to Tara. He caught a slight nod of her head and noticed a pink hue return to her face. What was going on between these two? he wondered. It was obvious Jessica was lying, but he hadn't time to investigate further.

'Will I call a doctor?' Jessica asked.

'No!' Tara was adamant.

'It's okay,' Boyd said. 'Stay calm. There are steri-strips here. I'll stick on a couple.' When he'd finished, he wrapped a bandage around the injured hand, fastening it with two plasters. 'There you are now.'

'Thanks,' Tara said, her voice weaker than the forcefulness of a moment ago.

The door burst open and Annie and Lottie rushed in.

'What happened?' Annie said.

Jessica trotted out the dishwasher story. Boyd noticed Tara drop her eyelids. Had something occurred between the sisters, causing one to lash out at the other?

Lottie moved forward and leaned down beside him. 'You've done a good job.'

'Dear God almighty,' Annie said. 'Shall I bring her to A&E?'

Boyd noticed she hadn't approached Tara but had remained standing just inside the door.

'He put steri-strips on the cut,' Jessica said, nodding towards Boyd before turning to finish loading the dishwasher. 'She's going to be just fine. As usual. Drama queen.'

'I need a drink,' Annie said, opening a cupboard. She found a bottle of brandy and a tumbler.

Boyd helped Tara to her feet. Something wasn't right here. He could feel it in his bones. 'I'll accompany you to your room. Is that all right with you?'

'I'm fine. I can walk,' she said, hiding a stumble.

'I don't think so. Here, let me link you.' He was surprised when she acquiesced to his request.

As they left the kitchen, Lottie leaned into his ear and whispered, 'See what you can get out of her.'

CHAPTER FORTY-FOUR

'Leave that alone for tonight,' Annie said sharply as Jessica banged plates into the dishwasher.

Jessica thumped the dishwasher door closed. 'Right, so. I'm off to my room.'

Annie sat at the table and Lottie wasn't sure what to do with herself. It was late and she had to get home to Sean. Chloe would have left for work. And she needed to talk to Rose about Ellen Gormley, but that would have to wait until tomorrow. Plus there were all the things on her wedding to-do list before Saturday morning. She silently groaned.

'Sit,' Annie said.

Lottie pulled out a chair. 'I was wondering if you could tell me more about the event that caused Tara to need therapy.'

'It was a long time ago, and honestly, Lottie, I prefer not to talk about it. It has nothing to do with your cases.'

Lottie was not to be deterred that easily. 'Dr Gormley came out here the day before we believe she was murdered. She was interested in the stables and according to a witness she seemed upset when she couldn't find them. The only connection I can make between Ellen and that visit is your daughter Tara.'

Annie took a pack of cigarettes from her dress pocket and placed it on the table. She tapped a long nail on it as if fighting an urge.

'There's only eleven months between Tara and Jessica.'

'Matthew told me that,' Lottie said.

'They were so close as youngsters.'

'But that's no longer so?'

Annie shook her head. 'When she was about nine or ten years old, Tara changed. It was so dramatic; it happened overnight. One day she was fun-loving and cheerful. The next, she wouldn't talk to anyone. Stayed in her room. Wouldn't eat for a week. Eventually I talked her round, but she was never the same.'

'What brought about this change in her?'

'I have no idea. She refused to tell us what was wrong. Things improved for a while. But Matthew, he couldn't cope with her, so when she was about to start secondary level, he decided to send her to boarding school.'

'How did that work out?'

'Terrible. She retreated into herself and refused to study, so we had no choice but to bring her home. We enrolled her in Jessica's school.'

'In Ragmullin?'

'Yes. They both finished school and went to college. And then her father offered Tara a job. I was sure she'd refuse. I think Matthew was even more stunned than I was when she accepted. And then … then she had another breakdown.'

'What caused it?'

Annie shrugged. 'She refused to discuss it.'

'Is that when Matthew got Ellen involved?'

'Yes, and she helped immensely. I wasn't privy to what they discussed in their sessions, but after a year, Tara told her dad she didn't need Dr Gormley any more.'

'Where were these sessions held?'

'Ellen had a private practice at her home. But as part of the therapy she would sometimes take Tara around the estate, as I mentioned earlier.'

Though it seemed unorthodox, Lottie assumed Ellen was trying to get Tara to deal with her childhood trauma. 'Do you think something happened to Tara here when she was young? In the stables?'

'Good God, no. This place was a ruin back then. We all used to live where Matthew now resides.'

There went her theory, then. 'That was your family home, where the girls grew up?'

'Yes.'

'Can I ask how Tara got her scar?'

Annie puffed out her perfect cheeks. 'Lottie, I'm at a loss to know how this conversation has anything to do with your murder investigations. These are private matters.'

Feeling tired, her head muggy, Lottie had no energy to pursue the conversation. 'Okay. One final thing. How did Matthew find Dr Gormley for Tara?'

Annie shook her head. 'I've no idea, but it's one of the few things he's done that I'm grateful for.'

*

Boyd felt as weak as Tara looked after climbing the stairs. He wondered if perhaps she should have gone to the hospital to be checked over. The cut on her hand was deep, but the steri-strips had stemmed the blood.

She stood outside a closed door that was taller than he was, almost touching the corridor ceiling. The house was huge, he thought. 'Are you okay now?'

'I'll be fine,' she said, opening the door. She stepped inside. 'Thanks for helping me.'

'Part of the service,' he said with a bow.

She laughed, and the upward curve of her butterfly lips lit her face like a beacon. 'You're very chivalrous in a time when it's in short supply.'

255

He liked the timbre of her voice. Soft and soothing. 'I hope you sleep well.'

Glancing inside, he saw a large bed covered with a plain quilt. On top of it were a plethora of teddies and dolls. Catching his look, she said, 'A throwback to my childhood. For some reason, I can't let go of that time.'

'A time of innocence?' he ventured.

She laughed, and it sounded child-like. 'My early days were even less innocent than my later years.'

'Why was that?'

'Oh, you'd need a career break to listen to my woes.'

'Lottie tells me I'm a good listener.'

'Are you and Lottie ... you know ...'

'We're getting married on Saturday.' Two more days, he thought with a smile.

'Congratulations. At least I know someone who's happy. I wish I could feel that emotion.'

'Care to talk about it?'

She ushered him into the room. He crossed the threshold, leaving the door open. She grabbed an armful of dolls from a low chair before dropping them on the floor. 'Take a seat.'

'Why are you unhappy?' He tried to make himself comfortable, folding his tall frame awkwardly into the low chair.

Tara sat on the edge of her bed, a sad-looking teddy bear in her hand. 'I think I was always the underdog in this family. Nothing I did was ever right. Not for my mother, anyhow. Have you any siblings?'

'A sister. Grace.'

'Nice name. You must know what sibling rivalry can be like.'

He didn't, because he and Grace were never rivals, the age gap too large, but he had seen something of it flare now and again between Katie and Chloe, Lottie's daughters.

'Tell me what it was like growing up.' He wasn't sure if this had anything whatsoever to do with anything, but it never hurt to get the backstory of potential witnesses and suspects.

'Jessica was always the brightest, the quickest, the wittiest in our family. I became something of a shadow. It's hard to break out from that. I tried. All my life I tried so hard, but I always ended up being the one who suffered the punishment.'

'Punishment for what?'

'Oh, kids' stuff. But the thing is, Jessica never got blamed, even when it was her fault. Once, when I was aged about ten, we had friends round. It got a bit boisterous over tea and the table was upended. Crockery smashed, food everywhere. I got walloped for it, but it was Jessica who had deliberately leaned on the side of the table she knew was unstable and made the whole thing collapse.'

'That's a bit mean, all right.'

'Yeah.' She dropped her eyes and squeezed the teddy tightly while nursing her cut hand to her chest. Then she smiled crookedly. 'Don't worry, one day I'll get my revenge.'

Boyd sensed that the story she'd told might actually be the other way around. He wasn't sure he believed her.

'You and Jessica aren't exactly friends, then?'

'Nope.'

'Do you have any friends?'

Her eyes filled with tears, and she bit down on her lip, forcing them away. 'I've had a few over the years, but I'm perfectly able to fend for myself now.'

'You remind me of a young girl I know. She has to fend for herself too. I think you'd be good for each other.' Boyd had no idea why he was saying this. Maddy and Tara were from completely different worlds, but there was something similar about them.

'I'm not a good Samaritan if that's what you're thinking,' she said.

Boyd felt heat burn his cheeks at his inappropriate suggestion. Lottie would have his guts for garters if she knew. 'Actually, forget I said that.'

'I never forget. So tell me, who is this girl?'

Where was the harm? he thought. Anyway, he wanted to see if Tara knew her. 'Have you ever met Maddy Daly?'

Tara scrunched up her nose like a child, thinking. 'Name doesn't ring a bell. Who is she?'

'She was one of the casual workers at your mother's restaurant party on Monday night.'

'I wasn't there. I was at the airport.'

'I'm only asking if—'

'No need to get stroppy.' She threw the teddy on the bed and curled her legs beneath her. 'Do you want me to make friends with her or something?'

'Not at all. Look, I'm sorry for mentioning her. I thought you might know her, that's all.'

'Okay.'

'What's it like working for your father?'

'Better than working for my mother.' She laughed. 'Dad is a pussycat. I can basically do what I like and ask for whatever I want. He never says a thing. There's no inquisition like with my mother.'

'She seems to be a hard taskmaster.'

'Don't get me wrong, Dad is a tough cookie too, but I can navigate my way around him.' She narrowed her eyes, vixen-like.

'What do you mean?'

'It's nothing.'

But Boyd knew it wasn't nothing. 'Tell me.'

'Are you trying to be my friend now?' She donned her child-like manner again.

'I don't like to see you unhappy.' He didn't like unhappiness in anyone.

'You don't know me.'

'That's true, but I can read your expression. What happened to you, Tara? What has made your life so sad?'

Her laugh didn't reach her eyes. 'You sound like Dr Gormley.'

'I never knew her,' Boyd said. 'What was she like?'

Tara picked up the discarded teddy again. 'She was okay, I suppose. Didn't say much. Wanted me to do all the talking. Sometimes we sat for the whole hour in silence. She still got paid. But it was kind of relaxing, you know, to be able to sit without having to say a word. That silence would drive my mother insane. She always has to be talking.'

'Dr Gormley had patience with you where your mother didn't?'

'I guess. Some days when she knew I didn't really want to be there, she'd get the car out and we'd go for a drive. Sometimes we'd come out here.'

'Did she seem to know the house, even though it used to be a ruin?'

'Yeah, suppose so. She said the lake was therapeutic. Not that we went down to it much. Once I suggested taking a boat out, but she nearly had a canary. She seemed to be afraid of the water. After that, we just walked around.'

'Was there any particular area that interested her?'

'She liked wandering around the stables.'

'How long since you met with Ellen?'

Tara shrugged. 'A while. A year, maybe.'

'Why did you finish the therapy?'

'My hand is sore. I think I need a painkiller.'

'Tara, I'll leave now but can you answer the question?'

She sighed long and deep. 'Mother said Daddy was wasting his money on a quack and that the therapy was doing me no good. It's all about money with her. Anyway, after a heated argument between them, I felt it was time to move on, so I cancelled my next session and never went back.'

'Do you know if either of your parents attended Dr Gormley themselves?'

'Are you kidding me? Mother wouldn't tell anyone her innermost secrets, least of all Ellen.'

'Why do you say that?'

'She hated her. Hated that I could speak freely with her. I think she was afraid of what I might tell her.'

'And was there something in particular your mother didn't want you talking about?'

Tara clamped her lips together and shook her head.

'Please, Tara, tell me.'

'I'm tired. I want to go to sleep.'

'Is it to do with something that happened to you when you were young?'

'I'm done talking for tonight. If you want me to meet this Maddy creature who you think is like me, then leave me her number and I'll chat with her.' She stood and kicked off her shoes. Boyd's cue to leave.

'Thanks for talking so candidly,' he said. He scribbled Maddy's number on his card and left it on the bed. He hoped this wasn't going to make its way back to Lottie. Then he had a worse thought. Could he have just put Maddy in danger? Shit. Too late. Tara was punching the number into her phone. 'Call me any time, okay?'

'Right. Thanks.'

As he left, he noticed her scrolling through her phone.

CHAPTER FORTY-FIVE

The clap of thunder seemed to rattle the few pieces of furniture in her bedroom. The mirror standing in a wooden frame on the dresser shattered as the front door banged downstairs. Seven years' bad luck, Maddy thought, and tugged the sheet up to her chin. A flash of lightning lit up the room as the rain drummed incessantly against the window. She ducked further down in her bed. A tear escaped from the corner of her eye and her entire body shook, the pain in her swollen and bruised arm excruciating. Her teeth chattered as if they were false, and another clap of thunder rocked the room.

Then, the pitter-patter of soft footsteps.

'Maddy, I'm scared.'

She pushed up in the bed. Little Trey was standing in the open doorway.

'Come here, pet.'

He ran over and jumped in beside her, landing on her sore arm. She bit down a scream but was unable to halt the flow of tears.

'No cry, Maddy,' he said, wrapping his arms around her neck. 'Trey mind Maddy.'

'It's okay, pet. I have to go downstairs for a pill because I have a bad pain in my arm. I need you to keep the bed warm. Can you do that?'

'Okay.' His eyes were already drooping with sleep as she slipped out of the room.

She heard Simon prowling around in the sitting room downstairs and hoped she could get in and out of the kitchen without disturbing him. Passing Stella's room, she heard the baby crying. Stella shushing her. Normal sounds. But these were not normal times. Was the pain making her delirious?

Creeping past the sitting room, she hurried into the kitchen and began rooting around in a drawer for paracetamol. As her fingers closed around an empty blister pack, she smelled him moving up behind her. She swung round. 'Stay away from me, Simon.'

'Who bit you on the arse?'

'I mean it.' She looked down to find she was brandishing a bread knife. Definitely delirious.

'Did you hear the thunder?' he said.

'Course I heard it. I'm not deaf. My arm hurts. I need paracetamol.' The ibuprofen the pharmacy had supplied her with were useless.

'I can give you something stronger. Wait there a minute.'

As he disappeared through the doorway with no door, she realised what he meant. Was he really into drug dealing? Stella should kick him out for good. The children! Oh God, she thought. Well, he could feck off if he thought he was getting her hooked on crack like half the town.

'Hey, Simon, keep it. I can suffer till morning.' She heard her phone vibrate on the floor above her head.

Back upstairs she saw that Trey was asleep and her phone had travelled under the bed with the vibration. She dragged it towards her through the dust and stared at the screen. It was a text.

YOUR SECRET IS NOT SAFE.

What the hell, she thought as the room lit up once again, quickly followed by the loudest clap of thunder yet. The rain continued, relentless.

*

After phoning her son to make sure he'd eaten dinner and finished his homework, Lottie sat in the car beside Boyd as he drove, and they filled each other in on their conversations with the Fleming women.

'It's too late to be calling on Matthew Fleming,' he said.

'Two women have been killed in their own homes. Someone had to be watching them. Checking out their schedules. Stalking them.'

'Brendan Healy has a history of stalking, allegedly,' Boyd said.

'He still hasn't been found, so we have to keep him on our radar.'

'Okay. I should have asked Tara and Jessica if they knew him.'

'Next time, don't forget. And tomorrow, check out if Tara actually had a flight booked to London on Monday night, and see if we can place her at the airport. Just in case.' Lottie yawned. 'I'm not sure what to think about Brendan Healy. He ran when we tried to interview him, but here's the thing. There was no sign of a break-in at the Mullen house and I doubt Rachel would have let him in, especially if he'd once stalked her.'

'We have no official report of the stalking even though Beth thought there should have been. Someone got into that house, somehow,' Boyd said. 'Perhaps if she'd had too much to drink, she might have opened the door. We do have a couple of witnesses from the party who thought she seemed either drunk or high.'

'She might have been just exhausted.'

'I'd really like to know why Healy ran when we tried to question him.'

'I agree. It made him look guilty. Maybe he's hiding something unrelated to Rachel's murder. Oh, I don't know, Boyd. This has been such a long day.'

'Yes, and like I said, it's way too late to be paying Matthew Fleming a visit.'

263

Lottie sighed loudly. 'Do you want to go home, then? You look tired. You don't want to overdo it. I can postpone this visit until tomorrow.' She glanced at Boyd. He looked worn out. His cheeks were cavernous and his eyes lacked the sparkle that had returned since his cancer treatment. She should be looking after him. Not making him drive the back roads of the county after a long day.

'I'll be fine,' he said. 'We're almost there, anyway.'

He took a right off the main road and negotiated the car up a narrow, winding lane that was little more than a dirt track with grass growing up through the tarmac. Matthew Fleming's house loomed in the arc of the headlights before Boyd switched them off.

Once she was out of the car, Lottie pulled up her hood. It did little to ward off the rain ricocheting against the ground like a volley of bullets. Wind whistled through the overhanging bare branches as she looked up at the creepy stone structure that Matthew Fleming called home. Gargoyles glared down from the walls, stained black from years of neglect. The windows were dark, like sightless eyes, except for one, which seemed to wink at her. She almost slipped on the green algae-like substance covering the tiled step of the porch. It was hard to believe this was the house where Annie and their daughters had lived before the separation.

She knocked loudly on the heavy door, smelling a distinct odour in the air.

'There's thunder and lightning on the way again,' she said with a sniff.

'Is your twitching nose telling you that?' Boyd said.

She nodded with a smile just as the heavens crashed loudly, rattling them both. The door opened silently on well-oiled hinges.

'Good evening, Mr Fleming,' Lottie said, needlessly flashing her ID badge. 'Can we come in, please?'

Fleming was dressed casually, thick tan cords hanging loosely on his hips. His mop of hair dripped moisture and his white shirt clung to his chest in damp patches. He held his phone in his hand but quickly pocketed it when he recognised his visitors.

'I'm not sure that's a good idea. Didn't I ask you to communicate through my solicitor?'

'You did, but I've just come from Annie's house and there are a few things I'd like to discuss urgently.'

He sighed loudly. 'I'm intrigued as to what Annie has been saying about me this time. You can come in for five minutes.'

He led them through a narrow hallway, at odds with the vastness of the exterior, and into what Lottie knew Rose would describe as a drawing room. Dark red leather armchairs stood either side of a stone fireplace. She smelled the smoke as it expelled in a down-draught from the chimney. A flash of lightning lit up the furniture in ghostly silhouettes, even though Fleming had switched the lights on.

'Can I offer you coffee? Something stronger?'

'No thanks,' Lottie said, answering for both of them.

'Take a seat. It's very unorthodox, calling to my home at this hour of the night, but I'm led to believe that's how you operate, Detective Inspector Parker.'

'Look, Mr Fleming, I know we got off on the wrong foot, but I need to talk to you about your daughter Tara.'

'You need to communicate through my solicitor.'

He was like the proverbial broken record. Lottie said quickly, 'I'd prefer it if you could speak to me. I'm interested in her relationship with Dr Ellen Gormley.'

'Why? Surely you don't think my daughter killed her therapist?'

'I don't know what to think, if I'm being brutally honest. I need facts.' She folded her arms. 'What happened to Tara when she was younger?'

'What are you talking about?'

'Annie told us—'

'Of course she spun lies about me. She's out to ruin me. Vindictive bitch.'

'Why don't you tell me the truth, then?'

'It was an accident.'

'What was?'

'At the quarry. Nothing I could do about it then and nothing I can do about it now.'

Lottie glanced over at Boyd. What was Fleming on about? Boyd cocked his head to one side. He hadn't a clue either.

'Which quarry?'

'It's adjacent to my land. It's no longer operational. Never was really. There were too many other functional quarries that I owned. Busy times.'

'Explain,' she said.

'He shouldn't have been anywhere near it, but boys being boys, he was.'

'I'm at a loss to know what you're talking about.'

Fleming blew out his cheeks, then paused, picking his words carefully. 'A young lad drowned in the stagnant water that had gathered in the quarry after a week's rain. Tara heard his cries. She ran out in her nightclothes, down the field. She almost fell into the abyss herself. Annie, or maybe it was Jessica, followed her and grabbed her just in time. I believe Tara saw the body in the water.'

'When was this?' Lottie wondered how Tara could have seen anything if it had been night-time.

'A long time ago. Nine or ten years now. Tara was about fifteen. Her old room faced the quarry across the field. She must have had the window open that night, because she heard the cries.'

'Where were you?'

'I wasn't at home.'

'And this was what caused Tara to need therapy?'

'I think it was part of it. Don't get me wrong, she was okay for a while. Just quiet and broody, like she was that time when she went into herself aged nine or ten. A stint in boarding school cured that upset. But following the quarry incident, I believe she cut herself – you've seen her scar, haven't you? After that, she seemed to internalise the trauma. It was only in her early twenties that it manifested itself again. That's when I got her into therapy.'

'Were the guards called out to the drowning?'

'Of course. There was a full investigation. Ruled as an accident or misadventure or something like that.'

'Did the quarry shut down?'

'It had already been closed at that stage.' He folded his arms. Defensive? Lottie wondered.

'What was the boy's name?'

'I can't remember it now, but it has nothing to do with your murders and my family have nothing to do with them either. You are way out of line trying to involve us.'

'I will be the judge of that.' She was thinking that it might have everything to do with Tara's current state of mind. 'Why would Ellen have brought Tara out to Molesworth House for some of her therapy sessions?'

'I don't know.'

'Did you know Ellen before you referred Tara to her?'

'She was a local woman. I would have known about her and her practice.'

'Any idea why she would have had an interest in the old stables at Molesworth?'

He pursed his lips. 'I don't know. Ask Annie. She seems to know everything.'

A puff of wind blew more smoke down the chimney. The smell irritated Lottie's nose, making her sneeze. She found a crumpled tissue in her pocket and blew her nose, then continued.

'Mr Fleming, two women have been murdered in the cruellest and most painful way. I need you to be honest with us.'

'I had nothing to do with either of them.'

She smothered a sarcastic laugh. 'On the contrary. You had a meeting with Rachel Mullen just hours before she was killed, and she was a teenage friend of your daughters. In relation to Dr Gormley, you referred your daughter to her a few years ago. There is a connection to you and your family whether you care to admit it or not.'

He stood with his bony back to the smoky fireplace. 'There could be a crazed killer out there stalking his next victim while you continue to victimise me and my family. It'd serve you better to do proper police work instead of intimidating innocents.'

'With all due respect,' Lottie said, 'I believe that if there is a tangible link to you, I will find it.'

'You do that. In the meantime, I request that you leave both me and my family alone. I will see you out.'

CHAPTER FORTY-SIX

Andy Ashe had two pints following a hard day at work then decided to swing round by Hazel's apartment. As much as she annoyed him, he was a little concerned that she hadn't been on the phone barking orders all day. It was unusual, to say the least. She never allowed an opportunity pass to let her staff know that she was in control, even when she wasn't.

At the turn for her complex, he lit a cigarette, shielding it from the spills of rain, then leaned against the wall and wondered at the logic of his actions. There wasn't a snowball's chance in hell that she would come visiting him if he'd rung in sick. No, she'd just make his life hell for missing work. So why was he bothering? He couldn't come up with an answer, his brain was dimmed with alcohol after a manic day on the shop floor. But something was tugging at him.

'Feck it,' he said aloud, and stamped the half-smoked cigarette into a puddle. A clap of thunder crashed overhead. He pulled up his hood, which offered him little respite from the torrential rain. If she doesn't answer, feck her again, he thought.

At her door, he knocked and waited. Nothing.

He put his lips to the letter box and shouted, 'Hazel, it's Andy. Just checking to see if you need anything.'

Silence.

He crouched, trying to see through the rectangular opening. But the letter box was fitted with brushes that stopped him from seeing a thing.

'Hazel? Are you okay?'

Silence. Not even the hum of a television. Probably asleep. Well, he'd done his bit.

But some internal warning system brought him around the side of her apartment. Just to make sure. He stood on the small square patio and put his hands up to the glass door. Pitch dark inside.

As he made his way out of the complex, he wondered if he should knock again. No, it was better if he minded his own business. She never did anything for him, did she?

Maybe another pint before he hit the hay. He still felt a pang of guilt. Tomorrow, if she wasn't at work, he'd call back to see if she needed anything. But for tonight, Andy Ashe felt he'd done more than enough for the bitch who made his life one long streak of misery.

*

The killer sat like a marble statue. Unmoving. Eyes unblinking, staring straight ahead in the darkness they had become accustomed to. The man's voice died away, as did the knocking on the door. Finally they were alone once more.

It had been a nuisance having to dip in and out of Hazel's apartment. Just as well they had cut a key from the spare Hazel kept hidden. The dose mustn't have been quite right. She had taken a long time to die. And it was so risky coming back like that. Someone could have seen them. But the risk was also adding such a high!

It was time to leave. The killer had things to do out in the real world that meant they could only come in and out at certain times. But now they were happy to have witnessed the struggle of her final breath being inhaled without another exhalation. The woman was dead.

With this, the killer experienced another kind of high. Sitting and watching was part of the game. A truly satisfying contest, though it was a one-sided event. It was not active or physical, more akin to sitting in a court chamber watching justice being meted out to the defendant. Innocent until proven guilty? Not in the killer's mind. They were all guilty from the time they had kept their lips sealed and their voices silent. Now they were silent for eternity.

The killer felt a slow smile crossing their face, and their chest cavity filled with pride, followed by a rush of adrenaline not unlike a sexual climax. Oh, it was good, so good. No! It was bloody brilliant. This was one thing they'd mastered and become skilled at. These actions might appear crazy to others, but they knew what they were doing. A sense of pride took hold of the killer as they stood up. Yes, this was so good.

Why did they have to exist in the so-called real world? This was as real and pure as anything they had ever experienced.

When the guilty one had finally arched and silently screamed, the killer had performed the final act. Inserting the piece of glass, broken from the old mirror.

It had been a successful hunt so far, but now that it was nearing a climax, the killer was not sure they could stop. They had been so precise and exact in all the deaths; why should they give up now?

CHAPTER FORTY-SEVEN

Lottie kissed Boyd goodnight, soft and lingering, then waved him off.

Inside, her house was quiet. She climbed the stairs and peeked in at Sean, surprised to see him already asleep rather than at his night-time ritual of online gaming. She needed to spend more time with him. Her son was a deep soul and she never knew what he was thinking. At least he had given her his blessing to marry Boyd. Sean loved Boyd. They got on so well together. It would be good for him to have a father figure in his life.

Chloe was not yet home. Back down in the kitchen, Lottie kicked off her boots and sat at the table, trying to clear her head before she went to bed.

There was a multitude of yellow Post-its laid out on the table. Chloe's wedding organisation. Idly, Lottie flicked through them. No, her mind was too full of questions about the two murder victims without clouding her brain with flowers, guests, hair and all that stuff. She searched for the Post-it pad, intent on writing up a few notes on the investigation, but when she found it, she couldn't locate a pen or pencil.

'Enough,' she told the empty room. Sleep was what she needed.

She realised she was sitting with her jacket still on, so she tore it off and debated having a quick shower but thought it might wake her up. She got up from the table and switched off the light. In the hall, she heard a key turn in the door. Chloe.

'Shift finished?' she asked.

'Yeah. Bit dead tonight. Have you seen the weather? Non-stop rain. Though there was a guy in talking shite. Mentioned you and Kirby.'

'Really? Who was it?'

'Andy something or other. Not a regular. Going on about his boss being a bitch and leaving him in the shit. He sounded drunk and angry.' Chloe hung her coat on the banister and kicked off her wet boots. She hauled her bag off her shoulder and fished out her phone.

'We interviewed an Andy Ashe as a witness in our investigation,' Lottie said, half to herself. 'Probably pissed off about it.'

'Did you go over the lists I left on the table for you?' Chloe said, halfway up the stairs.

'Yes,' Lottie lied. 'You have it all under control. Thank you.'

'Are you looking forward to Saturday?'

'I honestly can't wait,' Lottie said truthfully.

'Me too. Who's picking up Katie and Louis from the airport Friday morning?'

'Mmm …' Shit, she hadn't made any arrangements. 'Do you think we could ask Granny to do it?'

'Mam! Granny finds it hard to negotiate the straight road into town these days. It's okay. Leave it with me. I might know someone who'll do it.'

'And who might that be?' Lottie looked up the stairs at her departing daughter. Even after her evening shift in the pub, Chloe looked brighter than ever. Youth, she thought, wishing she had some of that energy.

'You don't have to worry about it, Mother. I'll sort it. Goodnight.'

'Goodnight, and don't let the bed bugs bite,' Lottie said to the air left in Chloe's wake as she heard her daughter enter the bathroom.

Locking the front door, she switched off the hall light and made her way upstairs. She plugged in her phone to charge and left it on the bedside cabinet. Then she stripped off, pulled on her cotton pyjamas and fell into bed. As the first wave of sleep tugged a curtain across her eyes the room lit up. More lightning? No. It was her phone.

Checking it, she smiled. Boyd.

She texted back. *I love you too.*

She was asleep in two minutes.

*

Beth couldn't sleep. She couldn't stop thinking of her sister. Walking around the empty house wasn't doing her nerves any good. On the one hand she was glad the forensic team had left, but on the other she was scared of being alone.

Rubbing her hands up and down her arms, she climbed the stairs and tentatively entered Rachel's room. It looked grubby. Fingerprint dust on the window frames and wardrobe door, even on the drawers of the locker. She ran her hand over Rachel's mattress, trying to get a sense of her sister's final resting place. The place where she had taken her last strangled breath.

No tears were left. She felt frozen inside. Drained of all emotion. Too frigid even to paint, which was her usual go-to in times of stress. Standing in this room of death, her skin tingled, the only outward sign of the evil that had been perpetrated on her last living relative. She didn't count her father. She'd tried calling Brendan, but his phone was switched off. She wasn't sure why he had absconded when the detectives had called. Guilt at his previous stalking of Rachel, perhaps? Maybe it was best to paint him out of this horrific picture.

She stepped backwards out of the room, thinking of all Rachel's plans that would never see fruition. Could she take up the project herself and try to make it work? Could she allow the SmoothPebble brand to die along with its creator? Rachel had been so enthused and excited, emotions that had shone brightly from her eyes and permeated Beth's skin. But now? Now all she felt was desolation and loneliness.

As she turned to descend the stairs, the doorbell shrieked. Jumping instinctively, she almost missed the top step and only saved herself by thrusting her hand out and grabbing the banister.

With her heart literally thumping up into her throat, she released the banister and leaned against the wall. It was late. She wasn't expecting anyone. She'd put off their friends, telling them she'd meet them tomorrow for a drink. No way her father would come. He had left their mother's funeral after one word with Rachel. The coward. Brendan? No, he'd run scared of the gardaí so it was doubtful he would return. She wondered again what had spooked him.

Someone was now thumping the door.

Feeling in her pocket for her phone, she took it into her hand, ready to hit the emergency number, and slowly descended the stairs.

Standing behind the front door, she said, 'Who is it?'

'Beth, I have to talk with you. Open the door. Let me in.'

'Who is it?'

'It's me. Tara.'

The mother watched her little girl rush away from the door. Why had she been spying on her father? Was he even in there? She'd thought he had left hours ago.

Something in the movement of the fleeing child told her to be wary. To be quiet. She slipped off her shoes and silently moved towards the door. It was open a crack, and the woman could see shadows moving around inside. The door always creaked. She knew that, but still she could not resist the urge to put her finger to the wood. She pushed it slowly inwards.

'Hello, darling,' he said in that fake voice that she knew proved he was guilty of something. Guilty of what, though?

Then she noticed the young woman, her face flushed and her untidy hair a mess, hastily doing up the buttons on her cheap blouse.

'What's going on?' she said, finding her voice.

'Just paying the staff,' he said as he scrawled his signature and tore a cheque from his chequebook.

'Thank you, sir,' the girl said, taking the piece of paper. She stood and pulled the hem of her skirt down as far as she could, covering her thighs, then began looking around the room frantically.

'Lose something?' the woman said. Probably her virginity, she thought.

'Erm, it's okay. My bag. I … erm … I think it's in the hallway.' Her voice was high. Squeaky.

The woman stood to one side to allow the teenager to pass. She turned and watched as she frantically searched through the coats and bags on the hall stand.

'Erm … ah … it's not here.' The voice echoed back.

'Try the kitchen.'

The woman remained at the door, studying her husband. There was no guilt written on his face, no contrition in his eyes. He was watching her as if willing her to accuse him of something, and she knew he had excuses ready, no matter what she said. So she did what she always did in situations involving him. She said nothing.

But that one incident was the turning point. That one incident poisoned their lives forever. That one incident gave her the strength to become the woman she'd always wanted to be. A separate entity from her husband.

CHAPTER FORTY-EIGHT

Thursday 23 November

It wasn't the way she'd have predicted her day would start, but Lottie was used to the unpredictability of her life, so once she'd ended the phone call, she hopped out of bed and dived into the shower.

She scrubbed life into her skin and shampooed her hair, forgoing conditioner. She'd suffer the fuzzy consequences of it in the name of her job. She pulled on faded blue jeans and a white long-sleeved T-shirt, and zipped up a black hoodie. Downstairs, she found her boots in the kitchen. They'd dried out during the night, a white line ingrained on the leather from the soaking they'd had yesterday. Not wanting to waste time eating cereal, she grabbed a battered banana from the counter and debated waking Sean. It was still too early to get up for school. He'd got up every morning this week on his own. He could do it again today.

She pulled on her jacket and hurried outside, dragging the front door shut behind her. She rang Boyd while she was starting the car, telling him to meet her at the house. He sounded like he'd been up for hours. Maybe he'd already been out for his bike ride. She hoped not, but now wasn't the time to tell him to slow down. Not when they both needed to speed up. Superintendent Farrell had made that clear.

She raced through the silent town, which was placid in the aftermath of the storm until she turned left towards Friar's Street. Fire trucks were parked haphazardly, with personnel draining flood water from the road. It was obvious to her that the river had burst its banks again. Cursing, she did a U-turn and headed back towards Gaol Street to drive the long way around. Hopefully the Brook Hotel hadn't been flooded. It stood on the banks of the river, and her wedding was due to be held there the day after tomorrow. It'd be just her luck, she thought, but for now she had more pressing things to attend to.

It was still dark, the street lights sheathing the complex in a hazy amber hue, giving it a ghostly appearance when she parked outside the red-brick apartment block. She signed in and handed the clipboard back to the muffled-up uniformed officer.

Garda Martina Brennan said, 'Morning, Inspector.'

'Is Jim McGlynn here?'

'He's been notified. Sam … Detective McKeown and I were first to arrive.'

Lottie raised an eyebrow and opened her mouth to ask the question, but closed it as quickly. She had more important affairs to concern her at the moment.

'Boyd is on his way,' she said. 'Tell him I've gone inside. Who found the body?'

Garda Brennan pointed to a young man sitting on a low wall. He had a foil blanket around his shoulders and was being interrogated by McKeown. 'Andy Ashe.'

'Right. Don't let him out of your sight.'

Lottie glanced at the victim's name scrawled in Garda Brennan's untidy script at the head of the page on the clipboard, then turned towards the doorway. As she walked, she thought of something. She had a copy of the third key from Rachel's key ring. Slipping it out of her pocket, she tried it in the door. No luck. Disappointed, she reminded herself to try it at Dr Gormley's house, just in case.

After donning her protective suit, overshoes, mask and gloves, she took a deep breath and proceeded inside. The lights were on. A narrow corridor led into a poky living area cum kitchen; not what she'd expected given the value of these apartments on the housing market.

She gagged.

A fetid stench caught in the back of her throat, despite the barrier of her flimsy mask. She eyed the takeaway Chinese food cartons lying on the counter and a hungry-looking cat licking the inside of one of them. The room stank.

'Shoo,' she said, but the moggy ignored her. She opened the patio door and shooed it outside, then closed the door again. She knew McGlynn would skin her alive for it, but she couldn't have the cat traipsing around the apartment any longer.

Noticing a skein of white powder on the small table, she shook her head, trying not to come to any impulsive conclusion, then made her way to the bedroom, averting her gaze from the young woman's body as her training forced her to initially concentrate on everything else.

The room was what she could only describe as a mess. Clothes had been flung everywhere. On the floor, on the bed and across a chair. A dress was hanging on the open door of the wardrobe. The area around the bed was a sticky mess of vomit. She remained standing by the door, reluctant to contaminate the scene she was witnessing, before at last allowing her eyes to linger on the body.

Hazel Clancy was dressed only in her underwear, the skin around her throat torn to shreds. Blood was smeared across the pillow, the sheets and her hands. Lottie could see it gathered around her broken nails. One hand was rigid, like that of Rachel Mullen, clutching her chest. Her hair was clogged with vomit. Her mouth was open wide in the scream that had died along with her soul, and her nose was bruised. Around her mouth, remnants of foam had hardened to her lips, chin and cheeks.

Leaning in as close as she could, Lottie peered into the woman's mouth. She gasped. Sure enough, lodged at the back of her tongue, something small and hard reflected back at her. A mirror shard.

She gulped loudly, unable to hold her breath any longer, and immediately felt faint. Dear God, she thought, who could do this to another human being?

She heard a sound behind her and swirled round on the balls of her feet. Boyd stood there, his face ashen above his mask, eyes wide and alert.

'Oh my God,' he said.

She was glad he hadn't added 'another one'. It was obvious that Hazel Clancy had died a death similar in pain and cruelty to those of Rachel Mullen and Ellen Gormley.

The room was cluttered and claustrophobic. Her eyes were once again drawn to the chair in the corner. 'I think whoever killed her sat there and watched her die.'

'Why do you think that?'

'Look at the way the clothes there are crushed. There are indents on them.'

'I'll tell McGlynn to examine them.'

'Are SOCO on their way?'

'Yes. And the state pathologist has been informed. McKeown is on the ball this morning.'

'I'm surprised he's able to concentrate.'

'Why do you say that?'

'Never mind.' She took a step closer to the bed.

'I really don't think you should—'

'I have to see if there are any puncture wounds on her arms. There's evidence of drug use in the kitchen.'

'Looked like cocaine. Do you think the killer forced her?'

'Maybe, or perhaps she was already a user. How do I know? Ashe might be able to confirm it for us.' She turned on her heel and pushed past Boyd, suddenly feeling the need to inhale the morning air.

Outside, she tore off the mask, gloves and overshoes and deposited them in a bag. Boyd joined her.

'Never thought I'd appreciate the fresh smell you get after rain.'

'Petrichor,' Boyd said.

'What?'

'The name given to the earthy smell produced following rain. Though it usually occurs when you get rain after a long spell of dry weather.'

'You never cease to amaze me, Mark Boyd.' She smiled and made her way towards Ashe.

'Andy,' she said.

'It's awful. Terrible. Brutal.' He shook off the foil blanket and pulled his sunglasses from the top of his head down over his eyes. Dawn had just broken. Lottie assumed this was a nervous habit.

'Why were you here this morning?'

'I called here last night too. Didn't go in when there was no answer. It was around half ten. You see, Hazel wasn't in work yesterday. Phoned in sick. But it was an unusual day …' He looked at Lottie, seeing her confusion. 'The thing is, whenever she's been off before, and it's not often, she'd be constantly on the phone, barking instructions at us. But yesterday there was silence.'

'You called round to see if she was okay?'

'Had a couple of pints and dropped in on my way home. But the lights were off, and I got no answer when I knocked, so I assumed she was asleep.'

'You went back to town for a few more pints after that, didn't you?'

'How do you know?'

'I'm a detective, Andy. What made you call to Hazel's home this morning?'

He scratched at his scalp, and dandruff flew in a snow shower. Removing the sunglasses, he twisted them between his palms. 'Hazel can be a grade-A bitch at times, but I had a feeling in my gut that something was wrong.'

'How did you get into the apartment?' Lottie hadn't noticed any damage to the door.

'I got a key from the management company. I was lucky there was someone already in the office. I didn't think to call them last night, not that I thought anything was wrong then, but you know … Oh God, what happened to her?'

Lottie tried to make him focus. 'Did someone accompany you into her apartment?'

'No, I told the man that I work with her. He didn't ask any questions.'

'Have you ever been in there before this morning?'

'Never.' His face paled in the dawn light. 'Sorry. It's awful. I'll never be rid of the image of what I saw.'

'Was it dark inside when you arrived?'

'What are you getting at?' He frowned in confusion.

'Did you have to switch on the lights when you arrived?'

'Yeah, yeah. It was still dark.'

'Why were you out so early?'

'I … I met up with someone last night and stayed at hers. I was heading home to have a shower and change my clothes before work when I decided … you know … to check on Hazel.'

Lottie had plenty more questions to ask him, but she was conscious of McGlynn's station wagon pulling into the area. She'd need to be quick. 'Andy, you were at the party on Monday night, the night Rachel Mullen was murdered—'

'Hey, hold on a min—'

'And your boss Hazel Clancy reprimanded you on Tuesday for an incident at work. Now she's dead. Seems to me—'

'I had nothing to do with either death.' He stood, his whole body shaking. 'God almighty, what do you take me for? I give out and swear and call Hazel names behind her back, but … that scene in there … Jesus Christ, I'm going to be sick.'

Lottie stepped back just before Ashe opened his mouth and deposited last night's drink on the ground.

'Get him cleaned up and take him to the station,' she told McKeown. 'Keep him there until I get back.'

'Sure thing,' McKeown said. He took Ashe by the elbow, stuffing a folded tissue into his hand. 'Come with me, sir.'

Lottie caught up with Kirby as he arrived, sleepy-eyed. 'Call into the management office,' she told him. 'We need all the security footage they have.' She'd spied small cameras in various alcoves. 'And organise door-to-door enquiries.'

'On it.'

As Kirby went off, all business, McGlynn approached, kitted out in his protective overalls, his heavy forensic case in his hand. 'Another poisoning, Inspector?'

'Good morning, Jim. It appears to be so. But here's the thing. I'm almost certain the killer sat in the chair in the corner of the bedroom and watched her die.'

'I'll have it examined. Anything else I need to be aware of, since you've been all over my crime scene?'

'Hazel Clancy, the dead woman, could be a drug user.'

'Right. Toxicology will determine it one way or the other.' McGlynn sniffed the fresh air from the rising breeze before moving on. 'You think her dealer had something to do with it?'

'Neither of the other murdered women had any evidence of drug use in their homes, so I don't know.' She shrugged, and the wind caught her hair. She swiped it away and stood to one side to let McGlynn pass.

'I'll notify you if I make a significant discovery,' he grunted. 'Has Jane been informed?'

'On her way,' Lottie said.

Boyd joined her. 'What next?'

She pulled up her hood and looked around the area. 'Honestly, Boyd, I haven't a clue.'

CHAPTER FORTY-NINE

Maddy stirred and turned over. She heard a whimper and her eyelids fluttered open. Trey. She'd forgotten the child was in the bed. She slipped out onto the floor and checked that he was okay. He slept on soundly. Listening to the stillness punctuated only by the boy's slow whistle of exhalation, she realised that all was quiet outside. The storm had passed.

She checked her phone. No new messages or missed calls. She could do with a shower to ease the pain in her arm, but she didn't want the water rattling through the pipes to wake the two-year-old, so before the goose bumps could take hold, she threw on yesterday's clothes, vowing to put on a wash later. The room smelled stale. Leaning over the child, she opened the top window an inch to let a little cool air circulate, then pulled the thin blanket up to his chin.

On the landing, she listened to see if either Stella or the baby were awake. Her sister's soft snores came from behind the door. No sound of Simon having stayed overnight. Good.

Downstairs, she plugged in the kettle and spooned coffee into a mug. She checked the cupboard, but there was no bread to make toast. She'd have to fly to the shop before Trey woke up. The kitty jar was empty.

'Fuck you, Simon,' she said. She usually blamed him for taking the little money they had. It wasn't even Stella's dole day. Damn.

As the kettle boiled, she didn't bother opening the refrigerator. She knew there was no milk. Staring out through the dirty window, she saw that the back garden had become an even worse swamp overnight. It was like living in a landfill.

'You're up early,' said a grouchy voice behind her.

'Simon. I thought you'd gone home.'

'Can't get rid of a good thing. Slept on the couch because Stella had a puss on her. Fill a mug for me, will you, love.'

'I'm not your love and you can make your own fucking coffee.'

'Grumpy face.' He slouched over to the counter, scratching his arse through his boxers. His bare chest was covered in hideous tattoos. Simon had no taste, Maddy thought, not for the first time.

'Can you lend me a fiver?' she said hopefully, taking out a mug for him.

'No, I can't. You're not a bit nice to me.'

'You'll have to get Stella to squeeze you out a drop of milk for your coffee.'

'Ah shite, is there no milk?'

'Nope.'

She sidestepped him as he opened the refrigerator in disbelief.

'Wait there a minute,' he said.

His grimy odour went with him when he left the room, and Maddy relaxed. She didn't trust him one bit, even though she knew she could kick him in the balls if he tried anything again. But it was too early to be fighting, and anyhow, she didn't want to start a racket and wake Trey.

'Here's a tenner. I want the change back,' he said, shoving a crisp new note into her hand.

'Any more where that came from?'

'Get the milk and be quick about it.'

The kettle whistled as Maddy left the house. She was on the road to the corner shop when she realised she'd forgotten to put on her coat. As if to remind her, she sneezed.

She picked up a two-litre drum of milk, just because Simon was paying, and a loaf of bread. She paid the twenty-two cents for a plastic bag. That made her happy. It wasn't her money. She made for the door.

'What's got that smile on your face today, missy?'

What was going on this morning? she wondered. The smart-arses were out in numbers.

'Hi, David. I'm picking up stuff for breakfast.'

She felt his eyes boring through the thin material of her T-shirt. For a moment she worried she'd forgotten to put on her bra, but she hadn't; he was just a dirty old man.

'Bread and milk,' he said. 'A pauper's diet.'

'Yeah, whatever,' Maddy said, inching past him.

'If you wait, I can walk back with you,' he said, holding the door open.

'I'm in a hurry. Trey is waiting for his breakfast. Sorry.' She wasn't in a hurry, and she wasn't sorry.

'I'll catch you again, so,' he said.

She escaped into the cold air, unable to shake the crawling sensation from her skin. It was like a thousand deadly ants had found a nest.

*

Beth Mullen held out a mug of coffee to her overnight guest.

Tara threw off the blanket and lowered her feet to the floor.

'Thanks a million,' she said, blowing softly over the hot liquid.

Beth sat in an armchair. 'You need to get that hand seen to. It must have bled during the night. There's blood on your shirt.'

'Don't worry about it. It'll be fine. Not the first time I've been cut and won't be the last.'

'Please don't talk like that. This can't go on. You need help.'

'My therapist is dead, so she's not going to be able to help me this time.'

'Find someone else.'

'Daddy will throw a fit if he thinks I'm cracking up again.'

'You're not cracking up. You're going through an emotional time. What with your mother opening her new restaurant and shoving it in your dad's face, and your dad sending you on wild goose chases to keep you busy, and—'

'Stop!' Tara held up a hand like a traffic warden, almost tipping over the mug in her other hand. 'I work hard for Daddy. He isn't just making up work to keep me busy. It's a real job looking after the environmental aspects of the quarries.'

'After all you've told me, I'm afraid your precious daddy is really not who you think he is.'

'We're not teenagers any longer, Beth, so why are you being mean to me?'

'I'm grieving for my sister. Look, forget it. Sorry.'

Placing the mug carefully on the coffee table, Tara leaned over and put a hand on Beth's knee.

'Hey,' Beth said, feeling the tingle of the other woman's touch on her skin. Maybe she should have put some clothes on instead of appearing in the cotton shorts and skimpy top she'd worn to bed.

'Oh, I'm sorry.' Tara clasped her hands together and squeezed them between her knees as though it was an effort to keep them still, grimacing as blood eased out of the cut. 'I'm on edge. I'm bored. I'm sad. I don't know what I am.'

'Last night I was thinking about Rachel and her work,' Beth said. 'All that effort going to waste. I'd love to get SmoothPebble up and running. But I couldn't do it on my own. I'd need financial backing, because lack of funds was what stalled Rachel. And I don't have a business brain, so—'

'Are you asking me to help?' Tara kept her head lowered, her voice even.

Beth looked at her. 'I think I am.'

'Sure. It will give me a purpose.'

'But I thought your work with your dad—'

'I can handle him. This will be a sideline for me. Oh Beth, this is exciting. Where shall we start? Do you have the SmoothPebble plans? The names and measurements of compounds and ingredients to make the products? How much money is needed?'

Bombarded by these questions, Beth realised how little she knew about Rachel's business.

'Compounds?'

'You know … the materials she was sourcing. I think Daddy might have wanted to be involved to give his company an environmental green star.'

'I don't understand.'

'Rachel wanted access to one of his quarries. You'll never guess which one it was.'

'Quarry? You don't mean … No. Not the one that caused you to … you know … She couldn't have. Could she?'

'I know she did.'

Beth slipped down on the armchair, her head abuzz with the implications of Tara's words. This put her sister's death in a whole new light.

Or darkness.

*

Annie watched her daughter as she walked barefoot into the kitchen. The girl looked weary.

'Jessica, you could do with smartening yourself up. We're back in the restaurant today, and I'm excited to get started. I've phoned David and he'll meet us there.'

'I had a bad sleep. Do you think I could take today off?' Jessica slumped onto a chair, pulling her silk robe tight about her waist.

'Have you lost your mind? Come on, chop chop. Eat your breakfast and follow me into town.'

Throwing the remains of her coffee down the sink, Annie turned the tap until the water ran clear into the drain. She looked over her shoulder. 'You've been very moody recently. Why is that?'

'I think you know why. A girl I went to school with has been murdered. Tara's therapist has been killed. And you want me to get up and dance a jig?' Jessica clamped her mouth shut as if it was filled with words she was afraid to utter.

'Darling, I don't mean just this past week. You've been like this for ages. I thought you'd be ecstatic with all that I've accomplished in such a short space of time.'

'I get that, but it's been too manic for my liking, if you want the truth.'

Annie slammed a wet hand on the table, causing Jessica to tremble. Good. She liked that she could still make her daughters uneasy. It kept them on their toes. Kept them in line. Even though Matthew had inched his claws into Tara, she wasn't worried about that. She had ways of winning the girl back.

'Being busy is the epitome of success,' she said. 'You can't sit back and let others swoop in and take your place. I do what I do for you. And for your sister, of course. You must know that everything is for both of you.'

Jessica stood, the crown of her head reaching Annie's chin. She threw back her shoulders. 'I don't think that's true.'

'You're talking rubbish.' Annie straightened up. Her high-heeled shoes caused her calves to cramp, but she wanted to show her daughter just who was boss in their relationship. 'This house has been in my family for generations. I will make it a success just as I'm going to make my restaurant a success. And no matter what you think, you will be by my side, working hard. I am certain of that.'

'Listen, Mum, I'm not sure that's what I want to do with my life.'

'If you walk away, Jessica, you're going to learn the hard way that family matters.'

'Family? Don't make me laugh. What about you and Dad? You're separated, heading for divorce. It seems to me that our family doesn't matter that much to you.'

Itching to lash out, Annie clenched her hands into tightly balled fists and kept them by her sides. 'When I talk about family, I don't include your father. He did his damnedest to ruin me with his affairs. But I stood up to him. I didn't let his wayward penis bring me to my knees. The things he did …' She unfurled her fists and held her hand to her mouth to keep the words from tumbling out.

'What did he do?' Jessica said. She must have seen the alarm register like a screech in Annie's eyes, because she stepped back, away from her mother, and appraised her with a swift shake of her head. 'Did he do something other than squeeze the boobs of teenage girls? Something other than abuse my friends? Is that what you're talking about? I know all about that. There's no need to hide it.'

'What are you talking about? Your father might have had a wandering eye, but he never touched your friends.'

'That's what you think.' Jessica folded her arms in a show of delight, demonstrating that she had succeeded in a mini triumph over her mother.

292

Annie quickly pulled her thoughts together before sitting. She patted the chair beside her. 'Sit down, Jessica. We need to talk.'

'I'm not talking to you without Tara present. She has to hear your lies as well. Where is she anyway?'

'She went out last night. It was late.'

'You let her go out in the state she was in? Didn't you see what she tried to do?'

'And what exactly was that? Do you want me to believe what you told that detective? Or did you attack her?' Annie couldn't wipe the smug smile from her face.

'You'll think what you like anyhow,' Jessica said. 'You always do. Not once in my life have you believed a thing I've said over what Tara might have told you. All that business when she was nine, telling lies about Daddy, and when I tried to tell you the truth, you wouldn't even listen to me. In your eyes, Tara is the star of this show, not me.'

'Why are you here instead of her then? Tell me that. And let me remind you, jealousy doesn't suit you, pet.' Annie wished she hadn't dumped her coffee down the sink. She could do with something to calm her nerves. She didn't want to fight with her daughter. Didn't want to fight with anyone, but Jessica had forced her hand.

'You're the one who's jealous,' Jessica spat. 'I'm sick of it. I kowtow to you all the time, knowing you're insanely jealous of what Daddy has achieved by expanding his quarry business into the UK. It's eating you up. It's ruining my life and I can't take it any more. You've tried to control us since we were toddlers. You almost ruined Tara, but she fought back, and now ... I don't know what you've said or done, but I think she's beyond help.'

Annie leapt off the chair and caught hold of her daughter's hair before she could leave the kitchen. Twisting the long locks around her hand, she tugged them tightly, pulling the girl towards her with a force she'd almost forgotten she possessed. With Jessica pinned against her, she whispered sharply into her ear, 'Others have paid for crossing me. Don't you dare, Jessica Fleming. Don't you bloody well dare.'

She released her, and watched as Jessica fled out the door, dragging her flailing silk robe in her hand. When she looked down, Annie was surprised to see she had long strands of hair twisted around her fingers.

She washed her hands in the sink with antibacterial gel, dried them furiously in a soft hand towel. Picked up her bag from the floor and eased it onto the crook of her elbow. Then, with a quick look in the hall mirror, she left for work.

CHAPTER FIFTY

Lottie parked behind the station and was heading around the side of the building when her phone rang.

'What's up, Chloe?'

'Oh Mam, you're not going to believe this. It's the worst thing that could happen to us.'

As her daughter broke into sobs, Lottie's skin prickled and she straightened her back, digging her fingernails into the palm of her free hand.

'Is it Sean? Is he okay? Bloody hell, Chloe, tell me.'

'It's not Sean. It's worse. Much worse.'

'Katie or Louis? For Christ's sake, spit it out.' Lottie paced a small circle, splashing up a puddle of mud, her heart thudding in her chest.

'The hotel is flooded, Mam. They rang me to cancel. They tried your phone, but it must have been off or on silent or something. They can't host the wedding on Saturday. Can you believe it? Oh my God, what are we going to do?'

Lottie expelled a gasp of air in relief. 'Is that all? I thought someone had died. I've enough corpses at work to last me a lifetime. Don't worry about it. I'll sort something out.'

'Sort something out? Mam! What are we going to do?'

'The wedding doesn't have to be this Saturday. It's a small affair anyhow. We can move it to another date.' Suddenly it didn't seem like such a bad idea. She was up to her ears in work, making little progress, and now they had Hazel Clancy's death to deal with. She was no nearer to having a handle on the killer, let alone handcuffs, than she'd been on day one.

'You will not postpone it,' her daughter cried hysterically. 'We need to find a new venue. And quickly. Shit, I'll have to notify everyone. Do you realise the amount of work involved?'

'Chloe, hun, it's no big deal. WhatsApp a message to the guests.'

'Katie is coming home specially for it, or have you forgotten? This is a disaster and I have to go to work later.'

'I'm busy too. Can we talk about it this evening? I can drop into Fallon's and chat to you there.' As Lottie paced a final circle, she saw Annie Fleming parking her car across the road. A seed of an idea began to sprout. 'Listen, Chloe, don't panic yet. I have an idea. I'll ring you back.'

*

A shrill wind cut through the thin material of her clothing and Maddy shivered, gripping the plastic bag with the milk and bread in her good hand. She felt weak and hoped she wasn't catching a cold. Hoped there wasn't an infection in her arm. But it wasn't cut, so why was she thinking silly thoughts? Pity she hadn't still got Ellen's bike. It would make her journey all the quicker. Maybe she could ask Detective Boyd if she could have it for keeps, if there was no one else to claim it. The idea put a spring in her step.

As she rounded the corner at the end of the terrace, she saw a man lounging against a damaged wall, his foot kicking up pebbles and water from a puddle on the path. He swung round, and their eyes locked in recognition. With her breath catching on the breeze, Maddy stifled a cough, deciding whether to turn and run or walk nonchalantly past him. Glancing over her shoulder, she saw David Crawley not far behind her. Which was the lesser of the two evils? David, probably.

Before she could react further, ponytail man stepped forward and caught her by the arm.

'Maddy, we really need to talk. I don't want to scare you, but I think you're in danger.'

'Yeah, right! Danger from you, arsehole. Let me go.' She tried to swing free of him, but his grip tightened.

'I swear I won't hurt you, but you need to listen to what I have to say. I knew Ellen. We talked a lot. She mentioned you. You made a huge impression on her and there's something you need to know. Please, Maddy.'

His eyes didn't look threatening; if anything, they were pleading. She heard David's footsteps slapping on the wet pavement.

'I don't know,' she said.

'I have a car.' He moved to the kerb and opened the door.

Was this going to be the biggest mistake of her life? She looked up the road towards her home and thought of little Trey waking up and Simon waiting for the milk for his coffee. What would Ellen tell her to do? Curiosity killed the cat, she knew the saying. But before she realised she'd reached a decision she'd scooted out onto the road and sat into the car.

As they pulled away, she spotted David, breathless, waving, calling her back. She stowed the bag with the milk and bread at her feet and snapped on her seat belt.

'What's your real name?' she said.

'I told you. Brendan. Brendan Healy and you're going to thank me for doing this.'

'I'm not so sure about that.'

'You took a risk.'

'It better pay off.' Or I'm dead meat, she thought.

*

Annie Fleming locked her car and ducked her head under a large black umbrella as the sky began to spit rain.

Lottie crossed the road. 'Hi, Annie. Can I help you?'

'I was hoping I'd see you here. I was wondering how the investigation is progressing. Rachel's death and all that.'

'It's early days. Lots to do. Loads of people to interview.'

'Surely you're seeing some results by now?'

'We are,' Lottie lied. Irritation nudged the hairs on her arms. She did not like to be pressured. 'When are you opening the restaurant?'

'Tomorrow night. I'm still worried, though. I wouldn't put it past Matthew to try something else.'

Lottie shook her head wearily and wondered what motive Matthew Fleming actually might have to sabotage Annie's work. 'I spoke with your ex-husband last night. Have you any hard evidence that he intends to harm your business?'

Annie held the umbrella over Lottie's head, drawing the two of them closer, like co-conspirators. 'No, but I have years of experience living with that sociopath. Mark my words, Matthew's grubby paws are all over Rachel Mullen's death, plus he probably did something to Dr Gormley.'

'I think you're treading on very dangerous ground making such an accusation.'

'I'm only telling *you*, Lottie, I'm not posting it on Twitter.' Annie smiled. 'Matthew and I have had our battles. Long and bloody, metaphorically speaking, and as far as I know he's never murdered anyone. He probably didn't directly or intentionally kill Rachel, but I can't help thinking he had something to do with it. Promise me you'll check him out thoroughly?'

'I'm checking out everyone who crossed Rachel's path.' Lottie took a step away and found herself standing in the rain again. Should she mention what she'd thought of when Chloe rang? Was it totally off the wall?

'That's all I can ask for, I suppose.' Annie sounded doubtful. Then her eyes brightened. 'Last night was such a treat, and I'd love it if you could come to my restaurant some evening. I'd like you to sample David's exceptional culinary talent.'

'I'll let you know.' Lottie's brain swirled with the possibilities and consequences of what she was about to say. 'Annie, I'd like to ask you something. It's a bit of a favour really.'

'Ask away.'

Was this even ethical? she wondered, but it would solve her problem. 'The thing is, the Brook Hotel flooded during last night's storm, and my wedding was to take place there on Saturday – just a small one, thirty or so – but now—'

'You don't have to say another word,' Annie said excitedly. 'I'm on it straight away. The restaurant is too small, but Molesworth House will be perfect. You can use the cottages for changing. Oh, and I never showed you the chapel house. It's perfect for your ceremony.'

'There's no need for a fuss. Like I said, it's a small affair. I don't want any big fanfare or a five-course dinner. Finger food will be grand.' Chloe would kill her.

Annie was having none of it. 'Leave it with me. I'll phone you later and tell you what I can do with such short notice. Oh Lottie, you've made my day.'

Lottie backed away as Annie made to hug her, the umbrella dripping large drops down her back.

'Here, I'll give you Chloe's number. My daughter's the organiser, not me.' She sent the number to Annie's phone.

'Perfect. And Lottie? Please do keep me informed of any progress with your investigation.' Annie pressed her key fob. 'It'd be great if you had it solved before Saturday and you could relax. My first wedding to organise! I can't wait to tell Jessica. Bye-bye.'

Lottie moved back to the shelter of the station door and watched the red tail lights disappear down the street. She was not at all sure if Annie Fleming was friend or foe. What ethical and professional line was she after crossing? To hell with it. If Annie could sort her wedding, she could be her friend for now. Afterwards, it was anyone's guess.

CHAPTER FIFTY-ONE

McKeown and Kirby looked excited as Lottie entered the office. She took off her wet jacket and shook it before hanging it on the back of her chair, then walked back into the general area.

'What?' she said.

'McKeown should get an Oscar,' Kirby said, an unusual gleam in his eye.

'Oh, who did you seduce now?' she said, immediately regretting her words. 'I mean …'

'It's okay boss,' McKeown said. 'I can flutter my eyelashes as good as the next one.'

'I'm sure you can.' Lottie glanced over to the corner to see if Lynch was listening to the conversation. She didn't want her words to be construed as sexual harassment. She had enough shit on her plate without that being added as a side dish. 'What did you find out?'

'I went to Dr Gormley's surgery after I brought Andy in. I was following up on the good doctor's patients. Her PA loves to gossip. Especially when it's her boss that's been murdered. She likes a cappuccino too.'

'You didn't!' Lottie said.

'I did. Brought her out for her tea break.'

'Bit unethical, isn't it?' Lottie said, and squirmed as she remembered her wedding arrangement with Annie Fleming. A snigger erupted from Lynch, and Lottie smiled, trying to take the harm out of her comment.

She knew she'd do the exact same thing as McKeown if she thought it'd help ignite a stalled case.

'Maybe, but I got something worthwhile, though there's no way to confirm it until we can acquire the information legally with a court order—'

'Jesus, McKeown, get on with it.'

'You're going to love this,' he said. 'Rachel Mullen was a patient of Dr Gormley.'

'Really? That's interesting,' Lottie said. Tara Fleming was also a patient, and Maddy Daly claimed to be the doctor's friend and a former patient. She had no idea how or if they all tied into something resembling a clue. Was someone targeting the doctor's patients? Was it as simple as that? If so, why and who?

'We need to expedite a warrant for Dr Gormley's patient records. They could all be targets.'

'Thought you'd be jumping up and down and throwing a party,' McKeown said. Lynch sniggered again.

'Yeah, thanks, I would, but I'm knackered. I've three dead women and a wedding in a few days' time. Don't think I have the energy to walk, never mind jump.'

McKeown ran his hand over his tightly shaved head. 'She also spilled another name. A woman who was invited to Monday night's party but didn't attend, and who is now dead too.'

'Oh crap,' Lottie said. 'Hazel Clancy?'

'Exactly,' McKeown said, his face glowing with pride. 'I threw the name out there and the PA said she was on the patient list.'

'We never actually interviewed Hazel Clancy,' Lottie said.

'Too late now,' Kirby said redundantly. 'I spoke to her on the phone the other day, though.'

'So far the only link is that Rachel and Hazel were both invited to the party on Monday night, and both attended the doctor for therapy. Were they killed because of something they spoke about to Ellen?'

McKeown said, 'I'll have another chat with the PA.'

'Can you talk with Jessica Fleming too? See if the Flemings knew Hazel?' She looked over at Boyd's empty chair. 'Where's Boyd? He was with me earlier at the Clancy apartment.'

'He was back briefly looking over his emails and calls,' Lynch said. 'Said something about checking in on Maddy Daly.'

'He sure has a bee in his bonnet about that young one,' Kirby said, fishing a chocolate bar out of his desk drawer and powering up his computer.

'Did you have your final suit fitting yet?' Lottie said, annoyance lacing her words. What the hell was Boyd up to? She had yet to tell him about the venue change.

'All done. I'll be like a stuffed turkey.' He shoved the last of the chocolate into his mouth. 'That reminds me, what's on the menu?'

'You'll be lucky if we have a menu.' She explained about the Brook Hotel flooding.

'What are you going to do?' McKeown asked.

'Chloe is sorting out a new venue.'

'Boyd won't be happy with the plans being upset,' Kirby said.

'I told you, it's almost sorted.' She changed the subject. 'Any luck with security footage from Hazel's apartment complex?'

'I left Garda Brennan with the manager of the complex to sort through a mishmash of CCTV footage. I wouldn't hold my breath on a successful outcome. It turns out Hazel owns her apartment but pays a fee to the management company for maintenance and security. That's why they had the key.'

'And then they hand it to Andy Ashe, just like that.' Lottie groaned. 'What about door-to-door?'

'Uniforms are doing it. I'll extract anything pertinent once the reports come in.'

'Okay. We need to trace Hazel Clancy's movements. Lynch, check her social media accounts and get Gary to interrogate her phone. Check if Tara Fleming had a flight to London Monday night. If so, we can then trace her movements if it becomes necessary. No point in wasting resources for now.'

'We have to interview Andy Ashe,' Kirby said.

'Right,' Lottie said, 'but back to Ellen Gormley for now. Has anyone made any headway on deciphering those pages found behind her bookcase?'

Kirby and McKeown shrugged. Lynch piped up. 'You said you'd look at them yourself, but if you like, I can do it.'

'Please do.' Lottie was glad to delegate her mounting workload. 'You'll find them somewhere on my desk. Has anyone followed up with whoever Ashe claimed he was in bed with last night?'

'Yes. His alibi checks out,' Kirby said.

'I'll need the post-mortem results to confirm Hazel's time of death. Call her workplace to find out when she was last seen there. We need to put a timeline on this.'

'I'll phone the state pathologist and confirm what time she has Hazel Clancy scheduled for,' Lynch said eagerly.

'Kirby.' Lottie turned to the door. 'Let's have that word with Mr Ashe now.'

Placing a mug of coffee in front of Andy Ashe, Lottie watched as he swallowed three large mouthfuls.

'Thanks,' he said. 'A brandy would be better, though.'

'You won't get that in here,' Kirby laughed. 'Budget cuts.'

He switched on the recording equipment and read out the usual mantra.

'Do I need a solicitor?' Andy said.

Lottie grimaced. She wanted to interview him without delay, and waiting for a solicitor would set her back an hour or two. 'This is a chat. Do you think you need one?'

'I haven't done anything wrong.'

'There you go, then,' she said.

Kirby went over the basic questions she'd already covered outside Hazel's apartment. When those were out of the way, she began in earnest.

'Andy, I need to ask you about the traces of drugs we found in Hazel's apartment.'

'I know nothing about that. My demon is alcohol. I never touched anything stronger in my life.'

Lottie noticed he was without his sunglasses, but his hand automatically reached to his head as if to pull them down over his eyes.

'We found a small amount of what looks like cocaine on her table. Was she a regular user?'

Ashe shrugged.

'You need to answer the question,' Kirby said.

'Okay. The thing is, I think she was on something.'

'Always, or just recently?'

He closed his eyes in thought, then opened them and stared directly at Lottie. 'About six months ago, Hazel changed. Her moods swung like a big dipper. I never knew from one day to the next what to expect.'

'Did she have a partner? Boyfriend or girlfriend?' Lottie said.

'Not currently. Do you think she was dumped and that affected her mood?'

'You tell me.'

'I don't know. She didn't talk about personal stuff. Not with me anyway.'

'Was there anyone at work she was close to?'

'I don't think so. None of us really liked her.' He blushed. 'I mean ... not so we'd kill her or anything. She was our boss, after all, but you know ...'

'I don't know.'

'We talked about her behind her back. That's usual with bosses, isn't it?' He winked at Kirby.

Lottie said, 'Andy, if you can remember who she was in a relationship with, I want to know now.'

'I told you. She never said a word. I just think something happened to change her mood. Recently she'd been worse than she ever was.'

'Because of whatever she was taking? Come on, Andy, I think you know more than you're telling us.'

He shifted one buttock on the chair, then the other, and bit his lip. Lottie resisted the urge to lean across the table and shake the answers out of him.

'Can I be arrested for it?' he asked eventually.

'Depends on what you're talking about.' Lottie's skin tingled, sensing she was about to get the break she craved.

'For giving her the name.'

'What name are you talking about?'

Ashe emitted a laboured sigh and clenched his hands tightly. 'One morning, a while back, Hazel was in the canteen. Crying. Hysterical, really. Snot running down her nose. Mascara all over her face. She was still wearing clothes from the day before, which was out of character for her because she loved to show off her style. I asked if I could help. She told me to fuck off.'

'And?'

'And I didn't. She was in such a state, I felt sorry for her. I thought someone had died. But she had no family. An only child, and her parents were dead. And she had no friends that I knew of—'

'Can you tell me what you talked about?' Lottie didn't need Hazel's life history at the moment. She wanted to know about the name he'd given her.

'Not much, to be honest. She was crying a lot. I put out my hand to comfort her, and she leapt off the chair and went for me. Drew her nails down my arm. It bled. I wondered if I needed a tetanus shot …' He seemed to catch Lottie's glare, and straightened his back. 'She said she needed something to fix her.'

'Fix her? What did she mean?'

'I asked her that, and she said she needed a hit.'

'A hit?'

'I assumed she meant weed, but that wasn't it at all. She wanted cocaine.'

'And you knew someone who could supply it?' Andy Ashe was more surprising than Lottie had first imagined.

'Yeah, I'd heard of a guy … I don't … I've never used anything like that in my life. I'm screwed up enough as it is.'

'Go on.'

'I'm an alcoholic. I recognise I have a problem. I was sober six months ago when this episode happened with Hazel. But in my dark days I met a lot of weird characters. Stoners and the like. I'd heard this name mentioned a good bit. When Hazel asked, I gave it to her.'

'What name?' Lottie held her pen tightly, eager to write. It might be nothing, but then again …

'Simon Wallace.'

'Simon?' Lottie said, trying to get a straight line in her thoughts.

'Do you have contact details for him?' Kirby said.

'I only knew that he drank in Fallon's from time to time.'

Lottie felt ill. Her stomach churned and bile rose to her throat. But in the next instant, she calmed herself mentally. Chloe was sensible. She wouldn't be influenced by the geezers propping up Fallon's bar or those handing out little plastic bags of powder in the toilets. Though she'd have a word with her anyhow.

'Did Hazel contact him?'

'She must have done. I saw the stuff on her table this morning.'

'How can we find him?'

'I told you. I know nothing about him.'

'And it was after that that she changed?'

'Yeah. She was snarky and contrary one day, and high as Everest the next. Harder to work for than ever before.'

Lottie glanced down at the few notes she'd made. Could Simon Wallace be the link between the victims?

'Andy, I want you to think very carefully when I ask the next question, because this is important.'

He nodded cautiously.

'Do you know a Maddy Daly?'

He put his head in his hands and then lifted it cautiously. 'The name does seem vaguely familiar …'

'Think. She worked at the party the night Rachel was murdered. Did Hazel ever mention her?'

He held his index finger in the air like he'd had a eureka moment. 'Yes! I remember it now. She was young. Tall, and thin as a whippet. Long black hair. It was in the shop. She had a sparkly dress in her bag. Hazel had been watching her and hauled her into her office.'

'What happened?' Lottie knew they had no record of Maddy on PULSE.

'She must've been in there no longer than five minutes when out she comes and walks out the main door brazen as you like.'

'Did you find out what went on?'

'I asked Hazel about it. She said it was all my fault. I was like "Why the hell is everything my bloody fault?" But she never told me the reason she let Maddy go. That's what Hazel was like. Unpredictable.'

Sitting back on her chair, Lottie stretched her arms in the air. She wanted to give a fist pump and shout 'Yes!' Instead, she interlocked her fingers behind her head and took a deep breath. Was this the break they needed? Maddy Daly was connected to all three victims.

'Thanks, Andy,' she said.

'Can I go?'

'Not yet. I've to make a call.'

Outside the interview room, Lottie phoned Boyd. No answer. Where the hell was he? They had to get Maddy into custody.

She raced up to the office.

'McKeown, we need to bring in Maddy Daly. And Simon Wallace while we're at it.'

'What's his address?'

'I'm sure you'll find Wallace on PULSE.' She paused to allow the adrenaline to calm down. 'Maddy lives in Cusack Heights.'

McKeown started typing Wallace's name into the database.

'And find Boyd.'

*

Boyd had had his fill of Stella Daly screeching at her boyfriend in a voice you could grate cheese on.

'Will you put on joggers or something?' she badgered him.

Simon ignored her. 'If Maddy doesn't come back with the milk soon, I'll have to drink black coffee,' he moaned.

The little boy, Trey, wandered in rubbing sleep from his eyes and asking for his breakfast.

'Why don't you put on *Paw Patrol* or *Fireman Sam*,' Stella said. 'Maddy will make you breakfast when she comes back.'

'If the little bitch ever comes back,' Simon grumbled, and lit a cigarette.

The smoke filled Boyd with a longing for nicotine. His phone rang in his pocket. Seeing the caller name, he hit decline. He could talk to Lottie later.

'What do you want with Maddy this time?' Stella said.

'Just want to make sure she's okay.'

'Why would you be bothered with the likes of us?' She snorted and shifted the baby from her shoulder to her knee. A fresh milky stain streaked down her back. She didn't seem to notice.

'I care about her,' he said, without offering further explanation. 'She's been gone a long time, if she only went to the corner shop.'

'I gave her a tenner,' Simon said. 'She's probably in Tesco, wasting it. I'll kill her.'

'Where'd you get a tenner from?' Stella said. 'I thought you were broke.'

Simon tapped the side of his nose.

Boyd's phone vibrated again.

Stella jumped up, almost dropping the baby. 'Did you rob the kitty jar?'

'I would have, if there was anything in it. Where'd you put the fifty Maddy earned Monday night?'

'I'm taking this call,' Boyd said, leaving the couple to argue over the money.

He went to pull the door for privacy before remembering there was no door. Outside, he stood on the step to take Lottie's call, but he'd missed her again. He was about to ring her back when he heard the siren. The squad car pulled to a stop in front of him.

'What's going on, McKeown?'

'I've to bring in Simon Wallace and Maddy Daly. Are they inside? I'm not going to ask what you're doing here.'

'I was checking up on Maddy, but she's gone to the shop. Simon's inside. What's he done?'

'We think he was Hazel Clancy's dealer.'

Boyd felt the brush of McKeown's shoulder as he pushed past. Following him inside, he heard Simon protest.

'What the fuck? You can't just barge in here like you want to have a garda party in my house.'

'It's my house, for your information,' Stella said, pushing the kitty jar back in the cupboard. The baby in her arms began to wail.

'Mr Wallace,' McKeown said in his best official voice, 'can you put some clothes on and come with me?'

'No, I can't.'

'Doesn't bother me. I can cuff you as you are.'

'What do you want with me anyhow? I done nothing.'

'Did,' Boyd said.

'What?' McKeown said, turning on him.

'Where's my clean joggers, Stella?' Simon said.

'On the line.'

He peered into the garden. 'There's nothing there.'

'Shit, the storm … There's a pair on the floor upstairs.'

As Simon elbowed his way out of the kitchen, Boyd stood inside the front door. He wasn't about to let Wallace do a Brendan Healy on him.

'Where's Maddy?' McKeown said.

'Corner shop,' Stella replied.

'Okay, we'll swing by there on the way.'

'It's okay, I'll go and look for her,' Boyd said, and escaped the crowded house to the sounds of Fireman Sam's jingle from the sitting room.

Garda Martina Brennan was propping up the door of the squad car when he went outside. She promptly straightened as he nodded at her. Deciding to walk rather than drive, he buttoned his jacket and pulled the collar up around his ears. The rain had been replaced by a biting north wind and he knew he had little fat on his bones to protect him.

When he reached the turn, he heard a shout from behind him.

'Mr Crawley, what's up?' he said as the chef rushed towards him.

'I saw her. Not too long ago.'

'Slow down. Take a breath.'

'Okay, sorry. It's just, when I heard the sirens, I came round from my house to see what's going on. Is it Maddy? Is she okay? Did that bastard beat her, or worse?'

'Nothing is wrong. Just routine.' Boyd waited a beat until the man's face leached of its high colour. 'Now, tell me, who did you see?'

'Maddy. She got in the car. He was a shady-looking character. Thought it might be one of Simon's friends. I waved at her and tried to stop them, but he sped off.'

'Who sped off?'

'The man. Driving the car.'

'Back up a bit. Start from the beginning.'

'Sorry. I met her at the shop. Even told her to wait and I'd walk with her. But she was having none of it. Said the kid was waiting for his breakfast. Milk and bread. That's no breakfast for a kid. Mine have bacon, eggs, mushrooms and—'

'Mr Crawley. David.' Boyd's patience had evaporated. 'Get to the point.'

'Yeah, well off she goes, and I get my bits and pieces and head for home. I was at the corner when I saw them. He was talking to her. Waving his hands around. Then he opens the car door and in she gets, brazen as you like.'

'A boyfriend, maybe?'

'Never saw him before in my life, and I see a lot that goes on around here. I could tell you a lot about that Simon character—'

'Later.'

'It was her face … little thin thing staring out the window at me. She looked confused, scared. I think she was terrified.'

'If she was terrified, why would she get into the car?'

'Maybe he had a gun or a knife,' Crawley said. 'Who knows around here?'

'Which direction did they go?'

'Up to the end of the road and then right. That's the way out of town.'

Boyd knew the town. Didn't need directions. He inhaled deeply, installing patience into his brain. 'Can you describe the man?'

'Maybe early thirties. He was taller than me. Smaller than you. A long dark jacket on so I couldn't see his clothes. Oh, and he had a short ponytail.'

Boyd gritted his teeth. Brendan fucking Healy. His instinct had been right all along. Maddy needed protecting. Or was she involved in something evil and dark? He shook his head and noticed Crawley staring at him. 'What kind of car?'

'Dark blue Mazda. Older model. Didn't catch the reg.'

Healy's car, which they'd been unable to locate.

'Thank you.'

'Do you need me for anything else?'

'If it's necessary for you to give a statement, I'll send a car later.'

As Crawley walked off with his shoulders straight, proud to have done his civic duty, Boyd scratched his head.

Where had Brendan Healy taken Maddy? And why?

CHAPTER FIFTY-TWO

As Lottie made her way back down the stairs to the interview room, she stopped halfway. This was all too easy. Andy himself had links to two of the victims; she'd have to ask him if he'd known Ellen Gormley as well. He could be spinning his story the way he wanted it spun, and she had to be careful not to get tangled in a web of lies.

Composing herself, she hurried on and re-entered the interview room.

Andy looked up as Kirby announced her return.

'You check it out, then? I'm right, amn't I? That Simon Wallace had something to do with it.'

'Leave the police work to us, Andy.' Seated again, she lined up her pen beside her notebook, the way Boyd might do it, and stared at Andy.

'What?' he said.

'Dr Ellen Gormley.'

'What about her?'

'Are you a patient of hers?'

'I don't know her.' He shifted uneasily on the chair.

'She's a psychologist, a therapist. No lies, Andy. I asked if you're a patient of hers.'

His face reddened. She had him. His voice was low as he said, 'When I was … you know … trying to sort myself out with the drink …'

Lottie had no time for his sob story. 'Who referred you to her?'

'Hazel.'

'Explain, please.' She glanced at Kirby, who was scribbling furiously despite the interview being recorded.

'Can I have another coffee?' Ashe said.

'Talk first.'

'Right. I was in a bad way with the drink. I desperately wanted to get off it. Hazel found me behind a rack of suits one day in a heap of sweat and tears. It was either lose my job or get help. She made a phone call. Turned out it was to Dr Gormley. Hazel said she was good, that she'd helped her out at one stage. The doc chatted with me and got me into the local AA. I was grand for a while. Then I relapsed, but I know I'm not lost. I'll sort myself out again soon. When all this madness is over.'

'Were you involved in drugs too? Is that why Hazel asked you about sourcing some for her?'

'Not at all. I told you. Alcohol was my drug. Still is. I suppose she felt she could ask me about the drugs because she'd got me sorted out with the therapist.'

'Did Hazel ever allude to why she'd been seeing Dr Gormley?'

'No. She never mentioned it again. Never even asked how I was getting on. But that's Hazel for you. Wrapped up in herself.'

'And you have no idea who it was she'd broken up with?'

'Erm … no.'

'You don't sound so sure.' She sensed he was holding something else back from her.

'I'm … yeah, I'm sure.'

'Is there anything else you want to share with us?'

He glanced over at the door, reached to his head for the sunglasses that were no longer there and said, 'Can I go now?'

'Detective Kirby will read back your statement and get you to sign it.'

As she left, Lottie was certain Andy Ashe had more to tell. What that was, she would do her best to discover.

*

McKeown had left to pick up Maddy and Simon when Lottie walked into the office. Lynch was on the phone, waving frantically. Lottie waited until she'd finished the call.

'Boss, I think I've sussed something,' Lynch said, her animosity apparently dropped for now. 'The map that Kirby found behind the doctor's bookcase: I checked the coordinates with the land registry, and it refers to a piece of land owned by Matthew Fleming.'

'Okay ...' Lottie waited for the punchline she knew was coming.

'But he didn't always own it.' Lynch grinned, her freckles stretching accordion-like across her nose. 'The land was previously owned by a Mervyn Gormley.'

'Any relation to Ellen?'

'Her father. It was then transferred to Ellen before being signed over to Matthew Fleming six years ago. Mervyn Gormley and his wife are now deceased.'

'Interesting,' Lottie said. But what did this mean? It had to have some significance if Ellen had gone to the trouble of hiding the map. She said, 'Not being sexist, though maybe I am, but why was it not bequeathed to Ellen's brother? When did he die?'

Lynch tapped a key. 'Aidan Gormley drowned nine years ago.'

'Ellen would have been twenty-one or so then. Can you check what age Aidan was when he died?'

Another few clicks.

'Holy shit,' Lynch said, pointing to the screen with a blue Bic biro. 'He was only seven years old.'

Lottie suddenly recalled the conversation with Matthew Fleming the previous night. About someone drowning in a quarry and how it had impacted on Tara.

'Where did he drown?' she asked.

'Want me to find out?'

'Print what you have and see what else you can discover. I want post-mortem and inquest records; where it happened; who found the child. I need every scrap of information. It might have nothing to do with anything or it might have something to do with everything.'

'On it.'

Lottie turned away, then stopped and said, 'Thanks, Maria. Good work.'

Kirby walked in and raised an eyebrow.

Lynch nodded and smiled.

Don't get too comfortable, Lottie thought. You're not out of the dark woods yet.

After Lynch had deposited the paperwork on her desk, Lottie made herself comfortable and read the information for herself.

Nine years ago, a seven-year-old boy had died in his father's quarry, a property that now belonged to Matthew Fleming. Had the death precipitated the sale? A wild thought flitted through her brain. Had Fleming killed the boy and was now killing those who might have either witnessed the drowning or knew something about it? Ellen would have been around twenty, and Rachel and Hazel would have been teenagers at the time. Matthew Fleming's daughters too. Did they all know the Gormleys?

'Lynch, check where Hazel Clancy is originally from and where she spent her teenage years. I want to know where she went to school too.'

'Sure thing.'

'Kirby, come here.'

'Yes, boss?' He ambled in chewing on the end of an unlit cigar.

'Look at these land registry printouts. That's a quarry, isn't it?'

He leaned over her shoulder. 'Yup. Sure is.'

'I want to know who owned all the surrounding land.'

She tapped her foot impatiently on the floor as Kirby left, and then remembered the other pages that had come from behind Ellen's bookcase. Lynch had given up on them. Dragging them from beneath a file, she squinted at them. Typical illegible doctor's script. She persevered, her nose twitching, hoping to find at least a name. But she was at a loss to make any progress. Only a doctor could decipher it. A doctor she could trust. She immediately thought of her friend Annabelle O'Shea, whom she hadn't seen in such a long time. That friendship had died a death following Annabelle's husband's arrest. She would try to convince Annabelle to help her.

'Boss,' Kirby said. At his desk, she looked over his shoulder. 'The Gormley family owned the land surrounding the quarry. Their house was situated two fields over from where Matthew Fleming lives.'

'Bingo.'

'What does it mean?'

'Something, Kirby. It means something.' She glanced over at Lynch. 'Anything further on the Gormley boy's death yet?'

'Working on it.'

She wanted to tell her to hurry the hell up, but McKeown appeared at the door.

'Good news and bad news,' he said.

'Spit it out.'

'Simon Wallace is downstairs.'

'What's the good news?'

'That was it. Boyd is looking for Maddy Daly. The bad news is she seems to have disappeared.'

CHAPTER FIFTY-THREE

The stink of body odour clogged the airless interview room. When Lottie walked in, Simon was chewing the inside of his cheek like he wanted to spit at her and was gathering saliva until he had enough to make an impact. McKeown immediately donned his serious face, making him look like a younger version of the Rock. Sean had mentioned that similarity to her after he'd first met McKeown, and even showed her a photograph, which she could not get out of her head. A bluebottle buzzed relentlessly around the room, the sound zinging in her ears.

After the introductions were made for the recording and Wallace's rights had been read out to him, Lottie took the lead.

'Mr Wallace … Can I call you Simon?' He shrugged and she took it as assent. 'We'd like to ask you a few questions.'

'Done nothing.'

'You don't know what I'm about to ask you.'

'Killed no one.'

'Will you let me ask the question?'

'No comment.'

She dug her nails into the palm of her hand and counted to five in her head.

'Hazel Clancy.' She left the name hanging in the air, studying Wallace's face. He battled to keep his features from reacting, but lost. He knew the name. 'I know you were acquainted with her, so you might as well talk.'

'Aqua what?'

'It means that you knew her.'

He chewed hard on whatever he had in his mouth, real or imaginary, before swallowing it. His Adam's apple appeared engorged as he said, 'Don't know who you're talking about.'

'I think you do.'

'You won't give up, will you? All right. She was into the hard stuff, wasn't she?'

Lottie glanced at McKeown. He placed a photograph of two large plastic bags containing white powder on the table.

'Where'd you get that?' Wallace said, his jaw dropping a few centimetres, showing his yellowed teeth, one crooked incisor. Lottie supposed he hadn't yet achieved the drug trade status where he could afford to fly to Hungary for a full mouth of dental work.

'At the Daly house. Under the mattress in the baby's cot.' McKeown's voice was cold.

'Fuck off, pig,' Wallace growled. 'You didn't have a search warrant. No warrant, illegal search.'

'We had probable cause, so it wasn't illegal, but this shit sure is.'

Lottie turned to McKeown. 'Enough for five years? What do you think, Detective?'

'Oh, much longer than that. With intent to supply, and depending on the judge, definitely longer.' McKeown was enjoying this. Wallace wasn't. He brought his hand to his mouth and chewed on a knuckle.

'Personal use,' he muttered.

'What kind of father hides his personal stash in his daughter's cot? Add child endangerment to the list, Detective,' Lottie said. 'And—'

'Hold on a minute—'

'With an inquisitive two-year-old roaming the house, make a note to call social services.' She turned back to Wallace. 'Don't think Stella will be too happy with that, Simon.'

'Fuck Stella and her kids. They're not mine.'

'We need to add a paternity test to the list.' She nudged McKeown's elbow and he wrote.

'You have to be shitting me,' Wallace said. 'What's your game, lady?'

'Oh, I'm a lady now, am I?'

'This is one hard lady,' McKeown said, leaning across the table conspiratorially. 'Want my advice? You don't want to cross her.'

'Shut the fuck up!' Wallace slammed the table.

'Hazel Clancy,' Lottie repeated.

Wallace restarted his chewing motion. Had he a wad of tobacco stuck there? Or a chunk of cannabis? He didn't look high, just pissed off at being caught.

'What's in it for me?' he asked, narrowing his eyes to a squint.

'First I need to hear what you know about Hazel Clancy.' Lottie made a celebratory fist under the table.

'What if I do know her? Guy in the pub told me she was looking for gear.'

'And you obliged?'

'If people want to pay, I can sell.'

She wanted to know more about his supplier, but she'd pass him off to the Drugs and Organised Crime Bureau when she was done with him. If he wasn't a murderer, he'd be the bureau's problem.

'When did you first contact her?'

'Must be six months ago. I called her and arranged a meet.'

He was talking like a kid from *The Wire*, not a thirty-year-old bum from Ragmullin.

'She gave you her real name?'

'Why not? She lives and works in town. I'd see her around, wouldn't I?'

'Suppose you would. You rang her. Then what?'

'Drooling for a high, she was. Would've sold her granny for it after the first few times.'

'Where did you conduct the deals?'

'At her apartment. The red-brick place on the way out to Lidl. Do you know it? Too fancy for her, if you ask me.'

'When did you last see Miss Clancy?'

'Hazel? She rang in a panic yesterday morning looking for … you know what.'

'What time was this?'

'Not sure. Could have been nine thirty or ten. It was just before midday when I got to her apartment. I know that because I had an appointment at the social at one.'

'Go on.'

'When I got there, she was chewing her nails off. I left the stuff. She told me to take what I wanted from her purse. She was tearing the gear apart when I left.'

'How much did you take from her purse?'

'Nothing. I didn't want her to accuse me of theft later on. I told her to pay me next time.'

'My heart bleeds for you,' Lottie said. 'I need the truth, Simon.'

'Okay. Okay.' He sighed. 'There was only a tenner in her wallet, so I took that.'

There was a ring of truth to his words, though Lottie doubted he'd achieve sainthood any time soon. 'Was that the last time you went to Hazel Clancy's home?'

'Yeah. Cross my heart and hope to die.' He grinned, his crooked tooth catching the light, transforming his face into a grotesque mask.

The fly buzzed loudly in the ensuing silence as Lottie formulated her next question.

'Can anyone verify your whereabouts from the time you left Miss Clancy's home until Detective McKeown picked you up this morning at Stella Daly's?'

Wallace glared at McKeown like he wanted to wring his neck. McKeown shifted on the chair and Lottie knew the thought was mutual.

'I was around,' Wallace said. 'Here and there. Out and about.'

'For shit's sake,' McKeown bellowed.

'It's the truth. I can do you a list.'

'Can you even write?' McKeown asked.

'You're some bastard. I take offence at that. Garda brutality.' Wallace leaned across the table towards Lottie. 'I want to make a complaint against him.'

'Simon, I haven't time for any more bullshit,' Lottie said. 'Hazel Clancy was found murdered this morning in her home. As far as I'm concerned, you were the last person to see her alive.'

She watched his mouth opening and closing, without a word coming out. Even the bluebottle went silent.

'I'm waiting,' she said eventually.

'She was alive when I left her. Did she overdose, or what?' He paused, screwing up his eyes. 'I don't think she had enough for that. Unless she had a heart attack or something.'

'It's the "or something" that I'm interested in. Hazel was poisoned.' She hoped Jane would be able to confirm cause of death soon, along with the type of poison administered and analysis of the piece of mirror she'd glimpsed in the victim's mouth. She still had no notion of what that symbolised for the killer. 'Did you know Rachel Mullen?'

'Never heard of her. Oh, wait a second. Isn't she that bird that was mentioned on the telly news? She was murdered.' His face dropped as he realised where Lottie was going with her questions.

'What about Dr Ellen Gormley?' she said.

'Ellen, did you say? The only Ellen I know is Maddy's friend.' His tone was more muted now, the seriousness of the situation resting heavily on his wide shoulders.

'One and the same.'

'You're shitting me?'

'I'm not. Do you know where Maddy is?'

'I've no idea, but you might be looking at another murder when I find her. She took my tenner.' His body shook with renewed anger. 'She went to the shop this morning to get milk for me, but maybe she had other plans. How the hell do I know what way that girl thinks?'

'What about Brendan Healy?'

'Who's he when he's at home?'

'He runs an art gallery in Dublin. He's from Ragmullin. Wears his hair in a ponytail.'

'That dude? He's the fellow who was following Maddy around yesterday. I think she was afraid of him.'

'How do you know she was afraid of him?'

'She must've been, or she wouldn't have asked me to walk with her.'

'Where was this?'

'Gaol Street car park. She was walking towards Gallagher's Lane.'

'Did you see him?'

'No. He'd gone by the time I arrived on the scene.' He winked. 'That's what the cops say, isn't it?'

'Anything else you care to tell me?'

Wallace was beginning to look bored. 'I never sold him drugs if that's what you mean. Don't know the guy. Never met him before.'

'Where were you last night?'

Shifting his buttocks on the chair, he said, 'I stayed at Stella's. On the couch. She had the hump. She'll tell you, if she feels like it. I never know with her. Anything else?'

'We're holding you on the drugs possession charge for now.'

'Fuck off. It's for personal use.'

'You admitted selling cocaine to Hazel Clancy.'

He folded his arms and rocked back on the chair.

If they believed Wallace, Hazel had been alive at midday yesterday. There'd been no answer when Andy Ashe called to the apartment last night. Had someone murdered her within that time frame, or later?

Lottie looked at McKeown. He shook his head slowly. Wallace hadn't the wit to carry out the murders with the planning required. Simon Wallace was a drug dealer. He wasn't their killer.

CHAPTER FIFTY-FOUR

Boyd drove around for an hour but there was no sign of the blue Mazda, Brendan Healy or Maddy Daly. Traffic reassured him they were on the lookout, but Boyd didn't hold out much hope.

He'd tried Healy's parents to see if they'd seen their son, but they weren't home. A neighbour told him they usually went to daily Mass, then afterwards to the Joyce Hotel for coffee and scones and maybe on to Lidl or Aldi. They were never home before one. Where would the gardaí be without inquisitive neighbours?

He caught up with Breda and John Healy in the foyer of the Joyce. They claimed not to have seen Brendan for a couple of days. John said his son had started to come home more often recently, and Breda thought he had a girlfriend. Boyd had to accept what they said.

Eventually he drove back to the station, where Lottie was in full boss mode.

'Where were you?' she said. 'Things have taken off at a gallop here. I wanted you to interview Simon Wallace, as you seem to be well in with the Daly household. Wallace is some bum. Any sign of the young one?'

'Young one?' Boyd's head was swimming. He needed coffee. Maybe he should have joined the Healys when they'd offered.

'Maddy,' Lottie said, swaying on the balls of her feet with impatience.

'She went off with Brendan Healy in his blue Mazda this morning. I can't find hide nor hair of them.' He blew out his cheeks. 'And before you ask, Traffic is on it.'

'This is a mess. Come on and I'll update you.'

Boyd followed dutifully and eased onto the visitor chair in her office. There were files everywhere. Pens strewn on the desk and floor, and the keyboard on top of the wastepaper bin. He itched for a free hour to tidy it up.

'You all right, Boyd?'

'Need a coffee, badly.'

'We'll get one in a minute. Before I get on to the investigation, I've something to tell you. About the wedding.'

'I got the suit. It fits grand.'

'Boyd, we nearly had no wedding.'

She was beaming, so he reckoned she had sorted whatever disaster she was about to relate to him. 'Tell me.'

'The Brook Hotel flooded after last night's storm.'

'I heard that.' The hotel had informed him first thing this morning, and he'd told them to ring Chloe. He'd been up to ninety every night for the last month, going over the spreadsheets and table settings, becoming a right groomzilla, and the news had stumped him so much that he had no idea how to tell Lottie. At least she now knew.

'Chloe was in a state when she rang, and then I bumped into Annie Fleming and had the best idea I've had in ages.'

An awful thought exploded in his head. 'Please tell me you didn't.'

'I did. Our wedding is going to be held at Molesworth House on Saturday. I gave her Chloe's number and she said she'll liaise with her. You don't have to be involved if you're thinking that the Flemings could be implicated in some way in the case.' She paused and must have caught his sceptical look. 'I agree with you, it's not ideal, but it's better than nothing.'

'Lottie, I want to marry you more than anything. And I know we kind of rushed the arrangements after the fright I had with my health

…' He paused, trying to form what he wanted to say correctly without offending her. 'But I think it's a bad idea.'

'What are you on about? I've sorted it. The wedding can go ahead as planned. Well, not as planned, but you know what I mean.'

'You're getting too close to Annie Fleming. Or have you stopped to think that maybe she's wheedling her way to be close to you? But whichever it is, you have to remember she could be a suspect in Rachel Mullen's murder. Even if she's not, her husband is. Possibly in all three murders.'

'The Flemings are separated. Annie professes to hate him and wants nothing to do with him. She even suspects him of some involvement.'

'Exactly. She's connected to the investigation, one way or another.'

'You're talking shite.'

'Lottie, you can't do this. You're compromising three murder investigations. Shit, you're compromising yourself.'

'And you're being sanctimonious and bitchy. Do you want to get married on Saturday or not?'

He leaned into the chair, feeling faint. 'I do, but I don't want to do it at the expense of our integrity. I'd rather postpone it if Annie Fleming is involved.'

'Really?' She stood, almost toppling her chair. She had no space to pace, with the mess on the floor. He groaned as he watched her roll her hands into fists and bang them against her thighs. 'Forget it. You're right. It's a bad idea. I'll ring Annie and knock the whole thing on the head.'

'Calm down for a minute.' He really could do with a coffee, and he thought Lottie could do with a sedative. No, not going there again.

'Calm down?' she said. 'I wish I could. I thought it was a good idea at the time. But listen, Annie's connection to the murders came about because Rachel Mullen was in her restaurant a few hours before she was poisoned. It's a coincidence.'

'And you believe in coincidences all of a sudden?'

'They happen.'

'Sure they do,' he said, unable to keep the sarcasm from his tone. 'Rachel was invited to that party. And I suppose it's a coincidence that Annie Fleming stepped in as the knight in shining armour to help you just when the Fleming family needed to be seen in a good light.'

'So what? Our wedding had nothing to do with her before today. She didn't phone the weather gods to bring a storm to flood the bloody hotel, did she?'

Boyd couldn't help a sad smile breaking out on his face. If Lottie didn't back down, she'd suffer the consequences and he'd have to pick up the pieces, but he hadn't the energy to keep the argument alive. 'Look, if it makes you happy, go ahead.'

'Thanks, Boyd.'

'Settled then. Argument over.' But he felt he had to get the last word in. 'Don't say I didn't warn you.'

'Oh, I'm certain you'll remind me many times if things go belly-up.'

At last she sat, and Boyd relaxed a little. She didn't appear as formidable while seated, but he wasn't fooled. He knew her too well. Loved her too much. Flaws and all. He was about to do something impulsive like lean across the desk to kiss her when Kirby bustled in the door.

'Boss, you're going to want to hear this.'

'What is it, Kirby?' Lottie scraped her hair from the nape of her neck and tied it back with a rubber band she found buried under a tower of files on the desk.

'I was chatting with Andy Ashe before he left just now, after he'd read and signed his statement. And you'll never guess what he said.'

'I haven't got all day.'

'He told me he was terrified to say the name while we were recording him.'

'What name?' Boyd said, unable to contain his curiosity.

'The guy Hazel Clancy had a relationship with.' Kirby ran a hand over his bushy hair, trying in vain to smooth it down.

'Who was it?' Lottie stood.

At last Kirby blurted it out.

'Matthew Fleming!'

CHAPTER FIFTY-FIVE

Maddy was on the verge of eating a dry slice of bread from the bag by the time Healy parked the car. He'd driven in circles around back roads, eventually ending up at the lake close to the big house where she'd been with Ellen last Saturday. That thought filled her with sadness for what must be the thousandth time that week. She was never going to see her friend again.

He got out of the car and lit a cigarette. 'Want one?' he said, blowing smoke into the car.

'Don't smoke, but I want to know why you've brought me all the way out here. And why all the back roads?'

'I think the guards are after me. They think I had something to do with Rachel's murder. I'm trying to stay low. Let's walk to the shore.'

'It's bloody freezing.'

'There's a jacket on the back seat. Use that.'

She watched as he strolled across grass flattened by the night's rain, up over the verge and onto the stony shore. She hadn't the energy to make a run for it. Anyway, it must be well over ten kilometres back to town, even on the main road. Sighing, she opened the plastic bag, took a swig of milk from the drum, then eased out a slice of bread and stuffed it into her mouth. She was starving.

With the waxed jacket pulled over her shoulders she joined him by the lake. The water was rippling around his feet, but he didn't seem to care.

'Why have you brought me here?' she asked.

'I wanted to talk about Ellen.'

'I found her body. It was awful.'

'I heard that rumour.'

'Ellen was my friend. How did you know her?'

'We met at an art exhibition in Dublin. We hit it off, and she loved the gallery. She seemed to have a thing about strays.'

'You don't look like a stray to me,' she said, appraising his designer jeans and wool jacket.

'She took me under her wing, just like she did with you.'

'You know nothing about my friendship with Ellen.'

'I know a lot.'

'She talked to you about me?' she said incredulously.

'She did.'

She kicked pebbles along the shore before bending down to pick one up. As she went to throw it into the water, a pain shot up her arm and she squealed.

'Are you okay?' he asked.

'It's only my arm. Had a bit of an accident. I'll be fine.'

'Maddy, do you know who killed Ellen?'

'No, but I'm beginning to think you do. Did you do it?' When she said the words, it didn't sound so fanciful, and for some reason it didn't make her afraid. If anything, she felt brave. 'Is this some sort of confession? If it is, I don't want to hear it. I've enough shit in my life, thank you very much.'

He laughed and sucked loudly on his cigarette before throwing it into the water. 'Do you know who owns that big house up there behind us?'

'Ellen brought me out to it last weekend.'

He turned and took a step towards her. 'Did she?'

Maddy stood her ground. 'Yeah. I thought it was just some fancy house. Couldn't see the attraction in it myself.'

'How did she seem to you?'

'What do you mean?'

'How did she react?'

'I'm not sure I know what you're getting at.' She paced along the shore a little way before turning and walking back to him. 'She seemed irritated.'

'Not angry?'

'Don't really know. She was interested in seeing the stables, but they're not there any more.'

'The stables,' he said, and stared out over the water. 'Maddy, I think I know who killed Ellen, but I need you to help me prove it.'

'Me? What have I to do with anything?'

'You can get close to the gardaí. You found Ellen's body. You were her friend. I need you to find out what they have, and once I get that information, I might be able to prove what I think I know.'

Maddy scuffed up more pebbles. Damp shingle stuck to the canvas of her shoe. A shiver shook her body, despite the heaviness of Healy's jacket on her shoulders. She didn't trust him. 'I don't like that idea at all.'

'You have to help,' he pleaded. 'It's partly your fault that she was killed.'

She stopped her scuffling and cocked her head towards him. 'You can drop that notion. Ellen was my friend.'

'The killer had to get to know her movements. To know when she'd be alone in her home. I think they followed you. Or monitored your conversations. Something like that.'

'You're talking shite. None of this has anything to do with me.'

'It has everything to do with you. You awakened a memory in Ellen. Something she'd spent years struggling with ... I'm trying to figure it out.'

'How do you even know her?'

'Doesn't matter.'

'Take me home now. I've heard enough of your bullshit.'

'You have to help me,' he said. He placed a hand on her arm. She shrugged it off angrily and the coat fell to the ground as she walked away.

Marching back to the car, she shouted over her shoulder, 'You're full of shit, you know that?'

She had been expecting violence. She was used to that, Simon being an example. But when she reached the car and looked back towards the lake, Brendan Healy was still standing where she'd left him, his shoulders heaving as he faced the grey water. Maddy hadn't a clue what to do. Start walking to town, using her thumb? Head up to the big house for help? Go back to Healy, who was clearly in distress? Or wait to see what happened next?

Running her hand up and down her painful arm, she leaned against the car and decided to wait. She had to learn more from him. She owed it to Ellen.

CHAPTER FIFTY-SIX

Lottie drove while Boyd read over the Andy Ashe and Simon Wallace interview transcripts and caught up on the information they'd discovered about the quarry on the map. The quarry where Ellen Gormley's little brother had drowned nine years ago.

'I want to have a look around that old quarry before we take Matthew Fleming in for questioning,' Lottie said.

'What do you think you'll find there?'

'Not sure, but it might be the key to everything.'

'Speaking of which, have you had any luck with Rachel's third key?'

'I sent Garda Brennan out to try it in Ellen's house. No joy. And it doesn't open Hazel's either.'

'It could be for an old lock that has been changed and she never got around to taking it off her key ring.'

'Probably.'

'What do you think you'll find at the quarry?' After straightening the pages, he closed the file on his knee. Lottie wondered if he would ever upgrade to using an iPad like McKeown. Probably not.

'From what Lynch and Kirby deduced, it hasn't been used in years, so it'll be a big fat hole in the ground with stones and water.'

'I think you're on a wild goose chase.'

'Land and power are great motivators, Boyd,' she said. 'And something happened to make Ellen's family sign that piece of land over to Matthew Fleming. Maybe the death of the boy, or maybe something else.'

'Maybe he just bought it.'

'Even so, it doesn't make sense. He already had a big quarry operation around Athlone at that stage. There has to be more to it.'

She took a turn off the main road that ran perpendicular to the road
to Matthew Fleming's house, steering the car carefully up a narrow
laneway. 'Have a look at Google Maps again. Make sure this is the way.'

'It is. I can see a rock formation up ahead. And the top of rusted
drilling equipment.'

When they reached the site, Lottie parked and they exited the
car. She zipped up her jacket and found a woollen cap in the boot,
which she tugged down over her ears. 'There's a spare hat if you need
it, Boyd.'

'I have a hood.'

'So do I, but it won't be much use up here. There's an east wind.'

She moved towards a relatively new gate. There was no lock on it,
so she slid back the handle and inched through the gap. The grass was
long and wet, the soil squishy beneath her boots until she reached an
area close to the quarry itself covered with damp sand.

A tall excavator-type machine with rusting chain pulleys stood
on the side of the crevice. She leaned over to see that the quarry was
three-quarters full of dense water.

'Careful,' Boyd said, reaching her side. 'One gust of wind and
you're gone.'

'It's so quiet, it's scary,' she said with a shiver.

'Abandoned a long time.'

'Yeah, but still … I don't know, it's giving me the heebie-jeebies.'
She drew back from the edge and walked slowly around the perimeter
as the wind whistled through the machinery. Large boulders lay discarded, untouched possibly for years. Algae and moss crept over the
limestone. 'Ellen Gormley's younger brother, Aidan, drowned in that
pit of horrible water. And eventually the quarry made it into Fleming's

ownership. I don't get it, though. I've asked Lynch to pull up anything she can find in relation to the drowning.'

'There would have to have been an inquest, so she should find those documents.'

'And a post-mortem.' Lottie walked a little further on. 'But has it anything to do with the three murders in the last week? If so, why now? Why those women? It makes no sense.'

Boyd shook his head slowly. 'We need to concentrate on Matthew Fleming. Everything swings back to him. And we need to ask him about his affair with Hazel Clancy.'

'Okay.' She didn't want to abandon her trek around the open crater, but she felt there was nothing to be accomplished here so she retraced her steps back to Boyd. 'Fleming's house is only across the hill. Want to hike it or drive the long way round?'

'Drive.'

She scanned the hillside one last time before following Boyd back down the trail to the car.

*

Lowering the binoculars, the killer considered this new twist in affairs. What had brought Lottie Parker to the quarry? The detective was no pushover, making connections without even realising she was doing it, a danger to the plans. It was possible she could scupper the entire operation before the endgame was reached. That wouldn't do.

The killer returned the binoculars to their case and wrapped it in green baize before clipping the case into a wooden box. They visualised putting Parker into a rectangle wooden box and lowering it into the bottom of the quarry, watching it disappear beneath the murky gloom of the caliginous waters.

A rightful resting place for one so detrimental to carefully constructed plans.

They checked the time, hoping Inspector Parker wouldn't miss the show that was due to commence shortly. And with any luck, she would become another victim.

CHAPTER FIFTY-SEVEN

Before Lottie could reverse and turn the car, she glanced in her rear-view mirror and saw a Range Rover tearing up the lane behind her.

'What's he doing here?' she said, switching off the engine and getting out of the car.

The Range Rover screeched to a stop and Matthew Fleming jumped out, bundled up in a suede jacket with a white lamb's-wool collar. On his head he wore a brown leather hunter's hat, complete with ear flaps. Comical-looking, but dressed for the weather, with green wellington boots on his feet.

'What are you two doing here?' His voice carried on the wind before he reached them.

'About to ask you the same thing,' Lottie said.

'You're trespassing on my land.'

'Really? I didn't see any warning signs at the head of the road.' She regretted having taken off her hat in the car, as the wind whipped across her face, numbing her skin.

'Yes, Inspector Parker, really. I have a meeting right here in a few minutes.'

'Bit cold for an outdoor meeting.'

'I'm finalising a deal to sell this heap of shit and I'd rather do my dealings alone, if you don't mind.'

He took off his hat as if it was the gentlemanly thing to do. Or maybe it made it easier to hear her.

'Don't see anyone else around,' Boyd said, getting in on the action.

'I'm early,' Fleming said, twisting the cap into a ball between his angular fingers. 'Part of being a good businessman. Getting set up before the opposition arrive.'

'Who is this opposition?'

'Not that you need to know, but it's an out-of-town buyer. I got an email late last night from someone wanting to meet. I'm intrigued to see who it is myself.'

'Can I have a word with you?' Lottie asked. 'I'll only take a moment of your precious time. We were actually about to visit you.'

'I haven't time for more of your inane questions.' He moved to push past her, but she caught his sleeve, gripping the tough material. She let her hand drop when he wriggled out of her grasp.

'Mr Fleming, you should be aware that new information has come to light. We need to interview you at the station.'

'Not now. I'm about to oversee a deal. I want to be shot of this damn place once and for all.'

'Is this the quarry Rachel was interested in using for raw material for SmoothPebble, her cosmetic range?'

'She did mention this location, but I told her it was out of commission. We talked about other areas she could access. I had intended that Tara would be the person she should deal with. Can I head on up now?'

'Can I trust you to come to the station after your business meeting is concluded, or should I sit in the car and wait for you?'

'I don't care what you do, just don't get in my way.'

'Why did you buy this quarry if you were going to decommission it? Not profitable enough for you?'

'Actually, I didn't really want it, but it was offered at a rock-bottom price and at the time it would have been stupid to refuse it.'

'You never operated it?'

'There were complications. The quarry business is subject to so much legislation and guidelines, it would make your eyes water. It's a small quarry, but even so I'd require planning permission to use it on a commercial basis.' He seemed to be in his element when talking about his business affairs. 'There's a lake over the hill and the locals were up in arms. Said if I reopened the quarry commercially, it would cause water and air pollution and every other goddam pollution they could pull from a hat. I'd have all the environmental agencies on my back, and I had other things to concern me at the time.'

'I've had a look up there,' Lottie said. 'Not much around it, is there?'

'I don't think there was ever enough product for an intensive mining programme. But with all the motorway developments, quarries had become lucrative developments. I was in the process of augmenting other quarry projects, so I put my efforts into those.' He waved a hand around. 'This place wasn't worth the hassle.'

'It used to belong to the Gormleys, isn't that right?'

'You've done your homework.'

'Why didn't Mervyn Gormley continue to use it?'

Fleming shrugged, his shoulders like tin plates, his face blue and chafed, his hair wild and unruly. He looked nothing like the cool businessman she'd met at his office a couple of days ago. She waited him out until he relented under her icy stare. 'Gormley's quarry was a small-time operation. I think he put most of the excavated stone and gravel into building his own house. Anyway, I had enough work in the pipeline to keep me busy in other areas of the country. Basically, I abandoned this place.'

'You mentioned last night about a drowning. Was it Mervyn Gormley's son?'

Fleming toed the ground with his boot before stretching his frame like a wiry oak tree. 'Inspector, that happened a long time ago. The inquest returned a verdict of accidental death. The boy just wandered out that night and drowned. It killed his parents. Literally. They died a few years later, one after the other, and once Ellen inherited the land, she wanted rid of it. Sold it to me for a nominal sum. Like I told you last night, the drowning incident fucked up my daughter. I regret the day I ever saw that hole in the ground. Doubly regret that I bought it. But if you let me get on with my business, I'm about to have it taken off my hands.'

'And you're selling it to someone you've never met?'

'I can't wait to sell. Anyhow, this deal has absolutely nothing to do with your investigations.'

She wanted to dispute this further, but the cold was biting and the wind rising. She questioned Boyd with a raised eyebrow and a steely look. He nodded.

'Okay,' she said. 'Do your deal. Come to the station straight after. I have questions for you about your relationship with Hazel Clancy.'

The cold blue hue leached from Fleming's face, leaving behind a whiteness to blend with his hair. 'Hazel? What's she got to do with anything?'

'She's been murdered, Mr Fleming.'

'What … I don't understand.' He physically stumbled before regaining his footing.

'I think you do.'

'Ah, for fuck's sake. You can't think I did anything to her, can you?' When Lottie remained stony-faced, he said, 'I swear to God, I didn't kill her.' He stomped an angry circle before coming to a stop in front of her. 'We had a fling. She was too intense. Couldn't see the fun in it. Truth be told, she scared me, and there's not much that scares me, I can assure you.'

'When did you last see Hazel Clancy?'

'It must be six months or more.'

'Can you account for your movements over the last forty-eight hours?'

He hesitated. 'Some of them. Probably. But I live alone when Tara is at her mother's. My PA can give you a list of my meetings, and,' his eyes brightened, 'you were at my house last night. Is that a good enough alibi?'

'No, it's not.'

They didn't yet have time of death. Lottie was still waiting on a call from Jane regarding the post-mortem. If Simon could be believed, Hazel had been alive before midday yesterday. The poison could have been administered any time in the last twenty-four hours, but Lottie was certain the killer had spent time watching her writhe in agony until she died. What type of person did that?

She appraised the crevices in Fleming's face, which were quickly cementing over with worry. Was his apparent shock at the news of Hazel's death a charade? Was he stronger than he looked? Was he a cold-blooded killer? Looks could be deceiving, but for some reason, she couldn't get a handle on Fleming.

He pulled his cap back on and tugged down the ear flaps. 'I give you my word, Inspector. On my daughters' lives, I will go straight to the station once I conclude my business here.'

Was she about to make a huge mistake? Another crack in her career wall? Feck it. She and Boyd could wait at the end of the lane. There was no way he was driving out of here without having to pass them.

'All right. Do what you have to do. Don't double-cross me.'

'You'd make a good business adversary, Inspector Parker. Despite my reservations, I have to admit I admire you.'

He gave her a sad-looking wink before trudging up the incline, his boots squelching on the moist sandy grass, his thin frame swaying in the wind like a willowy scarecrow that had lost its straw stuffing.

*

They sat into the car and Lottie drove a few metres down the lane before parking. She was trying to formulate her thoughts on how best to approach Matthew Fleming later on. She rang Lynch to see if there was any update on the drowning of Aidan Gormley. Nothing yet. Lynch was waiting for files to be emailed over. Jane Dore wasn't answering her phone, so Lottie would have to wait to see what Hazel's post-mortem threw up.

'I don't know if it's this case or what,' Boyd said, 'but I've had this awful urge all week for a cigarette.'

'Don't you dare. I made a deal with you. If you quit, I quit. Same goes if you take up the habit again.'

'Wasn't hard for you. You only smoked other people's.' He twisted to look at her. 'Lottie, I'm not going to smoke. I'm only telling you how I feel.' He turned towards the windscreen and tapped a finger on the dashboard.

She reached over and grasped his hand, squeezing tightly. 'You're such a strong person, Boyd. Never forget what you've been through. And I will be with you every step of the way in the future. I know I don't show it much, but I can't wait to marry you.'

'Never thought you could be such a romantic.' He flashed her his lazy grin and she had to beat down an urge to lean over to kiss him. What the hell, no one could see them.

She gripped his chin and turned his face to hers, a sense of longing taking root in the pit of her abdomen. Butterflies flapped around down there, and a rush of warmth replaced the freezing cold she'd been feeling, awakening sensations she was excellent at keeping hidden. It was a long time since she and Boyd had been intimate, because of his treatment regime, and for some inexplicable reason she wanted it now.

'We need to get our own place,' he mumbled.

'Shut up and let me kiss you again.'

Her entire body trembled beneath her jacket as he ran his fingers along her cheek to the nape of her neck and tried to untangle the rubber band from her hair.

'Stop, you're tearing my roots,' she exclaimed.

'There goes our romantic moment.' Boyd grinned. 'Ruined by a wonky rubber band.'

'Wonky rubbers have caused much more damage than that.' She laughed and added, 'Not to me, mind. All my children were wanted. Boyd, believe me, I'm really looking forward to Saturday.'

'I don't agree with the arrangement you've made with Annie Fleming, but as corny as this sounds, I can't wait for us to be husband and wife.'

She drew back a little. 'It's going to mean changes for us at work.'

'Feck it. We've overcome worse battles. You and me both. I love you, Lottie Parker.'

He leaned in to kiss her, but before she could reply, the air seemed to tremble, then shake violently, throwing them against each other, then tearing them apart. An almighty blast shattered the rear and side windows, glass shards pouring in on top of them. Lottie felt like she was flying as the car upended, hit a rock wall then flew towards the sky, flipping onto its roof before landing upright, its burst tyres submerged in a soggy field. She crashed down on top of Boyd, crushing him, her body spasming, her insides convulsing and contracting before all movement stopped with a shudder. Her heart thudded loudly in her eardrums, then there was an unnatural pop, followed by incessant ringing in her ears.

What had happened? Was she dead? Dear God, she pleaded, I want to see my children. I have so much to tell them. Adam, if you're up there watching, please don't let me die!

After a moment, she could breathe again. She assessed the situation. The car had flipped upside down and then the right way round again.

Blood. Pain. Noise.

A scream.

Had it come from her or from Boyd? But she was alive. She would see her children again. Thank you, God. She attempted to move, but the roof of the car pressed down, keeping her pinned on top of him. Somehow, the airbags had not inflated. Through the shattered side window, a smell carried towards her on the crest of a breeze. It was not unlike burning meat.

Rearing up a little to see through the fug of smoke and debris, she tried to comprehend what had happened. An uneasy silence settled around her.

'Boyd,' she whispered, blood pouring from her mouth where she'd bitten down hard on her tongue. A searing agony tore along her spine and she needed to scream again. A loud ringing deafened her ears further.

'Boyd? Are you okay?'

He was silent. She thought it was because she was deaf in both ears. His lips weren't moving. A trickle of blood seeped from his hairline and his body looked unnaturally twisted. She realised that her own weight was smothering him. With a few manoeuvres, she eased back and twisted round the right way.

Petrol! She could smell fuel. They had to get out of the car. Her door had smashed in on top of her. She couldn't open it. She couldn't climb across Boyd, and anyway his door was a bent piece of metal.

Criss-crossed cracks lined the windshield, but the glass remained intact. There wasn't much space, but she had to free Boyd and get them both out. The fuel tank could explode at any minute, she reminded her muddled brain.

Then she remembered something someone had once told her. Moving gingerly back to her own seat, she tugged hard in the confined space and released the headrest. Another bone-crunching manoeuvre and she crashed its steel legs into the windscreen, shattering the glass into tiny pieces. Most flew outwards, but some landed back in on top of them. She returned her attention to Boyd. How was she going to get him out?

He moaned, and his eyes flew open.

'Are you okay? Where does it hurt?'

His eyes glazed over.

'Boyd! We have to get out of the fucking car!'

'You don't have to shout. You're making me deaf.'

She knew she was shouting, even though she could hardly hear her own voice, such was the incessant drumming in her ears.

'I'm going to crawl through the windscreen space. Then I'm going to drag you. There's not much room. The roof and doors are crushed. Are you able to move?'

'Don't worry about me. Get out. Call for help.'

'Follow me.'

'Right, boss.'

With his assurance ringing in her ears along with the noise of the explosion, she hoisted herself out of the car, trying not to let the glass pierce her clothes more than it had already done. Outside, she stood up gingerly and leaned across the crushed bonnet, holding out a hand to Boyd. He grabbed it, and with all her remaining strength, she dragged him out through the gaping windscreen and onto the ground, where he lay panting, struggling for breath. He didn't appear to have any visible injuries, save for cuts on his face and hands and the blood from his temple. But what about internally? Could this trauma reverse his progress against the cancer? Shit and double shit. And what about herself? She didn't feel so bad at the moment, but experience told her tomorrow would tell a different tale.

'Can you stand up?' she said.

'Give me a minute. Bit dazed.'

'A minute? We might not have that.' She had no idea what had happened, but she wasn't waiting ten seconds longer, let alone sixty. She grabbed his hand, hauled him upright and looped his arm around her shoulder, then, half carrying him, stumbled away from the car. Boyd collapsed on the grass verge, shivering.

'What happened?' he said.

She shook her head, trying to restore her hearing. 'Don't know. Stay here. I'm taking a look.'

'Where?'

'The quarry.'

'Did someone blow it up?'

'I'm going to check.'

'Don't be a fool. Too dangerous. Call it in. Wait.'

'Matthew Fleming could be up there in need of help. Stay here.'

'Not going anywhere.' He pulled his phone from his pocket. The screen had a jagged crack. 'I'll call it in.'

She rubbed away some of the blood from his eye with her hand. 'Back in a minute. Don't move.'

'Couldn't even if I wanted to. Be careful. No heroics.'

'Famous last words.' She attempted a smile, but her face was too sore to accomplish the simple action. Instead she patted his blood-speckled hand and left him there.

With adrenaline spiking, she crossed the field, passing her battered car, which looked like it had been through a demolition derby. Apprehension laboured her breathing. What might she find beyond the wall a few metres up the lane? Gingerly she climbed over the crumbling stones and scanned the horizon.

Debris was scattered as far as she could see. The gate was no longer there. Matthew Fleming's Range Rover was a blackened carcass, a shell, glass blown out, the roof sheared upright, doors hanging off. Shards of steel and glass littered the surrounding area and further afield. A small fire burned in the shattered engine, but it looked harmless.

'Christ almighty,' she muttered.

She picked up speed, tripping as she moved over scraps of smouldering debris. Shrapnel of steel and rock. Lots of rock. Blood. Pieces of scorched flesh. Was that a singed finger part? Her stomach contracted; her guts churned. She forced an energy from somewhere deep inside.

'Fleming! Matthew!'

She screamed until her voice was hoarse, and then she began to run.

CHAPTER FIFTY-EIGHT

At the top of the crater, Lottie stared into the viscous water and wondered how divers would ever be able to search it. All around her she guessed there were chunks of Matthew Fleming's body, but she suspected the bulk of it was submerged below. She thought she could see his hat floating on the surface, but it was probably her imagination.

Through an increasingly thickening eye, she scanned the area, looking for signs of whoever Fleming had been due to meet. There was no one else about. No one had passed them on the lane. She hadn't the energy to hike over the mound-like hill, and decided someone else could do that. It would be irresponsible to continue. What if there were more bombs? Fuck!

As she made to return to Boyd, a thought struck her. Had Fleming planned this? Had he planted a bomb in his car and then stood at the edge of the quarry and detonated it, knowing it was powerful enough to blow him apart in a multitude of unmatchable pieces? Or had he exploded a device in the quarry itself? As she looked around, she noticed a huge crater not far from where she stood. Was that where the explosion had occurred?

Was Fleming their murderer? Had he decided to end his life thinking she was about to connect it all? Suspicions and circumstances were not enough to lead to a conviction. She needed evidence, and so far they hadn't much to point to Fleming, except that he'd had contact with all the victims. The only thing she had to rely on was her gut feeling, which at the moment was in a knot.

The air was pierced by the sound of sirens, heralding the arrival of the cavalry. She sank to her knees, feeling glass cut through her jeans and into her skin. All around her, pieces of wreckage lay sizzling. She hoped she wasn't kneeling on some small piece of flesh or bone that had once belonged to Matthew Fleming.

Dragging herself forward on hands and knees, she peered once again into the water. If Fleming had been meeting someone else, had that person also been blown to smithereens? The bomb squad and SOCOs would have to join the jigsaw pieces and show her the picture before she could know definitively how many people had been here. Perhaps Fleming had been alone after all. Could he really have detonated a hidden explosive? She should have insisted on him accompanying them to the station. But it made no difference now. What was done was done. She would suffer the consequences. That thought made her groan loudly.

The sirens grew closer, the rumble of heavy vehicles shaking the earth. A slither of rocks fell from the edge of the quarry and sank without trace. Perhaps an explosive device had remained from when the quarry was operational. Had something accidentally set it off? Maybe that was what had happened.

Skidding tyres and screeching brakes drew her thoughts back to Boyd. Better check he was okay.

All at once, an awful thought struck her. She got to her feet and began to run back down the lane. If someone had killed Matthew Fleming, could they still be here? Could they have gone after Boyd?

Irrational thinking flooded her brain as she floundered towards the traffic jam in the narrow country road. Then relief took its place as she saw two paramedics with their arms around Boyd, helping him walk to an ambulance.

The scene began to darken. Momentarily her sight was consumed by stars before the darkness returned and she felt her body sink to the ground.

'I'm fine. For God's sake.' Lottie tried to tear the blood pressure cuff from her arm. The paramedic's gaze was focused on the monitor beside the stretcher where she lay.

She was in an ambulance. She attempted to sit up. A firm hand pushed her down.

'Not so fast. We're trying to take a snapshot of your vitals. It'd speed up the process if you could remain still.' He smiled above his surgical mask. 'Think you can handle that?'

'Sure.' Letting her head ease back onto the rubber pillow, she said, 'My colleague. Mark Boyd. Is he okay?'

'He's in better shape than you are, if you ask me. A few cuts and grazes. No broken bones that our other team could determine without the aid of X-rays. He'll have nasty bruises in a day or two, as will you.'

'I'll be fine. I'm a tough cookie.'

'I'd agree with that.' *George*, his name tag read. He unwound the tight band from her arm.

'Thanks, George. Am I good to go?'

'I honestly don't know how the two of you walked away from that car. It's a total write-off. You must have an angel up there watching over you.'

Smiling sadly, Lottie held back a tear that was nudging towards the corner of her eye.

'Your BP is a little high and your heart is racing. A&E is your next stop. X-rays and maybe a scan. Same for your partner.'

'Those things take time I don't have.' She sat up and swung her legs to the floor.

'Seriously, you need to go to the hospital. Your colleague is already headed there.'

'Good. He's just finished six months of chemotherapy. He needs all the tests they can run. We're getting married day after tomorrow. He'd better be okay.'

George eyed his colleague, Amanda according to her badge. Lottie couldn't interpret the expression behind her mask, but from her eyes she'd guess it bordered on incredulous.

'Where's my jacket?' Her words were coming out all wrong. She couldn't give a fiddler's about the wedding. It was Boyd she was worried about.

'Your forensic guys took it.'

'It's bloody freezing. I'll end up with hypothermia.'

'Not if you come with us,' Amanda said stiffly. It was obvious the paramedics were used to belligerent patients. Lottie was about to become the icing on their proverbial cake.

'No can do. But thanks a million for checking me over. If I feel wobbly, I'll arrange for the tests.' She stepped out of the back of the ambulance to a cacophony of noise.

Just her luck. Superintendent Farrell was at the foot of the steps, apparently reading the riot act to Kirby.

'Ah, even though the Batmobile is a write off, Batman is okay,' Farrell said, taking the comedy route. 'Robin has been taken to hospital. Kirby, find a jacket for Batman here.'

'Thanks,' Lottie said. 'Look, Superintendent, I can explain—'

'I'm delighted you're both okay, but I have no doubt that you're about to concoct some dramatic play on events. Flying the car through the air? That's a new one even for you. I don't want to end up being the Joker in your pack, so I'm taking you back to the station for a proper explanation. Got it?'

'Yes, Superintendent.' Lottie dropped her head so that Farrell couldn't see her burning cheeks. Internally, every sinew was aching and seething in anger. Farrell wasn't going to interfere in her investigation. Not when the resolution was in sight. Just out of her reach for now, but she knew it was there, waiting to be grasped.

The superintendent paused. 'I knew Matthew Fleming. He was all bluster and business. I told you I had a run-in with him during my time in Athlone, but no matter what he was, he didn't deserve to end his life like this.'

'But what if he devised this scenario? What if he's still alive?' She didn't believe this herself and had no idea why she said it.

'This is not some James Bond spy thriller, Parker. But to pacify you, we will put a flag on his passport, and check airlines and ports.'

Kirby arrived with an oversized garda fleece jacket and held it out for Lottie to slip her arms into the sleeves. He turned her round and zipped it like she was a child, asking her with his eyes if she was okay. She nodded and side-eyed Farrell. Kirby smirked. He got it. She'd be fine once her hovering boss disappeared.

Composing her expression as best she could with her nose now starting to bleed, Lottie looked at Farrell. 'It's still possible Fleming detonated the explosive himself. There's a fresh crater blown into the side of the quarry.'

Farrell squared her shoulders, trying to make herself taller than Lottie, which was impossible. With her heavy-duty overcoat straining across her chest, she said, 'Are you joking me?' She gave Lottie a derisory look.

Head buzzing, Lottie made to step around her. Farrell grabbed her elbow.

'Inspector Parker, I'm not impressed at being kept out of the loop. I'm on my way to inform Fleming's family, and I want you in the station in half an hour with a full explanation as to why you and Sergeant Boyd were out here on a hillside with Matthew Fleming, resulting in possibly one dead man, and a hole the size of a cathedral in said hill. Plus, you better have progress on the three murders you're supposedly investigating.'

Lottie watched her stomp off to her car, mud splatter staining the backs of her black tights.

'I think you better do what you're told for once,' Kirby said.

'I need to know what happened.'

'Leave it to the experts. The army bomb disposal unit is on its way.'

'That means SOCOs can't go near the site until the army declares it safe. Damn.'

'The whole quarry could be booby-trapped.'

'Kirby, this is not Northern Ireland in the seventies.'

'Yeah, but this area was once an IRA stronghold. And these older quarries used to use dynamite and Semtex. It's possible there are still explosives on site.'

'Oh for God's sake.' Lottie ran her hand through her hair. It came away streaked in blood. 'Okay. You win. Can you drive me back to town?'

'Sure. I'm parked down there. Almost on the main road. Can you walk that far?'

'I'm Batman, didn't you hear? I can fucking fly.'

'Ha ha.'

'You won't be laughing when I ask you to stop at Matthew Fleming's house on the way.' Lottie took off in front of Kirby.

*

Brendan Healy eventually trudged back up to Maddy as the breeze turned into a howling gale and the waves lashed foam over the pebbled shore. She kept her head down, ignoring him.

'The stables are the key to it all,' he said.

'I haven't a clue what you're talking about.'

'It was something Ellen said. But I don't know what it means.'

'How do you expect me to know, then?'

'Have you met Beth?'

'Who's she?' Maddy said.

'Rachel Mullen's twin sister.'

'The same Rachel who was poisoned after Annie Fleming's party?'

'Yeah.'

'I was working at that party. In my sister's place. She's had a baby and … well, you don't need to hear about my family terrors. What about this Beth?'

'The Mullen twins were friends with the Fleming girls when they were teenagers. You've met Tara and Jessica?'

'I met Jessica on Monday night.'

'I think we should go talk to Beth, and if she won't speak to us, we'll give Tara and Jessica a go.'

'Wait a minute.' Maddy wasn't at all sure she wanted to get involved in Healy's amateur detective lark.

'What?'

'I need to go home. Trey hasn't had his breakfast and I have the milk and stuff.'

'I'm sure he's eaten by now. Look, Maddy, the guards think I had something to do with Rachel's death, and possibly Ellen's. But I promise you I did not kill either of them.'

Digesting his words, Maddy felt her stomach curdle the milk she'd swallowed earlier. 'Why would they think that?'

'It's complicated. Get in.'

She stepped away from the car. 'I'll take my chances hitching back to town, if you don't mind.'

'I do mind. I can't put my finger on it, but I think you are the key to this mess. Something about you resonated with Ellen, something to do with her past, and if I can figure it out, then I'll be off the hook.'

'You don't need me for that.' She rounded the car, putting a little distance between them. 'I want to go home.'

He lit another cigarette. 'What am I thinking of? You're just a kid. A poor confused, stupid kid. Get in.'

She wanted to tell him he was right on the poor bit, but that she was far from stupid. 'What are you on about?'

'I'm taking you home.'

The clouds had darkened to an inky black and a downpour thundered to earth. As she sat into the car, she thought: maybe I am stupid after all, but at least I'm dry.

CHAPTER FIFTY-NINE

Kirby skidded the car to a halt into a puddle and a hail of pebbles. 'That house is a monstrosity.'

Lottie silently agreed. She wiped more blood from her nose as fatigue settled into her muscles. The ache in her back intensified following the short but bumpy car ride. She gingerly swung her legs out of the car as Kirby held out a hand to help her.

'You're going to get us both fired,' he said, slouching up to Fleming's front door.

'Might as well be hung for a sheep as a lamb,' she said, quoting one of Chloe's favourite idioms, stolen from her granny Rose.

'Then I'd rather be a cow when our superintendent finds out about this.' Kirby's voice wheezed as he caught up with her. 'How will you get in?' He handed her protective gloves and pulled on his own.

'Let's see if there's a key under the mat.'

'Boss, can't this wait?'

'I don't want anyone making evidence disappear before we get our act together.'

'Who do you mean?'

'We have to get in first.' A tremor of anger laced her words. She needed to calm down. There was no key under the mat. Or under the flowerpot with the stump of a long-dead plant. 'Try the back door,' she said. 'I'll wait here.'

With Kirby out of the way, Lottie felt the adrenaline that had been fuelling her dissipate, and her body seemed to fold in on itself. She leaned against the porch wall, using it to keep her upright, and looked at the Yale lock. Could it? Really? Searching in her jeans pocket, she pulled out the copy of Rachel's third key. No harm in trying.

She stuck it in the lock. Twisted it.

'I don't believe it,' she said as the door opened.

Without stopping to think why Rachel had a key to Matthew Fleming's house, she entered. Maybe it made sense of the overnight case in the boot of her car. They must have been in a relationship or embarking on one.

Inside, there was little natural light. She flipped a switch and a yellow hue emerged slowly. With no idea what she was looking for, she made her way down the hall and entered what looked like a study.

The leather-topped desk was clear of paperwork, except for an envelope propped against a pen holder.

To whom it may concern, printed in black ink on cream vellum paper.

Small, square, neat letters. Her heart pounded. She wanted to tear it open. Had Fleming left a suicide note, or had the killer of three women left a tantalising message? She should wait for SOCOs. She should wait for it to be dusted for fingerprints and tested for DNA. She should wait, full stop.

There were a lot of things she should do, but with her index finger and thumb, she picked up the envelope by its corner.

The door creaked behind her and she started, almost dropping it. 'Jesus, Kirby, you scared the shit out of me.'

He blundered into the room, a cobweb entwined in his hair. 'You could have told me you got in. I nearly burst a gut trying to shoulder in the back door.'

'You didn't break it, did you?'

'No, I came looking for you and found the front door open. What's that you're holding?'

'God himself only knows. Do you think it could be a suicide note?'

'How would I know? Are you going to open it?'

'What should I do?'

'You're the boss.'

'I'm asking for advice here, Kirby.'

'Don't open it.'

'Thought you'd say that.' She laid it flat on the table. 'We could use a kettle to steam it open.'

'Now you're taking the piss.'

'Feck it.' She slid a finger under the flap and was surprised to see it lift easily.

'What does it say?' Kirby stood too close. Cigar smoke permeating his clothes made Lottie hide a gag. She needed to lie down. To sleep. To wake up from this nightmare. To check her kids were okay. Was Boyd even okay?

She slid out the single sheet. The same cream vellum as the envelope.

'"Sorry."' She read the word aloud, a sense of anticlimax taking the wind out of her sails.

'Is that all it says?' Kirby said.

'You can read as well as I can. Fetch an evidence bag from the car.'

While Kirby retreated, she stared at the note. Somehow it didn't sound like Matthew Fleming. From the little she knew of him and the couple of times they'd met, she thought he'd have left a full explanation for his actions. But what did she know any more? She'd walked into a bomb site. She'd almost got herself and Boyd killed. She should have insisted on taking Fleming to the station and not let him wander into the quarry to his death, whether it was by his hand or that of another.

When Kirby returned, she slid the envelope and note into the evidence bag. She watched as he scribbled the date, time and location on the outside before signing it with a scribble.

'Rachel's key fitted into Fleming's front door lock,' Lottie said. 'She had an overnight case in her car. If she was planning on spending the night with Matthew, what changed her mind? Why did she go home? And if she was in a relationship with him, what reason had he to kill her? It's all a bit weird, Kirby.'

'Sure is. You want to have a further look around, or will we high-tail out of here?'

'A quick look. Two minutes.'

'Might be more bombs.'

'There's not. This note was left to be found.'

Leaving the study, she climbed the stairs.

*

Maddy convinced Brendan Healy to bring her home, telling him she'd go to Beth's later. She needed to ensure Trey was being looked after. She didn't trust many people in her life, and she definitely didn't trust Simon.

'Give me the address. I'll go there as soon as I get Trey fixed up.'

'How long will that take?'

'As long as it takes.'

'What kind of a name is Trey?'

'You're a dose, you know that?'

'I can call back for you if you like. In an hour? Beth lives in Green-field Drive. That's a bit of a walk away from you.'

'Not if I take a shortcut over the back field and cut down behind a few housing estates.'

'But that's …'

Healy's voice trailed off, his eyes fixed on her house, then he put his foot on the accelerator and sped past the end of the road.

'Hey, stop! I live up there.' Maddy twisted round to see what had spooked him.

'There's a garda car outside your house,' he roared. 'What have you done?'

'It must be Simon.'

'Who's Simon?'

'My sister's boyfriend.'

'Shit.'

'Pull up here. Let me out.' She grabbed the handle, ready to jump out if he didn't stop. 'I have to make sure the kids are okay.'

He slowed the car. 'This is unreal.'

'Let me out. I need to go back.'

Eventually he pulled up on a grass verge, engine still running, his face puce and nostrils flared. 'If you double-cross me, so help me God, I won't be responsible—'

'Christ almighty, can you stop and listen to the shite pouring out of your mouth? You're such a dose.' She stepped out of the car, her heart beating too fast and her hands shaking like mad.

'You're a nutcase, Maddy Daly. I don't know why Ellen ever wanted to be a friend to you.'

'Whatever,' she said, and slammed the door. Her head buzzed with all that had happened.

'I'll be at Beth Mullen's. Don't let me down,' Healy shouted as he gunned the engine and took off.

Rushing back up the road, Maddy wondered if she'd escaped one potential lethal drama only to walk head-first into another.

CHAPTER SIXTY

While Kirby dropped off the note and envelope to be forensically analysed, Lottie phoned Boyd.

'I'm still alive,' he said. 'I must have used at least three or four of my nine lives by this stage. You won't get rid of me yet, though.'

'It's no time for gallows humour.' Lottie gasped with a wave of relief. He sounded fine. 'Did you have your X-rays yet?'

'You should see this place. It's like everyone in Ragmullin decided to get sick today. I'll walk out of here with the flu! Seriously, though, I've had a few stitches, and a very patient nurse gave me painkillers. I'm on a list for radiology. How are you?'

'Sore but fine.' She wanted to talk to him about Fleming's house and whether the man could have orchestrated a series of murders culminating in killing himself, but now was not the time.

'You sound tired,' he said.

'Nothing eight hours under a duvet won't cure.'

'When did you ever have eight hours under a duvet?'

'Mmm.'

'Can I join you?'

'I'll call you later. Make sure you stay there until you're discharged. We can manage here. No heroics,' she said, repeating what he'd told her earlier.

'I've had enough heroics to last me a lifetime, Lottie.'

She ended the call and stepped into the incident room.

'Are you okay, boss?' McKeown said.

'I'm fine.'

'And Boyd?' Lynch asked.

'A few bruises,' she said, though in reality she didn't know. Should she have gone to the hospital to check up on him? He could fake it over the phone. She'd check in on him after the team update. 'Any progress?'

'SOCOs aren't allowed on site until the army bomb disposal crew complete their work,' McKeown said.

'Then we're no nearer to knowing what actually happened other than that an explosion occurred, is that correct?'

'About right.'

'Superintendent Farrell is waiting for me, but I want to fill you in first. Kirby and I did a detour via Matthew Fleming's house. Remember the third key on Rachel's key ring? It fits Fleming's front door.'

Lynch said, 'They must've been in a relationship. Remember, I did an inventory of Rachel's suitcase on day one. It contained a change of clothes, nightwear, underwear and some cosmetics.'

'I had a look upstairs. There was a room that possibly belongs to his daughter Tara.'

'She lived with her father from time to time, didn't she?'

'Plus, I found what might be a suicide note in Fleming's study.'

Kirby appeared at that moment.

'Did you get a photocopy before you handed it over?' Lottie asked.

'Sure did.' He pinned it to the board.

Lynch moved closer to have a look. '"Sorry." One word. Could mean anything.'

'I know, but it's all we have until the army declare the scene safe.' Lottie studied the note. 'Let's park it for now. Anything else turn up while I was getting my arse bombed?'

Lynch smiled but shook her head.

McKeown said, 'I got hold of CCTV footage from the management company at Hazel Clancy's apartment complex. Tapes start from last weekend. Working our way through it.'

'Good. Let me know as soon as you have anything.'

'Will do,' McKeown said.

Lottie heard Superintendent Farrell before she saw her.

'My office,' Farrell said, and turned on her heel.

Lottie caught up with her and entered her office, a spiel at the ready. But Farrell wasn't having any of it.

'First off, I'm glad you're okay, and Boyd too, but what's this about you defying my orders to come straight back to base?'

'I don't know what you mean.'

'Don't play the innocent card. I bumped into Kirby in the corridor. Can't hold his water, that man.'

Shit, Lottie thought. What had he said?

'And you needn't go blaming him either. This is on your head. Yours alone.'

'I fully accept that.' Lottie yearned to sit down, but Farrell was standing with her back to her, staring out the window. She leaned against the nearest wall, letting her spine take her weight, which wasn't really a good idea because her back ached in protest. 'I can explain.'

'You bloody well better.' At last Farrell turned, straightening her tie before taking a seat behind her desk. She still didn't ask Lottie to sit.

'I had a copy of this key since day one. It was on Rachel's—'

'I know about the key. I know about the note. I know about you entering a dead man's home illegally and compromising evidence. And to cap it all, your partner is in hospital, lucky to be alive.'

That wasn't exactly true. Boyd would be fine, but Lottie erred on the side of caution and kept her mouth shut.

'So, Inspector Parker, what have you to say for yourself?'

She wanted to say that she needed to go home, have a long shower and sleep for twenty-four hours straight. 'I accept what you're saying, but these cases are evolving quickly, and with so little evidence to point to any one individual, I had to do what I saw fit at the time. Hence trying the key in Matthew Fleming's door. I was surprised when it worked. I entered the house and saw the note. I felt it could be too important to wait for SOCOs, who are already overstretched.' Without allowing Farrell time to cut in, she continued. 'I admit I should have insisted on Matthew Fleming coming to the station instead of allowing him to walk to his death. But I'm not psychic, so how was I to know what was about to happen?'

'You may not be psychic, but I'm increasingly of the opinion that you might be a psycho.'

'That's totally unfair.' Lottie catapulted herself from the wall, her bones creaking as she moved towards the desk. 'Superintendent Farrell, I apologise if things were not done by the book, but I have to get to the bottom of this before anyone else loses their life. Please, you have to listen to me.'

'Sit down,' Farrell relented at last.

Lottie didn't wait to be asked twice. 'Thanks.'

'What do you propose for the next move, bearing in mind I have to face the media in less than an hour?'

'Access to Fleming's personal effects, his finances and diary would be a good start. We need to determine if he was actually meeting someone at the quarry; if so, that person is our prime suspect for his death. If he had no meeting, then he orchestrated this whole debacle himself.'

'Did he murder those three women?'

'If he killed himself, then I'm inclined to say yes. But what was his motive? I can't get my head around why he'd do it. He could just be a murdering psycho, though they don't normally kill themselves, do they? Or it could be something from the victims' past.'

'The piece of glass lodged in their throats is odd too. What's that all about?'

'I honestly don't know yet. The glass might be from a mirror, but unless we find the source, we have nothing to match it to.'

'What else?'

'It'd be interesting to see his will. That might help with a motive if he was murdered. But the women's deaths? Nothing clicks.'

'You have a lot of questions with no answers.'

'You have to appreciate how hectic this week's been,' Lottie said wearily. 'Three murders, and now Fleming.'

'This is not a criticism, or maybe it is, but you've been going around in circles. You need to find a straight line and follow the damn thing to its destination. Find a resolution.'

'I know. Have you informed Annie Fleming of her husband's death?'

'Yes, and not a tear. Like a statue, that woman.'

Lottie considered her next words very carefully. Should she speak up now or remain silent? It had been one of those days, so why not?

'Superintendent, there's something I have to tell you. I don't think you're going to be impressed, but I can explain how it might help the investigation.'

Farrell sighed. 'Go on, tell me.'

Lottie took a deep breath and explained about the change in her wedding plans.

CHAPTER SIXTY-ONE

Boyd was discharged with a prescription for painkillers and an appointment for a scan the following Monday in Tullamore Hospital. He was strongly advised to take complete bed rest for seven days to allow his body time to recover from the trauma and shock of the explosion.

'You're very lucky.' The doctor scribbled his signature on the forms.

'I am,' Boyd said, biting his tongue in case he admitted he was getting married on Saturday. He was halfway out the door and didn't want to be hauled back in.

Instead of calling Lottie, because he could do without a lecture, he phoned Kirby to pick him up. He arrived within five minutes.

'Home?' Kirby said.

'I want you to go by Maddy Daly's house first.'

'What for? Simon Wallace is in custody. Possession with intent to supply drugs. Other charges might follow.'

'I just want to reassure myself that Maddy got back home. Last I knew she was driven off by Brendan Healy.'

'I can check it out.' Kirby reached for the radio.

Boyd was having none of it. 'Do me a favour and swing by her house.'

Kirby grunted but did as he was told. 'If you ask me, you look like shit and shouldn't have been allowed out of hospital.'

'I didn't ask you.'

'God almighty, you're as belligerent as your future wife. Do you think the wedding will be postponed now?'

'Ask Lottie. How is she anyhow?'

'Contrary as hell. She's been in the super's office for the last half an hour. Some shit storm there.'

Boyd remained silent for the short drive over to Maddy's estate. Lottie was well able to look after herself in front of Farrell. After telling Kirby to wait in the car, he acknowledged the garda sitting in the squad car outside the house.

He knocked on the door. No answer. Raised voices carried through the letter-box. Females. Child crying. Baby screaming.

As he knocked again, he noticed the door was off its latch. Pushing it inwards, he stood into the hall as Maddy came racing from the kitchen.

'What are you doing here? You've caused us enough trouble already.'

'Maddy, can I have a word?'

'No you bloody well can't. I've had it up to here with you lot.' She grabbed the banister and made to storm up the stairs, but he caught her arm. 'Ouch! Jesus! Did you have to do that?'

'Give me one minute, Maddy. Please.'

She relented and sat on the third step, rubbing her arm with fingers that looked devoid of blood. He sat on the bottom step, his legs aching as he bent his long frame into the small space.

'What happened to you?' she said. 'A row with Iron Man?'

'Row with an explosion,' he said.

'Jesus! What's this town turning into?'

'That's a good question.' Boyd smiled, and at last she did too.

'Are you okay?' she asked.

'I've survived worse.'

'People like you always survive.'

'I hope so. What about you?'

'I'm grand.'

'Your arm—'

'It's fine.' She cradled it carefully and he was sure it was far from fine.

'What's wrong with Stella?' he said, as her sister's cries continued unabated from within the house.

'You should know all about that.'

'Tell me.'

'Simon is in jail. Drugs. The dope-head. He's a dose.'

'Did Stella not know about his drug dealing?'

'I suppose she did, but you never think you're going to get caught. But listen. Simon may be a twat, and a dealer, but he's not a murderer.'

'I tend to agree with you,' Boyd said. 'He had no reason to cut off the hand that was feeding him.'

'What?'

'You know, like if—'

'I know what you mean. I'm just surprised you don't consider him a murder suspect.'

'I think the murders were too well planned, and from what I've heard about Simon Wallace, he doesn't seem to be all that organised.'

'Nailed it in one.' She smiled, and he liked how it lifted away some of the darkness from her eyes. It made her look her age.

'Tell me why you had to attend Ellen Gormley originally.'

Her face closed up, like a clothes-peg snapping shut. 'It's private.'

'It might have something to do with why she died.'

'It doesn't.'

'How do you know?'

She chewed her bottom lip in silence.

When it was obvious she wasn't going to talk, he tried a different angle. 'Tell me about Brendan Healy.'

Ceasing her chewing, she opened her mouth to say something before shutting it as quickly.

'Come on, Maddy. People are dying in awful circumstances. I need to know your relationship to Healy.'

'You're having me on. There's no relationship. I never met him before this morning. No, that's not exactly true. He followed me in town yesterday. Wanted to talk about Ellen. I didn't know who he was, and I was scared, so I got away from him. I got a weird text last night. Might have been from him. But how would he have my number? Anyway, he just turned up here this morning ... he was kind of persuasive.'

'Did he harm you?' Boyd's eyes dropped to her arm.

'Not that way. It was the way he was talking.'

'Where did he take you?'

'Out to the lake. Close to that Molesworth House place. He wanted to know why Ellen was interested in it.'

'Do you know why she was?'

'I already told you, I don't.'

'And Healy took you on a drive and then brought you back? Hard to believe.'

'You needn't believe it if you don't want, but it's true.'

'Did he say he knew Ellen?'

'Kind of. In a roundabout way.'

'Explain.'

'I don't know what he meant.'

'And he dropped you home to your door?'

'He saw the garda car and freaked. Drove off but let me out around the corner. He wants me to meet him at Rachel Mullen's house.'

'What for?'

'To talk to someone called Beth. He says he thinks he knows what's going on and he says you think he's involved, and he wants to nail the killer and clear his own name. Some shite like that.'

'You're to stay here, Maddy. I'll get a car to pick him up.'

'He'll think I'm a snitch.'

'There's no harm in telling the truth.' He eyed her intently, his neck creaking from twisting round on the stairs. 'You are telling me the truth, aren't you?'

'Yeah.'

'So tell me why you went to Ellen that first day.'

More biting of the lip.

'It's nothing to do with what's happened to her. I swear.'

'Let me decide then.'

Maddy tore at the hole in the knee of her jeans, keeping her eyes downward. 'It was all my fault and I couldn't handle it. Couldn't sleep or anything. Stella ... well, she was great about it and sent me to the doctor with the last few euros she had that week. The doc, Ellen, she was so nice. Said she could help me just by talking. I'd no money but it didn't seem to matter. She said her sessions were free to me. Something about it being a public practice. It was nice of her.'

'You started therapy?'

'If that's what you want to call it. Chats, I'd call it.'

'What did you talk about?'

'Confidential.'

'Maddy, I can't help you if you don't tell me.'

She stood quickly and looked down at him. 'I don't need your help. Trey needs me. Stella and Ariana need me. I owe them big-time. I'm sorry I ever met you at all. If it wasn't for Ellen's poxy bike ...' A sob caught in her throat. 'Can you go now?'

'Please, Maddy.' Boyd got slowly to his feet. 'You have to talk to me. I think you could be the key to all this.'

'That's what Brendan Healy said. But you're both mistaken. I'm just getting caught in the crossfire. Go, please go.'

A wail carried from the sitting room. Trey ran into the hall, the streak of hand prints on his bare legs. Maddy scooped him up and patted his hair, whispering, 'It's okay, pet. Your mummy's just tired.'

With the child's arms tight around her neck, she traipsed up the stairs without looking back.

Before leaving, Boyd glanced into the sitting room. Stella was on her knees, changing the baby's nappy.

Without looking up, she said, 'Don't blame Maddy for anything. She's suffered enough. I made her suffer, but nothing's her fault and that's the truth.'

Boyd wanted to question the distraught young woman further, but the sight of her tears falling on the baby's bare belly stopped him. He glanced around at their miserable existence. One photo in a frame on the mantelpiece was the only nod to decoration. He stepped closer, wondering why there were no other family photos around.

'Nice photo, though all little kids look the same to me,' he said.

Stella sniffed away her tears, finding it difficult to summon her hard-girl act.

Boyd's head thumped, and he rubbed his forehead, his fingers nicking the stitches just below his hairline. The child in the photo looked too old to be the baby. 'Is this Trey?'

Stella swallowed loudly, snapped the babygro buttons closed and lifted her daughter, then stood and joined Boyd at the mantelpiece.

'No, it's not Trey.' She leaned over and blew dust from the frame.

With his head pounding like there was an army of ants hammering for their lives to escape, Boyd felt his vision cloud over. He clutched the mantel to steady himself. His fingers brushed the frame, causing it to fall. The glass smashed on the marble surround and Stella screamed.

'What have you done? You broke my baby.'

He heard thumping on the stairs and Maddy ran into the room. She grabbed Boyd by the arm and led him past the chair with the cigarette burns on the arms and out to the front door.

'Can you not keep your nose out of other people's business?'

'I've no idea what I did to cause her to react like that.'

'It's family stuff. Now please leave. I'm stressed, Stella is stressed, and you look like a truck ran you over.'

'I want—'

'I'll talk to you tomorrow, okay? I need to calm Stella down.'

'Right so.' Feeling guilty that a fifteen-year-old was able to take control of the situation when he was not, he added, 'Before I go, can you tell me what you know about Hazel Clancy?'

'She's a bitch, that's all I know.'

'She's dead.'

'Good enough for her.' Maddy crossed her arms, her face a mask of resolve. He knew he wasn't going to get anything else out of her in her current mood.

In the car, Kirby said, 'What have you done now?'

'I usually ask Lottie that question.' Boyd looked up at the house. 'Let's call to see Beth Mullen.'

'No can do. Under orders to get you home.'

'Kirby, please. Then I'll go home. I promise.'

'I don't know who's worse, you or the boss. You're going to make a great couple.'

The way he said it, Boyd couldn't figure out if Kirby was being serious or sarcastic, and he was too tired to even try.

*

Chloe was more than a bit pissed off with her new boyfriend. He showed up when he felt like it, then other times he fawned over her so much it was sickening. She wasn't sure she wanted to stay with him – she didn't see him that often anyhow – but she needed someone to be by her side at her mother's wedding. Otherwise she'd end up babysitting Sean and her nephew Louis. Weddings were for drinking, having fun. No way she was going to waste the day.

She polished the bar counter and served pints of Guinness and shots and craft beer until she couldn't see past the heads of the Thursday-night clientele.

By 10.30, the crowd had thinned as the young people headed off to find late-night bars or nightclubs that would allow them in. That was when she saw him. By the window with a frizzy-haired, pale-faced, funkily dressed woman. She looked older than Chloe but younger than him. What the hell was he doing bringing another woman into her bar?

She turned to the head bartender. 'I need a minute's break.'

'Sure,' he said.

Folding the J-cloth on top of the glass washer, she smoothed down her black apron, sidled out past a couple hugging the end of the bar and approached him.

He looked up and smiled. 'Chloe. Couldn't see if you were working or not. Great crowd in tonight.'

She ran her tongue along her teeth, trying to ensure her voice had a nonchalant air when she spoke. 'Didn't think you were going to show up tonight. Who's your friend?'

'This is Beth. She needed to get out of the house. Her sister died and she's in a state. Could you get us refills while you're at it? Good girl.'

Without lifting their empty tumblers, Chloe fumed her way back to the bar. The audacity. The bare-faced cheek of him. She was done with him.

But as she slammed glasses onto the shelf, she rethought her decision. She needed company for the wedding. She'd dump him after that.

CHAPTER SIXTY-TWO

When Lottie opened her front door, she nearly passed out at the sight of him.

'Jesus, Boyd, you look how I feel.'

'Need to sit down. Bit dizzy.'

'Where've you been?' Hustling him into the sitting room, she shouted up the stairs. 'Sean, come down and put the kettle on and make tea.'

'Thanks. Tea would be good. Hi, Sean,' Boyd said when the boy stuck his head around the door.

'You look like shit,' Sean said, and disappeared into the kitchen.

'He's right, you know.' Lottie plumped up the cushions and lifted Boyd's feet onto the coffee table. Sean would have something to say about that.

'I'll be fine. Kirby dropped me home after the hospital, but I didn't want to stay on my own in case I passed out.'

'You still drove over here?'

'Think I did, anyhow.'

'You're impossible. You can stay here. Katie's bed is free for another night at least.'

'I was thinking of yours.' He smiled crookedly.

'And I'm thinking you need a spacious bed and a good night's uninterrupted sleep. Take Katie's bed. You have the rest of your life to share mine.' She gave him a wink and squeezed his hand. He leaned over and kissed her gently on the lips.

They pulled away when Sean came in with two mugs of milky white tea.

'I put a heap of sugar in yours.' He fished two Kit Kats out of his pocket and left them on the arm of the couch, then glanced at Boyd's feet on the coffee table, questioning Lottie with his eyes. One rule for Boyd and another for him, he was saying. Lottie shook her head. Now was not the time for that argument. He shrugged and left them alone.

'I'm having a hard time remembering stuff,' Boyd said, after he'd taken a slug of tea.

'A good night's sleep will help.' Lottie sipped her own. 'Why did you call to Maddy's?'

'How do you know about that?'

'Kirby.'

'Figures.'

'You're obsessed with that girl, Boyd.'

'There's something about her. I feel … I want to protect her.'

'She could have something, or everything, to do with the murders, you know.'

'I think she was just in the wrong place at the wrong time.'

'She appears to have been in a lot of wrong places at wrong times, then. What's her story about Healy?'

'She told me he wanted to know about Ellen and stuff like that. I can't remember all of our conversation. She kicked me out. I went to talk with her sister, but she threw a hissy fit over a photo I knocked over. Then I got Kirby to drive round by the Mullens' house, but there was no sign of Beth or Healy. Next thing I remember is Kirby manhandling me into my flat.'

'Maybe you should go back to the hospital. Have a brain scan in case you have concussion.'

'I'm allergic to hospitals.'

'If you're not remembering stuff, that's serious.'

'This tea is doing the job.'

Lottie cosied up beside him. She had intended to tell him about her conversation with Superintendent Farrell, but for now she just wanted to sit in silence and listen to his heartbeat. Tomorrow was time enough to talk about work, and the wedding.

*

Her daddy was nice to her for a while. A week or so really, but in her nine-year-old world it felt like an eternity. It was hard to keep a secret, and somehow she knew it was a secret. She didn't run to tell her mother or go around telling everyone 'Guess what I saw Daddy doing in his study?' No, she kept what she had witnessed firmly locked inside her head, inside her heart, fearful in the knowledge that only she had witnessed her father's misconduct.

It made her feel afraid, if she was honest. It unsettled her so much that for three whole days she couldn't keep her food down. She vomited up every morsel she put into her mouth. Her mother fussed over her, which was nice because the little girl had never before been made a fuss of. And that was when she realised something profound. Though she lived in a large house full of people, she was always alone.

About two or three weeks after the event, as she now thought of it, she was sitting on her swing in the garden when she looked up to see him strolling over the lawn towards her. A cool breeze seemed to precede him, and the blades of grass shuddered with each step he took. She heard the flutter of leaves and the chirps as the birds in the tree above her head took to the sky. He didn't look angry. He didn't look sad. Years later she would assign a label to the look. Bland.

'Honey? Are you okay?' he said as he sat on the matching swing beside her. He never called her by her name. Always honey or sweetie or pumpkin or some other term of endearment that meant absolutely nothing to him.

She stifled a giggle. He was way too big for the swing. Would he break it? No! She hoped he didn't fall and hit the ground. She wouldn't be able to lift him up. She was too little.

'What's the smile for, sweetie?'

'Nothing, Daddy.'

'You like keeping secrets, don't you, honey?'

'Suppose so.'

'Some secrets should never be revealed. Not to anyone. Do you under-stand what I'm saying?'

'Think so,' she said. Deciding to be brave, she added, 'Do you mean the secret from your study, Daddy?'

'Shh.' He looked around wildly and the iron frame of the swing rattled. She twirled the chain around until she was facing him. Mistake. His face was bright red and air was whistling from his nose. He looked like a squashed-up version of the adult he was, sitting on the swing, and she was glad he wasn't towering over her or she might not have been so brave.

'Honey, you have to go away. It's for your own good. I'm sorry, but I can't have this hanging over me.'

She didn't understand. 'Why can't you go away? Why has it to be me?'

'Don't be cheeky. I'm the boss of this house and whatever I say, you do.'

'But Daddy, what if I tell Mammy the secret? Who's the boss then?'

He jumped off the swing and grabbed the chain of hers and twisted and twisted. He moved so fast, she didn't know what he was doing until she felt her breath stick in her throat with no escape. He lowered his head, his eyes dark pins of hate. They scared her more than anything he could do. She felt her face was going to explode before he rewound the chain one turn.

When he spoke, his voice was low and gravelly.

'Listen to me, you little demon. You will never tell anyone. Do you hear me? Never. It is none of your business. It has nothing to do with your mother. She can think what she likes but she never saw anything. I know what you saw because I know everything, but it's my business alone. Remember, this is my house and I can do what I like here.' He paused and undid another twist on the chain, bringing his face so close that she *could smell the scrambled eggs he'd had for his breakfast and see the piece of fluff stuck to a link of the gold chain that always hung around his neck.*

'I could kill you right here, you know,' he whispered. 'I could say you twisted the chain so tightly that it got stuck in your hair and choked you.'

He grinned at her then, and traced his finger down from her eye over her burning cheek, letting it linger on her bulging lips denied any air before he wound the chain the opposite way, freeing her. Falling to her knees onto the dry clay, she coughed and coughed. She felt something bitter rise up from her empty stomach, and she spat it out and kept spitting, again and again, until there was nothing left inside her.

'I'm sorry, honey. I didn't mean that. I'll make it up to you. When you're older. You'll understand then. I just wish you could be as good as your sister.'

When she was able to breathe, she looked up. He was walking back towards the house, one hand hitching up his trousers at the waist, and wiping the other up and down his leg, as if touching her had left some blemish on his skin. She watched the blades of grass settle as if in relief after each of his footsteps.

Lying back on the dry ground, she stared up at the green leaves on the tree above her head and waited for the birds to return to sing her a song. But the day was ruined. He had ruined it. They had all ruined her life. Every last one of them was poison.

CHAPTER SIXTY-THREE

Friday 24 November

The mirror did Lottie no favours. She'd felt like the Tin Man from *The Wizard of Oz* when she'd swung her legs to the floor and attempted to stand. Ouch. The shower did little to ease the creak across her shoulders or the ache pricking her spine. And now the mirror mocked her.

A bump over her right eye and a black and yellow crescent beneath it. She found some of Chloe's foundation and smeared it generously to cover the worst of the damage. She was lucky. She had to remember that. And so was Boyd. Boyd!

She opened the door to Katie's room to find it empty. The bed-clothes had been stripped and bagged into a pillowcase. Typical Boyd. She fetched clean sheets to dress the bed before Katie arrived. A lump threatened to burst her heart as she thought of seeing her daughter and grandson again. She checked the time. Not long now.

With the bed done, she heard the front door open below. She wanted to run down the stairs, but her legs protested, so she descended slowly.

She burst into tears as two-year-old Louis ran into her arms. She whipped him up and smothered his hair with kisses, feeling his tears dampen her shirt. He'd got so tall!

'I've missed you so much, munchkin.'

'Nana! Love you, Nana.'

His arms tightened around her neck, and all at once she regretted her actions of the last twenty-four hours. How could she continue to do this job? She loved her family so much, and she was constantly in danger, constantly putting them in danger too.

'Hello, Mam. Bruised and bashed as usual.' Katie rushed to embrace her mother.

'Oh Katie. Have you been eating at all? You look so … adult! Come in,' Lottie said. 'I've missed you so much.'

'You're letting the heat out,' Rose said, arriving with a Spiderman rucksack on her shoulder. 'Come with me, Louis. Let's see what your great-grandma can cook for your breakfast.'

She bustled the child into her arms and made for the heat of the kitchen. Lottie hugged Katie again.

'It's so good to have you home.'

'Are you excited?' Katie said.

'Excited?' Lottie held her daughter at arm's length, seeing worry lines around her eyes. Katie was ageing too quickly. So much had happened in her twenty-one years. It wasn't fair.

'Mam! Your wedding. Tomorrow. I can't wait.'

'Did Chloe tell you about the change of venue?'

'She did. Do you realise how impossible it is to organise anything when you're away from home?' Katie waved her arms dramatically. 'I'm sick of video calls and texts. And don't get me started on Chloe. Do you think she listened to one thing I told her? Wanting to do everything her way, all the time. Drama queen. But I'm here now and I'll get it sorted. Where is she?'

'I'm here,' Chloe said, from the top of the stairs.

'Katie!' Sean shrieked from behind Chloe and almost hurled her down the stairs as he thundered past, taking two steps at a time. As he flung himself into Katie's arms, Lottie could see he was in tears. Her family. All together at last. And after tomorrow, Boyd would be part of her family too.

'I've a fry beginning to sizzle on the pan,' Rose said. 'First come first served.'

'I've missed an Irish breakfast so much,' Katie said.

When Lottie was alone in the quiet hall, the smell of cooking drifting from the kitchen along with the happy chatter of them all talking at once, she felt a surge of happiness flush through her body and settle in her cheeks. Was it right to suddenly feel this contented? She knew it could all go pear-shaped. She had to learn to live for every moment of every day. Adam would want her to do that. So how did her job fit into that scheme? But before she could think of such complexities, she had to eat.

'Leave a sausage for me.'

*

When Jessica Fleming entered her sister's bedroom, she tried to hide her shock by folding her arms and using the wall for support.

Tara sat, naked, her knees to her chest, her arms hugging her legs. She was balled up like a ceramic egg. Like a small child. Rocking. If she fell over, she would surely crack and break into smithereens. Jessica knew she had to do something.

'Jesus Christ, Tara, get a grip on yourself. People will be arriving soon. You need to get dressed.' She pushed away from the wall and threw open the wardrobe doors. 'What do you want to wear? Something sombre. Black. Not much here. Why do you keep so many of your clothes at Dad's house? Bloody nuisance now with the guards crawling all over it like soldier ants.' Standing back, appraising her sister's meagre selection, she grabbed a hanger. 'This trouser suit will do the business. Now, what shirt?'

'Get out!' A guttural screech came from the mouth of her coiled sister. Tara's eyes were streaked with blackened tears, her hair wild and uncombed.

'This cotton thing will have to do. It's creased, but you can keep your jacket buttoned up. God, Tara, you look a state. Shower first. I'll leave these out on the bed. You can find your own underwear.'

'Get out!'

'And after you've washed and dressed, you better get downstairs. Mum is worn out, plastering an insincere mother-of-sorrows expression on her face. I don't know how she does it. And don't forget we have a wedding ceremony and reception tomorrow. Last-minute planning. I know you hate Mum's side of the business, but this calls for all hands on deck.'

Tara unwrapped her arms from around her legs and curled her hands into fists. 'So help me God, I'll tear every hair from your head, pluck your eyes from their sockets and smash every bone in your body if you don't get the fuck out.'

'I'm glad to see you've got some spirit left. I have to talk to David about the wedding menu. You can help Mum.'

'We have to arrange Daddy's funeral, in case you forgot.' Tara banged her fists against her knees.

Jessica couldn't help the sneer crossing her face and her lip curling, while at the same time she felt her eyes clouding over. 'I can never forget anything to do with Daddy. Just because he's dead, don't think you can paint him in bright colours. He was a sex addict. A fraud. And a murderer.'

'Liar!' Tara snarled, standing up, her skin shredded from her nails. 'You don't know what you're you talking about.'

'I do, and you do too. Now get dressed. It's going to be a really big day!'

*

Tara found it took all her strength to turn on the shower. She stood under the thundering jet but had no energy left to wash herself. The thought of having to raise her hands to shampoo her hair filled her with weakness and she felt her knees buckle. No, she had to be strong. For Daddy. He had made mistakes, but nothing warranted the way in which he'd died. That was what everyone was saying, anyhow.

Once she'd found her focus, she switched off the shower, stepped onto the fluffy mat and slowly dried herself. After wiping steam from the mirror, she chanced a look at her face. A monster stared back at her. Blonde hair with dark roots showing, wild and wiry and wet. Face still streaked with mascara. Sorrow laced her eyes and her downturned lips refused to move.

Opening the cabinet drawer, she found nail scissors and, without thinking of the consequences, furiously cut off locks of hair.

'This won't do,' she told her reflection.

In the bedroom, she picked up the larger scissors from the dresser. Without bothering with a mirror, she hacked chunks of hair from her skull. Running a hand over her scalp, she felt a few stray tendrils sticking out. She cut those too.

Back in the bathroom, she appraised her work.

A razor would finish it off. Nice and tight to her skull. She found a neck shaver with the battery fully powered and finished the job. Through tear-misted eyes she acknowledged the result. She liked it.

Her daddy was dead. Nothing could bring him back. But now, with the gatekeeper no longer around, was there any way to stop the secrets spilling out?

'Tara!' Her mother's voice echoed from downstairs.

Shaking her head wearily, Tara dragged mismatched underwear on to her damp body and dressed hurriedly in the clothes selected by her damn sister. Why should she wear sombre black, even if Daddy was dead? But she hadn't the time or the will to choose anything different. The suit would have to do. Searching for shoes, she noticed her muddy boots in the corner behind the door. She could not recall having worn them recently, so why did they look damp and dirty?

'If you're not down here in three minutes, Tara, I'm going to haul you out of that room myself.'

She had no doubt her mother would do as she promised. Feeling too drained to rebel, she hunted for shoes to lend her additional height and a sense of importance over her mother, all the while trying to ignore the boots behind the door.

'Tara Fleming!'

'Coming,' she said, and took another look in the full-length mirror. Black suit, blue velvet stilettos, shorn hair. The perfect image of the unstable daughter.

A smile curled at the corner of her lips. She knew something none of the others knew. Her smile turned into hysterical laughter. Her mother and sister did not know that the girl who had struggled most of her life with that awful burdensome secret thrust upon her shoulders was about to inherit what was left of her father's wealth. She winked at her reflection. At last she was smarter than her mother and sister.

Things were about to get a whole lot more complicated for the Fleming family, and Tara couldn't wait to see how it all played out.

CHAPTER SIXTY-FOUR

Lottie had dragged herself reluctantly away from her reunited family and into the station. Only a few hours, she'd promised, crossing her fingers behind her back. She was determined to find the resolution to the week's horrors. Otherwise, how could she go ahead with the wedding celebration tomorrow?

As she climbed the stairs to the office, she met McKeown.

'Brendan Healy is in interview room one.'

'Oh, did he just walk in off the street?'

'Exactly. Beth Mullen is with him.'

'Give me one minute and I'll join you.' She flew into the office and dumped her jacket and bag. She took a second to switch on her computer, but it was so slow she didn't bother to wait to see her emails load.

As she skidded towards the door, she saw Lynch waving at her from the corner.

'Good morning.' Lottie waved back.

'Have you a minute? Something came up and—'

'When I get back.'

In the interview room, Lottie sat down heavily. Beth Mullen looked like she'd lost a stone in the last few days. Healy sat with his arm around her shoulder. Protective or controlling? The next few minutes would tell.

After the recording equipment was ready and formalities completed, Lottie said, 'You made a hasty exit the other day. We've been looking for you, Brendan.'

'Sorry about that. I panicked.'

'Didn't make a good impression.'

'Yeah, I get that.'

'Why did you run?'

He remained silent.

Beth said, 'Go on, Brendan, you've nothing to lose. Tell the truth.'

Lottie waited while he removed his arm and interlocked his fingers on the table. He bit the inside of his cheek before he opened his mouth to speak.

'I don't know where to start.'

Lottie shook her head dramatically and was immediately sorry as her neck creaked from the effort, sparking the memory of yesterday's explosion.

'Brendan, when Detective Sergeant Boyd and I were in Beth's house the other day, we were investigating her sister's murder. You fled. That leads me to believe you had something to hide.'

'I'd nothing to hide. I mean, I'd heard on the car radio that a therapist had been found dead. When I heard the location, I knew it was Ellen. I ran because I wanted to find out all I could, because of Ellen.'

'How did you know her?'

He took a deep breath. 'I used to be her boyfriend. I thought you'd start looking into me and find out about me supposedly stalking Rachel and put two and two together and get five.'

'You stalked Rachel and she's now dead. You're telling me you were Ellen's boyfriend and she is also dead. You have some explaining to do, Mr Healy.'

'He didn't kill them,' Beth said. 'He's only here because I told him it was best to tell the truth.'

'Then you also abducted Maddy Daly and—'

'Hold on a minute,' Healy said. 'I asked her to come for a drive to chat, and she came willingly. I brought her back, didn't I?'

'Why did you take a fifteen-year-old girl off in your car?'

'Jesus, you twist everything.' He stood, turning to Beth. 'I told you they'd do that.'

'Brendan, please. Sit down.' Beth put a hand on his arm, and he resumed his seat, shaking his head.

'Okay, let's start again,' McKeown said. 'Where were you Sunday night?'

'What's Sunday got to do with anything?' Healy said.

'Were you in Ragmullin last weekend?' Lottie said.

'I … don't think so. I was getting ready for the exhibition in the city.'

'That's Dublin, right?' Lottie said.

He sniffed and curled his lip. 'Right. I came home Tuesday morning. What's with Sunday?'

'That's when we believe Ellen was poisoned.'

He shook his head slowly. 'I didn't do it. It's not right, what happened to her. She was a great person. My mother says she was too good for this world.'

'You say you used to be in a relationship with Ellen,' Lottie said. 'Tell me about it.'

'After the … you know … after being accused of stalking by Rachel …' he glanced at Beth, then back at Lottie, 'Dad got me an apartment in Rathfarnham from a friend of his, with a rent I could just about afford once I started working in the gallery. That's where I first met Ellen. At an exhibition. We had a drink and became involved. She only ever wanted to meet me when she was up in the city. That suited me fine.'

'How long had you been seeing her?'

'Little over a year.'

'In secret all that time?'

'Yes. We broke up about six months ago.'

'Where did you used to meet?'

'She came to my apartment. We usually cooked or ate takeaway with a bottle of wine or two. She wanted to keep our relationship a secret.'

'Why was that?'

'I'm not sure. I didn't question her on it.'

'Did that weigh heavy on you?'

'I don't know what you mean.'

'It became such a burden that you had to kill her.'

'I didn't kill Ellen. I've hardly seen her in the last six months. She was very troubled. She'd become obsessed with Maddy Daly.' He looked sideways at Beth before continuing. 'Ellen knew it was wrong to talk about her patients, but Maddy was no longer a patient. She was enamoured with the girl. She never told me the specifics of why Maddy had attended her for therapy, but whatever it was, it had a huge impact on her. She just wanted to help her. That's the impression I got. Maybe it had something to do with the fact that Ellen's brother died when he was seven and he'd be just a little older than Maddy now if he was still alive. Though I could be wrong there.'

'I think that's a bit of a stretch. There has to be more to it.'

'If there is, I don't know what it is.'

'Right,' Lottie said. 'Why did you take Maddy yesterday?'

'It was an impulse. I thought Ellen might have told her something that'd help me find her killer. I knew that once you discovered I used to be her boyfriend, and with my history with Rachel, I'd be your prime suspect. I was right there.'

Lottie didn't tell him that she'd only discovered his relationship with Ellen when he'd told her about it. What other secrets were hidden inside Ellen's world?

'And did Maddy shed any light for you?'

'She's just a vulnerable teenager in a rotten situation. She knows nothing.'

'Do you know Matthew Fleming?'

'Not personally, but Ellen often spoke of him. In a nutshell, she hadn't much time for him.'

'Why not?'

'Something to do with a quarry, but she was vague.'

'You do know Matthew Fleming is dead?'

'Heard about it this morning. That's what convinced Beth that I had to come in. Too many bodies accumulating and she thought I'd get the blame if I didn't come clean.'

Lottie wondered what element of truth, if any, was couched in his words. 'Did you know Hazel Clancy?'

'No. Why?'

'She's dead too.'

'Holy fuck, what's going on?' he said.

Lottie wanted an answer to that question too.

Beth said, 'Rachel and I were friends with Hazel in school. I knew she worked in town, but we hadn't met up in years. And now she's dead. Holy God. This is a shit show.'

Brendan said, 'If I was to hazard a guess, and not talking ill of the dead, I'd say Matthew Fleming is the root cause of everything. I believe Ellen hated him with a vengeance.'

'Can you elaborate?'

'Not really. When Ellen spoke about Maddy, she nearly always mentioned Fleming straight afterwards. But she never expanded on it. That's why I asked Maddy to come for a drive. I thought maybe Ellen had told her something important.'

'And had she?'

'Not that I could discover. Maddy only said Ellen wanted to see the stables at Annie Fleming's house but they were no longer there.'

'Do you know the relevance of that?'

'No idea.'

Lottie turned to Beth. 'Do you know, Beth?'

The young woman kept her eyes down, focused on a speck of dirt on the table. 'Not really. When we were teenagers, Rachel and I, sometimes we went to the old Molesworth ruin with Tara and Jessica. Hazel hung around with us too. We messed about and smoked weed in the stables once or twice. That's all.'

'Was Ellen with you?'

'God, no. She was maybe five or six years older than us.'

'Do you know anything about Ellen's younger brother?'

Beth seemed to pale. 'He drowned, didn't he?'

'What do you know about that?' Lottie pressed.

'Heard rumours about it.'

'Care to elaborate?'

'I don't know any specifics. Just what adults said at the time.'

'And what was that?'

'I think they said he wandered off one night and drowned in a quarry.'

Lottie folded her arms, thinking. Trying to form the straight line Farrell had told her about. It wasn't working. Everything was tangled like tinned spaghetti.

'Okay, do either of you want to add anything to what you've already said?' McKeown tapped his iPad.

'No.' Healy shook his head.

'That's it,' Beth added.

'I hope so,' Lottie said.

*

When they returned to the office, Lynch said, 'The CCTV from Hazel Clancy's apartment complex has shown up something.'

McKeown said, 'Meant to tell you, boss, but I got sidetracked with Healy appearing.'

'Show me.' Lottie sat on the edge of his desk with Lynch by his other shoulder.

'This is from Tuesday night,' he said. 'It's a camera on an outer wall close to the road. You can see someone standing in the bushes. Hazel walks around the side of the apartment, apparently having locked herself outside the patio doors. The person coming out of the bushes is dressed in black and the face isn't visible. They seem to approach Hazel and then they both disappear. Might have gone back inside.'

'Who is it?'

'No idea. Maybe that person was the killer and they were taken by surprise when Hazel unexpectedly appeared around the side of the house.'

'Possibly, but we know Hazel was alive the next day, per Simon Wallace's statement.'

'That camera appears to have been broken the next day.'

'Opportune.'

'Yeah,' McKeown said. 'The camera at the front of the complex captures numerous comings and goings. Most to other apartments. A few we can recognise as being callers to Hazel's. Simon Wallace and Andy Ashe but one will surprise you.' He let the images run, stopping when someone appeared.

'Who is that?'

'It looks very like Tara Flaming!' Lynch said triumphantly.

'Tara? What the hell?' Lottie said. 'We need to have a word with her.'

McKeown picked up his iPad and tapped. 'This came in from the search team at Matthew Fleming's house. They found boxes of rat poison behind a panel at the back of the wardrobe in the room we believe to be Tara's.'

'That's enough for me.' Lottie said, slapping him on the shoulder excitedly. 'Come on, McKeown, let's talk to Tara Fleming. Lynch, prepare the documents to secure an emergency search warrant for Molesworth House.'

'Hasn't your wedding been moved there?' Lynch said.

'It will hardly go ahead now.'

'What won't go ahead?' Boyd stood in the doorway. He looked terrible, bashed and bruised.

Lottie swept up her jacket and bag and tugged his elbow. 'You can come with us and I'll explain.'

On the drive out to Annie Fleming's house, Lottie told Boyd about the morning's events. As she spoke, she digested what Healy and Beth had said – or, more pertinently, not said. And she mulled over the evidence now pointing to the possibility of Tara Fleming being the murderer. They might have circumstantial evidence, but they still had no motive.

'You sure you're okay, Boyd?' she said.

'Bit sore,' he replied, 'but I'm fine. Hospital rang me and my bloods are okay. Hard to kill a good thing.'

Annie led them into the large room where Lottie had first met her and Jessica. Inside the door, Lottie stalled, unable to keep her mouth from dropping open.

Sitting on a chair in the far corner of the room, Tara was unrecognisable from the girl she'd met at dinner two nights ago. Her scar seemed to blaze, and her hair had been hacked off. Her eyes were dead pools of grief. In her current state, she revived memories of the hard times Lottie had had with Chloe in the years after Adam had died. She pitied Annie having to cope with the struggles ahead. Her mission here was about to make that all the harder.

'I'm sorry for your loss,' McKeown said, and crossed the room to sit beside Jessica, who nodded and bowed her head.

'I'm sorry, Annie,' Lottie said.

'Thanks,' Annie said. 'I appreciate you taking time out of your schedule for us. No matter what I thought of him, Matthew was still my girls' father.'

'It must be very traumatic for you all. Can we have a chat?'

'Come to the kitchen. I'll make coffee.'

'No, Annie. I'd like a word with you all together.'

'Sure,' Annie said nervously. 'Sit down.'

As prearranged, Boyd sat beside Tara, with Lottie closer to Annie, where she had a good view of both girls. She decided to cut to the heart of their visit. 'I have a sample of notepaper here. Do any of you recognise it?'

'It's Daddy's,' Tara said quietly. 'He uses it for special, hand-written letters.'

'He still used that?' Annie scoffed.

'Where did you get it from?' Jessica said.

'Your father's study.'

'What were you doing in there?' Annie asked, her face a shadow of the vibrant woman from the previous days.

'We were following up on his death,' Lottie said, her eyes darting from one woman to the next.

'Don't you need a warrant for that?' Jessica said.

'When can we have Daddy's body home?' Tara said.

'The army bomb disposal team only gave the all-clear at the quarry late last night. A recovery mission is under way at the moment.'

'Recovery?' Tara said. 'You mean they're going around with spoons and picking up pieces of my daddy?'

Something like that, Lottie thought, shocked by Tara's words. 'When Matthew's post-mortem is completed, the state pathologist will tell us when he can be returned home.'

'Thanks,' Annie said, before Tara could say anything else.

'When will Mr Fleming's will be read?' McKeown said. Lottie noticed how close he sat to Jessica, with the young woman's thigh touching his. She'd have to have a word.

Annie said, 'Later today, maybe. I have to contact the solicitor. Why? Is it important?'

'Everything is important until it's not,' Lottie said.

'Doesn't matter,' Tara said. 'Daddy changed his will. He left everything to me.'

'Don't be ridiculous,' Annie said, looking down her nose at her daughter. 'We hadn't yet divorced. I am the main beneficiary of Matthew's estate.'

'No, you're not. I drafted the will with Daddy. Everything is mine. So there.' A smug expression replaced what had looked like grief on Tara's face.

'You don't know what you're talking about.' Annie stood, phone in hand. 'I'm ringing the solicitor straight away. There's something in family law to protect me, I'm sure of it.'

'No need to ring anyone,' Tara said, and whipped out a sheet of paper from her pocket. It was the same cream vellum as the note on Matthew's desk. 'I have a copy. Witnessed and all.'

Lottie crossed the room and took the sheet of paper. 'If this is legal, she could be right, Annie. Matthew bequeathed his entire estate to Tara.'

'Let me see that!' Annie snapped the page from Lottie's hand. 'This is a fake. It's a copy of nonsense.'

'Go ahead, ring Daddy's solicitor. You will find it's perfectly legal.' Tara crossed her arms defiantly.

'Stay a moment, Annie,' Lottie said, as the woman made for the door. Annie's face had a resigned look when she returned and sat. Was it a simple case of Fleming being murdered for his money? Could Tara really have killed her father? But if that was so, why had she to kill three women? They still had to discover whether the explosion had been detonated by Matthew himself or by someone else. 'Do you know of anyone who would want to harm Matthew?'

'How long have you got?' Annie said. 'He was a shrewd business-man, but he rubbed people up the wrong way. I spent a lot of time ironing out problems for him. It wore me down to my sinews. But I knew a lot about his business, and I don't think his death is related to his work. I think he did it to himself, the selfish bastard.'

'Mum!' Jessica said, while Tara sniggered like a ten-year-old.

Lottie wondered about the bomb. If Matthew didn't detonate it himself, that meant it had to be someone who knew how to handle explosives. 'What about in a personal capacity?'

'He was a womaniser,' Annie said with a downward eyelash flutter. 'He hurt a lot of people, but I don't think he hurt someone badly enough for them to blow him to pieces.' She shook her head.

'He knew all three murder victims,' McKeown said.

'He knew a lot of women, Detective,' Annie said, tight-lipped.

Lottie stood. 'I need you to draw up a list of people you think might have held a grudge against him.' She stood in front of the two sisters. 'You both knew Rachel Mullen, Hazel Clancy and Ellen Gormley. Did anything happen in your past that might have resulted in their deaths this week?'

She was met with a silence so strong she could hear it.

'What do you mean?' Annie said eventually.

'Like a teenage pact?' Lottie kept her eyes on the girls; she was grasping at the proverbial straws.

'You've got to be joking.' Tara laughed, but Lottie thought it sounded nervous.

'I'm not.'

'We weren't real friends with those girls,' Jessica said, 'and Ellen Gormley was much older than us.'

'We couldn't stand Rachel or Beth back then,' Tara said.

'What about Hazel Clancy? Did you like her?' Boyd said, his voice soothing, as if trying to calm Tara.

'I haven't thought about her in years, to be honest.'

'Really?' Lottie raised an eyebrow. 'We have evidence of you visiting Hazel on Tuesday night. CCTV images.'

Tara bit down hard on her lip and remained silent.

'Why did you go and see her?'

'Okay, okay. It was just something Ellen said in therapy. After Rachel's death, I just wanted to check in on her.'

'Ellen was a slut,' Jessica said, changing the subject.

'Why do you say that?' Lottie turned to her.

'Because she fucked our father when she was a kid,' Tara screeched. 'A teenager. Whatever. And you, Jessica ... this is all your fault!' She stood up, pulled a pair of scissors from her pocket and lunged across the room, aiming straight for Jessica's throat. Boyd followed her as McKeown put his arm on Jessica's shoulder and thrust her to the floor.

'You're a bitch!' Tara shrieked.

Boyd caught her arm, twisting the scissors from her grip. They fell harmlessly, clattering on the expensive floor.

Tara tore at her head, as if trying to pull her hair out, then, realising she had shorn it off, she turned and ran from the room, dodging past

Lottie's flapping arms. Boyd took after her, skidding on the polished wood as he careened around the door.

'Got her,' he yelled from the hallway. Lottie looked out to see him with Tara in an arm grip and cuffs in his hand. 'Calm down, Tara,' he said. 'Everything is going to be okay.'

Don't think it is, Lottie thought, and called for backup.

'What is her problem?' Jessica said, as McKeown helped her to her feet.

'Your sister is consumed with grief,' Annie said. 'You need to talk to her.'

'I always have to mop up her mess.' Jessica seemed reluctant to leave McKeown's side.

'What do you mean?' Lottie asked.

Annie interjected, talking as calmly as if it had only been a harmless spoon dropping to the floor and not an attack with scissors by one daughter on another. 'Oh, that's just Tara's normal behaviour. She's prone to outbursts. Now she's totally overcome with grief for her father. She'll be fine in a few minutes. Fetch her medicine, Jessica.' Annie turned to Lottie. 'Now, let me talk to you about tomorrow.'

Are you for real? Lottie thought. 'Annie, this isn't the time for that conversation. But to be clear, I don't want it to go ahead.'

'Rubbish, of course you do. It will take our minds away from more morbid affairs. Your Chloe is a lovely girl. She's been out here and had a look around. Everything is in order. The cottages will be ready when you arrive first thing in the morning.'

'It can't go ahead.' Lottie was mesmerised by the woman's attitude. Shock? Maybe.

'Of course it can. My first event,' Annie said. Lottie didn't like to be wrong-footed, and now she had to arrest the woman's daughter. But Annie continued before she could get a word in. 'Along with catering at the restaurant, Jessica is working hard with David on the wedding menu. It will be fab. So exciting.'

'Annie, will you stop and please listen to me,' Lottie said as Boyd returned with Tara, the distraught girl's hands in cuffs. 'We are arresting Tara for the murder—'

'No! That can't be right. Tara, what are you doing to me?' Annie exclaimed. 'You didn't kill your daddy, did you?'

Lottie noted that Annie did not run to her daughter.

'It's a mistake,' Tara said mutinously.

'I don't think it is,' Jessica said. 'You've wanted to get your greedy paws on Daddy's money for a long time. The only way you could get it quickly was to kill him. But to blow him up like that … what type of monster are you?'

Tara gritted her teeth, snarling as Boyd led her out.

Annie stood resolutely tall beneath the paintings of her grim ancestors. 'Lottie, I am torn every way at the moment. This is so hard to digest. My own daughter! God, it's too horrible to make sense of. What will people think? It's a disgrace on my family.'

'I think Tara will need you to be strong for her,' Lottie said, at a loss to know what else to say.

'I will be, and I'll get this misunderstanding sorted. But don't you worry, I won't let you down. Believe me, your wedding will be an extravagant affair.'

Lottie knew that now wasn't the time to argue. Annie was compensating. Ignoring the fact that her daughter was being taken into custody. She was definitely in shock. Even so, Lottie wondered what kind of woman could coldly think of business while her daughter was led away in cuffs having been accused of murdering her own father for money and three women for God knows what reason.

As they left the house, officers arrived with Lynch's hastily acquired search warrant. Lottie sat into the car beside Boyd, with McKeown remaining behind at the house, keeping a close eye on Jessica and Annie. She had yet to figure out the significance of the shards in the victims' mouths and Tara's motive for killing her childhood friends and her therapist. Sometimes the answers took a long time to evolve.

But they had their killer, hadn't they?

She leaned over and laid her hand on Boyd's.

'Case closed,' he said.

'I hope you are right, Boyd. I really hope you're right.'

CHAPTER SIXTY-FIVE

Saturday 25 November

'Oh my God! Mam! You look amazing.'

Chloe grabbed Lottie's hands, twirling her around the room. She couldn't believe how beautiful her mother looked. Bruises all covered up with thick make-up, her hair divine. It had taken a lot of cajoling to get her to agree to allow the wedding to proceed, but a few opportune tears had worked, and Lottie had given in. Probably for a quiet life, but what the hell!

Chloe was so proud of her mother and wanted to hug her forever. But then Lottie turned away to talk to Sean. The favourite. Ah well, Chloe had her boyfriend today – though maybe not for much longer – so regardless, she was going to have fun.

As Katie fetched the bouquets from the kitchenette, Chloe went on ahead. Despite the early-morning packing and rushing to get to the venue, she still couldn't believe the beautiful day they'd woken up to, after the storms they'd had all week. Crossing her fingers, she looked skywards.

'Daddy, please make this day special for Mam.'

She waited while Katie, Sean and her mother left the cottage. After the drama following the Brook Hotel flooding, things had worked out okay, even though she wasn't sure what to make of Annie Fleming. She had held her breath for hours after Annie's husband had been killed and her daughter arrested, thinking everything would be cancelled. But the woman had a game face on, insisting she wanted the event to proceed. Jessica, though, was a different kettle of fish, as Granny Rose would say. Ice queen, Brendan called her.

Where *was* Brendan? She scanned the crowd and her heart stopped. Why wasn't everyone inside?

She rushed up to Granny Rose. 'Granny, what's wrong?'

'Apparently the groom hasn't appeared.' Rose rushed past her with Boyd's sister Grace.

'Boyd? What's up with him?' She instantly wondered if the explosion had affected him more than they'd thought. She watched as Lottie talked first to Grace, then Kirby.

Her mother rushed into the studio cottage Boyd was to use to get changed. Chloe followed, and as Lottie fell in a faint, she caught her in a flounce of chiffon and lace.

'Water!' she yelled. 'Get her water. Mam! Mam! Wake up. It'll be okay. Oh God, someone, do something.'

Slowly Lottie opened her eyes, her face white, her hands shaking. 'I need to find Boyd.'

'Where is he?' Chloe said, taking a tumbler of water from someone and holding it to her mother's lips.

'Help me up,' Lottie said.

'Kirby, make yourself useful.' Chloe took one arm and Kirby the other, and together they got Lottie to her feet.

'What does the note say?' Kirby asked.

Once Lottie was placed on a chair, he read it aloud. '"Before you make the biggest mistake of your life, meet me. If you don't, her blood will be on your hands. She is with me. You know where to find us." Boss, that's the same notepaper we found in Matthew Fleming's house.'

'We need to figure out who sent it to know where he's gone,' Lottie said. 'When did you last see Boyd?'

'Mmm.' Kirby shuffled his feet. 'We had a few drinks last night, seeing as there'd been no stag, so it must have been around midnight. Not sure. I'd had a good few by then.'

'He arrived here this morning, because his suit and bag are here,' Lottie said. 'Find out what time anyone last saw him.'

Chloe sighed. And they called *her* a drama queen? Boyd was next in line for that accolade, she thought. As she backed out of the room, Superintendent Farrell pushed her way inside.

*

Lottie groaned as the trouser-suited woman made her way into the cottage. The superintendent looked almost human.

'What's this about a note?' Farrell said.

Lottie handed it over. 'I'm trying to think who sent it.'

'It can't be Tara Fleming, because she's in custody. Everything pointed to her, didn't it? The evidence you found in the room at her father's house. The poison boxes in the wardrobe. The notepaper. The muddy boots in her bedroom here. And, of course, her father's will. She stood to inherit everything he owned.' Farrell paused for breath. 'Damn it, I knew this was a bad idea. What was I thinking of? I should have prevented you proceeding with this circus. Slap bang in the middle of a family embroiled in murders and secrets.'

'No crime was committed at Molesworth House,' Kirby said, 'and all we found here were the muddy boots.'

'What he said,' Lottie said.

'You convinced me that allowing the wedding to proceed at this location might bring skeletons clattering out of the cupboards. I didn't

think they'd escape bringing one of our own with them. I need a drink.'
Farrell shook her head and went to fill a glass with water.

Lottie waited while Kirby shooed everyone else out of the over-crowded room. McKeown and Lynch arrived, and the detectives stood around Lottie. Another wave washed over her and she didn't know if it was shock, hunger or fear.

'Someone fetch my phone.'

'I'll do it,' Kirby said, escaping.

Rising to her feet, she wanted to tear off the dress and find a pair of jeans. 'Boyd's phone! We need to put a trace on it.'

McKeown said, 'I'll do that.'

Kirby returned brandishing her phone like a sword. 'There's a heap of messages on it.'

'Get Katie to bring my jeans, jumper and jacket. Tell everyone to head for a drink or something.'

'I'll talk to the guests,' Lynch volunteered.

'And locate Annie and Jessica Fleming. We need to secure the interested parties.'

Lynch scurried out.

Farrell rounded on Lottie. 'Interested parties?'

'Like I explained to you after the arrest yesterday, I had my doubts about Tara being the perpetrator. Since she had to be sent for a psych evaluation, we haven't yet had an opportunity to interview her. But everything fitted in too nicely.' Lottie took a deep breath to see if her words were sinking in, then continued. 'I believe it's possible Tara was set up to take the fall. Look, if she's convicted and consigned to prison, she won't inherit her father's wealth. And whatever event instigated the murders, she either can't or won't talk about it. She might have had a motive to kill her father but what was her motive to poison and kill Ellen, Rachel and Hazel? I'm certain there's a killer still out there.' She tried to get her thoughts straight. She'd sensed something was going to happen, but she'd never envisaged Boyd being dragged into it. Where the hell had he been lured?

'How do you propose we find Detective Sergeant Boyd?' Farrell said.

Lottie scanned the messages on her phone. All congratulations. Feck them. Ignoring the email notifications, she tapped Boyd's number and listened to the silence. 'His phone's off. Didn't I just ask someone to get it traced?'

Kirby returned, followed by Katie carrying an armload of clothes. 'Mam, what can I do?'

'Take Louis, Sean and Chloe and go home. Granny and Grace too. Lock the doors. Stay there till I get home. Kirby, organise a driver for them.'

Katie hugged her tightly, then nodded and ran from the room, Kirby on her heels. Lottie had never seen him so animated.

'Give me two minutes,' she said, escaping to the bathroom, where she tore off her dress and the clips from her hair and pulled on her familiar clothing. She ran cold water from the tap and splashed her face; her make-up smeared, but she had no care for that. She had to find Boyd. Once she felt steady on her feet, she returned to the main room, where Farrell was conducting a post-mortem on the morning's events.

'If Tara's not our killer, we have to assume that whoever is behind the murders lured Boyd somewhere,' the superintendent said, her face puce and her arms folded.

'But who?' McKeown said, frowning in confusion.

The doorway darkened as Lynch rushed in. 'There's no sign of Annie or Jessica Fleming. We've searched everywhere.'

'Shit,' Lottie said. 'When were they last seen?'

'The staff say Annie was here around seven this morning. The chef, David Crawley, says she finalised the menu, then said something about Matthew's funeral. No one remembers seeing Jessica, and her car is gone.'

'Put out an alert on the car.'

'Will do,' Lynch said.

'McKeown, tell me what you've learned about Jessica.'

'What?' His shaved head reddened.

'This is no time for embarrassment. You interviewed her here the other evening and talked to her yesterday after we arrested Tara. What do you think of her?'

'She's as cold as ice. I couldn't find any empathy in her at all. Narcissistic to a fault. Between the lines, I think she hates her mother and sister but blamed her father for everything.'

'Interesting.'

'Do you think she set out to frame her sister?' Farrell said. 'Is Annie involved?'

'I don't know what to think.' Lottie paced in circles. 'Why lure Boyd away? If Tara has been set up and is in custody, why show your hand like this?'

'If it is the sister, perhaps she's craving more limelight?' Farrell suggested.

'Or she has unfinished business.' Lottie scratched her head, nicking one of the cuts beneath her hairline. A trickle of blood tracked along her frown. 'Let's think logically while the killer is acting illogically.'

Kirby returned. 'Your family are on their way home. Chloe wanted her boyfriend to go with them, but he refused.'

Lottie thought for a moment how she had yet to meet Chloe's boyfriend. 'Who's he?'

Kirby blushed and scraped the floor with his toe. 'Brendan Healy.'

'Oh for shit's sake,' Lottie said. Farrell had called this a circus, but it was turning into a ridiculous carnival. Healy must be twelve years older than Chloe. What was his game? 'I don't believe it. Bring him to me if you can find him.'

Kirby scuttled out of the room.

Farrell's eyes threw sharpened knives in Lottie's direction, but she hadn't time for her boss now. This was a clusterfuck of the highest order.

'McKeown, we need to speak to Tara. It's time she bloody well started talking to us.'

'She's still awaiting the psych evaluation. Hasn't said a word so far. I wouldn't be hopeful.'

'Just get the bloody car.'

'She'll need her solicitor present.'

'For Christ's sake, McKeown, phone ahead.' Lottie paused for breath. 'Any word on Boyd's phone yet?

'I have people working on the trace.' He raced out.

While she was waiting, Lottie checked the emails on her phone to see if there was anything to help her. Maybe Jane Dore had completed Hazel's post-mortem. She could do with results.

Scrolling, she noticed a reply from her friend Dr. Annabelle O'Shea. It was her translation of the illegible script from the pages found in Ellen's house. Lottie began to read, her eyes opening wide as her jaw dropped. At last, something to work with. Now she had the whole picture.

'McKeown!' she yelled, racing for the door. 'Where's McKeown? Where's the bloody car?'

CHAPTER SIXTY-SIX

With her anger rising, Maddy tried hard to make sense of the situation.

Ellen was the only person she had ever told about what she'd done when she was thirteen. That had been the biggest mistake of her life. Ellen. Her friend. Yeah. Some friend. Mouthing off to others. Using her. For what? Well, it had ended up in a bloodbath. All because of her personal misfortune.

But had it really been her fault? At that first session, Ellen had tried to convince her it hadn't been, that it had been an accident. Then at the next visit she had gone all weird. Talking about her own life. About Aidan, her little brother.

None of that mattered now, Maddy thought. It was all about perception. And she would pay the ultimate price for her error of judgement. For her mistake. With no one else prepared to take a stand against the injustice of it all, she had to step up. She just had to wait for the right moment.

CHAPTER SIXTY-SEVEN

The car would not move fast enough. Lottie bit her nails to the quick.

After ten minutes that felt like ten years, McKeown screeched the car to a halt. She was out of it and heading for the steps when he caught her arm.

'We need backup,' he said.

'She's in there, I know it. Boyd too.'

'Boyd is smart. He'll know how to handle the situation, but we may need the armed response unit.'

'You think she has a gun?'

'No, but she might have explosives. Remember what happened at the quarry. Unofficial report says there was enough Semtex used to blow up half of Ragmullin. You were lucky.'

'Shit!' Lottie tore her hair. What to do? 'If we come in with the armed response unit, she could do anything. If I go in alone, try to reason with her, maybe we have a chance.'

'You can't reason with a psychopath.'

'I can try.' She went to the car boot and pulled on a Kevlar vest. Her gun was locked in the safe in the station. So much for her wedding day. Who would have thought she'd need to be armed?

'Please, boss, it's too dangerous.'

'Call the armed response unit. I'll give you a signal if I think there's a potential risk of an explosion, and then you can bring in the bomb disposal unit. I'll have your number ready. If it rings, you know you have to act.'

'I don't think you—'

'The weapon of choice so far has been poison, except for Matthew. Look, McKeown, everyone inside could be dead. I have to go in. I *am* going in. Radio for backup.'

She walked through the gateway with no gate towards the battered door that led into the house with no sitting room door. Standing on the step, she put her ear to the front door.

A voice.

Someone was inside. Still alive. She pushed the door inwards. The sad hallway opened up before her.

With a final nod over her shoulder to McKeown, she knew she was on her own.

She entered the house.

The first person she saw was Boyd.

Thank God. He was alive. Sitting on the floor in the corner by an empty fuel basket, a cable tie around his wrists in front of him. His skin was grey, highlighting the bruises he'd suffered in the quarry explosion.

Stella looked to be asleep, lying on the couch, her chest rising and falling as her baby suckled. No, she wasn't asleep. A large bump on her forehead told Lottie the girl had been attacked. She couldn't see any other wounds, and the baby seemed fine.

Maddy sat close to Boyd, two-year-old Trey's little arms wrapped around her neck. Why were the children so quiet?

'Ah, you worked out the note then? Glad you could join us.' Jessica Fleming looked quite different, her eyes wild behind her spectacles. 'I didn't think you'd figure it out so fast. I wanted you to discover them in tiny pieces, like shattered glass.'

'It doesn't have to be like this,' Lottie said, wondering what the young woman had planned. She didn't appear to be holding a gun, and there was no explosives vest attached to her chest. That was one positive in an otherwise shit situation. Jessica wore faded jeans with a thick black leather belt around her waist, flat black boots and a navy shirt. Her dark hair, tied in a high ponytail, swished as she approached Lottie.

'You have no idea what I'm about to do.' Jessica's voice was high-pitched, unnatural.

'Whatever it is, it's not worth it. You can't get away with it any longer. I know what you did to Ellen's little brother.'

Jessica's eyes flared like black shards of coal. 'You can't prove anything.'

Lottie thought over Annabelle's email containing her transcription of Ellen Gormley's words. It wasn't proof, but it gave her a good idea of what had sparked Jessica into a murderous campaign.

'You thought you'd got away with it, didn't you? All those years ago. Killing Aidan, a little boy, out of spite, because his sister was having an affair with your daddy.'

With her lip curling in disgust, Jessica sucked in her cheeks. She grabbed Maddy's hair and dragged her to the centre of the room, kicking out at Trey, who immediately released his grip on his aunt's legs. With his still bound hands, Boyd reached up and brought Trey to his knee. Lottie knew he was trying to tell her something with his eyes. What? Hopefully she would figure it out before it was too late.

Jessica sneered. 'If you want a murderer, here she is. The wretch who lives in this shithole and sucks up the sympathy of your fiancé. *She* is a killer.'

'It was an accident,' Maddy cried.

Lashing out, Jessica hit her so hard across the face that Maddy dropped to her knees with a screech. Lottie felt it would be impossible to overpower Jessica at the moment. She appeared to be in control. Had she planted an explosive device? What was her weapon? Lottie was finding it hard to think straight, let alone plan what to do.

'So you say, Maddy.' Jessica reached behind her back and carefully extracted a steel canister from a clip on her belt. 'But I despise troublemakers. That's what they all were. Pretending to be my friends while laughing behind my back. Ellen thought we could be the perfect babysitters while she screwed my daddy. She left her little brother with us regularly. We were only kids ourselves. I knew where Daddy took her in his flash car, playing the big-shot quarry man.'

'Where did he take her?' Lottie knew she had to keep Jessica talking. Give the armed response unit time to arrive.

'He brought her to Molesworth, to the stables. Filled her head with plans of what he was going to do with the place. Ha! It belonged to Mum. Turned out she was the one with the balls to renovate it. Not him. Anyway, the point is, Ellen threatened to take him from us.'

'If your father was a philanderer, I'm sure he had other women besides Ellen. She couldn't have been anything special to him.'

'She used to babysit us when we were kids. He first screwed her over his study desk when she was only fifteen!' Jessica screeched. 'Tara saw them. She told me, and I didn't believe her. That's when she went a little crazy for the first time. Then, when we were teenagers, not much older than fifteen ourselves, he started up the relationship with Ellen again. I knew then that she was special to him. She had to pay.'

'How did she pay?' Lottie kept her eyes fixed on Jessica's face, not allowing her gaze to wander towards the canister she held in one hand. It couldn't be explosives, could it? No, she guessed it held strychnine.

Did Jessica plan to poison them? How would she manage that? She had to keep her distracted.

Jessica's eyes lost their flare and she stared flatly at Lottie, as if she was in another realm. 'The best way to make someone pay is to take away the only thing they love. Daddy took Tara from me when he sent her to boarding school. She came home like a shell. Turned against me. I loved my sister, but things were never the same after that.' She sighed and brought herself back into the room. 'Now you have taken her from me and I'm going to take your precious Boyd, just like I took Ellen's precious brother.'

'Aidan was seven years old!' Lottie couldn't keep her rage suppressed any longer.

'It worked. The *tragedy* split them up. Ellen blamed herself for not caring for her little brother while she was trying to take away our father. And the kid's death eventually killed her parents. Great result.'

'But still your father favoured Tara over you. Did you tell your sister what you'd done? Is that why she had a breakdown?'

'Why destroy one person when you can take down two at the same time?' Jessica's laugh was a deranged cackle.

'What did you do to Tara?'

She seemed to relax, reliving her manipulative past. She ran her fingers up and down the canister and leaned back against the mantelpiece. Lottie noticed a small fire burning in the grate as Maddy crawled over to sit beside Boyd. Stella was still unconscious, her baby now asleep.

'We'd all been drinking that night,' Jessica said, her eyes darts of ebony. 'You know what teenagers are like, alone with a bottle of vodka. No one cared that we were supposed to be watching the kid. So easy to control him. I told him he had to go home. Pitch black out that night.

Little shit was wetting himself. I told him his mum and dad had come home early because they missed him so much. He wasn't to know they were away for the whole weekend. The others were well into the vodka by then, so they didn't see me slip out after him.'

'So you pushed a seven-year-old boy into the quarry, then went back to your house, and when Ellen returned, you told her he must have missed his parents and wandered home. Across the fields in the pitch dark. You played the guilt card on her.'

'Something like that.'

'And the others didn't miss you when you went after the boy?'

'Told you, they were drunk.'

'What about Tara?'

'When I got back from the quarry, I poured more alcohol into her. She was so drunk she could hardly stand up. I told her he'd gone home. She didn't know what she was doing and crawled out of the house to look for the little shit. Found him in the quarry and started to scream. Mum arrived home just then, I've no idea where she'd been, and heard the commotion. When the fuss had died down, and Tara came home, I tucked her into bed like a good sister and she went unconscious. Once again, she was the centre of attention. I was so mad I broke a hand mirror and drew a shard down her face.' Jessica's eyes glazed over at the memory, and Lottie felt a piece of the puzzle click into place.

'When Tara eventually woke from her drunken stupor, she couldn't remember anything. It was easy to convince her it was all her fault. I told her she'd fought with the little shit and he'd cut her with the mirror and run off home. That he'd drowned as she followed him, and she was to blame. Easy to manipulate people who are already broken.'

'Tara kept silent, all these years?'

'She went nuts, didn't she? Believing she was at fault. Then, years later, Daddy sent her to his ex-lover, the shrink, for therapy.'

'But what could she tell Ellen?' Lottie knew from Ellen's notes what she and Tara had spoken about, but she wanted to keep Jessica talking. The young woman was revelling in how she'd carried out what seemed to be the perfect murder, followed by years of deception.

'It was her.' Jessica pointed at Maddy.

'That's ridiculous,' Lottie said. 'Maddy would have been even younger than Aidan back then. She has nothing to do with this.'

'Fate intervened,' Jessica snorted. 'If you believe that shit. Care to tell the inspector, Maddy?'

The girl bit her lip and shook her head.

Boyd spoke up. 'Maddy told me that her one-year-old nephew, Jacob, drowned in a plastic paddling pool in their back garden three years ago. Because of that, she ended up in therapy with Ellen.'

Lottie took up the story, recalling Ellen's scrawl. 'Maddy blamed herself, because she was supposed to be watching the child that afternoon. It was an accident, but Maddy's sessions caused Ellen to revisit what had happened to her brother. She used Maddy to understand her own guilt and to delve deeper into Aidan's tragic death. By then, Tara was beginning to doubt the story she'd been told, so Ellen worked with her recollections too.'

'You're bright for a boring detective,' Jessica sneered. 'My perfect sister even spoke to Hazel about it, and that got Hazel talking to my dad, as she was bonking him at that stage. Such a den of iniquity.'

'And Rachel, what did she ever do to you?'

'She'd been there the night the kid drowned too. More recently, she was having an affair with Daddy. Did I say he liked bonking my old friends? I couldn't take any chances. She was a loose thread. Better out of the way before she could unravel the remainder of my life. Every one of them had become a mirror reflecting my past back at me.'

'But there was no proof you killed little Aidan. You had nothing to fear. So why? Why all the murders?'

'Why not?'

'Come on, Jessica.' Lottie took a step closer. 'I don't buy that.'

Jessica ran a finger up and down the steel canister. 'Ellen, or maybe it was Hazel, told Daddy what she believed happened that night. Daddy quizzed Tara and then told Mum. Mum spoke to me. I denied it, of course, but they were ganging up on me. I couldn't risk them destroying my life. I thought Mum and Dad would divorce, but they were too slow moving on to that phase. I knew that if I got rid of Daddy and the others, and with Mum and Tara out of the way, I'd inherit the Fleming fortune and my secret would never be told.'

Lottie swallowed down her horror. Annie had known what was going on all this time. And where the hell was she? 'Did you know your father had changed his will?'

'When those bitches told him what they thought had gone on ten years ago, he wrote me and Mum out of it and put in my scarred bitch of a sister.'

'You concocted all this, including brutally murdering your own father, to keep your role in Aidan's death secret and to inherit Matthew's wealth?'

'And to hurt those who loved him, or thought they loved him. Genius, don't you think?'

'We all know what you've done,' Lottie said, casting a hand around the room.

'Ah, but you're not going to be able to tell anyone.' Jessica held out the canister carefully. 'My time studying chemistry before I switched to business has stood me in good stead. I outdid myself at the quarry; now all I have to do is set this on fire and you're all extinct.'

Lottie didn't understand what chemical was in the canister or how it might work, but she'd witnessed the results of Jessica's handiwork at the quarry and wasn't about to dispute her words.

'There's no need for that.' Her heart was beating so loudly she was sure Jessica could see it thumping through her Kevlar vest. 'Ellen left detailed notes. Even if you destroy everyone here, my colleagues have evidence. And once Tara is well enough, she'll tell the truth. You can't get away with this.'

'I can get away with anything I want.' Jessica's eyes blazed and her hand gripped the canister tighter.

The room was too silent. Lottie said, 'Where's Annie?'

'Oh, my dear mother. She had a little too much to drink. I drove her to the lake. Left her there to puke her guts up. Won't help her, because we all know the results of strychnine poisoning.'

'Jessica, hand me the canister. We can sort this out at the station.'

'I'm not stupid. I have an escape plan.'

Lottie tried desperately to think of a way to defuse the situation. 'Let the children out of here, at the very least.'

'What do I care about kids? I killed one, didn't I? But that bitch,' she pointed at Maddy, 'couldn't keep her guilt to herself and woke up memories in Ellen, motivated her to question *everything*! I had to take action.' With a shrug, Jessica turned towards the fire. 'It's her fault. Not mine. I'm too clever for the lot of you.'

It was time. Lottie didn't stop to ponder on the narcissism spewing from Jessica's mouth. She'd caught Boyd's eye and noticed a twist of his wrist and the glint of steel in Maddy's hand as she quickly cut the cable tie. The rumble of heavy vehicles drawing up outside gave her the chance to act.

With a nod to Boyd, she lunged for Jessica, grabbing her around her knees and hurtling her against the mantelpiece. She heard the woman's skull crack as Boyd caught the canister and Maddy lunged with the small knife in her hand. There was no need for it. Jessica Fleming was unconscious.

Trey screamed and the baby woke up with a cry. Stella roused from her slumber, holding the bump on her head, and an empty gin bottle rolled out from under the couch when she drew her feet to the floor, clutching her daughter.

'What happened?' she said groggily.

The room quickly filled up with armed response personnel. Too many people in such a confined place. Lottie wanted to escape. She carefully handed the canister to someone dressed in a hazmat suit. 'It might contain a chemical, maybe nitroglycerine. Or it might only be dirty dishwater.'

'Won't take any chances.'

Lottie's claustrophobia intensified and she was unable to breathe. Then she felt the reassuring pressure of Boyd's arm on her shoulders.

Once she got her breath back, she said, 'What the hell just happened?'

Tara Fleming was no longer a little girl, but the horrors of her past waltzed before her eyes like a tapestry of characters at last coming to life.

Back then, she'd felt the cracked mirror scrape along her cheek, and through a vodka-induced sleep she'd thought she saw her sister smiling down at her. Jessica?

The little boy. Aidan.

Now, years later and after a fortune in therapy, she realised how she had lived the lie her sister had whispered in her ear that night.

Oh dear God! Jessica had pushed the defenceless little boy into the deep quarry waters. And all her life since, Tara had been led to believe it was she who had drowned him. Though his voice had been silenced way too young, the boy had a name, Aidan Gormley, and she vowed to make sure it was never forgotten.

She rose from her disturbed sleep. She looked in the mirror. The scar no longer seemed to mock her. It was now a reminder of how her sister's love had transformed into hate. Feeling stronger than she had since she was nine years old, she pledged to wear her scar with pride and to do something with her life to benefit others who lived in the mistaken belief that they were to blame for another's actions.

Never again would she fear her own reflection in the mirror.

She would be true to herself, the voice of the silenced.

CHAPTER SIXTY-EIGHT

Maddy cradled Trey in her arms in the station canteen while Kirby fetched them a meal from the chipper. Stella had sobered up quickly and sat sullenly on the other side of the table, baby Ariana in her arms.

'I never blamed you, Maddy,' Stella said.

'I blamed myself. I loved Jacob as much as you, and I should have cared for him better.'

'No, I should have cared for him. I know I was very young when I had him, but you were just a child yourself when he died.'

Lottie sipped tepid coffee while she listened. 'It's not your fault, Maddy. You just happened to get caught up in the fall-out. Ellen loved Aidan too, and she was good for you, even if you did open her Pandora's box.'

'I know. But I can't help blaming myself.'

'I blamed myself after my husband's death for things I thought I should have done differently. But I had no control over it. I'm learning to move on. You have to do the same.'

'You and Boyd are strong people. You come from good homes. I have nothing. I'm nobody.'

Boyd tapped the table lightly with his knuckles. 'Maddy Daly, you are one of the strongest fifteen-year-olds I've ever met. The events of the last week demonstrate how resilient you are. You can make something of your life.'

'Suppose so,' Maddy said. 'How is Annie Fleming?'

'Recovering,' Lottie said. 'We found her in time, though she has internal tissue damage. Tara is doing okay too. She'll need residential treatment, but she's committed to helping Beth Mullen get Smooth-Pebble off the ground, rebranding it as Rachel's Dream. She wants you to work with her when you finish school. You have to go back to school. That's part of the deal.'

'I don't mind school. I love learning. Just haven't attended much this term. Is Tara really innocent in all of this?'

'Yes, she is,' Lottie said. 'We have CCTV of her at the airport on Monday night and at the M4 toll booth on her way home. She visited Hazel on Tuesday night and had drinks with her, trying to get her to talk about the night Aidan Gormley died. She also visited Beth. Tara didn't trust her recollections of that night, but she had no way of proving anything while the girls remained silent. It was Jessica who decided no one would be around to reveal the truth.'

Boyd stood and went to the door. He returned a second later wheeling in a High Nelly bike festooned with ribbons and bows. 'We know Ellen would have wanted you to have this.'

Maddy bit her lip and brushed her chin on Trey's head. 'Ellen was such a good friend. Now I have no one.'

'Me, Maddy,' Trey said. 'I'm your friend.'

'You sure are, bud,' Maddy said, and sitting him on the other chair, she stood and took the bike from Boyd. 'Will you teach me how to fix a chain?'

EPILOGUE

Her mother, Rose, had booked a surprise honeymoon for Lottie and Boyd. Two nights in a luxury hotel in County Mayo.

'Lottie,' Boyd said, his hazel eyes reflecting seriousness in the firelight, 'my first wedding reception was held at that hotel. Please forgive me when I tell you I can't go there.'

'Don't be silly,' Lottie said. 'We all have memories to overcome. Mine were happy and loving until Adam's diagnosis, and then it was a car crash. Yours may have been a demolition derby, but I'm not turning down two nights of luxury. You're either with me or not.'

'I'll always be with you.'

'We can get married any time, anywhere. But I really need the break.'

'Okay, I'll go with you,' he said. 'I could do with a good night's sleep.'

She winked at him. 'Who said anything about sleep?'

'I'm serious. The doctor told me I need seven days of bed rest.'

'Suits me just fine.'

The sitting room door opened, and Louis raced in waving a book. 'Nana Lottie, bed.'

'Okay.' Lottie took her grandson's hand. 'Only one story.'

'Two.' Louis held up one finger.

'Don't go away, Boyd,' Lottie said. 'I'll be down in a few minutes.'

'Take your time,' he said, yawning.

'And don't fall asleep there.'

'Where else can I fall asleep?'

'The girls put new sheets on my bed and covered them with flower petals.'

'You're joking me?'

She winked. 'Of course I am. See you in a minute.'

Climbing the stairs with Louis snuggled in her arms, Lottie paused to listen to her children laughing in the kitchen and smelled the food that her mother was cooking for their tea. She still had to talk to Chloe about Brendan Healy and get a handle on how she'd met him and what was going on between them. That huge age difference for a start! But she parked it for now.

Her wedding day might have been ruined, but she was happy. And that scared the shit out of her. Because even though it was a cliché, Lottie Parker believed some things were too good to be true.

A LETTER FROM PATRICIA

Hello, dear reader,

Sincere thanks to you for reading my ninth novel, *Silent Voices*.

I had so much fun creating this story and I hope you enjoyed reading it as much as I enjoyed writing it.

I recognise that it's been a trying and difficult time for millions of people around the world and I hope that you have been able to suspend reality for a few hours and lose yourself in the world of Lottie Parker and Ragmullin.

I'm grateful to you for sharing your time with Lottie, her family and her team in this the latest book in the series. I hope you enjoyed *Silent Voices* and I'd love it if you could follow Lottie throughout the series of novels. To those of you who have already read the other eight Lottie Parker books, *The Missing Ones*, *The Stolen Girls*, *The Lost Child*, *No Safe Place*, *Tell Nobody*, *Final Betrayal*, *Broken Souls* and *Buried Angels*, I thank you for your support and reviews. And if *Silent Voices* is your first encounter with Lottie, I hope you are in for a treat with the previous books in the series.

I'm always delighted when readers leave reviews, so it would be fantastic if you could post a review on Amazon or, indeed, on the site where you purchased the eBook, paperback or audiobook. It would mean so much to me. And thank you so much for the reviews received so far.

You can connect with me on my Facebook author page, Instagram and Twitter. I also have a website, which I try to keep up to date.

Thanks again for reading *Silent Voices*.

I hope you will join me for book ten in the series.

Love,
Patricia

        f trisha460

        🐦 @trisha460

        📷 patricia_gibney_author

        🌐 www.patriciagibney.com

ACKNOWLEDGEMENTS

I somehow wrote this book during the summer of 2020, in the midst of the COVID-19 pandemic. At times, during lockdown here in Ireland, I thought I'd never be able to write another word. But with the comfort of friends and family, and the encouragement of my agent, Ger Nichol, and my editor, Lydia Vassar Smith, I succeeded in getting the story down on the page. In one way it has never been so difficult to write a book, but in another way, writing it was hugely therapeutic.

I want to start by thanking you for reading *Silent Voices*. To everyone who continues to follow Lottie's journey, thank you for reading my books.

Special thanks to a friend who lived in my estate years ago, and whom I still meet regularly around town on her white bicycle. Antoinette (Bracken) Wims, your bicycle was the inspiration behind Ellen's High Nelly!

My agent Ger Nichol of The Book Bureau has been a constant source of encouragement to me and is always available to chat and listen. Thank you Ger and also Marianne Gunn O'Connor. Thanks to Hannah Whitaker, at The Rights People, for sourcing foreign translation publishers to publish my books.

I am honoured to have Lydia Vassar Smith as my editor. Lydia is professional and astute and, like Ger, always ready to listen. That means a lot to me as an author, because I write in an environment that at times can feel like working in solitary confinement! It is important to have people you trust at the end of the phone. Thank you, Lydia.

Thank you to Kim Nash, head of publicity at Bookouture, Sarah Hardy and Noelle Holten for all the PR work, and your encouragement and support. Thank you, Kim, for checking in on me. Thanks also to those who work directly on my books at Bookouture: Alex Holmes (production) and Hamzah Hussain (publishing), Alex Crow and Hannah Deuce (marketing). I'm forever grateful to Jane Selley, who has worked on almost all of my books, for her excellent copyediting skills.

Thank you to all at Sphere and Hachette Ireland, who publish my books in paperback, and thanks to all my foreign translation publishers for bringing my books to readers in their native languages.

Michele Moran is the incredible voice on the audio format of all my books. Michele brings Lottie to life in the ears of those who listen on audio. Thanks, Michele and your team at The Audiobook Producers.

Book bloggers and reviewers help readers find my books, and I am grateful to every reader who has posted reviews, because you all make a difference. The writing community is very supportive of me and my work. Thank you to all who have listened to me, chatted and advised me, especially my fellow Bookouture authors. Thanks to local bookshops, libraries and the media for spreading the word!

Special thanks to John Quinn and Rita Gilmartin for responding to my pleas for clarification and advice. Inaccuracies are all my own. I tend to fictionalise police procedures to add pace to the story. It is fiction after all!

Thanks to Patricia Ryan and Denise Collins for providing me with the remote cottages in Sligo and Kerry in which to write. The tranquility of those areas is perfect for enhancing the creative spirit.

Thanks to my friends for all their support, especially in these unpredictable times. Antoinette Hegarty, Jo Kelly, Jackie Walsh, Niamh Brennan, and Grainne Daly, thank you for being on the end of the phone. Hopefully we will get to travel again soon.

Thank you, Kathleen and William Ward, my parents, for being a constant support throughout my life.

Thanks to my mother-in-law, Lily Gibney, and her family, for all your support.

My sisters and brother support me in all that I do. Thank you, Cathy Thornton, Gerry Ward and Marie Brennan. Marie has become an integral part of my writing process, always on hand to help me with my edits, and for her sins, she is the reader of the terrible first drafts! Thank you.

In these uncertain times, family is crucial, even when personal contact is not allowed. I want to say a special thanks to my children, Aisling, Orla and Cathal. You all looked after me so well when I was ill at the start of the pandemic, and I am eternally grateful for the fine young adults you have grown to be. Your dad, Aidan, would be so proud of you all, as I am. I am thankful to have you in my life. I'm even more thankful to you for bringing me boundless love in the form of my four grandchildren, Daisy and Caitlyn, and Shay and Lola. I know Aidan is smiling down on us and guiding us through life and spreading his love through each one of us. I love you all.

All the characters in my books are fictional, as is Lottie's town of Ragmullin. I was born and live in Mullingar, which is situated in the heart of Ireland. The support I've received from everyone here is invaluable. I can't thank you enough.

Finally, dear reader, *you* make it all worthwhile. I am forever grateful to you.

Now I have to write book ten in the series!